The Getaway Special

Tor Books by Jerry Oltion

Abandon in Place
The Getaway Special

The GETAWAY SPECIAL

JERRY OLTION

TOR®

A Tom Doherty Associates Book
New York

This is a work of fiction. All the characters and events portrayed in this novel are either fictitious or are used fictitiously.

THE GETAWAY SPECIAL

This book is printed on acid-free paper.

Design by Heidi Eriksen

A Tor Book
Published by Tom Doherty Associates, LLC
175 Fifth Avenue
New York, NY 10010

www.tor.com

Tor® is a registered trademark of Tom Doherty Associates, LLC.

Library of Congress Cataloging-in-Publication Data

Oltion, Jerry.
    The getaway special / Jerry Oltion.—1st ed.
        p.   cm.
    "A Tom Doherty Associates book."
    ISBN 0-312-87777-3
    1. Interplanetary voyages—Fiction.   2. Space flight—Fiction.
3. Space ships—Fiction.   4. Scientists—Fiction.   I. Title.

PS3565.L857 G4   2001
813'.54—dc21

                                                2001041538

First Edition: December 2001

Printed in the United States of America

0   9   8   7   6   5   4   3   2   1

FOR THE WORDOS

Acknowledgments

Special thanks to Eleanor Wood for being wonderful, Bob Gleason for being patient, the Oregon Writers Colony for refuge from the real world, and Pat Dooley for writing a computer program to calculate the Tangential Vector Translation Maneuver.

PREFACE

I owe you an explanation.

If you've read another book of mine called *Abandon in Place*, you've met a character named Allen Meisner. He's a genuine mad scientist, a card-carrying member of the International Network of Scientists Against Nuclear Extermination, and he helped a couple of astronauts figure out how to make a spaceship out of goodwill and wishful thinking.

He's in this book, too. In fact, he actually came from here first. The first section of this book predates *Abandon in Place* by about fifteen years. I wrote it as a short story back in 1984, and it was published in *Analog* magazine in April of '85.

That was before the Soviet Union collapsed and the Berlin Wall came down. The Cold War was still in full swing, and people were afraid the world could go up in a mushroom cloud at any moment. I wanted off the planet, and I wanted off *now*. From that impetus, "The Getaway Special" was born.

People liked the story. They kept asking me to write a novel based on it. I tinkered with it a little here and there, but years passed without much progress. In the meantime I wrote *Abandon in Place*, and I needed a mad scientist for that book, so I borrowed Allen from here. Never mind that the two books describe wildly different universes; Allen seemed adaptable enough, and he wasn't doing much over here. He had to leave his invention behind, but that was okay, too; there was plenty of wonky science for him to do in *Abandon*.

But playing with Allen again got me to thinking about *The Getaway Special*, and Tor expressed an interest in publishing it, so here I am writing it after all. The world is a different place than it was when I wrote the original short story, and Allen has been living in an alternate universe for a while, but that's okay. Reality has never been all that easy to pin down anyway.

The short story that started everything became the first part of this book. I adjusted it for the politics of the day, but there was surprisingly little change necessary. The Soviet Union may not be the Evil Empire anymore, but the pieces it left behind are still a nuclear threat—in many cases a more dangerous threat than the parent country. The International Space Station that we were talking about building in the '80s is still not up and running, and nobody seems to know what we'll call it when (if) it is. The space shuttle is still our only way to put people into orbit, despite the steady aging of the fleet. And so on.

In 1984, Allen Meisner saw all this and said, "Enough!" Now it's 2000 and he's back from a consulting job in another universe, still eager to get on with the business of busting humanity out of the cradle. So am I. I'm glad to have him back.

The Getaway Special

Allen Meisner didn't look like a mad scientist. He not only didn't look mad, with his blonde hair neatly brushed to the side and his face set in a perpetual grin, but—at least in Judy Gallagher's opinion—he didn't look much like a scientist, either. He looked more like a beach bum.

But his business card read: "Allen T. Meisner, Mad Scientist," and he had the obligatory doctorate in physics to go with it. He also had a reputation as an outspoken member of INSANE, the politically active International Network of Scientists Against Nuclear Extermination, and he held patents on half a dozen futuristic gadgets, including the electron plasma battery that had revolutionized the automobile industry. He had all the qualifications, but he just didn't look the part.

That was all right with Judy. In her five years of flying the shuttle, most of the passengers she had taken up *had* looked like scientists, or worse: politicians. She enjoyed having a beach bum around for a change.

Right up to the time when he turned on his experiment and the Earth disappeared. She didn't enjoy that at all.

It started out as a routine satellite deployment and industrial retrieval mission, with two communications satellites going out to geostationary orbit and a month's supply of processed pharmaceuticals, optical fibers, and microcircuits coming back to Earth from Space Station *Freedom*. It was about as simple as a flight got, which was why NASA had sent a passenger along. Judy and the other two crewmembers would have time to look after him, and NASA could reduce by one more the backlog of civilians who had paid for trips into orbit.

Another reason they had sent him was the small size of his experiment. Since the shuttles had begun carrying payloads both ways there wasn't a whole lot of room for experiments, which meant that most scientists had to wait for a dedicated Spacelab mission before they could go up, but Allen had promised to fit everything he needed into a pair of getaway special canisters—small cylinders designed for schoolkids' experiments and the like—if NASA would send him on the next available flight. After all the bad publicity they'd gotten for nationalizing the space station and carrying the laser and particle beam weapons into orbit, they'd been glad to do it. It would give the press something else to talk about for a while.

They had even stretched the rules a little in their effort to launch a scientific mission. Most getaway specials were allowed only a simple on/off switch, or at most two switches, but they had allowed Allen to plug a notebook computer into the control line for his. It had seemed like a reasonable request at the time. After all, he would be there to run it himself; none of the crewmembers needed to fool with it.

Officially his was a "Spacetime Anomaly Detection and Transfer Application Experiment." One of the two canisters was simply a high-powered radio transceiver, but the other was a mystery. It contained a bank of plasma batteries with enough combined power to run the entire shuttle for a month, plus enough circuitry to build a supercomputer, all wired together on a hobbyist's integrated circuit board three layers deep. That in turn was connected to a spherically radiating antenna mounted on top of the canister. Rumor had it that someone in the vast structure of NASA's bureaucracy knew what it was supposed to do, but no one admitted to being that person. Still, someone in authority had vouched for it, and it apparently held nothing that could interfere with the shuttle's operating systems, so they let it on board. It was Allen's problem if it didn't work.

So on the second day of the flight, as Mission Specialist Carl Reinhardt finished inspecting the last of the return packages in the cargo bay with the camera in the remote manipulator arm, he said to Allen, "Why don't you go ahead and warm up your experiment? I'm about done here, and you're next on the agenda."

Discovery, like all the shuttles, had ten windows; six wrapping all the way around the flight controls in front, two facing back into the cargo bay, and two more overhead when you were looking out the back. Allen was blocking the view out the overheads; he'd been watching over Judy's shoulders while she used the aft reaction controls to edge the shuttle slowly away from the space station and into its normal flight attitude. He nodded to Carl and pushed himself over to the payload controls, a distance of only a few feet. In the cramped quarters of the shuttle's flight deck nearly everything was within easy reach. It was possible— if you floated with your feet in between the pilot's and copilot's chairs and your head pointed toward the aft windows—to strand yourself without a handhold, but to manage it you had to be trying. Allen had put himself in that position once earlier in the flight, and he'd gotten the worst case of five-second agoraphobia that Judy had ever seen before she could rescue him. After that he kept a hand-hold within easy reach all the time.

Judy finished maneuvering the shuttle into its parking orbit and watched the shadows in the cargo bay for a few more seconds to make sure the shuttle was stable. She checked Carl's progress as he latched down the manipulator arm, glanced upward through the overhead windows at the Earth, then turned to watch Allen.

Here, in her opinion, was where the action was on this flight. For years NASA had promoted the image of the shuttle as a space truck, and that's what it had become, but for Judy the lure of space was in science, not industry. She wanted to explore, not drive a truck. But she was thirty years too late for Apollo, and by the looks of things at least thirty years too early for the planetary missions. If they happened at all. Driving a space truck that occasionally did science projects was the best she could hope for.

It hadn't always been that way. For a while, when she'd first joined NASA, the future had looked as bright as ever. The collapse of the Soviet Union had left the entire defense industry without a purpose, so it seemed only logical that its vast experience with rockets and supersonic aircraft and other high-tech gadgetry would be put to use in space. Logical to people like Judy, at least. But the military, unused to peace, kept right on preparing for war, and just as Allen's group had predicted, they had soon enough found another enemy. Dozens of them, in fact. It sometimes felt as if the Pentagon had joined the Enemy of the Month Club. The Middle East seemed to have taken on Evil Empire status, but that was just the tip of the iceberg. Europe was chock-full of unstable countries and becoming more so by the moment as individual economies collapsed under the weight of the foundering Eurodollar. France was especially hostile at the moment; they had already blamed America for most of their cultural woes, so it was easy to lay blame at the same feet for their financial problems as well. The final straw had apparently come when the Premier's daughter, after a vacation to San Francisco, had brought home a $250,000 credit card bill and when her father had asked what she had bought, she had answered, "Je ne sais . . . whatever."

It had all been downhill from there. France had plenty of sympathizers, too. Never mind that most of Europe had been American allies through two world wars; the Russians had been allies before the Cold War, too. They'd been friendly again after the Berlin Wall came down, but that hadn't even lasted long enough to finish building the space station. Now the only thing the French and the Russians were putting into orbit was laser weapons.

It seemed like the only country that *hadn't* sided against the U.S. was China, but everyone knew you couldn't trust the Chinese.

Judy thought the whole thing was ridiculous. Humanity had been given one final chance to get into space before they ran out of resources for good or bombed themselves back to the stone age, and they had blown it. She was one of the last generation who would get into space at all; she was willing to bet that after the shuttles wore out there would be no replacement for them. The military would keep a few unmanned boosters flying so they could keep sending up "defense" satellites, but that would be the end of it. And eventually, if INSANE was right, the world's nuclear-equipped nations would use their arsenals on one another and pave the way for cockroaches to take over the planet.

So she planned to enjoy every minute of her time in space while she still could.

She was looking over Allen's shoulder now. He had Vel-croed his computer onto a corner of one of the interchange-able panels that had been installed for controlling yesterday's satellite launches. Beside it was a simple toggle switch, which he flipped on. He watched a self-check rou-tine on the computer's display, then when it gave him the okay he pushed a function key labeled "Transmit/Time." The computer gave a loud beep, a beep echoed over the ship-to-ground radio link, and the top line of the display began counting forward in seconds. Allen nodded and pressed an-other key, which reset the counter to zero, then he tapped a few more instructions into the keyboard. Judy saw a series of numbers flash on the display. They were in groups of three, but she could see no particular meaning to them.

"What are those numbers?" she asked.

"Coordinates," Allen replied.

"Coordinates for what?"

Allen smiled and pushed the function key labeled "Jump."

"Us," he said.

The radio beeped again. Carl, who was still looking out the aft windows into the payload bay, shouted something like "Whaaa!" and leaped for the attitude controls.

Judy's flinch launched her headfirst into the instrument panel in front of her. She swore and pushed herself over beside Carl. "What happened?"

He pointed through the overhead windows, but it took

Judy a second to realize what he was pointing at, or rather what wasn't where he was pointing. In normal flight the shuttle flew upside down over the Earth, making for an excellent view of the planet overhead, but now there were only stars where it should have been. She pushed off to the front windows and looked out and to either side, but the Earth wasn't there either.

Allen said, "Don't worry, it's—"

"Not now," Judy cut him off. First thing in an emergency: shut up the passengers so you can think. Now, what had happened? She had a suspicion: Allen's experiment had blown up. It had to have. She pulled herself back to the aft windows to get a look down into the cargo bay where the getaway special canisters were attached, next to the forward bulkhead. She couldn't see that close in, but there was no evidence of an explosion, nothing that could have jolted the shuttle enough to flip it over. Besides, she realized, nothing had. They would have felt the motion. The Earth had simply disappeared.

A long list of emergency procedures reeled through her mind. Fire control, blowout, toxic gasses, medical emergencies—none of them applied here. There was nothing in the book about the Earth disappearing. But there was always one standing order that never changed. *In any emergency, communicate with the ground.*

"Don't use the jets," she said to Carl; then, turning to the audio terminal, she flipped it to transmit and said, "Control, this is *Discovery*, do you copy?"

Allen cleared his throat and said, "I don't think you'll be able to raise them."

Judy shot him a look that shut him up and called again. "Control, this is *Discovery*. We have a problem. Do you copy?"

After a couple of seconds she switched to another frequency and tried again, but still got no response. She was at the end of her checklist. What now?

Allen had been trying to say something all along. She

turned around to face him and said, "All right. What did you do?"

"I—ah, I moved us a little bit. Don't worry! It worked beautifully."

"You moved us. How?"

"Hyperdrive."

2

There was a moment of silence before Judy burst out laughing. She couldn't help it. *Hyperdrive?* But her laughter faded as the truth of the situation started to hit her.

Hyperdrive?

Behind her, Carl began to moan.

As calmly as she could, Judy said, "Put us back."

Allen looked hurt. He hadn't expected her to laugh. "I'm afraid I can't just yet," he said.

"Why not? You brought us here, wherever here is."

"We're somewhere between the orbits of Earth and Mars, and out of the plane of the ecliptic, but we could be off by as much as a few light-seconds from the distance I set. We shouldn't try to go near a planet until I take some distance measurements and calibrate—"

"Whoa! Slow down a minute. We're between Earth and Mars?" She felt a thrill rush through her as she asked the question. Could they really be? This was the sort of thing she had always dreamed of. Captain Gallagher of the Imperial Space Navy! Hopping from planet to planet at her merest whim, leading humanity outward from its cradle toward its ultimate destiny in space . . .

But right behind it came the thought, *I'm not in command of my ship.*

Allen said, "If my initial calculations were correct we are. We'll know in a minute."

"How?"

"I sent a timing signal just as we jumped. When it catches up with us I'll know exactly how far we moved. It should be coming in any second now."

Judy looked toward the computer. The top line of the

display kept counting seconds and the radio remained silent. Allen began to look puzzled, then worried. He began typing on the keyboard again.

"Stop!"

He looked up, surprised.

"Get away from there. Reinhardt, get between him and that panel."

Carl nodded and pulled himself over beside Allen.

"I'm just checking the coordinates," Allen said. "I must have mis-keyed them."

After a moment's thought, Judy said, "Okay, go ahead, but explain what you're doing as you go along. And don't even *think* of moving the ship again without my permission." She nodded to Carl, who backed away again, then she suddenly had a thought. "Christ, go wake up Gerry. He'd shoot us if we didn't get him in on this too."

A minute later Gerry Vaughn, the copilot, shot up through the hatch from the mid-deck and grabbed the back of the command chair to slow down. He looked out the forward windows, then floated closer and looked overhead, then down. He turned and kicked off toward the aft windows, looked around in every direction, and finally backed away. Then, very quietly, he said, "Son of a bitch."

Allen beamed.

"Where are we?"

Allen lost some of his smile. "I'm not sure," he admitted. "We're supposed to be two and a half light-minutes from Earth in the direction of Vega, but we either missed the signal or went too far."

"Signal?"

"Before we jumped, I transmitted a coded pulse. When the pulse catches up, we'll know our distance. Next time we jump I'll send another pulse, and as long as we jump beyond the first one then we can triangulate our position when they arrive. That way I can calculate the aiming error as well as the distance error."

"Oh," Gerry said. He looked out the windows again as

if to assure himself that the Earth was really gone. Finally he said, "Look at the sun."

"What?"

"The sun."

Judy looked. It was shining in through the forward windows. She had to squint to keep it from burning her eyes, but not much, and now she could see what Gerry was talking about. The solar disk was about a fourth the normal size.

Carl, floating just above the mid-deck hatch, looked too. He made a strangling sound, looked over at Judy as if he was pleading for help, then his eyes rolled up and he went slack.

"Catch him!" Judy yelled, but it was hardly necessary. People don't fall when they faint in free-fall.

Neither do they faint. Blood doesn't rush away from the brain without gravity to pull it. So what had happened to him?

As she debated what to do, the answer came in a long, shuddering breath. "Oh," she said. "He forgot to breathe." She laughed, but it came out wrong and she cut it off. She wasn't far from Carl's condition herself.

Get it under control, she thought.

"Gerry, help him down to his bunk."

Gerry nodded and pushed Carl back through the hatchway into the mid-deck. When they had gone below, Judy said, "Well, Allen, this is a pretty situation you've got yourself in."

"What do you mean?" he asked.

"I mean hijacking and piracy."

"What? You've got to be—" He stopped. She wasn't kidding. "All right, I can believe hijacking, but piracy?"

"We're carrying a full load of privately owned cargo, which you diverted without authority. That makes it piracy. You should have thought of that before you started pushing buttons."

Allen looked at her without comprehension. "I don't get

it," he said. "What's wrong with you people? I demonstrate a working hyperdrive engine and Carl curls up into a ball, and now you start talking about piracy? Where's your sense of adventure? Don't you realize what this means? I've given us the key to the entire universe! We're not stuck on one planet anymore! The human race can have some breathing room again. And what's more, I've ended the threat of nuclear extermination forever!"

Judy hadn't even thought of that angle. She'd been too busy trying to suppress the hysterical giggles that kept threatening to bubble to the surface. Hyperdrive! But now she did think about it, and she didn't like what she came up with. "Ended the threat of nuclear extermination? You idiot! You've probably caused it! Do you have any idea what's going on at Mission Control right now? Full-scale panic, that's what. They've lost an orbiter—gone, just like that—and it's not going to take long before somebody decides that the Russians or the French or somebody shot us down with an antisatellite weapon. I think you're smart enough to figure out what happens then."

She watched him think it through. He opened his mouth to speak, but he couldn't.

Judy said it for him: "We've got to get back within radio range and let them know we're okay, or all sorts of hell is going to break loose. So how do we do that?"

"I—without calibrating it we shouldn't—"

"I just want you to reverse the direction. Send us back the same distance we came. Can you do that?"

"Uh . . . yes, I suppose so. The error in distance should be the same both ways. But I don't think it's a good idea. We could be off in direction as well as distance. We could wind up in the wrong orbit, or underground for that matter."

Judy tried to weigh the chances of that against the chances of nuclear war. Since France had put missiles in Quebec in response to American missiles in England, both sides were on a launch-on-warning status. If somebody decided they had already used an A-sat weapon . . . ?

She was starting to feel like a captain again. At least she felt the pressure of being the one in command. Four lives against six billion, hardly a choice except that she had to make it. She heard herself say, "It's a chance we'll have to take. Do it."

Seconds later she was convulsed in laughter. It was an involuntary reaction. The giggles had won.

Allen stared at her for a moment before he ventured, "Are you all right?"

Judy fought for control, and eventually found it. She wiped fat globules of tears away from her eyes and sniffed. "Yeah," she said. "It just hit me." She pitched her voice in heroic tones and said, " 'I'll take that chance, Scotty! Give me warp speed!' God, if only the *Enterprise* had flown."

Allen looked puzzled for a second before comprehension lit up his face. "The first shuttle. Okay." He laughed quietly and turned to his keyboard. As he typed in the coordinates he said, "You know, I did try to buy the *Enterprise* for this, but I couldn't come up with the cash."

"I'm surprised you didn't build your own ship out of an old septic tank or something. Isn't that the way most mad scientists do it?"

"Don't laugh; I could have done it that way. The hyperdrive engine will take you directly into space from the ground if you want to. But I didn't think a flying septic tank was the image I wanted. I thought a shuttle would be better for getting the world's attention."

Judy felt a shiver run up her spine. "Well you definitely did that. I just hope we can patch things back together before it's too late. Are you ready there?"

"Ready."

"Let's go, then."

Allen grinned. "Warp speed, Captain," he said, and pushed the "Jump" button.

Earth suddenly filled the view again. It was at the wrong angle, but just having it there made Judy sigh in relief. She tried the radio again.

"Control, this is *Discovery*. Do you copy?"

Response came immediately. "*Discovery*, this is Control. We copy. What is your status, over?"

"Green bird. Everything is fine. We've had a minor, uh, navigational problem, but we've got that taken care of. No cause for alarm. What is *your* status, over?" She realized she was babbling. There would be hell to pay when she got back on the ground, but she didn't care. Warp speed!

The ground controller wasn't much better off. "Everything is under control here too," he said. "Barely. What is the nature of your navigational problem? Over."

She suddenly realized that she had another big choice to make. Half the world must be listening in on her transmission; should she tell them the truth? Or should she do the military thing and keep it a secret? There were code words for just such a contingency as this.

It was a simple decision, even simpler than the one to return. She said, "Dr. Meisner has just demonstrated what he calls a hyperdrive engine. I believe his description of it to be accurate. We went—"

There was a violent lurch, followed by the beep of Allen's radio pulse, and the Earth disappeared again.

Judy turned away from the radio to see Allen lifting his finger off the keyboard. "Damn it, I told you not to touch that until I gave the word! Get away from there!"

Allen looked hurt. "I think I just saved our lives," he said. "Somebody shot at us." He pointed out the aft windows into the cargo bay, where a cherry-red stump still glowed where the vertical stabilizer had been. Hydraulic fluid bubbled out into vacuum from the severed lines.

Judy took it all in in less than a second, then whirled and kicked herself forward between the commander's and the pilot's chairs to look at the fuel pressure gauges. They remained steady, but the hydraulics and the auxiliary power units that drove them were both losing pressure fast. It hardly mattered, though; both systems were used only during launch and descent, and there could be no descent without a vertical stabilizer.

She shut off the alarms and clung to the command chair

for support. "That was stupid," she said. "Of course the laser satellites would fire on something that suddenly pops into orbit where it doesn't belong. Damn it! Now there really is going to be a war." She turned around to face Allen. "Take us back again, but this time put us short of the Earth. I don't want to go into orbit; I just want to be in radio range."

Allen hesitated. "I—I don't think we should—"

"Do it! The end of the world is about fifteen minutes away. I don't care what it takes, just get us within radio range. And *outside* laser range."

Allen nodded.

While he punched numbers on his keyboard, Judy tried to compose what she was going to say. She wouldn't report the damage yet, not until she was sure everybody had their fingers off of the missile launch buttons. Ground control would know by their telemetry that something was wrong, but they wouldn't know how it happened, and the military would know that the Russians or the French or the Chinese had fired an A-sat weapon, but they wouldn't know at what. Or—she had a sudden thought. Who said it had to be an enemy A-sat? It had to have been an automatic shot; that made it a fair chance that it was an American beam.

It hardly mattered. Either way, it would mean war if she didn't explain what had happened.

Allen looked over at her and said, "I've cut the radial distance by one percent. I don't know where that will put us, but it should at least be out of Earth orbit."

Judy nodded. "Okay. Do it." She turned to the radio.

The hyperdrive did its trick again, but the Earth didn't fill the view. In fact it took Judy a moment to find it: a gibbous blob of white reminiscent of Venus seen through a cheap telescope. At least she supposed that was Earth. A bright point of light that might have shown a disk if she squinted had to be the Moon beside it. They were too close together, though, or so she thought until she remembered that the Moon could be between the ship and Earth, or on the other side of it, and the apparent distance would be shorter than it really was.

She shook her head. "Too far," she said. "We'd never make ourselves heard from this distance. You'll have to take us closer."

Allen was starting to sweat. "Look," he said. "I can't keep moving us around without calibrating this thing. Every time we jump we're compounding our error, and we get farther and farther from knowing where we are."

"I know exactly where we are," Judy said. "We're too far for radio communications. Take us closer." She waited about two seconds while Allen hesitated, then added, "Now."

"All right," he said. He tried to throw his hands up in a shrug, but he overbalanced and had to grab on to the overhead panel to steady himself. He pulled himself down again and began to work with the keyboard.

Judy heard the radio pulse and the view changed again. Earth was larger, about the size that it would be when seen from the Moon, though it showed only a crescent now. She didn't see the Moon out the front windows, but when she looked back through the cargo bay windows she found it. It was bigger than the Earth. Much bigger. They couldn't have been more than a couple thousand miles from it. She watched the surface for a few seconds, trying to determine their relative motion. Was it getting closer? She couldn't tell.

All the same, as she plugged her headset into the radio she said, "Get ready to move us again." This time Allen didn't argue.

"Control, this is *Discovery*, do you copy?"

She had forgotten about the time lag. She was about to call again when she heard, "Roger *Discovery*, we copy, but your signal is weak and you have disappeared from our radar. What's happening up there?"

"We're not in orbit any longer. Doctor Meisner's experiment has moved us to the general vicinity of the Moon. I repeat, Doctor Meisner's experiment is responsible for our change in position. There is no cause for alarm. Do you copy?"

A pause. "We copy, *Discovery*. No cause for alarm. You bet. We'll tell the President to get his finger off the button, then. Hold on a second—uh . . ." The timbre of Control's voice changed, and Judy realized he was reading. Someone had evidently handed him a note. He read: "Due to a state of national emergency, the Pentagon has taken control of this mission. You are now a military flight. Any information concerning the nature of Doctor Meisner's experiment is now classified top secret. Do you copy?"

Judy had been expecting that. She laughed into the microphone and said, "Don't tell the world that we've got hyperdrive? You know where you can tell them to put it, Control. Kindly remind the idiots at the Pentagon that I am a civilian pilot, and that my loyalty goes to humanity first, nation second. What they request is tantamount to suppressing knowledge of the wheel, so you can tell the Pentagon to stuff it deep, over."

Judy saw motion out of the corner of her eye and turned to see Allen applauding silently. He said, "I sent e—"

Judy held up her hand to quiet him as Mission Control responded. She could hear the cheering in the background. "Roger, *Discovery*. We copy and concur. Your, ah, hyperspace jump seems to have messed with the telemetry. We're getting low pressure readings in the hydraulics and APUs. Do you confirm, over?"

"Your readings are correct. We have sustained damage to the vertical stabilizer. We won't be able to re-enter. Request you reserve space for us on the next flight down."

"Roger, *Discovery*. What kind of damage to the stabilizer?"

"It's been vaporized. Completely melted away. We assume it was either a particle beam or laser antisatellite weapon, automatically fired. We do not consider ourselves to have been attacked. Please be sure the Pentagon understands, over."

"Roger, *Discovery*. I'm sure they'll be glad to hear that."

Allen butted in. "Uh, Commander?"

"I'll bet they will. Hold on a sec." She turned off the mike. "What, Allen?"

"I think we should get away from here. We're picking up

velocity being this close to the Moon. It'll make it hard to put us back into orbit."

"Velocity? How?"

"Gravitation. We're falling toward the Moon. When we make our next hyperspace jump the velocity we gain will still be with us. We'll have to cancel it before we can go into Earth orbit."

"Oh. Right." Judy tried to visualize the situation in her mind. Too close to the Moon; well, "Can you put us on the other side of the Earth?"

"I don't want to fool around near the planets any more. I need to calibrate it. I think the danger of war is past, is it not?"

Judy nodded. "Okay. Give me a minute to explain what we're going to do, then you can take us wherever you want. Within reason," she amended quickly. She turned on the radio again and said, "Control, this is *Discovery*. Doctor Meisner says that the Moon's gravitation is causing us to build up unwanted velocity. We'll have to make another hyperspace jump in order to leave the area, plus another series of jumps to calibrate the engine. We'll be out of radio contact for a while. Promise you won't let them blow up the world while we're gone? Over."

"We'll do our best, *Discovery*. Things are a little hot down here."

Judy imagined they were. If the ground controller didn't have a Marine holding a pistol to his head within the next couple of minutes she would be very surprised. "Just keep the lid on until we get back," she told him. "Remind the President that this would be a really stupid time to go to war."

"We'll do that. Good luck, *Discovery*."

"Good luck to you. *Discovery* out." Judy switched off the radio, turned around, and screamed.

3

"Be calm," Gerry said as he floated up through the mid-deck hatchway with the .45 from the emergency survival kit in his hand. "Allen, you may continue with your jump. Judy, you will please come away from the controls."

"What do you think you're doing?" she demanded.

"I'm appropriating this vessel for the Russian Federation. You won't be harmed so long as you do as I say."

"Come off it, Gerry. You're not going to fire that thing in here. One stray shot and you'd lose all your air."

"There is that risk. I'd have preferred a less destructive weapon, but the survival kit doesn't carry a dart gun. I'll just have to be careful not to miss, won't I? Now come away. Slowly, that's it." He reached out and stopped her in mid-air, leaving her floating where he could see her move long before she reached anything to push off against.

He glanced out the aft windows at the surface of the Moon beyond the cargo bay and said, "Allen, you may move us away now." He kept the gun aimed at Judy as he spoke.

Allen swallowed. "Right." He turned to the keyboard and began keying in coordinates.

"Why are you doing this, Gerry?" Judy asked. "You're not a Russian."

"That depends on your definition. I've been a sleeper agent since before I entered the space program, since before the Union collapsed. In any case, my nationality is not the issue. What matters is my belief that the Federation should have this device."

Allen cleared his throat. "I, uh, I was planning on giving it to everybody. You see, part of the reason I did things the way I did was to get everybody's attention so they wouldn't think it was a hoax when I sent the plans out over the internet."

Gerry shook his head. "A noble thought. Unfortunately, the world isn't ready for it. Russia will have to keep your idea secret until the rest of humanity is sufficiently civilized to handle something this dangerous."

"Bullshit," Judy said. "You can't believe that. You want to keep it for yourself. You want Russia to be a big superpower again, and you think this will—"

Gerry waved the pistol at her. "Be quiet. Allen, you will make the jump now."

Allen turned back to his keyboard and pushed the transmit key. The radio sent its timing pulse, but nothing else happened.

"What—?" He looked out the window, pushed the key again, and again. Still nothing changed.

"I must have mis-keyed it," he said. He entered the coordinates again, canceled the timer and reset it, and hit "Jump" again.

Still nothing.

"Something's wrong."

"Allen." Gerry had the gun pointed at him now.

"I'm not lying! It's not working! It's hardly surprising, with all the jumps we've been doing in a row. Something's probably burned out. It's still an experimental model, you know."

"Then you will find the problem and fix it." Gerry glanced out the window and added, "I suggest you do it quickly."

Judy followed his glance. The Moon's surface was definitely closer now.

Allen said, "You'll have to go out and get the canister."

"Not until you've exhausted the possibilities inside. The problem may be in the computer."

"It isn't. The signal is reaching the radio, and all the data uses one line. The problem is in the canister."

Gerry thought it through and nodded. "All right, but

Judy will go out and get it. I prefer to remain here where I can watch you."

The Moon was larger still by the time Judy stepped out into the cargo bay. She had cut the suiting-up time to its bare minimum, but it still took time breathing pure oxygen to wash the nitrogen out of her bloodstream, and even Gerry with his pistol couldn't force her to go outside before she was sure she was safe from the bends. Once she was out she took time for one quick look—she could see their motion now, the cratered surface growing inexorably closer by the minute—then she unfastened the "mystery" canister and climbed back into the airlock with it under her arm. When she got back inside she handed it to Allen and started to pull off her helmet.

"Leave it on," Gerry said. Judy could hear the tension in his voice even through the intercom. She understood the reason for it, and for his order. She wouldn't have time to become uncomfortable in the suit. If Allen found the problem she would have to take the canister back outside, and if he didn't they would crash into the Moon; either way she wouldn't have to worry about the suit for very long.

Allen floated over to the wall of lockers in the mid-deck and opened the one holding the tool kit. Then he opened the canister and held it so the light shone down inside. Judy looked over his shoulder and saw a maze of wires and circuit boards. Allen looked at them for a minute, then reached in and pushed a few wires around. He let go of the canister and left it floating in front of him, looked up, and said, "I think I've found it. Judy, could you help hold this a minute?"

She nodded and reached out to take it from him.

"Here, over on this side," he said, pulling her around so she was on his left. Gerry floated to his right with the gun at the ready. Carl was still unconscious in his bunk beside Judy; evidently Gerry had given him a sedative when he had the chance.

Allen handed the canister to Judy, positioning her like a piece of lab equipment until she held it at the right angle, then he pulled a screwdriver out of the tool kit, reached into the canister's open end with it, and looked sideways at Gerry.

"I've just taken over the ship," he said. "Now float that gun over here, very gently."

Gerry didn't look amused. "What are you talking about? Get busy and fix that before I—"

"Before you what? I give you ten seconds to surrender or I take this screwdriver and stir. Shoot me before I make the repairs and you get the same result. Maybe they'll name the crater after you."

Gerry shifted the gun to point at Judy. She felt her breath catch, but Allen shifted his head to be the target again. "Won't work. You can't risk hitting me and you know it. Float the gun over. Five seconds." Allen slowly threaded the screwdriver in between the wires until his hand was inside the canister, saying all the while, "Four seconds, three seconds, two seconds, one—very good, Gerry. Judy, catch that."

She let go of the canister and fielded the gun, sandwiching it between her gloved hands, but she couldn't get her finger in the trigger guard. Her heart pounding, she said, "Allen . . ."

He saw the problem. "Trade me," he said, letting go of the canister and taking the gun from her. "Get in the bottom bunk, Gerry."

Wordlessly, Gerry drifted over and slid into the bunk. Allen closed the panel after him, then hunted in the tool kit until he found a coil of what looked like bell wire and used that to tie the panel shut. Then he gave the gun back to Judy and began looking inside the canister again, poking and prodding around.

"What are you doing?" Judy asked.

"Looking for the problem."

"I thought you said you'd found it."

"I lied. I didn't figure there was much point in looking until we had Gerry safely out of the way."

"But what if—never mind. Just hurry. We don't have much time."

"It won't take long. If it isn't something simple I won't be able to fix it anyway. I don't have any test equipment. All I brought along were spare parts."

Judy propped herself against the lockers, her back against the wall and her feet out at an angle against the floor. She'd discovered the position on her first flight. It almost felt like gravity, at least to the legs, and it had the added advantage of holding her in place. She said, "I can't believe you. Do you have the slightest idea what this means to the human race?"

"I think I do, yes."

"Then why are you risking it like this? You should have made it public the moment you realized what you had. Good god, if the secret dies with us now, we—"

"It won't. I arranged an internet mailing to every member of INSANE, triggered by the first pulse from the timing beacon. The plans should be arriving in people's email all over the world just about now." Allen raised his voice so Gerry could hear him, too. "There are thirty-seven Russians in INSANE, Gerry. They each got the email, too. So you see, none of this really would have made much difference in the long run anyway. This was just a public demonstration so they wouldn't waste time trying to decide if it would really work. I've asked everyone to put the plans on their web sites, too, so anybody can download them. I don't think any elite group should have a monopoly on space travel, not even INSANE." He paused, squinted inside the canister, and said, "I think I've found it. All those jumps in a row overheated a voltage regulator."

He opened his personal locker and got out a baggie full of electronics parts. He fished around until he found the one he needed, a half-inch square with three legs, and replaced the one in the canister with it. He put the lid back on and held it out. "Okay, you can put it back now."

Judy took the canister and pushed herself toward the airlock. Before she closed the door, she said, "Why don't I stay out there while you try it? It'll save time if we have to bring it in again."

"Good idea."

She closed the airlock door and began depressurizing it. It seemed to take forever to bleed the air out, but she knew that it only took three minutes. She could hear her own breathing inside her helmet, just the way she'd imagined she would when she was a little girl dreaming about space. The suit stiffened a little as the outside pressure dropped. When the gauge reached zero she opened the outer hatch and stepped out into the cargo bay.

The Moon was a flat gray wall of craters in front of her. She watched it for a moment, thinking, *This is what it looked like to the Apollo crews. And I thought I'd never get to see it.*

What sorts of other things would she be seeing that she had only dreamed of before? The other planets, almost certainly. Other stars? Why not? She knew she was going to be in trouble when she got back, but Allen's invention practically assured her that the trouble wouldn't last. Space-trained pilots were going to be in very short supply before long. NASA couldn't afford to ground her now, but even if they did she knew she could get a job flying somebody else's ship. Or even her own, for that matter. Anything that would hold air would work. She wasn't above flying a pressurized septic tank, if that's what it took to stay in space.

Judy heard a nervous voice over the intercom. "Having problems out there?"

She shook herself back to the present. The Moon was drawing closer by the second. "No. Hang on." She fastened the getaway special canister back to the cargo bay wall and plugged in the data link to the ship. "How's that?"

"I'm getting power. Let me run the diagnostic check." A few seconds later, Allen said, "Looks good. I'm keying in the coordinates."

"You sure you don't want to stay and admire the view?"

"Uh . . . some other time, maybe."

"Right." Judy reached out to steady herself against the airlock door. She tilted her head back for one last look at the Moon, so near she almost felt she could touch it. Someday she would. Someday soon. She cleared her throat. "Whenever you're—"

But it had already disappeared.

4

"Your hyperdrive engine," Carl said, "is the worst disaster to befall the world since the invention of the nuclear bomb." He'd finally awakened from the drugs Gerry had given him, and was hovering over Allen's shoulders in the aft crew station, glancing nervously out the overhead windows from time to time, as if the Earth might slip by without his knowledge unless he were diligent in watching for it.

He was a nervous man anyway, thin and hatchet-faced. At least he looked that way on the ground. In orbit, the normal pooling of fluids in the upper body that came with zero-gee rounded out his features, making him look almost normal. Judy, watching him from the command chair where she'd been trying to assess the damage to the ship, wondered if that was why he liked spaceflight so much: because it improved his appearance.

Allen stood at his control panel, his feet tucked into floor grips so he wouldn't have to hold himself down every time he pushed a button. He'd been there for nearly an hour, running diagnostics on the hyperdrive engine and using the shuttle's navigation equipment to figure out where they were before he moved them anywhere else.

It was taking much longer than he'd expected, partially because of Carl's interference. At this latest proclamation, Allen tilted his head back, looked at Carl upside down, and said, "You know, it amazes me how a Luddite could work his way so high in the space program. If you really think a major breakthrough in spaceflight is a disaster, why aren't you back in Florida blowing up the Vehicle Assembly Building or something?"

Carl's eyes bulged. "Luddite! I don't have to be a Luddite

to see what this will do to the world economy. If you give hyperdrive engines to everyone at once, people are going to use them all at once, and when they all leave their jobs to go gallivanting around the galaxy there won't be anybody left to run the machinery. Our whole industrial society will grind to a halt."

Allen laughed. "Oh come on, now. Our whole society? I'd be surprised if one person in a hundred actually goes anywhere. One in a thousand is probably a high estimate. All I've done is give the adventurous the option to get off an overcrowded planet. That doesn't seem like a recipe for disaster to me."

"It wouldn't." Carl wiped spittle from his lips. "Look, it doesn't take a big upset to shake the world economy. Remember cold fusion back in the eighties? The stock market went berserk right after Pons and Fleischmann announced their discovery. If they hadn't been proven wrong almost immediately, we would have had a major depression. These things need to be eased into use so people can adapt to them slowly, not dumped on us without warning."

"That's what they said when I introduced the electron plasma battery," Allen said. "Everybody was worried that it would knock out the auto industry because it was such a better power source than the internal combustion engine, but it didn't. What it did was give Detroit another chance to build something that would compete with foreign cars, and it incidentally helped clear up the air across the entire *planet*. The only people who were hurt were the ones with no faith in human ingenuity who bet against the auto industry in the stock market and lost."

Carl reddened, and Judy wondered if he was one of those people. He didn't let it derail his argument, though. He dismissed it with a wave of his hand and said, "You got lucky. This time there's a lot more at stake."

He glanced reproachfully at Judy as well. Before Allen could respond, she said, "Don't look at me that way. There's careful dissemination and there's suppression. The military wanted full suppression, and there's no way I'd go along with that."

"You don't know what they wanted," Carl said.

"Wanna bet?"

Allen said, "Look, you're both missing the point. Humanity isn't some homogeneous mass that reacts like *this* or like *that* when something happens to it. It's a bunch of individual people, living individual lives. Trying to manipulate their reactions to something is ridiculous. Worse than ridiculous; it's fascist."

"Oh, so now I'm a fascist Luddite?" Carl glanced out the windows, then back at Allen, who turned back to his computer and tapped another instruction into the program that analyzed the data from their previous jumps.

"That's what it sounds like to me," he replied.

Carl snorted contemptuously and reached for a hand-hold to pull himself closer to Allen. "Listen here, mister physicist. I'm probably a bigger proponent of freedom and technology than you are. That's why this business has me so upset; I can see what's going to happen to the space program from here on out."

"Why should you be upset?" Allen asked.

"Because it's going to die, that's why! People aren't going to spend money on space stations and orbiting colonies when they can zip off to Alpha Centauri on a wish and a prayer."

"Hmmm," Allen said, scratching his chin. "I never looked at it quite that way, but even so, I really don't think—"

"That's the problem! You really don't think. You're so hot for glory that you can't be bothered to consider—"

"Carl."

He glanced over at Judy, and the look in his eyes made her glad he was clear across the flight deck from her. Still, she didn't want him around Allen anymore, either.

"I want you to inventory the consumables. We don't know how long we're going to be out here, so we need to figure out how long we can stretch it before we run out of food and air."

Allen turned toward her. "Don't worry, I'll get us back before we run out of anything. I'm just about to start the calibration runs."

"And then how long before we can get back into the right orbit for a rescue mission, and how long before they can *send* a rescue mission?" Judy asked him. "No, we're going to start conserving now, while it will do the most good."

"I—"

"Save it, Allen. Carl, go below and do the inventory."

Carl looked as if he wanted to protest, but apparently he wasn't ready to add mutiny to the list of troubles he imagined awaiting him back on Earth. "Aye aye, Captain," he said sarcastically, but he shoved away from Allen and pulled himself headfirst through the hatchway in the floor.

When he was gone, Allen said, "I meant it; the calibration shouldn't take more than another couple of hours, and once I've done that I could put us back in orbit in no time. Of course, as long as we're out here, we could just as easily do a grand tour of the planets."

They could, couldn't they? See the whole solar system in one mission. Somewhat reluctantly, Judy said, "I don't know if that's such a good idea."

"You too?"

She unbuckled her seatbelt and floated closer to him. "I don't know what to think. I think Carl's overreacting, but he does have a point. We may be moving too fast here. It could be too much for people to adapt to all at once."

"We've already demonstrated what we can do," Allen said. "The question now is whether we take advantage of it ourselves or let someone else."

"That may be a good enough reason to slow down. Leave something for the next people to do. We don't want to look greedy." She looked at his notebook computer Velcroed to the workstation. The lettering was nearly worn off the number keys, and there was a semicircular streak on the screen where he had tried to clean it with a damp cloth. Nothing fancy about it. There were millions of computers just like it all over the world, and from what she'd seen inside the getaway special canister, the parts for the hyperdrive engine wouldn't be hard to come by, either. It wouldn't be long at all before someone else tried it.

"How many people did you send the plans to?" she asked. "Everyone in INSANE?"

Allen nodded. "There's over three hundred of us."

There would probably have been more if the organization had a different name, Judy thought. Three hundred wasn't exactly a lot. As she thought about it, she felt the hair on the back of her neck start to tingle.

"You realize every member of the group is going to be a target now?" she asked.

Looking back to his computer, Allen said, "They will be if they don't forward the email. I mentioned that in my letter. It's a powerful incentive to share."

"You're assuming they get the chance to share," Judy said.

"It takes about three mouse-clicks," Allen pointed out.

"You need unbroken fingers to click a mouse."

He frowned. "What do you mean by—"

"Email is hard to intercept, but snatching three hundred scientists would be a piece of cake. I'll bet every spy agency and secret police force in the world is trying to do just that. A lot of them probably have plans in place just for this sort of contingency, so their response is going to be about three mouse-clicks away, too." It seemed farfetched, but if she agreed with Carl about anything, it was that Allen's hyperdrive was a big enough deal to rattle governments. And when governments got rattled, they usually became ruthless in trying to ensure that they wound up on top.

Allen's eyes had gone wide. "You—no, that's impossible. You're talking about a globally coordinated kidnapping effort, timed to happen before *anyone* forwards the email. Once it's out on the internet, it'll spread like wildfire. Nobody can stop it."

Judy sighed. "I don't know. Maybe I'm worried about nothing. When I first realized what we were dealing with, I was afraid we'd be killed before we could get the secret out, but now I'm starting to wonder how many people are going to be killed *because* of it."

"Nobody," Allen said. "The word is spreading as we speak, and it's spreading way too fast to stop."

"You hope."

"I know."

He turned back to his computer. "I'm ready to test it."

"You've figured out where we are?" Judy squinted out the windshield at the sun. It was a tiny, bright circle against black space.

Allen shrugged. "Close enough. We're somewhere past Jupiter's orbit. Jupiter is clear around on the other side of the Sun right now, but that's how far we are. I think."

She gave him a sidelong glance. "I thought you were going to do your testing between Earth and Mars."

He shrugged. "I thought so too, but with the Sun the size it is, we can't be there. Evidently I miscalculated."

A shiver ran down Judy's back. What if he'd miscalculated on something more dangerous, like the diameter of the space warp his engine created, or whether people could live inside its sphere of influence? He could have killed them all the first time he pushed the "Go" button.

He might kill them yet. If something else burned out in the hyperdrive, they could be stranded millions of miles from help, and even if they did manage to make it back to Earth, there was no guarantee they could achieve orbit again. And if they managed that, they still couldn't land the normal way. Not with the vertical stabilizer vaporized. *Discovery* would need major repairs before it could ever negotiate the atmosphere again.

Judy dreaded the investigations she would have to endure once—if—they landed. Maybe it was just Carl's pessimism getting to her, but she was beginning to regret her rash defiance of authority, if only for the inconvenience it would cause her before she could actually use Allen's device for exploring. But the alternative—letting it become a military secret—felt infinitely worse.

She took a deep breath and said, "Go ahead and do what you have to do."

5

As Allen keyed in coordinates, he said, "I'm going to set it for one-tenth of a percent of our first jump. That should cut our distance down to a few light-seconds, and put less strain on the engine."

Judy nodded. "Good."

He pressed the "Go" button. The radio beeped, but the view out the windows remained the same. Judy didn't know whether that was because they hadn't gone anywhere, or because they just hadn't gone far enough to change the scenery. Without planets close by, that would take a long jump. They would have to leap clear across the Solar System before the stars would even start to shift position.

Seconds crawled by while they waited for the radio pulse to catch up with them. Judy said, "Are you sure your receiver is—" but then the radio beeped again and Allen said, "Aha, got it! We went . . . three and a half million miles. Holy cow."

He keyed in more coordinates, then took them through hyperspace again. After five or six seconds, the radio beeped again, then about ten seconds later it beeped again. "Okay," he said, "we've got our triangulation, and that at least looks good. No aiming error. But that distance . . ." He trailed off, keying in more coordinates.

He took them on three more jumps in rapid succession. Every time Judy heard the beep of the radio beacon, she felt a shiver run up her spine. It wasn't the sound, but the momentary disorientation of the jump that went with it. Each time it happened, she imagined herself being torn apart atom-by-atom and squirted through some higher dimension to someplace else. Allen had sworn it didn't work that way, but her subconscious mind evidently didn't believe him. She wished he would at least get the thing calibrated so she wouldn't keep wondering if the next jump would take them halfway across the galaxy.

But after their fifth jump in as many minutes, he was still frowning and scratching his head. "What's wrong?" she asked him.

"It doesn't make sense," he said. "It's taking far less energy to create the space warp than I calculated it would. It's almost an order of magnitude off, except for the jumps from Earth and the Moon. Those were only four or five times as efficient as I expected. But that still translates into distances anywhere from ten to a hundred times as far as I intended to take us."

"You mean you can't predict where you're going to go?"

He smiled reassuringly. "Sure I can. It's repeatable; we demonstrated that earlier. I can figure out the energy/distance correlation by trial and error if I have to, but I'd much rather be able to calculate it ahead of time, especially for long jumps. When we start going light-years at a stretch, we don't want to wind up in interstellar space with no idea of where we are."

Judy shivered. "You're right about that." She didn't even like not knowing where in the Solar System they were, but to be lost light-years away from home would be terrifying.

Allen drifted up to the overhead windows and looked out. "Hmm. I wonder . . ."

"What?" A cooling fan turned on in the control console; Judy pulled herself closer to Allen so she could hear better.

"I wonder if mass has anything to do with it. I did all my initial tests in vacuum chambers at the bottom of Earth's gravity well; maybe it doesn't take as much energy to punch a hole in space when you're not close to a large mass."

Judy felt her breath catch in her throat. She had to swallow before she could say, "*Maybe* mass has something to do with it? You don't *know?*"

He shrugged. "How could I? This is my first chance to get away from it."

"But—didn't your theories predict anything like this?"

He smiled cheerfully. "What theories? I stumbled across the effect while I was working on the electron plasma battery. I puzzled it out enough to make the engine, but I don't have anything like an all-inclusive theory to explain it." He pushed himself back down to the keypad and typed in another set of numbers.

"What about relativity?" Judy asked.

Allen laughed. "If relativity could predict something like this, we'd have been using hyperdrive since 1925 or so. No, it's a completely new phenomenon." He pulsed the engine again, and while they waited for the timing signal to catch up he said, "I'm betting it won't contradict anything we already know, but we'll probably have to modify our existing theories to account for it. In the meantime, if we can figure out how it works experimentally, we'll be miles ahead of the theorists."

"So to speak," Judy said.

The radio beeped, and Allen said, "Okay, another three million miles. Now we go back near a gravity field . . ." He punched in more coordinates, and when he pressed the "Go" button Earth blinked into view again, this time at least half a million miles away. The Moon was just a small sphere beside it.

Allen didn't wait for the timing pulse to catch up. He set up another jump, and this time Earth shifted across the star field. They'd apparently gone sideways, rather than toward or away from it. When the timing pulse from that jump arrived, Allen nodded and said, "Two hundred thousand. Much shorter. So gravity *does* affect it. Now we just have to figure out how much." He began to whistle softly as he set to work analyzing the data.

After a few minutes, he said, "Hang on; I'm going to see if I can actually hit a target this time."

"What target?" Judy asked immediately, but he'd already pushed the button. She looked out the windows and gasped in surprise. Saturn had swelled into view like a soap bubble rising from a cosmic bathtub toy. The planet itself looked about the size of the full Moon seen from Earth, with its rings more than double that width. The shuttle had materialized over one of the poles, so the rings went all the way around.

"Very funny," Judy said.

Allen looked out the window and grinned. "Good old inverse-square law. You've got to love it."

Anybody who knew how to calculate an orbit knew the inverse-square law: the gravitational attraction of a given mass dropped off with the square of the distance from it. The same rule worked for light intensity, sound volume, and just about any other quantity that issued from a point source. Judy tried to imagine how it applied here. It was hard to think with Saturn just outside the window, but she forced herself to look away and concentrate on what Allen had said. "So did jumping to Saturn just now take more energy than the same distance in flat space, or did it take less because we were going downhill?"

Allen shook his head. "More. Apparently whenever you get near mass, it takes more energy to create the warp field, no matter which way you go. You've got to warp it twice, see, once at the point where you leave the normal universe and once where you drop back in." He wrinkled his forehead, thinking, then said, "In fact, if it took less energy going toward a big mass, then we'd probably have wound up inside a black hole on our first jump."

Judy winced at the thought, but Allen didn't notice. He said, "The good news is, distance is just a minor factor in the equation, so as long as we don't try jumping directly from planet to planet, we can make interstellar jumps without having to take along a nuclear reactor for power."

"I thought you said you could jump directly from the surface into space."

"You can. You just don't want to go very far on the first jump, or it uses more energy. So you make a short jump to get outside the gravity well, then a long jump to someplace near where you want to go, then another short jump to land.

Well, actually a bunch of short jumps, because you can't go all the way to the surface."

"Why not?"

Allen had been waving his arms as he talked; he reached out to one of the remote video monitors to steady himself. "Two reasons. When you jump, you keep your initial velocity, so unless you match it perfectly with the spot on the ground you're trying to land on, you'll be moving when you get there. But the other reason is that you can't appear where there's already something in the way. Even air is too thick. So you have to appear outside the atmosphere and fall the rest of the way in with a parachute."

"Or fly in," Judy said. She looked out at the stump of the vertical stabilizer. *Discovery* wouldn't be flying anywhere for a while.

She shuddered to think what would have happened if the A-sat weapon had hit the crew module instead of the tail. Or if they'd been just a few more minutes in repairing the hyperdrive, or if the space warp it generated hadn't been big enough to take the whole shuttle along with it. They were lucky to be alive.

Saturn lured her attention again. Part of her, the little girl who'd dreamed of space travel, boggled at the sight, but the part of her who captained the space shuttle was thinking, *He didn't even know how it worked before he yanked us out of orbit.*

Maybe knowing how many things could go wrong on a space flight made her paranoid, but the knowledge that Allen was flying by the seat of his pants didn't inspire confidence. What if he'd missed something else equally obvious? In fact . . . "Wait a second. Are we outside Saturn's radiation belts?"

"Radiation belts don't extend over the poles," he said.

"You're sure?"

He nodded. "Relax. I know what I'm doing. And now that I know how to correct for mass, I can put us back in Earth orbit any time we want."

Provided the hyperdrive didn't burn out again. Judy imagined them falling into Saturn if it failed. Or would they starve first? How far away were they, anyway, and how strong was Saturn's gravity at this distance? And even if they didn't fall into Saturn, what about the unwanted velocity they'd picked up from their time near the Moon? Aloud, she said, "You don't have any idea what our actual vector is, do you? Like you said, we could pop into the right place, but doing seventeen thousand miles an hour straight at the ground. Even if we start out a couple hundred miles up, that doesn't give us much time to react."

Allen looked out over Judy's shoulder. He didn't say anything for at least a minute, and when he did speak it was only to say, "We're farther out than anyone has ever been. Seeing something nobody else has ever seen. Doesn't that mean anything to you?"

The rings looked like tie-dyed silk. Specks of brightness just beyond them had to be the shepherd moons. Judy could almost hear the theme from *2001: A Space Odyssey* playing in the background.

She shook her head and the music stopped. "Sure it does," she said, "but it also means if something goes wrong, we're dead. I'm just trying to keep that from happening."

Carl chose that moment to float up through the hatchway, an even more worried than usual look on his face.

"What's wrong?" Judy asked.

"We've got eight days of consumables," he said, "but the toilet's broken, and Gerry's got to go. At least he says he does."

"Oh, great." The power of suggestion made Judy suddenly notice the pressure in her own bladder, too. She tried to ignore it, but she knew it wouldn't be denied for long. Nor would Gerry's. "Well, he'll just have to use a waste bag," she said. "For that matter, he'd have to use one anyway, because I'm not letting him loose again."

Carl scowled. "We can't keep him in that bunk forever."

"We're not going to. Allen is just about done here, and I think we've pushed our luck far enough for one flight. As soon as we're sure it's safe, we're going back to the space station."

"Good," Carl said. He pulled himself down into the mid-deck again without even looking out the window.

Allen did. Judy found her gaze following his, once more drawn to the spectacle of Saturn floating just outside. The planet was half in light and half in shadow, the soft texture of its cloud layers giving it the puffy three-dimensionality of an overstuffed pillow. Its rings, on the other hand, were so flat an abstraction that they looked unnatural, like a collar drawn with a felt-tip marker on a hologram of a cat.

"Sure you don't want to stop off at Mars?" Allen asked softly.

She took a deep breath, then sighed and looked away. "Not this time. Let's go home."

6

"It'll take three jumps to put us back in orbit," Allen said. "I already figured out how to do it weeks ago. I call it a 'tangent vector translation maneuver.' "

"That's kind of a mouthful," Judy said. She and Carl were looking over his shoulders again as he programmed the coordinates into his computer.

"It's descriptive," Allen replied. "When you're in orbit, your vector is always tangent to the point you're occupying at the moment. So to slip into a particular orbit, you have to translate your current vector into one that's tangent to the orbit you want. What we do is jump to within a few thousand miles of Earth, where we're close enough to use the tracking satellites and ground radar to establish our vector but far enough away to keep from hitting anything if we're aimed the wrong direction. Then once we know how fast we're going and what direction we're headed, we jump to the right point over the planet for gravity to warp our trajectory into the right one for where we want to be, and then we pop into low-Earth orbit with just the right vector. It's a piece of cake."

"Famous last words," Carl said.

Allen ignored him. "First translation coming up." He pressed the "Jump" key.

The radio beacon beeped. Judy looked out the forward windows just in time to see Saturn vanish like a switched-out light, and Earth pop into existence to the right of where it had been. It was much larger, filling about sixty degrees of view, which meant they were closer than the Moon, but still way beyond normal orbital altitude.

"Checking our position . . ." Allen said slowly. "Hah! I was less than fifty kilometers off target."

"Good for you," Carl said in a voice that said just the opposite. He turned away and pulled himself past Judy into the copilot's chair.

"What are you doing?" she asked when she saw him reaching for the radio controls.

"I want to find out how much damage we've done on the ground."

Judy wasn't sure she wanted to know, but she supposed there was no point in delaying the inevitable. "All right," she said, "but no transmissions just yet. Let's find out how much trouble we're in before we let them know we're back."

"They'll spot us quick enough with radar," Carl pointed out.

"If they're looking out here. We must be ten thousand kilometers up."

"Twelve," Allen said.

"Won't matter," Carl said, but he set the radio to receive only and started sifting through the commercial frequencies, switching on the cabin speaker so all three of them could hear.

There weren't many stations with the power to punch a clear signal that far into space, and there was a lot of static from stations that had just enough signal to create interference, but Carl managed to tune in an English-language station long enough to hear the end of the Beatles' "Yesterday."

"Appropriate," he sneered. The deejay came on and told them that the weather was partly cloudy and fifty-seven degrees out with a slight chance of rain in the higher elevations. Judy chuckled as she always did when she heard that phrase from space, but her breath caught in her throat at the deejay's next words.

"Here's an update on the new computer virus that . . ."

Whatever else he had to say was lost in static.

Judy felt her heart lurch. "Get that station back!" she ordered.

Carl tried, but atmospheric conditions had apparently

changed enough to block it. He tuned on across the spectrum until he heard another snippet:

". . . extremely virulent email virus has apparently mutated into three different forms already. The original 'hyperdrive plans' form hit less than an hour ago, but the Internet Virus Watch Consortium has already detected two variations, one with a subject line reading 'Wait, it's real!' and another one reading simply 'Hoax.' These are very dangerous virus programs that can apparently cause irreparable hardware damage to your computer if you even open them, so the only safe course of action is to delete them unopened, even if it appears that they were sent by someone you know."

Judy looked over at Allen, whose mouth was open wide enough to stick his foot into. "Impossible, is it?" she asked.

"It—I—how could they do that so *fast?*"

"Like I said earlier, they've probably had contingency plans for something like this ready to go for years. A real virus they can rename to mimic your email and send out from thousands of sites all at once; it would overrun the entire net within minutes."

"It wouldn't be a virus," Carl said happily. "It's an email worm. Reads the address book on the target computer and sends out more copies of itself to everyone listed there."

She glared at him. "Virus, worm, whatever; the important thing is that somebody's managed to do an end-run around Allen's email."

"Yes, they have, haven't they? They've given us a second chance."

"Second chance, my ass! This is a power grab, pure and simple. Whoever did this is trying to keep it all to themselves. You don't really think they're going to tuck the plans away and never use them, do you?"

Carl shook his head. "Of course not. There'll be controlled experimentation, cautious exploration, and—"

"By whom? The CIA? Carl, do you really want *them* to be the ones who lead humanity into space?"

That took a little of the wind out of his sails, but not

enough. "It's a moot point," he said. "They've won."

"No they haven't," Allen growled. He tapped at his keyboard, the radio beacon beeped again, and Earth shrank to a third its former size.

"Where did you take us?" Judy asked.

"Geosynchronous orbit."

The communication satellite, like practically everything the shuttle carried into orbit, looked like a cylindrical tank with solar panels and antennas attached to it. Judy had seen dozens of them in her time as a pilot, but never from her current vantage point: just behind one in orbit 36,000 kilometers from Earth. In normal operation the shuttle never got that high; the satellites were released in low orbit and had to use their own engines to climb into position.

It had taken *Discovery* another two jumps to reach it, but that was just to fine-tune their orbit. The extra velocity they had picked up during their fall toward the Moon had been almost exactly what they needed.

Now Allen was outside in a spacesuit, tethered to the end of the shuttle's manipulator arm while he plugged his computer into the satellite's diagnostic port. Judy, watching through the payload bay windows, could see him tapping the keys with a screwdriver off his tool belt because his gloved fingers were too thick to type with.

"How's it going?" she asked over the intercom.

"Just about got it," he replied. "I've got all five hundred channels ready to accept my input when I give the command, so now all I need to do is hook up the video stream."

The black-and-white screen beside the back windows was showing an old rerun of *Space Rangers* at the moment. Normally it was used to watch the manipulator arm at work, but they could patch any signal they wanted to it. Allen had strung an antenna out in front of the satellite so they could monitor its broadcast, and Judy had tuned through the microwave channels until she had found an unscrambled show. "I can't believe it," she said. "You can just plug in your computer and take over an entire communications satellite?"

He laughed. "Well, it helps if you've got the control program already loaded."

"And where did you get that?"

"Friends in high places."

Carl, who'd been glowering from the copilot's chair all the while, laughed derisively. "Another nut case from INSANE, no doubt. I hope he hangs alongside you when the Feds catch up with him."

Allen didn't bother to reply. Neither did Judy. She was just as tired of shutting him up as she was of listening to him. The only reason she hadn't locked him into a bunk alongside Gerry was because she knew he wouldn't do anything to stop her or Allen from what they were doing. He'd lost the argument, but he wasn't the type to try forcing his way. He would wait for the courts to exonerate him, and in the meantime he would snipe at them and make them feel guilty.

Judy would have felt guiltier if she believed him, but she still didn't buy his rationale. There might be some economic disruption as people got used to the idea that they weren't stuck on one planet anymore, but throwing the internet into chaos to stop the plans had probably caused more financial damage than the hyperdrive would. And as for the personal consequences, she might lose her job for failing to follow orders, but she couldn't believe she'd be in any real danger when they got home. This wasn't the seventeenth century, after all, and unlike Galileo, neither she nor Allen would have to recant their beliefs on pain of death. Once the secret was out, scientists everywhere would confirm it, and when that happened the government would have far bigger things to worry about than prosecuting Judy and Allen for giving it away.

"Okay, I'm ready," Allen said. "Here goes." The notebook computer was dangling at the end of its data cable; he grasped it in his left glove while he pushed the "Enter" key with his right index finger.

Space Rangers whirled into static, replaced by a bright blue screen with white words: "Emergency Alert. If you have videotape equipment, set it to record the following program." Allen's calm, classical-station-disk-jockey voice read the message aloud, then the screen cleared to show Allen himself, dressed in a white spacesuit liner, in a sequence that Judy had filmed just minutes earlier with one of the shuttle's public relations cameras. They had stored the image digitally on his computer's hard drive, and he was playing it back now through the video interface.

"By now you may have already heard that the Space Shuttle *Discovery* has demonstrated a revolutionary new device, a faster-than-light engine for traveling through space. I am Doctor Allen Meisner, the inventor of that device, and I've interrupted your program today to give you the plans for it." He smiled wide for the camera, and Judy winced at how goofy he looked. Nobody was going to believe him. People all over the world were no doubt switching channels already, sure that he was selling something.

But then, he was on all the channels. They could switch satellites if they wanted, but even then they would probably encounter him on at least half the channels there. All the communications satellites were linked these days, relaying signals around the globe. Even the European satellites were part of the system. They could be taken off-line from the ground, but Judy knew not all of them would be. Not in time, anyway. The ones under private control—like the one they had hijacked—probably wouldn't go off-line at all. After all, this was news, and none of the networks would want to be the only ones *not* carrying it.

The video zoomed in on the computer screen, which showed an image of the circuit diagram that Allen had attempted to email to everyone. In a voice-over, he described how to assemble it and how the finished engine worked. The whole thing took less than ten minutes, including the last-minute addition that he had hastily cobbled together to explain the distance calibration. The presentation looked like a bad high school physics film the way he—or more often just his hand—pointed out various parts of circuit diagrams, but as Judy watched him describe how to build and operate a hyperdrive engine, she couldn't help but be impressed. Some people, anyway, would record it, and that's all that mattered. It wouldn't take long for them to realize it was genuine, and once the secret was in private hands, it would spread throughout the world just as fast as an email virus.

The radio came alive with frantic calls from Mission Control the moment the television broadcast began, but Judy switched it off. She already knew what they would have to say. Her skin prickled as she waited for a laser blast from the defense satellites, but she didn't really think that would happen. This was an international communications satellite, and unlike the automatic shot that hit the shuttle's tail fin, shooting at them now would take an executive decision to authorize. She was willing to bet nobody would stick their neck out to do that, not without thinking it over very carefully, by which time Judy and her crew would be gone.

They let Allen's video repeat once before they unplugged it and let the satellite resume its normal programming. Judy brought the arm and Allen down into the cargo bay again, then moved the shuttle away with the maneuvering engines as soon as Allen was in the airlock. A few minutes later he had removed his spacesuit and joined her on the flight deck. "Where to now?" he asked, taking his position at the hyperdrive controls.

"The space station, I guess," Judy said. "I think we've done about all we can do from out here."

Carl snorted. "Believe me, you've done more than enough."

7

Space Station *Freedom* had not lived up to its designers' dreams. That was less the fault of the architects and the engineers than it was the fault of the waffling politicians and the vociferous minority they represented, but whatever the cause, administrative costs and "tactical compromises" had eaten so much of the budget that there was little left for hardware. So little, in fact, that the astronauts had taken to calling it *"Fred"* in order to save forty-three percent on the cost of the name.

For a while it had lost its name entirely. When the Russians had been part of the project, NASA had decided that calling it "Freedom" might be considered a slap in the face to the former Soviet power, so some poetic genius in the front office had decided it should be referred to by the totally uninspired, bureaucratically functional title of "the International Space Station" instead. The Russians, who had poetry in their souls, had hated that even worse than "Freedom," but they were too polite to say so.

Then, after the inevitable political split, NASA revived the old name and tried to pretend that the alliance had never happened. Never mind that billions of dollars had been poured down the drain on hardware that was now useless without its Russian counterparts; the official dogma was that we had never counted on their help and didn't need it now.

That was true enough, Judy supposed. The place held air and six crewmembers. But it was a far cry from what it could have been.

Even so, when the lumpy row of habitat modules and their crosswise boom of solar panels blinked into existence only a few miles away, Judy felt a strong sense of relief. With the vertical stabilizer missing there was no hope of landing, and with the toilet stopped up they only had a few hours before they had to break out the waste bags. Whatever else its shortcomings, at least *Fred* had working plumbing.

But more than that, as soon as they docked she could turn over the hyperdrive to someone else. She wouldn't be responsible for it anymore, and wouldn't have to keep making decisions that would affect the whole human race.

She switched the radio to the ship-to-station frequency and spoke into the tiny microphone that snaked around the side of her face from her communications carrier. "*Freedom*, this is *Discovery*, do you copy?"

The voice in her headset was female. That would be Mary Hunter, the station commander. She didn't sound excited about the call. "Roger *Discovery*, this is *Freedom*. We copy, and have you on radar. What is your status?"

All business, eh? Judy shrugged and said, "Nominal, except our vertical stabilizer is damaged beyond repair. And the toilet is backed up again. Request permission to dock and wait for the next shuttle."

"Ahh . . . *Discovery*, be advised that the United States government has issued a warrant for your arrest. If you dock here, we'll have to confine you to quarters and turn you over to the Feds on the next flight down."

Judy laughed. "Confined to quarters? Mary, the habitat module is thirty feet long. Where are we going to go?"

"With Doctor Meisner's device on board, who knows? I don't particularly want to find out, and besides, we have orders."

Judy looked over at Carl in the copilot's seat, strapped in for the thrust they'd never needed. Normally Gerry would be sitting there, but he was still locked into his bunk. He'd given them plenty of reason, but suddenly it didn't seem quite so unlikely that Mary would do the same to them.

"Told you so," Carl said smugly.

Turning around so she could see Allen in the equipment bay behind her, Judy said, "Well, it looks like we're in for a long wait in a closet until they have another shuttle ready to fly. Unless you have another trick up your sleeve."

He shook his head. "It wasn't supposed to work this way. People were supposed to be overjoyed. We were supposed to go home to parades and speeches."

Carl laughed. "Oh, there'll be plenty of parades, all right, with our heads on spikes out in front of 'em."

"Not funny," Allen said petulantly.

"Neither is upsetting the global economy," Carl said. "Or giving every country on Earth an instantaneous delivery system for nuclear bombs. Or—"

"It can't be used for that," Allen said. "You can't open a pathway into the atmosphere; there's too much matter already there."

"How long you want to bet it'll be before somebody figures out how?"

"They won't, because it's impos—"

Mary's incoming voice cut him off. "What are your intentions, *Discovery*?"

I intend to stay free, Judy thought, but aloud she said, "I don't see that we have much choice."

"Neither do we. Do I have your word that you'll submit peacefully to arrest?"

"No," Judy said automatically. "I mean, give us a minute to talk this over. We weren't expecting quite this kind of reception." She turned off the radio. "Well?"

Carl said, "Well what? We don't have any other option."

"Sure we do," Judy said. "We've got over a week's supplies left, don't we?"

Carl nodded reluctantly.

"We've got twice as much oxygen as we'll ever need now that we can't use the OMS engines for landing, and the fuel cells will keep providing water, so we could actually stay two or three weeks before we *have* to give ourselves up. The question is, would we be any better off if we did that?"

"Nope," Carl said. "You'll still be guilty of treason and piracy. They'll just add resisting arrest to the charges."

"If they can catch us. Allen, isn't there any way you can

use that drive of yours to set us down on the ground? Someplace out of the way, where we'd have time to escape before they caught up with us?"

Allen shook his head. "Like I told you before, it won't put something into a space that's already got something in it. Not even air. It takes too much energy to open the gateway. I could maybe drop us down to thirty miles or so above ground, but anything below that would burn out the engine."

She felt a moment of irrational annoyance. What good was a hyperdrive if you couldn't land once you got where you were going? She pushed the thought aside and tried to visualize the problem. "Can't you transport what's there into space, and put us in the vacuum left behind before it closes?"

Allen shook his head again. "No. Not without another engine on the far end, and split-second timing. And you'd have to have the calibration down *cold*, to within a foot or two, or it wouldn't work. I suppose it might be possible, eventually, but with the way the jump field is affected by mass you'd have to account for so many variables that it'd take forever to calculate. The density of the air itself would probably affect it, and the composition of the ground below, and—"

"Okay, okay, I get the picture." Judy looked out at the space station, its habitat module shining white in the direct sunlight. The airlocks sticking out of either end were surrounded by machinery and tool lockers; placed where they would be easy to reach during EVAs. Half a dozen emergency descent modules clustered around the airlocks as well, poised for quick evacuation in case the habitats lost pressure or came under enemy fire. Nobody had ever actually ridden one down from orbit, but they were basically the same system as the old Gemini capsules, two-seat re-entry vehicles with ablative heat shields and parachutes. NASA had originally intended to build a miniature shuttle for a lifeboat, but the X-38 program had fallen to the budget axe along with so much else.

Judy eyed the descent modules critically. "Carl, what's our ground track, anyway?" she asked.

He called up the display on the center monitor. The station and shuttle were over western Australia, heading northeast. Not good. If they were to de-orbit now, they'd wind up in the north Atlantic, or worse, in the Middle East. But in one more orbit they would pass over the U.S. If they timed it right, they could make like they were going to dock with the space station, then grab an EDM and be gone before Mary and the rest of the station crew could react. The modules were mostly composite material; radar couldn't track them. If Judy and Allen switched off the emergency beacon, they stood a good chance of making it to the ground without detection. NASA could only calculate where they would land to within a few dozen miles; that was a big area to search. With any luck at all, they could make a clean escape.

Provided they survived the descent.

Judy flipped on the radio again. "Mary, you still there?"

"Still waiting. Have you made a decision yet? Ground control is getting a little nervous."

"We're still thinking about it. Have you got any idea just what they've got planned for us?"

Mary laughed. "Well, what do you expect? They were willing to give you a simple trial and execution until you pulled that stunt with the communication satellite, but now I think they're leaning more toward public humiliation and stoning."

"Not funny," Judy said. She looked out at the descent modules again, wondering just how far off the mark Mary was. Not far enough, she was afraid. All right, then, time for plan B.

"I'm willing to stand trial," she said, "but I want some assurance I'll *get* a trial. If the President promises us safe conduct, we'll surrender." There, that ought to ensure a long enough delay to get them into position.

In the meantime, she made Allen keep breathing oxygen so he could get back into his spacesuit when the time came, and she began washing the nitrogen out of her own system as well. Normally a transfer from shuttle to space station didn't require suits, but Judy explained that she wanted to be ready in case they had docking problems, and she made Carl and Gerry breathe oxygen, too, so they wouldn't suspect her real plan.

But ten minutes later, Mary came back on the radio and said, "Switch over to ground control. The President is waiting."

If Judy had needed any assurance that she was in deep trouble, she'd just gotten it. President John "Private Interests" Stevenson didn't respond that quickly to a call from his stockbroker.

That was his voice on the radio, though, saying, "Well, Miss Gallagher, you've certainly caused a ruckus, haven't you?"

Judy was beyond being impressed by politicians. She said, "It seems to me that whoever spread the virus on the internet is the one who caused the ruckus."

"That will be a matter for the courts to decide." He cleared his throat, then said, "You've asked for my word that you'll be treated fairly when you return. I can assure you that you will receive the full protection of the law in your prosecution for high treason, piracy, hijacking, computer hacking, and violation of Federal communications regulations."

He had to be reading that from a note card. Good. If she ever wound up in court, Judy would subpoena the document and every memo that led up to it. There were bound to be some interesting surprises in the paper trail.

She didn't plan to let it get that far. She said, "Thank you, Mr. President," and switched back to the space station frequency. "All right, Mary, we've got what we asked for. I'll bring it in for docking, but I'm going to take it slow. That hit we took could have screwed up our maneuvering engines."

Mary evidently didn't want to risk a shuttle crashing into her space station, either. She said, "Understood, *Discovery*. Take your time."

Judy did, using the aft work station controls to inch the shuttle closer to the habitat's airlock with tiny bursts of the smallest thrusters. She managed to stretch it out for over an hour, which gave them just fifteen minutes before they would be in position to make their break.

Carl had been watching her work, criticizing her timid piloting all the while. She'd been counting on that; when the shuttle was still a couple hundred feet away, she turned to him and said, "All right, then, you finish it," and pushed away from the controls. He leaped to the task like any back-seat driver given a chance to prove his superior talent, and while he concentrated on the docking, Judy pulled Allen with her down into the mid-deck.

"Okay," she said when they were out of Carl's hearing. "You get a choice. You can go back on the next shuttle and stand trial, or you can leave with me in one of *Fred*'s emergency descent modules. We've got a twenty-minute window of opportunity opening up about ten minutes from now."

Allen blinked in surprise. "You mean there's another way down?"

From his bunk, Gerry said, "No, there isn't. Those things were never meant to be used. They were meant to make the public think NASA was doing something for safety."

Judy had been filling her spacesuit's pockets with valuables from her personal locker; she stopped and looked over at Gerry. "The cynical spy speaks," she said.

"Spy or not, I'm trying to save your lives. If you take an EDM, you'll burn up in the atmosphere."

"What makes you so sure of that?"

"I was on the committee that approved them."

Was he? Judy tried to remember, but astronauts were on so many committees she could never keep straight who was on what. But even if he was, should she believe him about the modules' safety? NASA would never approve an emergency system that didn't work, would they? If an emergency ever happened, it would make them look even worse than if they had no system at all.

Gerry said, "I mean it. Judy might survive if she goes

alone and skips a couple of times before she takes the final drop, but Allen, you're fifty pounds too heavy. Even if you take your own module, you'll go down like a meteor the whole way."

Judy finished loading her pockets. "Bullshit, Gerry. The EDMs are old technology. It worked with the Gemini capsules, and it'll work now. Allen, put on your suit."

He didn't move. "Are you sure, Judy? What's Gerry got to gain by lying to us?"

"I'll tell you what he's got to gain," Judy said as she straightened out the bottom half of her spacesuit, did a half somersault, and stuck both feet at once through the waist ring into the legs. "Two more scapegoats to share the blame with. Without us, all the heat's going to fall on him."

Allen didn't look convinced, especially not when Gerry laughed and said, "Nice rationalization, Judy, but it doesn't change anything. Those EDMs are death traps."

Judy didn't have the time to argue with him. She would have just ignored him, but Allen wasn't suiting up, and they had to be out the airlock before Carl docked the shuttle with the space station; otherwise their airlock would open directly into captivity. So she said the only thing she could think of to convince him.

"All right, Gerry, I'll call your bluff. How about if I let you come with us?"

"What?"

"If I turn you loose, I'm betting you'll opt for an EDM, too."

Gerry bit his lip, then laughed. "No way. Besides, there's only two spacesuits."

"I'd carry you in a rescue ball. Unless those are bogus, too." Rescue balls were another cost- and weight-saving idea: instead of providing spacesuits for the entire crew, the shuttle carried half a dozen yard-wide airtight balls. In an emergency, the odd men out climbed inside them with portable oxygen tanks, zipped them tight, and had the astronauts with spacesuits carry them through the airlock to safety.

Gerry thought it over for a long moment, then he said, "All right. Let me go."

Judy nodded. "Okay, just a minute." To Allen she said. "There, you see? He was lying. Put on your suit."

Allen looked once more at Gerry, clearly not convinced, but he began to suit up. Judy reached for the top half of her own suit and pulled it on, linking the waist rings, then putting on the gloves.

"Let me out first," Gerry said. "I'll get the rescue ball."

"Hold on," Judy told him. She helped Allen on with his own suit and gloves, then before she set his helmet in place she said, "Don't use the radio. Carl will overhear us if you do. I don't want him to know we're there until we're already out the airlock."

Allen nodded. Judy secured his helmet and helped him into the airlock, then started to follow him. She was lowering her own helmet into place when Gerry shouted, "Hey, let me out of here!"

She twisted around to face him. "You lied to me, I lied to you. Consider us even, Gerry."

He growled and tugged at the sliding panel that held him captive, but the wire tying it shut held fast. "I wasn't lying about the descent modules!" he shouted. "I never planned to get that far! I was going to take over the ship again and fly it to *Mir*."

Mir II was a duplicate of the old Soviet space station, launched by the Russians in a fit of nationalistic pride when they got kicked off the American project, but they had quickly run out of money to maintain it and had to sell it to the French. Judy supposed Gerry could still get political asylum there, if he ever made it that far. But he never would, and he knew it. He'd be a sitting duck for days while he transferred from *Freedom*'s orbit to *Mir*'s. If the U.S. didn't shoot him down, somebody else was sure to.

"Sorry, Gerry," she said as she pulled herself into the airlock, "but I just don't believe you."

"I hope you go down in flames!" he shouted. "I hope you feel it the whole way down! I hope you—"

She slammed the airlock door and cut him off.

8

Two people in an airlock made for a tight fit. "Are you sure about this?" Allen asked, his voice about half an octave higher than usual. Even with full air pressure around them he was barely audible with two layers of glass between his mouth and her ears; she read his lips as much as heard the words.

"Sure I'm sure," she said with exaggerated mouth motions. She turned the airlock depressurization control knob to 5 psi, held it a minute to make sure the suits weren't going to leak, then turned it to zero. While they waited for the air to bleed out, she turned her head until her face was right in front of his and said, "As soon as we get out, grab your hyperdrive canisters and follow me to the descent module."

I can't hear you, he mouthed, leaning in to touch his helmet against hers.

"That doesn't work," she said. "You have to read lips."

It doesn't work? He looked like a kid who'd just learned that the Tooth Fairy wasn't real.

"Not enough surface area in contact," she said.

I'll be damned, it doesn't work. What did you say?

She spoke slowly and enunciated each word separately. "I . . . said . . . get . . . your . . . hyperdrive . . . canisters . . . and . . . follow . . . me."

Right.

When the airlock pressure fell to half a psi, Judy opened the outer hatch. The last of the air puffed out in one final whoosh, and she let it pull her out. Swinging around the edge of the hatch, she helped Allen through, then pulled herself down onto a flat package in the cargo bay where she could get a good solid surface to kick off from toward the space station overhead. It was only twenty feet away or so; Gerry had nearly held them back too long.

They didn't have time for the Manned Maneuvering Unit, the thruster chair that they normally used for moving around in space, nor did they have time to set up a cable and traverse the distance with carabiners. They would have to jump free. While Allen unstrapped his hyperdrive engine, Judy kicked off. For a heart-wrenching moment she was sure she'd screwed up and would miss the space station entirely and drift off into space until she ran out of air, but at such a short distance she'd have had to be trying hard to keep from hitting something. As it was, she'd gone nearly straight up; she had to push off from the station's airlock and scramble along handholds to reach the descent modules.

Carl had seen her pass over his target. The radio came to life with his frantic call, "Judy, what the hell are you doing out there?"

She didn't answer. Every second counted now. If the station had someone suited up and waiting in the airlock, he could still stop them.

"Judy, answer me."

She pulled herself up against the closest descent module, opened the hatch, and climbed inside. It was a tiny thing, barely big enough for the two seats it held. Judy crawled into the one farthest from the door and studied the control panel. It was simple enough; a power switch, a switch to blow the bolts holding the module to the station, a joystick to control the attitude thrusters, and a single red button labeled "Retro." Gauges and radio controls and manual overrides for the retro jettison and parachute release systems filled up the rest of the panel, but she had seen more complicated kitchen appliances. She flipped the switch that put the emergency locator beacon in manual mode, made sure the manual switch was set to "Off," then she flipped the main power switch and smiled when the green light above it lit up.

"Who do you think you are?" Carl demanded. "Butch Cassidy and the Sundance Kid? You're in space, for god's sake! You can't just steal a horse and ride out of town!"

"Wanna bet?" she muttered, but her mic was still off. She leaned back out the hatch to see how Allen was doing. He had one of the canisters loose, and was working on the other. Judy waited nervously while he got the second one free, tucked one under each arm, then tilted his head back to see where she'd gone. She waved at him from the hatch of the descent module.

He waved back, but nearly lost the canister under his right arm. He grabbed it again, but that motion lifted him off from the cargo bay and started him tumbling. He realized his predicament instantly, but instead of waiting for Judy to come get him, he kicked out with his left leg, evidently hoping to at least get himself moving toward her.

It didn't work. Judy watched, helpless, as he tumbled away at a forty-five degree angle. He'd managed to do the nearly impossible; it looked like he was going to miss the entire station, and there was nothing Judy could do to help him. If she jumped to intercept him, they'd both float off into space, and if she took the time to clip her safety line to a handhold, she'd never reach him.

The radio was a confusion of voices, Carl calling "Man overboard," Mary shouting orders to someone else inside the station, and ground control demanding to know what was going on. Judy was about to switch on her transmitter and tell them to shut up and do something useful, like send someone out with an MMU, when Allen did the only thing he could do to save himself: he took the canister from under his right arm and threw it as hard as he could out into space.

Judy gasped. The hyperdrive! Or part of it, anyway. She hoped Allen had saved the valuable half. It didn't look like he'd even stopped to consider it, though; he'd just thrown what he'd had in his hand.

The canisters weighed nearly a hundred pounds each; the reaction was more than Allen had expected. He nearly swept by the station on the *other* side, but Judy scrambled out of the descent module, gripped a handhold, and stuck her feet out in his path. He grabbed her boot on his way past and pulled her over backward hard enough to pop joints in her spine, but she held on and let him climb down her body until he reached the handhold.

He paused with his helmet next to hers and mouthed a single word: *Thanks.*

"Any time," Judy replied. "Come on, let's go before Carl sends the cavalry after us." She pointed inside.

She let Allen climb in first this time, motioning for him to sit in the far seat with the remaining canister on his lap, then she climbed in after him and pulled the hatch shut. She flipped the separation switch, and the module shuddered as the explosive bolts freed them from the station. With the joystick, Judy rolled it over until she had a clear shot out through the payload bay; then she used the forward thruster to move them free of both the station and the shuttle. She kept up the thruster burn until they were moving away at a couple dozen feet per second; at that speed they could fire the retros in less than a minute without damaging anything with their exhaust.

She checked her suit's oversize digital wristwatch. They were about halfway through their descent window. Good; that meant if they missed a little they'd still come down somewhere in North America. Judy hoped it would be someplace rural, but she would take what she could get.

Carl and Mary and ground control were all still shouting at her. Their combined voices were nothing but a distracting babble, so Judy switched them off. She swung the descent module around until the nose was pointed backward in their orbit, and when she was sure she had it lined up right, she pushed the big red "Retro" button.

Acceleration slammed her back in the seat. The shuttle spacesuits weren't designed to be sat in under thrust; Judy felt all the internal hoses and seams pressing into her back and legs, and the waist ring drew a painful line between her kidneys. She tugged at it until it fit into the hollow of her back.

The thrust died away as the retro rocket burned the last of its fuel, and they were once again in free fall. Judy nudged the joystick left a little to keep them lined up properly, and waited for the first contact with the atmosphere.

It came as a gentle rocking, easily corrected with the thrusters. Then a little heavier, buffeting rather than rocking. Judy corrected for that, too, keeping the heat shield beneath them aimed straight into the onrushing air. She could feel the drag now, pushing her into the seat the same way the retro rocket had. Only this time the force didn't stop at one gee. It built up, two gees, three, more.

With the gee force came the fireball. Long streaks of flame shot past the hatch window, engulfing the entire capsule.

Judy looked over at Allen. He was looking out at the flames with eyes as wide as fried eggs, and his mouth was gaping open. Judy couldn't tell if he was screaming or just hyperventilating.

"It's all right," she told him. "It's an ablation shield. It's supposed to do this."

Then a big flaming chunk of something swept past the window, and the capsule pitched violently to the side.

9

Judy tugged hard on the hand controller, trying to right the capsule before it started tumbling. For a moment the attitude jets strained against whatever force had pushed them to the side, but just as the jets seemed about to win, the capsule gave another lurch and tilted the other way. Judy felt them go completely over, the seat harness digging into her shoulders and the capsule shuddering ominously as they plowed headfirst into the atmosphere.

That should have been impossible. They were weighted all wrong for that attitude. The center of gravity was down below the seats in order to keep them aimed bottom-first in their descent. To turn them the other way, something had to be trailing away behind them like the tail of a kite, and as soon as Judy realized that, she knew what it was. The retro rocket. It hadn't jettisoned automatically after firing, and since all her experience had been with the reusable shuttle, she hadn't done it manually, either. Now it was back there on the heat shield, disrupting the air flow and holding them at the wrong attitude.

Judy reached forward to the violently pitching control panel and flipped the manual jettison switch, but nothing happened. The electrical connection to the explosive bolts had already burned through. Unfortunately the bolts themselves hadn't gotten hot enough to blow, or their problem would have been solved.

They only had a few seconds in their headfirst attitude before the capsule would burn up. Judy shoved the controller hard to the side and the capsule pitched over, but with the retro rocket trailing behind, it wouldn't go all the way. She rolled the capsule to the other side, the motion throwing her hard against Allen, who held the getaway special canister tight to his body to keep it from flying loose and bouncing around inside the capsule. Judy had to roll the descent module back and forth twice more before the straps or fuel lines or whatever was holding the engine on gave way and the capsule once again flipped around to ride blunt end first.

Another piece of flaming debris swept past the window, but this time instead of pitching to the side, the capsule steadied out and fell smoothly through the rest of its descent.

The gee force grew stronger as they dropped into thicker air. It didn't feel at all like the gees the shuttle pulled on launch and descent; this felt far more personal, as if the universe had invented a brand new force just to torment Judy and Allen. Judy gritted her teeth and concentrated on not blacking out.

Terror helped immeasurably. Her heartbeat stayed up around 200 or so as she waited for the heat shield to burn through, and as she wondered how much damage those few moments of headfirst re-entry had done. The parachute was packed into a compartment in the nose of the capsule, and if that had gotten too hot—if it had melted in there, or if the release mechanism had warped enough to jam—then they were as good as dead.

She'd know in another couple of minutes, because they were coming out of the fireball now. The bright orange flames quit roaring past the window, giving way to blue sky. They were in the lower atmosphere. Judy rolled the capsule around so she could see the ground, but was startled to find only water below.

They'd *missed*. They were supposed to land somewhere in the United States, but somehow they'd missed the entire North American continent. Not only that, but Judy had no idea whether they'd overshot or undershot. She'd seen the ocean dozens of times from this vantage, but there was no way to tell whether this was the Pacific or the Atlantic.

Then the shoreline swept past and she laughed with relief. It was a lake! Probably Lake Michigan—no, there were snow-covered mountains to the east of it. That had to have been Salt Lake, then, in Utah.

The mountains rushed past below, giving way to high plains, then desert. Not good. The Air Force had no doubt tracked the fireball on the way down, and even though the descent module was invisible to radar now, they could calculate within a few dozen miles where it was going to land. In a forest or a city, Judy and Allen might have time to escape before anybody could get a helicopter out to capture them, but if they landed in the desert they might as well just switch the emergency beacon back on and wait to be picked up. Especially in this desert; Judy could see snowdrifts in the lee of whatever vegetation was down there. Even the most inept tracker in the world could follow them through snow.

The attitude jets wouldn't alter their ground path enough to matter, and the only engine that could—the retro rocket—was a burned-up lump of metal falling on its own trajectory miles away. The only thing Judy could do to change their course would be to deploy the parachute early, and hope they had already slowed down enough that the shroud lines wouldn't snap the moment the 'chute filled out. Assuming it opened at all.

Not yet, though. The gee force was easing off, but they were still braking, which meant they were still way above terminal velocity. Judy looked over at Allen, who was trying to say something to her, but the capsule was bouncing too much for her to read his lips and the interior was still in vacuum so his voice didn't carry. That wasn't good either; atmospheric pressure from outside could crumple the walls if there were any weak spots.

There should have been a valve to allow air to bleed inside, but if there was, then it had melted shut or been plugged by debris. All the same, they needed to equalize the pressure, so Judy did the only thing she could think of under the circumstances; she blew the hatch.

She'd trained for explosive decompression before, but

never for the reverse. Even at their high altitude, air rushing to fill the vacuum slammed her sideways into Allen, then shoved him against the wall of the capsule. Sound returned, the sound of wind shrieking through the open hatch frame, tugging at the canister in Allen's lap and flapping the loose ends of their harnesses against their heads and shoulders.

Nuts to this, Judy thought, reaching out to the parachute switch and flipping the toggle. She heard the bang this time, and a moment later a jolt as the drogue 'chute streamed away, filled out, and pulled the main 'chute after it.

The main parachute opened with a bone-jarring snap. The capsule had been traveling nearly parallel to the ground; there was a moment of freefall as it swung around like a pendulum to hang downward instead, and a sickening few seconds of oscillation before Judy used the attitude jets to stop their swing. The jet made a loud hiss in the air, but when it cut off, the capsule was nearly silent.

Is . . . is it always like that? Allen asked. She still had to read his lips. Even though there was air around them again, his voice didn't make it through his helmet.

She tried not to let her laugh become hysterical. "Are you kidding?" she replied when she could breathe again. "I was sure the whole way down that Gerry was telling the truth."

She loosened her harness and leaned over to look out the hatch. The ground was still a couple miles below them. Judy could see another lake to the west, with some green that might have been scrub pine on the hills around it, but when she looked straight down she saw a whole lot of bad-lands and not much else. Snow covered the low ground and drifted in the lee of anything tall enough to provide a wind-break, but there was plenty of reddish-brown dirt sticking through.

"Well, we don't have to worry about hitting anybody," she said, straightening up and tightening the straps again.

They swayed slightly as the capsule descended through the different layers of air over the high desert. The para-chute was oversized, designed to bring them in slowly so they would survive a landing on solid ground. Judy kept reminding herself that the Russians had done it that way for years, but as the horizon crept upward into view outside, she thought for a moment she could see the face of her father in its outline, then when she blinked she saw her mother in the clouds.

My god, she thought, your life really does flash before your eyes.

Then the capsule slammed into the ground, tipped over backward, and rolled, clanging against rocks and kicking dirt and snow inside the hatch. Judy saw sky, then ground, then sky again, then a sagebrush jammed momentarily through the opening, then finally, after about three complete revolutions, the capsule came to rest with the hatch pointing up into the air.

"You okay?" Judy asked. She dangled sideways, only her harness keeping her from falling on Allen.

I think so, he replied, his helmet still muffling his voice.

Judy realized it wasn't just her harness that was squeezing her. Atmospheric pressure was pressing her spacesuit tight against her body as well. She shut off her oxygen flow and opened the equalization valve, then reached up to her helmet, twisted it sideways, and slid it off. She took a cautious sniff. The air was cold, and stank of scorched metal, carbon composites, and sagebrush. After days of canned air on board the shuttle, it smelled wonderful.

Allen was lying on his side on what was now the floor. He had to struggle to get his hands free so he could pop his own helmet off, but even then he was having trouble. Judy loosened her straps so she could help him, and together they managed to lift the bubble from his head.

"This reminds me of a car wreck I had once," he said.

"That's encouraging," she muttered. She released her harness completely, bracing herself against the control panel, then climbed up on the seat backs and stuck her head and shoulders outside, wiggling sideways to get the life-support backpack past the hatch frame. It had been easier in zero-gee.

The capsule had come to rest on a sagebrush-covered hillside. The ground between plants—and there was a lot of open space—was reddish dirt, scattered with rocks and covered spottily with snow.

"It looks like we went to Mars after all," she said.

"What?"

"Never mind."

She hoisted herself out and slid down around the capsule's curved side to stand in the dirt. The snow immediately around the capsule had melted, and little puffs of steam still rose from beneath the hot metal to blow away immediately in the breeze. Judy was glad for the snow; if they'd landed in the summer they might have started a fire. As it was, the capsule had gotten plenty hot. Soot streaked its sides, and the rivet heads holding it together had actually begun to melt. It was already cooling, though, with the air blowing onto it from the snowbanks.

The parachute had tangled in the sagebrush. Good thing it had; there was enough wind for it to drag the capsule for miles if it hadn't. But now it was a huge orange-and-white target for anyone flying over. That was no doubt the designers' intent, but it was the last thing Judy wanted. She gathered it up while Allen tossed their helmets out through the hatch, then hoisted the getaway special canister up for her to take. The capsule teetered precariously when he stood up, so Judy wadded the 'chute between it and the ground to steady it, then took the canister from him and lowered it to the ground.

"Is this the valuable one?" she asked, "or did we go to all that trouble just to save the radio beacon?"

"I don't know," Allen said. He slid to the ground, then unscrewed the canister's top. Judy looked over his shoulders and was relieved to see the same nest of wires and circuitry that she'd seen inside the shuttle when he'd had to fix it.

"We've got the right half," Allen said.

"Good. I think. On the other hand, if we're going to get caught, I'd just as soon they don't find that."

Allen said, "Let's try not to get caught." He looked at the

blackened capsule. "I wonder if we can camouflage this thing." He tried breaking off one of the sagebrush stems, but the gnarled wood refused to give, even when he twisted it round and round like an apple stem.

"Wait a second," Judy said. "The parachute." She pulled it back out from under the capsule and shook it out.

The orange and white stripes were three feet wide. She and Allen had to fold it in layers so only the white showed, but they had plenty of material to work with, and plenty of shroud lines to tie it down. When they had finished, the descent module was just a white lump in a vast red-and-white desert.

"Now what?" Allen said. He turned once around, scanning the horizon, but there was little more to see in the distance than at their feet. Sagebrush, rock, dirt, and snow went on in every direction. Presumably it did, anyway; the hillside they had landed on blocked their view to the north. At least Judy thought it was north; her direction sense was usually pretty good. If it was, then the sun was just a little west of south, so they still had a few hours of light. Not too many, though; the sun set early in the winter in Utah. Or had they gone all the way into Colorado?

"Let's climb up to the top and see if we can see any sign of civilization," she said.

10

It was slow going in their spacesuits, with the bulky arms and legs restricting their motion and the weight—especially the life-support backpack—throwing them off balance, but they needed the insulation. They would when they stopped exerting themselves, anyway; as it was they were panting and sweating when they reached the top, Judy carrying both helmets while Allen carried the hyperdrive engine. They hadn't been in space long enough to lose much muscle or bone mass, for which Judy was grateful; after a long flight she was sometimes exhausted just climbing a set of stairs.

She had expected to see just more sagebrush and snow from the top of the hill, and that was nearly all they did see, but a couple miles to the north there was a straight line that might have been a fence or a road. It was hard to tell from this distance, but it was something artificial, anyway. The only other straight line, and it really wasn't that straight, was the pair of footprints leading from the capsule to the top of the hill. Judy wondered how long it would be before somebody spotted it, and them. She looked up in the sky, but she only saw two contrails, and they were way too high to be search planes.

"Man, that's the bluest sky I've ever seen," she said.

Allen had set the canister on the ground. "We must be pretty high up," he said, panting a bit from the exertion. "The sky gets darker with altitude."

Judy almost told him she knew that already, but bit her tongue. No sense annoying him. But why was it, she wondered, that scientists all figured only they knew why the sky was blue?

She pointed at the line in the distance. "We might as well try for that."

He nodded tiredly. "I guess." He picked up the canister and they trudged down the north face of the hill.

They spotted the first search plane about half an hour later. They'd been keeping to low ground whenever they could, finding that their oversize boots made walking in snow much easier than climbing up and over the hills, so they heard the sound long before they saw the black arrow in the sky.

"Fighter plane," Judy said the moment she heard it. The tearing-fabric sound of its engines practically screamed "military" at her. "Find a big patch of snow and lay down in it."

"*Lie* down," Allen said automatically, but he was already moving to obey. He set the canister in a drift in the lee of a waist-high sagebrush, scooped snow over it, then fell forward in the same drift and wiggled down into it. Judy was amazed at how quickly he disappeared from sight; his white spacesuit blended in perfectly.

Except for his butt. The fabric where he'd slid down over the scorched side of the descent module had been smeared with soot. Judy threw a couple more handfuls of snow over it, then sat backward in another drift a few feet away. She lay on her back and scraped snow up over the control panel on her chest with her arms, feeling a little like a child making a snow angel.

The plane roared past a couple miles to the south, heading west. Judy got just a brief glance of it as it flashed across her field of vision: a wedge-shaped dart, throttled down to just above stall speed, but still moving fast. Not the best search plane, but the Air Force had evidently scrambled whatever they had ready to fly. She waited for it to turn around and circle them, or the capsule, but it kept on going.

When its engine noise had faded below the level of the

wind through the sagebrush, she stood up and helped Allen to his feet again. "One down," she said.

Allen brushed the snow off his spacesuit. "How many more do you suppose there'll be?" he asked.

Judy looked at the sky, once again empty except for the high contrails, and shrugged. "Your guess is as good as mine."

The line they'd seen from the hilltop turned out to be a gravel road. It hadn't been plowed, but a single set of tire tracks broke through the foot-high snowdrifts that crossed it at a thirty-degree angle. More blowing snow had nearly filled them in; Judy guessed they were half a day old at least.

"I wonder which way they were going," she said, bending down to see if she could find any clues in the tread pattern, but the inch-wide ridges angled one way on one side of the tracks and the other way on the other.

Allen set the getaway special canister on end in the gravel and sat down heavily on it. His breath came in great wheezing gulps, and a vein on his forehead pulsed way too fast.

"Hey, are you all right?" Judy asked, kneeling down beside him.

"Fine," he said. "I'm just . . . in terrible shape. Too much . . . time in the lab."

"Yeah, well this will take a few pounds off, that's for sure."

Allen didn't speak for a few minutes. When he did, his voice was closer to normal. "We're going to be running out of daylight pretty soon. I wonder if we should start thinking about shelter."

Judy had never considered the possibility that they would last until dark without finding someone or being found, but it was beginning to look like they might. The sun was quite a bit lower in the sky now, and though a few more planes had passed over high in the sky, all but one had looked like commercial flights. The odd one had been another military jet, also flying a straight east-west swath, but it had been far to the north. Judy wondered why there weren't more of them, but she supposed a couple dozen planes could be out there searching and still not cover a tenth of the possible ground track. These badlands were *big*.

So should they make an igloo or something? The wind had picked up, and it felt colder, too. Judy was glad for the snoopy hat, the communications carrier that held the microphone and headset for the radio, but she knew she would have to put the helmet back on eventually if it got much colder. And if they had to do that . . .

"I don't think it matters much. These suits will insulate us from practically anything, and we can seal them up for another five hours or so if we have to. I think we'd be better off walking."

"I was afraid you'd say that. Which direction?"

Judy looked both ways down the road. She could only see about a mile to the west before it dropped behind another hill, but she didn't need to see that way to know what was out there. She'd seen it from the air, and there was nothing for a *long* ways. It didn't look much better to the east, but she could only see five or six miles that way.

"East," she said.

Allen stood up, groaning, slung the canister over his shoulder, and said, "Let's get moving, then. The sooner we find someone, the sooner I can get out of this damned spacesuit."

They had only walked another mile or so when they heard the whine of a motor ahead of them. This one was on the ground, and electric by the sound of it. The crunch of gravel beneath the tires was almost as loud as the motor. Judy took a step toward the side of the road, half expecting it to be a military jeep, but as it drew closer she saw a regular civilian pickup truck. Well, not so regular; it had been jacked up until the undercarriage sat nearly level with the tops of its oversize tires. It was painted deep red, and sported a chrome bumper with a winch on the front, chrome wheels, chrome footsteps, and a chrome roll bar behind the cab—bristling with chrome spotlights. All six lights had yellow smiley-face covers over their lenses.

Judy considered jumping into the barrow ditch and hiding, but this was the only sign of life on the ground they'd seen all day, and she was getting tired and hungry. They were just going to have to take their chances with the locals.

She stayed put in the middle of the road and waved her arms. The pickup rolled toward her, crashing through the snowbanks and swerving with each blow until it looked like the driver might career right into her, but he finally noticed the white-suited astronauts and stamped on the brakes. The truck slid to a stop sideways in the road about twenty feet away from them, and the driver—a heavily bearded cowboy, by the looks of his black, potato-chip-shaped hat—stared in open-mouthed wonder at the sight before him.

Judy couldn't resist. She marched up to the pickup, her spacesuit creaking in the cold air, and waited until the cowboy rolled down his window.

"Take me to your leader," she said.

11

His name was Trent. It turned out there was a passenger in the truck, too, a blonde, thin, heavily made-up girl named Donna, but she'd been sitting so close to Trent she hadn't been visible from outside. Judy wondered if they were on a date or if they were married, but she didn't think it would be polite to ask.

And Trent and Donna were nothing if not polite. After Trent's initial startled exclamation, "Where the heck did *you* come from?" and Judy's explanation that they had made an emergency re-entry from the space station, he had offered them a ride to town, treating them like any other random hitchhikers.

Squeezing four people in the cab would have been impossible with two of them wearing spacesuits, so they took them off and stashed them in back, along with the getaway special canister, under a black vinyl cover that stretched drum-tight with more snaps around the edge than a satellite's thermal shroud. Now, wearing just their spandex liners, crisscrossed with the cooling and ventilation tubes, Judy and Allen sat in the cab and held their hands out toward the heater coils while Trent drove.

They covered the same distance Judy and Allen had walked in just a couple of minutes, and continued on westward. Okay, Judy thought, so she'd guessed wrong. It wouldn't have mattered. As they drove, she realized they could have walked for days in either direction at the rate they'd been going and never have reached anything.

The pickup shook its passengers almost as badly as the descent module. Rather than plow straight through the snowdrifts, its wide tires rode up over them, then rebounded off the road when they came down the other side, magnifying every bump and making Trent struggle for control every fifty feet or so. The laser-sighted rifle in the gun rack behind their heads rattled against the back window and threatened to fall free with every jolt, making Judy fear for a head injury from behind as well as from the front.

To keep her mind off the imminent crash, she asked as nonchalantly as she could while bracing herself on the dashboard, "So what town are we heading for?"

"Rock Springs," Trent said, then when he realized that didn't mean anything to her he added, helpfully, "Wyoming."

"Ah," Judy said, trying to decide whether that was good or bad. Was this Rock Springs big enough to hide a couple of astronauts in, or would they stick out like polar bears in a tar pit?

Whatever its size, it had to be better than standing out in the sagebrush with the sun going down.

Allen had been burning to say something ever since they saw the truck. He'd resisted for a couple of miles, but after maybe the hundredth time they surged over a snowdrift, then bounced two or three more times on the fat balloon tires, he could contain himself no longer. "You know," he said, "narrow tires are actually better in snow."

Trent thought about that for a bit, then said, "Depends on what you call 'better.' Smoother ride, I'll grant you. But we didn't come out here for a smooth ride." He grinned.

"Why did you come out here?"

Trent glanced to Donna, who was leaning against his side as if glued there, then said, "Oh, just a little four-wheeling."

"Ah."

They rode in silence for a minute or so. Trent had obviously been burning with barely suppressed questions himself ever since he'd seen them, but he'd been minding his own business admirably. Allen's unsolicited advice had broken the unspoken compact, though, and finally he asked, "So, what kind of emergency did you have up there on the space station, anyway?"

Judy had been trying to decide how much to tell him. She looked to Allen, who shrugged and said, "The whole reason we're here is because we wanted to get the word out."

Trent was immediately apologetic. "Look, if it's none of my business, I don't want to know."

"Yeah," Donna added, the first word she'd said besides "Hello." She was chewing furiously at a wad of gum, and evidently had taken to heart her mother's advice not to speak with her mouth full.

"No, it's all right," Judy said. "It's everybody's business. The government may not think so, but damn it, this is supposed to be a democracy."

Trent narrowed his eyes, and coming from under a black Stetson the way it did, and with a full beard hiding the rest of his face, his gaze looked cold and mean. But his words gave just the opposite impression. "Now I'm really not sure I want to know," he said. "Government secrets can be bad news."

"No, no, it's nothing like that," Judy said. "Well, actually, maybe it is, but—" She realized she was babbling. "Look, the reason we're here is because Allen invented a hyperdrive engine."

Trent looked at her without saying anything.

"A faster-than-light spaceship drive," she said. "He tested it on board my shuttle, and took us out to Saturn in no time at all."

"Is that so?" Trent asked rhetorically.

"Yes, it is," Judy answered anyway. "And when we got back into orbit, the military wanted us to keep it secret."

"Why?"

Allen said, "Because it'll give everybody on Earth the chance to go exploring the galaxy on their own, that's why."

"How's that again?" Trent asked.

Allen laughed. "You heard me right. Anybody can build one. It's cheap, and easy, and it'll take you to Alpha Centauri as quickly as it'll take you to the Moon."

Trent laughed nervously. "Well, partner, it looks like this time it took you to Wyoming."

Judy laughed with him. "That wasn't the hyperdrive," she said. "We came down in an emergency descent module, like a Gemini capsule. First time anybody's ever used one."

"That must have been a pretty wild ride."

"That's an understatement."

Judy leaned back in the seat and described their re-entry, then backed up and filled Trent and Donna in on the rest of the flight. They listened to her with ever-growing astonishment, and when she was done, Donna said, "You were actually up there, looking at Saturn's rings, *today?*"

Allen, who had been helping embellish Judy's story, said proudly, "That's right. And we could have gone even farther if we hadn't been worried about the world going up in flames while we were gone. Plus we had to get back and spread the word before the government could put a lid on it."

Trent shook his head. "Man, that just burns me up. But it's just like 'em to go suppressing things they don't want us to have. They've been doing it for years. They sat on a hundred-mile-per-gallon carburetor since the nineteen-fifties because they were afraid it would upset the automobile industry, but they wouldn't release it even when everybody switched over to electric."

Allen looked thoughtful for a minute, then said, "A hundred miles per gallon? Isn't that beyond even the theoretical limit for efficiency?"

Trent frowned. "Not the way I heard it."

Allen opened his mouth to pontificate, but Judy elbowed him in the side and shook her head and he closed it again without saying anything.

The gravel road led down one last hill, then joined up with a paved and—mercifully—plowed road leading north-south again. Trent slowed a bit for the turn, headed north, then fed power to the motor until the truck reached a hundred and started to drift from side to side on its balloon tires. Evidently he wasn't comfortable driving unless he was just barely in control.

Rock Springs turned out to be a medium-sized town, filling a two- or three-mile-wide low spot in the prairie where a river evidently ran through, and spilling up over the sides into the surrounding hills. When they were still about a mile away from the outskirts, Trent slowed the truck to a crawl and turned off the road, then flipped the switch for four-wheel drive and they bounced along over sagebrush and rocks as he climbed a hill.

"Where are we going?" Allen asked.

"Lookin' for roadblocks," Trent answered.

The sun had already set, and he'd been driving with his lights on, but he switched them off again and drove by the faint evening skyglow until they were just below the crest of the hill. From that vantage they could see the town spread out below them, most of its street lights already on and headlights streaming along the roads. They could also see police cars, their red and blue strobe lights flashing, on all the roads entering town, including the interstate highway that circled it to the north.

"Well now," Trent said, "It looks like time for a little more four-wheeling." He didn't sound dismayed at the prospect.

Judy and Allen hung on to the dashboard and the door and each other as Trent backed up and drove the truck around the back side of the hill, staying high enough to keep out of the worst of the snow, but low enough not to call attention to themselves. The truck tipped alarmingly, and every time they hit a bump with the uphill side Judy was sure they would go over, but Trent evidently knew just how much he could push it. The uphill side got pretty light a couple of times, but the wheels never actually left the ground.

The only sound was the soft whine of the motor, and an

occasional klunk or rattle when they bounced over a rock. It reminded Judy of what driving the lunar rover must have been like. She wondered if she would ever have the chance to find out.

Eventually, about the time it was getting too dark to drive without lights, they rounded one last hill and came to a trailer court. There had once been a chain link fence surrounding it, but kids with bicycles and motorcycles had long since torn down a section of it at the end of the last street. Trent squeezed his pickup through the gap, switched out of four-wheel drive, turned on his lights, and drove through the trailer court. The police cars with their flashing lights were only a few blocks away; as he turned onto the main road and accelerated away from them, he grinned and said, "Hah. Roadblocks."

Even so, he made Judy and Allen hunch down in the seat so they wouldn't be spotted while he drove on into town. Judy tried to keep track of their turns, at least, so she would have some idea of what part of town they were in, but the streets twisted and veered apparently at random even when they were obviously in a residential area, until she was thoroughly lost.

"What did they do, pave the cow trails?" she asked.

Trent laughed. "Yep. That's exactly what they did."

He drove up a steep hill, zigzagged down a couple more streets, and pulled into a driveway in front of a light pink single-story house. A bare-limbed tree stood in the middle of the front yard. There was an attached two-car garage to the left of the house; Donna pushed the button on the remote control clipped to the sun visor, the door slid upward, and Trent drove the pickup inside. Donna pushed the button again, and the door closed behind them.

Their joints popping, Judy and Allen climbed down out of the pickup, sidled around a more conventional-looking, boxy car parked next to it, and followed Donna into the house. Trent paused long enough to plug the truck's recharger into the wall socket before he came in.

As soon as they got inside the house, it became apparent

that Donna ruled within its walls. Frilly curtains, kitchen wallpaper with strawberries on it, shelves full of knick-knacks in the living room—everything bore the stamp of femininity and comfort. To Judy, after hours in the cold and another hour or two in the bucking pickup, it looked like a little slice of Heaven.

12

After she and Allen had showered, put on clothing borrowed from their hosts, and eaten their first meal in half a day, they turned on the TV to see what kind of story the police had concocted to explain their roadblock. It turned out they hadn't. The news didn't even mention it, and the more Judy thought about it, the more ominous that silence felt. The government evidently still thought it had a chance to cover up the whole hyperdrive affair, or they'd have at least admitted that a couple of astronauts had made an emergency landing. As it was, Judy suspected that if she and Allen were caught, they would never be heard from again.

The announcer did mention the television broadcast they had made from the communications satellite, but he attributed it to a hoax played by a couple of Caltech students taking advantage of the confusion caused by the computer virus. There were even pictures of a mobile TV van surrounded by police cars, and two kids coming out the open back doors with their hands on their heads.

The international news was a little more accurate. The European Coalition admitted that one of their anti-missile satellites had fired on an unknown object that had appeared on their radar, and the U.S. admitted that they had gone on red alert until the "misunderstanding" had been cleared up, but neither side would explain what had caused the incident in the first place. Except for one U.S. senator who suggested that the Europeans had staged the whole thing to test the American defenses.

"They missed an obvious connection," Judy said when a commercial came on. "They should have said the search planes were looking for a couple of French spies who parachuted out over Wyoming. It would have tied their story together perfectly."

"They probably didn't think of it," Allen said. "They're scrambling to keep ahead of the truth. But it's all futile. They can't keep a lid on it forever. People all over the country have already taped our broadcast. And not all the email messages that got sent out are the virus. *Somebody* is bound to try building the circuit, and it'll only be a matter of time before everybody realizes it's for real."

Trent was sitting with Donna in the loveseat to one side of the screen. "That may be so," he said, "but what are you going to do in the meantime?"

Allen said, "Well, I'll probably try to contact somebody from INSANE, though I'm not sure they'll be able to do us any good, since they're probably under close surveillance themselves. On the other hand, we've still got the hyperdrive. All we need are a few car batteries and a spaceship and we can go anywhere we want."

"Oh, well, sure," Judy said. "Just a couple of batteries and a spaceship. No problem. I'm sure they have dozens of both on clearance down at Wal-Mart. Or do you get them from a used spaceship lot? I forget."

Allen shook his head. "We're going to have to redefine our idea of what makes a spaceship. With the hyperdrive, just about anything that can hold air will do the job, as long as it'll survive a parachute landing."

"Oh," said Judy. "Well, in that case we've already got a spaceship, unless the Feds have found it."

Allen nodded. "I suppose we do. It's kind of cramped, though. It wouldn't hold much gear."

"True." Judy yawned. "Excuse me. It's way past my bed-time."

Donna jumped up immediately. "Oh, I'm sorry! I forgot, you must be on Florida time, aren't you? I'll make your bed."

Judy got up too. "I'll give you a hand."

When they were alone in the spare bedroom, Donna worked up her courage and asked, "Um, do you guys need separate rooms, or . . . ?"

With everything else that had happened to her that day, Judy hadn't even thought about sleeping arrangements. She did now, and was a little surprised to realize she didn't mind the idea of sharing a bed with Allen. There wasn't any privacy on board the shuttle; she and he had already slept within a couple feet of each other. And they'd pretty much linked their fates together for the foreseeable future; if she insisted on modesty it would just complicate things even more.

Besides, he was kind of cute, and making the great escape with him had somehow made him even more attractive. Judy had no idea if he felt the same about her, but she supposed there was one direct way to find out.

"One bed is fine," she told Donna.

When Allen came into the room a few minutes later, he paused in the doorway and said, "Are, uh, are you sure you, uh, want company tonight?"

Judy had already undressed and slid under the covers. She raised up on one elbow, holding the sheet over her breasts with her free hand in a way she hoped looked both modest and sexy, and said, "Look, if nothing else, we need to talk. We need to come up with a plan."

"Yeah." He stepped on into the room and closed the door behind him. Judy watched him undress until she realized she was making him self-conscious, so she lay back and watched the shadows on the ceiling until she felt him slide in beside her. He lay straight as a board, careful not to touch her.

"So," he said. "What sort of plan did you have in mind?"

She laughed, and rolled over to face him. She didn't bother to keep the covers tight against her body this time. He glanced over at her, then looked back at the ceiling, but she'd seen his pupils dilate.

Business first, though. "Well," she said, "let's look at the situation. I don't know about your career as a scientist, but my shuttle piloting days are pretty much over. We're halfway across the country from anyplace familiar, we have practically no money, no clothes of our own, and we're probably the most wanted people in the world right now. What do you suppose we ought to do first?"

He crossed his arms over his chest. "Well, when you put it that way, maybe we ought to go undercover. Get jobs. I could probably flip burgers somewhere, and you could wait tables. Or I could charge batteries at a service station and you could clean windshields."

"Why don't *you* clean windshields while I charge batteries?" Judy asked him.

"Because you'd get better tips than I would, and nobody tips the battery guy."

"Oh."

Allen looked over at her again. "Or there's one other possibility."

"What's that?"

"We could build ourselves a spaceship and explore the galaxy."

Judy shivered. "Yeah, we could, couldn't we?"

"I think so. It probably wouldn't even cost that much to get set up for it. What do you think? You want to?"

"Yes," said Judy, so fast her response had to have been reflex. She shivered again.

Allen laughed softly. "Sounds like we've got a plan, then." He let his gaze drift downward for a moment to where the sheet had fallen away from Judy's breasts, then he looked back into her eyes. "What else did you have in mind?"

The bed squeaked. They made love slowly, deliciously, at first to keep from embarrassing their hosts, but they soon forgot all about their surroundings in the pleasure of exploring each other's bodies. That, as much as anything, had been Judy's true intent when she'd decided to seduce Allen. She needed an escape, however temporary, from the immensity of the changes in her life.

Afterward, when they lay back against the pillows and Judy rested her head on Allen's chest, she whispered, "Thank you. That was nice."

"Mmm hmm."

"It was a good way to end a really strange day."

Allen didn't say anything for a long time, and Judy had just decided that he must be one of those men who don't talk after sex, when he said, "I have to admit, when I woke up this morning, I didn't really expect to wind up quite like this."

"I hope you're not disappointed," Judy said.

"Only that we didn't try this in free fall when we had the chance. Our starship is likely to be a little cramped."

Judy snuggled closer, sighed. "Free fall is good for acrobatics, but it's hard to just hold someone there."

"Oh." He was silent a while longer, then said, "I wonder what other myths about spaceflight we're going to wind up disproving once we start doing a lot of it?"

Judy had been drifting toward sleep. She surfaced just long enough to consider his question, but her answer, if she ever came up with one, got lost in her dreams.

13

Trent and Donna both worked day jobs. Trent ran a construction crew, building new houses to replace the ones that had been destroyed when Bitter Creek—normally a trickle at the bottom of a crumbling gully—had flooded after a week of intense thunderstorms the previous summer; and Donna sold jewelry in the White Mountain shopping mall on the west side of town. They had both offered to stay home and help Judy and Allen plan their next move, but there was really very little they could do, and besides, calling in sick could cause more suspicion than it was worth. So they left their guests in the house when they went out in the morning, with instructions to make themselves at home. Judy thought she saw a vague what-have-we-gotten-ourselves-into expression on their faces when they left, but if they were thinking that, they never betrayed it in their words or actions.

As soon as their cars had rolled away up the street, though, she turned to Allen and said, "We've got to find a place of our own. We can't impose on them forever."

Allen said, "Right. Fish and visitors stink after three days. But if we're lucky, we won't have to be here much longer."

"Oh?"

"I've got friends all over the world. Somebody's bound to be able to help us." He went to the closet by the front door and rummaged through the coats there, eventually pulling out a brown and black leather jacket for himself and a puffy pink nylon coat for Judy. Hers had a hood with a fur ruff around it; to cover his own head he took one of two well-used black cowboy hats off the closet shelf.

"Where are we going?" Judy asked him, eyeing the coat dubiously.

"We need to make some phone calls that can't be traced back to here."

They cut the map out of the phone book so they could find their way around town, then bundled up and headed out into the winter cold. Judy looked like a flamingo in Donna's pink coat, and Allen looked like a beach bum doing a Clint Eastwood imitation, but nobody on the street paid them any special attention. Evidently people in Wyoming were used to funny-looking clothes, or else too polite to mention it.

There was one advantage to cowboy clothes: anyone looking for two downed astronauts would have a heck of a time getting past their first impressions to even bother looking at Judy's or Allen's faces.

There wasn't much snow on the ground in town. By the low, dirty drifts in the lee of houses, it looked like most of it had blown away. It certainly hadn't melted. The morning air felt like liquid oxygen in the lungs, and ice crunched underfoot where patches of it still clung to the sidewalks.

As they walked along the residential streets, their breath drifting away in white clouds behind them, Judy found herself thinking about the Earth under her feet. Not just the concrete and the dirt, but the whole planet. She could feel its mass pulling her against it, could feel the rock resisting her footfalls, transferring the force of her leg muscles deeper and deeper into its crust until it was lost in the myriad criss-crossing forces that echoed through its mantle and core. When she looked out through the bare branches of people's yard trees, she saw undulating hills and gullies all the way to the horizon—a horizon that blurred to indistinct haze in the distance—and she felt for the first time the immensity of the planet she called home.

Yet only yesterday she was so far away she couldn't even see it. The thought boggled her mind. She had been farther away from Earth than anyone else in the history of the human race, and here she was home again less than twelve hours later, walking on a sidewalk with her hands in her pockets like anyone out for a stroll around the block.

She'd never been to Rock Springs before, but it felt like home. Compared to where she had just been, how could anything on Earth *not* be home? Astronauts always liked to say that you couldn't see national boundaries from orbit, but when you couldn't even see the planet, the artificial boundaries that people put up between each other seemed even less important. She felt the irrational urge to run up to a total stranger and give him a big hug just to reaffirm her connection with humanity.

"Are you, uh, feeling a little weird right now?" she asked.

Allen cupped his hands together and blew into them. "Cold," he replied. "Otherwise okay. How about you?"

"I think I'm in shock."

"Oh?"

"Everything looks different to me all of a sudden. Not physically different, but sociologically. Like I'm seeing it from a different perspective now."

Allen smiled. "Yeah, I'm getting a little of that. Maybe not as much as you, 'cause I knew what we were going to do up there, but I know what you mean."

"I wonder if this is how the Wright brothers felt," she said. "It's like having a leg in the past and a leg in the future at the same time."

"Maybe. But the Wright brothers didn't really expect—whoa!" Allen's left foot shot out from under him as he stepped on a patch of ice. He windmilled his arms and caught himself before he fell, but his hat flew off and rolled out into the street just as a dark brown General Electric van approached. The driver swerved, but the hat rolled right under the tires. It made a soft *flap flap* as they squashed it flat, then the driver hit the brakes and the van screeched to a stop.

He opened his door and looked back at Judy and Allen. He looked to be in his forties or so, and he wore a hat almost identical to the one he had just run over. "Sorry," he called out. "I tried to miss it, but it was too quick."

"That's all right," Allen said, stepping out into the street to retrieve the hat. He punched the top out into a dome and bent the sides upward into their potato-chip shape again. "There," he said. "Good as new."

The driver shook his head. "Nice try. Well, you're a darn sight more calm about it than I'd be, that's for—" He suddenly narrowed his eyes and peered at Allen as if he'd just switched to x-ray vision. Judy grabbed Allen's arm and was just about to make a break for it when the driver said, "Uh . . . let me give you a little piece of advice. Dent the top in again so you don't look like a Mountie, and pull the brim down low in front until you can get yourself a pair of sunglasses or something to hide those eyes. Your face is all over the papers this morning."

"Uh . . . thanks," Allen said.

"Any time." The driver shut his door and the van started to roll on down the street, then it stopped again and the driver stuck his head out the window. "Hey, was that business on the TV yesterday for real?"

"Yep," Allen said.

The man whistled softly. "I'll be damned. My sister recorded it." He put the van in reverse and backed up until he was even with them. "Hey, you two need a ride somewhere?"

Allen looked over at Judy. She glanced into the back of the van. No SWAT team huddled there to grab them. Just an empty baby seat and a bunch of plastic kids' toys in bright primary colors.

"We're looking for a phone," she admitted.

"I can help you with that right here," the driver said. He reached onto the dashboard for his cell phone and held it up, then he nodded his head sideways and said, "Come on around and get in where it's warm."

Allen twirled the hat around in his hands a time or two, then ran his thumb along the top until it once more had the three deep creases it had started out with. "Does everybody in this town help out fugitives, or are we just lucky?" he asked.

The driver shrugged. "It's a pretty friendly town."

"I guess."

Judy and Allen walked around to the passenger side and got in. There were just two big bucket seats in front, so Judy climbed in back and sat behind Allen. From there she could keep an eye on the driver, too.

"Name's Dale," he said, twisting around and holding out his hand toward Judy. "Dale Larkin."

"Judy Gallagher," Judy said. When they shook, his hand felt amazingly warm against her cold fingers.

"Pleased to meet you. And you're Allen Meisner. Whee-oo. Wait'll Lori hears about this! Here, make all the calls you want."

He handed Allen the phone and drove on down the street while Allen switched it on and started dialing, but Judy had a sudden thought.

"Hey, wait! Disable the caller ID before you dial."

Allen nodded. "Good idea. What's the code for that?"

"Star-six-seven," Dale said.

"Does that disable the emergency locator, too?"

"Yep. So they say. Mine doesn't work anyway, so you're okay."

Allen punched in the code, then tried calling his fellow mad scientists while Dale drove them down a steep hill into the center of town, but nobody was home at the first two numbers he tried. He tried a third, and a second later he broke into a big grin.

"Gordy! Hey, Allen here. I . . . yeah. No, we're okay. I can't tell you that. I can't tell you that, either. Listen, I need some help here. I'm going to have to buy some stuff, and I can't use my own credit card for obvious reasons. I . . . yes, we're going to . . . no, I really can't tell you that. Somewhere in Colorado, all right?" He frowned. "Wait a minute. You've got federal agents breathing down your neck, don't you? Don't bullshit me, Gordy! They're in the room with you, aren't they?"

"Hang up!" Judy said.

Allen shook his head. "Listen, tell them . . . I don't care about that; tell them it's too late. The word is out, and by this time tomorrow, we will be, too. Out in space, you dumb shit! Yes, I know what the economic—oh, forget it." He growled in the back of his throat and punched the phone's "Off" button.

"Is he all right?" Judy asked.

Allen shrugged. "Sounded like. Sounded like Carl got to him first, though. Why is it," he asked Dale, "half the people who hear about this are terrified that the world is going to fall down around their ears?"

The streets were labeled alphabetically, just "A," "B," "C," and so on. Dale turned right on A Street and headed up a bridge over the railroad tracks. "Maybe they've got too much invested in the status quo," he said.

Judy looked at him a little more closely, surprised to hear the phrase "invested in the status quo" coming from underneath a cowboy hat. "What do you do?" she asked. "For a living, I mean."

He grinned. "Rob banks."

"No, really."

"I really rob banks."

14

The guy sounded sincere. There was an uncomfortable silence while Judy tried to think how to respond, but she could only come up with one question: "Why did you tell us that?"

"Because I can," said Dale with a wry smile. "You're probably the only total strangers in the world I can trust with the truth. You're not going to turn me in, 'cause you're on the lam yourselves."

Allen turned the phone over in his hand and popped open the peripheral slot cover. "You pulled the GPS receiver," he said.

Judy had heard the phrase "grinning like a thief" before, but she had never realized what it meant until now. Dale was proud of his accomplishments, and happy to have found someone he could brag to about them. "Yep," he said. "I don't know for sure if switching it off actually disables it, so why take the chance?"

He brought the van to a stop at a red light on the far side of the overpass. Judy considered jumping out while they were stopped, but she had no idea how to get back to Trent and Donna's house from here, and she wasn't getting danger vibes off of Dale. She looked at the kids' toys and the baby seat beside her. Did he actually have a kid, or were they just props to remove suspicion from his vehicle?

"Why do you do it?" she asked.

He shrugged. "That's where the money is."

"Yes, but . . ."

"But it's wrong. I know. So's ripping up the ground to get the coal out from underneath it, or cutting down a whole forest for the lumber, or selling tennis shoes made in third-world sweatshops. I decided to cut out the hypocrisy and go straight for the target without screwing anybody along the way."

"Sounds like the banks get a pretty good screwing," Allen pointed out.

Dale shook his head. "Actually, not. They're insured, so the individual bank never loses any money. The cost is spread out over thousands of banks, and millions of depositors. And it's not like I knock one over every week. I live modestly. People lose more money under their sofa cushions than what I cost them."

"But . . . you're still stealing from them!" Judy protested.

"So's every industry that uses public land or non-renewable resources. At least I don't steal from the future."

"Yes, but . . ." She stopped. A police car pulled up at the light from the side street to their right. Dale signaled for a right turn, waited for the light to turn green, then waved as he drove past the cop. The cop waved back.

"Always cultivate a friendly relationship with the Federales," Dale said. "But not too friendly. That draws even more suspicion than hostility." He nodded toward the phone that Allen still held in his hand. "You going to call anybody else?"

It took Allen a few seconds to shift mental gears. "There doesn't seem like much point," he said. "If they got to Gordy, they got to the rest of us."

Dale drove them along a street lined with light industrial businesses: welding shops, a glass shop, several auto repair garages. "What do you need besides money?" he asked.

"A spaceship," Allen replied.

"Well, I can't help you there. But if you need cash, I've got plenty of that."

"You'd just give it to us?" Allen asked.

Dale laughed. "Easy come, easy go. The nice thing about having a realistic attitude toward money is it doesn't rule your life anymore. Besides, you guys just gave the whole world something that's worth a hell of a lot more than what

I'm offering you. Maybe I'm feeling generous 'cause of your example."

Judy shivered, but it had nothing to do with the cold. They did need money, but she couldn't imagine taking any that came from a bank robbery. It was hard to bring herself to speak, but she made herself say, "I don't think I'd be comfortable with—"

"I didn't figure you would." Dale had lost some of his smile. He bit his lower lip, thinking, then said, "How about this? Suppose you give me your credit card number, and I give you cash. I've got a dummy corporation I set up for laundering my proceeds; it would be simple to bill a few thousand to your card. Then it's actually your money you're spending."

"I don't know," Judy said. "It seems to me we'd still be spending the bank's money."

"They're not marked bills. And you'd be out a dollar for every dollar you spent, so it's not like you'd be getting something for nothing." Dale turned left at another cross street and drove slowly past more businesses.

Allen said, "You'd be mobbed with FBI agents before you finished typing the number in."

Dale smiled again. "You haven't had much experience with this sort of thing. If the Feds ever come knocking, they'll find that you bought a computer by mail order from a company in Virginia. So long as you don't challenge the charges, they can't cancel the payment, and the money trail stops at a numbered Swiss account so they can't trace it to me."

Allen shook his head in reluctant admiration. "Pretty slick, all right." He turned sideways in his seat so he could look at Judy. "What do you think?" he asked.

"Honestly? I don't like it. No offense, Dale."

He shrugged. "No skin off my nose either way. I'm just trying to help the only way I can."

Allen wrinkled his forehead, thinking. "I'm trying to see how this would be any worse than taking grant money from a tobacco company or Microsoft or somebody like that, and I have to admit it seems a lot less questionable."

"It's apples and oranges," Judy said.

"It's money," Dale put in. "The whole damned concept is so full of moral trouble, you can burn out your brain doing what you're doing. You need cash, I got cash, and I didn't kill anybody to get it. That should be all you need to worry about."

Judy heard the anger in his voice, but she didn't let it stop her from saying, "No, it's not. I don't think robbing banks is right, and I don't think I want to—"

"Look here, miss high and mighty. You've already done more damage to society than I ever could. The fact that you've given us something in return is a point in your favor, but it doesn't undo the damage. Maybe my offer is an attempt to atone for my sins, I don't know, but I do know that you're on pretty shaky moral ground yourselves to be turnin' up your nose at it."

"Maybe so, but I—"

"Stop!" Allen said. Judy was so startled that she closed her mouth, then she opened it again to blast him for trying to shut her up, but he said "Stop the car!" and she realized he wasn't even talking about her.

"What's the matter?" she asked him as Dale pulled over to the curb.

"Nothing. I think I just found our spaceship." He pointed into a lumber yard across the street.

She tried to see what he was looking at, but all she saw were stacks of boards, pallets of concrete blocks, and three big yellow plastic igloos five feet high and half again as long.

"Where?" she asked.

"There. That water tank. It looks like the walls must be half an inch thick. I bet if we seal it up, it'll hold atmospheric pressure."

A water tank? Judy looked at the igloos again. It looked pretty cramped inside. No room to stand up in. No room to store more than the barest of necessities. There weren't any windows, either; just a couple of pipe fittings the size of her thighs sticking out either end. She and Allen might be able to make portholes out of them, but they would also have to cut a hole for a hatch and figure out how to seal that after they were inside, and they would have to drill more holes to mount their controls and their acceleration couches and their equipment lockers. They'd also have to mount steering rockets on the outside, plus a parachute and who knew what else. By the time they were done, the thing would look like a wiffle ball. Either that or they'd have to glue everything down, and she could imagine how well that would work the first time they landed hard. They would have better luck going back for the emergency descent module.

Dale didn't seem to think much better of the idea than Judy did. He was chuckling softly and shaking his head.

"What?" asked Allen.

"What you got there is a pretty specialized kind o' tank," Dale said. "I don't think many people would want to go gallivantin' around the galaxy in one."

"Why not?" Allen said. "A tank is a tank, isn't it?"

"Sure it is," said Dale. "Except when it's a septic tank."

"A septic tank?" Allen tilted his head sideways, as if maybe seeing it from another angle would make it look like something else.

"Yep," said Dale. "Made for stickin' in the ground and fillin' with shit. Not exactly what I'd call spaceship material."

Judy couldn't help laughing, but Allen's earnest expression didn't change.

"Why can't it be?" he asked. "Just because it's designed for one purpose doesn't mean we can't use it for another. I've spent my whole life thinking of things in different terms, and that's why I've gotten where I am today."

Dale snorted. "In a minivan in the back side of nowhere, with no money in your pocket and the Feds hot on your ass. Yessir, that's an accomplishment."

"Look who's at the wheel," Allen said quietly. "You're two for three yourself."

That took a little wind out of the bank robber's sails, but not all of it. "I'd debate that with you if it mattered," he said.

"The Feds have no idea where I am, and there's nothing to link me to any of the robberies even if they did. But that's not the point; the point is, they *are* after you, and you've got no money and no vehicle to make your getaway. I think you're nuts, but if you want to make a spaceship out of a septic tank, my offer still stands. Cash for credit, or I could just buy the tank for you outright. Your choice."

Or they could just get out of the van right now and forget they'd ever met this guy, Judy thought, but she knew they weren't going to do that. For one thing, it was a long, cold walk back to Trent and Donna's house, if they could ever find it from here. For another, they really did need to make a clean getaway, and soon. After the trouble the government had already gone to in suppressing Allen's invention, they weren't going to stop until he and Judy were in custody, or dead.

And despite her misgivings about the source, how many people could she reasonably expect to offer them the money they needed? They'd been incredibly lucky so far, but they couldn't count on luck forever.

"All right," she said. "Buy us the tank."

15

They didn't buy it then and there. For one thing, something that large would have to be delivered, and they had no idea what address to give the driver. It would be pushing Trent and Donna's hospitality considerably to ask them to give up their garage for a spaceship assembly building, and Judy and Allen couldn't very well do it in the back yard, either. All it would take would be one curious neighbor—or a cop driving by in the alley—to blow their cover.

They needed a workshop, but Judy wasn't about to ask Dale for help with that, too. She wrote down his cell phone number, then had him drive her and Allen back to the spot where he'd picked them up.

"We'll get in touch when we're ready," she told him.

"Good enough," he said, tipping his hat slightly to her as she climbed out of the van. "Glad to help whenever I can."

The cold air made her cheeks tingle again the moment she stepped down to the street. She shoved her hands in her pockets and hunched her shoulders to pull her collar tight around her neck.

As they stood on the sidewalk and watched Dale drive away, Allen said, "Does that guy have a Robin Hood complex, or what?"

Judy grinned. "I think he's just trying to out-do you."

Allen started walking back toward Trent and Donna's house. "Maybe. Whatever his motives, we've got a financial backer. That's better than we had this morning."

"We've got a sugar daddy, is what we've got. And I still don't like how he got his money. But I guess beggars can't be choosers."

"Nope."

Allen led them past the street the house was on, then turned in at the alley beyond it. Judy looked behind them, half expecting to see Dale's van or a black sedan full of FBI agents tailing them, but there was nobody in sight. A dog barked from behind a high board fence, but it stopped as soon as they were past.

Judy looked at the packed gray dirt of the alley, at the dingy snowbanks with strands of windblown brown grass poking through. It all seemed so normal, so mundane. If the memory of yesterday's flight weren't so fresh in her mind, she could almost believe she was a little girl again, exploring the neighborhood around her house with the boy from across the street.

Then again, maybe she was doing just that. Or getting ready to, anyway. It was just a bigger neighborhood than she was used to.

"Are we really going to use a septic tank for a spaceship?"

Allen kicked at a loose rock, which skittered a few feet ahead of them down the alley. "Unless you can think of something better. A septic tank is designed to hold up against the weight of half a dozen feet of dirt; it's probably the sturdiest pressure vessel we're likely to find on short notice."

"I guess." She kicked at the rock, but it veered into a snowbank in the lee of a garbage can. "What about the emergency descent module? We hid it pretty well. It's probably still out there, and we *know* it'll hold air."

"That's about all it'll hold. We want something we can at least pack a lunch in. We're talking about traveling to another star, not—"

"We're talking about building a spaceship out of a septic tank," Judy said. "I'm just thinking maybe it would be smart to start with something that was actually designed to be used in space."

"The hyperdrive was designed to be used in space," Allen said with a wounded tone to his voice.

And it nearly smashed them into the Moon, Judy thought, but she didn't say it. "We could at least rob it for parts," she said. "The parachute, if nothing else. And maybe the acceleration couches."

Allen nodded. "Good point. I might be able to use some of the switches and stuff, too. Is this the right house?" They had reached a pink house with light blue trim, but from the back it was hard to tell if it was the same house they had left.

The garage was on the right side. The big elm tree in the back yard looked familiar. Judy looked at the house's windows and compared them to the arrangement of rooms she remembered. "I think this is it." She opened the gate and walked up to the garage's side window, standing on tiptoe to look in without stepping in the flower bed next to the wall. There was nothing growing in it at the moment, but she didn't want to compact the soil over any of Donna's bulbs.

She had to shield her eyes from the sun to see inside, but when her pupils dilated enough, she could see the spacesuits piled in a heap on the floor beside the workbench.

"This is the place."

They went around to the front and let themselves in, stamping the snow off their boots at the door. The warm air inside the house was a welcome reprieve from the winter day outside. They hung their borrowed coats in the closet and Judy went into the kitchen to make something hot to drink.

There was still half a pot of coffee from breakfast on the warmer, but Judy wasn't really that fond of coffee. She opened the pantry to look for tea, but she spotted can of Swiss Miss on the top shelf and decided on that instead. There was even a bag of mini-marshmallows to go with it.

It felt odd to help herself to things in someone else's kitchen, but Donna had told her to make herself at home, and at the moment she desperately needed to feel at home somewhere. She was trying not to dwell on the enormity of what she and Allen had done, or of what they intended to do yet, but when she let her guard down she could feel it hovering at the edge of her mind, waiting for its chance to overwhelm her.

When she carried the two steaming cups of chocolate into the living room, she found Allen sitting in front of their hosts' computer, downloading something off the internet.

"What are you getting?" she asked, setting the cup down beside the keyboard.

"The email I sent to INSANE. I wanted to see how hard it would be to get. Plus I need a copy of the control software. I had to leave my notebook on the shuttle."

"The files are still available? I would have thought the government would have shut down any site that offered them."

Allen took a sip of his chocolate. "Mmm. Thanks. Nope, they can't do that. There are too many private servers to shut 'em all down. They're trying to overload the net so nobody can connect, and they're spamming everybody's email, but the local server is too small for them to give their full attention. I got right on and went to their virus alert page, and there were the attached files I emailed to INSANE. Labeled 'Dangerous, do not open' of course, but they were there."

"You're sure they're the right files? I wouldn't put it past the government to screw with them so they won't work even if people do realize what they really are."

The files finished downloading. Allen opened the one called "Hyperdrive.pdf" and scrolled through it. "This is the file that describes how to build the drive," he said. "It looks right. It still has all my typos, at least. And that's the file I would have expected to be altered if they were going to. Screwing with the drive design would just keep it from working, but altering the control program could get people killed."

Judy wondered if some of the cloak-and-dagger types in the CIA would see that as a bad thing. If the hyperdrive proved deadly, that could work in their favor.

The memory of dropping into the atmosphere in a ball of flame made her shudder so badly she had to set her cup of chocolate down to keep from spilling it. "People are going to get killed even if the drive and the control program work perfectly," she said. "Space isn't a forgiving environment. One mistake can kill you even if all your equipment is working fine."

Allen looked up from the computer screen. "Just like cars," he said. "To most people, the benefits are worth the risk. It'll be the same with hyperdrive. Better, actually, since you're not nearly as likely to kill an innocent bystander if you lose control."

True enough, but she couldn't help wondering how many would-be astronauts would weed themselves out of the gene pool in the next few weeks simply by underestimating the danger. They were going to be dropping like meteors across alien skies, and even if they made it to the ground intact, they wouldn't have the equipment to survive long on a completely unexplored planet. Hell, most people couldn't survive long if you dropped them in a wilderness area on Earth.

But some people could. Some people could survive in Antarctica with only a backpack full of food and a pair of skis. And those were the type who were most likely to go into space.

Yeah, right. Like herself.

Now she understood what Carl had been thinking yesterday on board the *Discovery*. He wanted to go into space just as badly as she did, but he wanted to do it slowly, carefully, a step at a time. He wanted the vast infrastructure of NASA and the military industrial complex behind him. He wanted hardware that had been tested thousands of times under every conceivable condition, and he wanted redundant systems that would back it up if anything went wrong. He wanted safe, reliable spaceflight, glamorous and interesting but no more dangerous than being an actor or a musician.

He wanted exactly what she wanted.

Neither one of them were going to get it. Flying the shuttle was hardly safer than flying a fighter jet in combat, and it was the safest spacecraft ever built. Judy had struggled to overcome her terror every time she went up. The only reason she'd done it was because she couldn't have lived with herself if she didn't. In that regard, Allen was right: the benefits were worth the risk.

He had opened the control program and was examining the code. "Looks clean to me. I can run simulations to be sure, but I'm nearly certain this is the original article."

"Good," said Judy. She picked up her mug and forced her hands to be still while she sipped her hot chocolate. The web browser's window peeked over the top of the program window, and she read the top line banner: *Nasdaq down 500 points*. As she watched, the number changed to 550.

"Holy shit," she said, pointing. "Look at that."

"It'll rebound," Allen said.

"It had better. Most of my retirement money is in technology stocks."

"Switch them to septic tank manufacturers," Allen said with a smile. "Or seed companies."

"Seed companies?"

"Sure. People aren't just going to use this to explore. We're going to see a wave of colonization that'll make the American West look like a practice run. They're going to need seeds for crops, harvesting equipment, farm animals, medical supplies, toothbrushes, soap, clothing, music, books, and who knows what all else." He held out his hands, palms up. "People are going to be buying everything it takes to reconstruct civilization somewhere else. And since it'll be just as easy to come back for more equipment as it will be to get wherever they're going, people will keep buying stuff on Earth for years to come. The economy will *boom*."

"I'll be damned." Judy sipped at her chocolate, glad for the warmth of the mug in her hands. "So what sort of stuff do we need to take with *us*?"

"Good question. Let's do a little brainstorming." Allen disconnected from the net and opened a blank email document.

"Who are you emailing?" she asked him.

"Nobody. It's just the easiest way to get a text document."

"Oh."

"So let's think about what we need for our trip." He typed: *Equipment manifest*, then said, "How about if we organize according to Maslow's hierarchy of needs? Air first." He typed *compressed oxygen*. "Then water, then food. The ship will be our shelter." He added each item to the list as he named it.

Judy tried to think what would be the next most important thing after basic survival was assured. "Energy," she said, remembering the half of the hyperdrive that Allen had thrown away to change his vector during his jump from the shuttle to the space station. "Specifically, batteries. Lights. Heat." What else did they need that would require power? "Another notebook computer."

"Right. The spacesuits. The parachute from the emergency descent module. Some kind of servo or explosive bolt system to release it on command."

Judy sat down on the edge of the couch next to the computer desk. "Acceleration couches," she said.

"Wait up," Allen said, still typing. He caught up, then added *security cameras* without saying it aloud.

"What's that for?"

"Electronic windows. If we mount cameras outside and have a monitor inside, we don't have to cut holes for windows. Or worry about them blowing out."

"Oh. Good idea."

"Of course. I thought of it." He grinned.

"We're drifting off Maslow's list," she said. "What have we skipped?"

"Sex," Allen said. "But I'm assuming we can generate that locally when we need it."

"You are, are you?"

"Hope springs eternal," he replied, blushing slightly.

"True enough," she said, remembering who had maneuvered whom into the sack last night. She still tingled when she thought about it. Who would have thought that a mad scientist could be such an accomplished lover as well?

They looked at one another with undisguised lust for a moment, and she allowed herself to fantasize about ripping his borrowed clothes off right there in the living room, but she finally shook her head and said, "Spaceship first. What else do we need to take with us?"

"Zip-together sleeping bags," Allen said.

"Okay."

"Cooking equipment."

"Right. And a camp stove."

He wrote that down. The first item on the list scrolled off the top of the screen.

"Toilet paper," she said. "And a shovel."

16

They were still at it when Trent and Donna returned home from work. Trent showed up first, leaving his pickup parked on the street and walking warily to the front door rather than parking in the garage like he had last night. Judy met him at the door, and he looked past her into the living room before he spoke.

"Everything okay?" he asked.

"The coast is clear."

He nodded slowly. "Good. Be right in." He went back out to his pickup and drove it into the garage. Judy could see him talking to someone on a cell phone as he went past the window. Had he arranged for backup if there was trouble waiting for him at home? It certainly looked like it.

He came in from the garage a couple minutes later, his right hand in his coat pocket. Judy thought the bulge there was bigger than his hand alone would make.

"How, um, how was your day?" she asked.

"Okay," he said. "How was yours?"

"Pretty good. We've been making plans. We have a fair idea of what we need to do, and it looks like we can get the money to do it with."

Trent looked over at Allen, still seated in front of the computer. "Have you checked the news yet?"

"Off and on," he said. "Looks like the stock market is down. The government is still trying to blow a smoke screen, but the real news is spreading just as fast as the lies."

Trent nodded. "Radio was full of it all day. They're calling you crazy. Say you're armed and dangerous."

"Crazy is probably accurate," Allen admitted. "Maybe

even dangerous, depending on the circumstances, but I'm armed only in the biological sense."

Trent thought it over, then pulled his hand free of his coat pocket. There was still a sizable lump left behind. He opened the closet by the door and hung his coat inside, rummaging around a bit longer than was necessary. Judy bet the gun wasn't in the same coat anymore.

His hands were empty when he closed the door and stepped into the living room. "It was pretty hard to concentrate on roofing today, knowin' you two were here."

"I imagine so," Judy said. "We're sorry to be causing so much trouble."

"I didn't mean it like that," Trent said quickly. "I don't mind seein' things get shook up a little around here. It's kind of fun knowin' something nobody else in town knows."

Judy heard tires crunching ice in the driveway, and looked up to see Donna's car rolling past the window. A minute later she emerged from the garage, her cheeks glowing rosy from the cold and her arms full of groceries.

"I picked up some stuff on the way home," she said. "I hope you like pork chops."

Judy went into the kitchen and helped her unload the bags, then set to work peeling potatoes and boiling them while Donna and Trent cleaned up and changed into more comfortable clothes. Trent popped open Budweisers for everyone, handing the cold aluminum cans around without even asking if they wanted any, but Judy was glad to have it. The alcohol took the edge off her nerves, and the smell of food cooking made everything seem homey and safe, at least for the moment.

"So," Trent said, spinning a kitchen chair around and straddling it backward, "what's your plan?"

Judy looked at Allen. Allen looked at her, then at Trent. "We've, ah, found a suitable pressure vessel," he said. "We've come up with a pretty extensive list of equipment we'll need to turn it into a starship, but it's mostly stuff we can buy locally. Except for the ultralight airplanes. We'll have to have those delivered."

"Ultralight airplanes?" Donna asked over the crackle of frying meat.

"Yeah. If we actually find a habitable planet, we figure we'll want some kind of transportation when we get there. It would be a shame to go all that way and then be stuck exploring what we can reach on foot."

"Good point," Trent said. He cocked his head to the side, thinking, then shrugged and took a pull off his beer. "Lots of ways around that," he said, "but a plane ought to do. Have you flown before?"

Judy laughed, "Yes. I'm a shuttle pilot, remember?"

"Oh, right."

Allen cleared his throat. "We were wondering if you'd be amenable to going back out where you found us and seeing if our emergency descent module is still there. If nobody's found it yet, we could use a lot of the hardware off of it."

Trent took another drink of his beer. "We could do that. Gets dark awful early this time of year, though. We'd have to do it with headlights, unless the Moon's out."

Judy tried to remember what phase the Moon was in. It had looked full the last time she'd seen it, but that was because she'd been practically on top of it. She closed her eyes and visualized the geometry in her head: the Earth had been out the forward windows, a bright crescent cradling a dark ellipse, and the sun had been on the west side from her point of view, so that meant the Moon was about halfway between first quarter and full.

"It should be up until about three," she said.

Trent nodded. "All right, then. I guess we'll do a little midnight four-wheeling tonight." He grinned at the prospect. This was clearly not a hardship as far as he was concerned. "How big is this thing?" he asked. "Will it fit in the back of the truck?"

She took the measure of it in her mind. "No problem."

"How about weight? Can two guys lift it?"

Weren't she and Donna invited? Donna had been out with him before, but Judy didn't know what the protocol was in four-wheeling. Or maybe he was thinking to protect the women from danger if the Feds had staked out the EDM.

It didn't really matter to her. Bouncing over sagebrush wasn't her idea of a good time anyway, and she was long past the stage where she would let feminism make her do something she didn't want to do just to prove a point. Let Trent and Allen hoist the thing into the back of the truck. "You could probably skid it up a couple of planks," she said.

"Good. What about this whatchacallit . . . pressure vessel of yours? Will it fit in the garage?"

"Probably," Allen said. "But I feel bad taking over your place like this."

"Don't worry about it. You won't be here that long. And if you'll show me how to build a starship of my own, I'll consider it a fair trade."

There was a loud clatter from the kitchen as Donna dropped the spatula she was using to flip pork chops.

"You okay in there?" Trent asked.

"Fine," she said. "Why don't you make yourself useful and set the table?"

"Yes ma'am." He set his beer on the table and got four place mats from the top of the refrigerator, set out plates and silverware and napkins, then sat back down while Judy helped Donna mash the potatoes and make gravy. By the time they put the food on the table, Judy's stomach was growling like a cornered wolf.

Trent finished his beer and crushed the can with a single squeeze of his right hand, then tossed it in the garbage can under the sink. Allen tried to copy him, but it took two hands. Trent didn't even let on that he'd noticed; he just set out fresh beers all around, and when everyone had taken a seat he held up his can and said, "Here's to going where no man—or woman—has gone before."

"Hear hear!" Allen said, and everyone drank. Judy caught Donna's eye and raised an eyebrow in question, but Donna just smiled and offered her the first pick of the pork chops.

Trent and Allen took off right after dinner, leaving Judy and Donna to clean up. Domesticity was new to Judy, but she found a certain pleasure in the simple repetition of washing dishes. At the moment, that was all she wanted to do. She and Donna talked about inconsequential things: the weather, Donna's job in the mall, family. They compared genealogies and discovered that they were distant relatives, either third cousins or cousins thrice removed, neither knew which. Judy said she wasn't surprised, given that everyone on Earth was supposedly only six degrees of separation from everyone else, and then they played that game for a while, trying to see who was more closely connected to various celebrities. Judy won practically every round—being an astronaut put her in some far-ranging circles—but Donna surprised her with one connection.

"You're only two people away from the Dalai Lama?"

"Yep," Donna said. "My brother went mounting climbing in Tibet with someone who knew him." She laughed, then said, "But here's the question nobody can answer me: when he dies and gets reincarnated somewhere else, are we still only two degrees apart or do we have to start all over again?"

Judy thought it over for a moment while she dried the last of the silverware. "Well, you can just rock me to sleep tonight," she said at last.

Donna smiled. "It's a stumper, isn't it?"

When they finished in the kitchen, they went into the living room to watch the news. Judy and Allen were the top story on every channel, but the official word was still that the whole hyperdrive thing was a hoax. Judy felt her blood starting to boil as one anchor, a fifty-ish man with the network standard touch of gray at the temples and the "trust me" dark blue suit, said in his officious voice, "NASA investigators have uncovered evidence of a conspiracy between Gallagher and Meisner that was hatched nearly two years ago, just months before Meisner applied for a crew position on board the space shuttle. It is still unclear what role the computer virus plays in their conspiracy, but top government officials . . ."

He stopped speaking, but his eyes continued to scan left and right, obviously reading ahead on his teleprompter. He narrowed his eyes, then said, "Who wrote this crap, anyway? We all know that's not true. The truth is, the Space Shuttle *Discovery* disappeared from radar yesterday, reappeared eleven minutes later in a completely different orbit, got hit by a missile defense laser, then went to the Moon. We've got confirmation of that from half a dozen different sources, including NASA's own flight telemetry. And the original email message wasn't a virus at all. I've checked it out myself and it appears to be exactly what it says it is: detailed plans for the engine that allowed—"

A loud beep drowned out his voice and the picture swirled into static, to be replaced a moment later by a text message in white on a blue background: *Network Difficulties: Please Stand By.*

"Network difficulties, my ass," Judy said. "The only difficulty they've got right now is the government trying to stomp all over the first amendment." She looked at the message on the screen, imagining the chaos in the TV studio at the moment. Was the anchor being sacked? Arrested? Were there soldiers rushing through the station with automatic rifles, shooting up the broadcast equipment?

Suddenly she didn't feel quite so smug about the anchor's slick persona. If he'd had any idea how much trouble he was getting himself into, he had just shown the courage of a war correspondent.

She looked over at Donna, who was sitting beside her on the couch with the remote control in her hand and a surprised expression on her face. After a moment Donna switched the channel, but the other news stations were still regurgitating the official story. "This is starting to get scary," she said after the fifth or sixth reassurance that nothing unusual had happened in space.

That was the understatement of the year. Judy felt goosebumps on her goosebumps, and she wasn't even cold. "Allen and I should go," she said. "We're putting you and Trent in danger."

Donna switched the channel back to the "Network Difficulties" screen. "No," she said. "I won't send anyone out in the cold to fend for themselves when I can help them. And we're not in nearly as much danger as you are."

Judy wasn't sure if she should take heart at that comment or not. Donna was right, but only because Judy and Allen were in more trouble than practically anybody.

"Well, I can't argue with you there," she said. "But all the same, I don't want to drag you into something just because you were nice enough to pick up a couple of hitchhikers."

"You didn't. Trent and I talked about it last night, and we want to help."

Judy bit her lower lip, trying to decide whether to say anything more or not, but Donna saw her indecision and said, "What?"

"I was just thinking that it sounds like Trent wants to build a spaceship of his own. How do you feel about that?"

Donna laughed. "I've been living in this one-horse town all my life. I used to dream about going off to college or running away to Los Angeles and trying to get into the movies, but I never did. Once in a while I'll drive down to Salt Lake to go shopping, but that's about as exciting as it gets around here. If Trent wants to take me to Mars, I'm all for it."

"It's dangerous, you know. More dangerous than you can imagine."

"I know." Donna took a deep breath and let it out slowly. "We'll read up on it. Well, I will. Trent's not much of a reader. But I'll make sure we're ready before we go anywhere." She hesitated a moment, then added, "And I'd listen to any advice you want to give me."

Judy leaned back in the couch. What advice did she have for someone who had never been into space before?

"Take Dramamine."

17

Trent and Allen returned just after midnight. The pickup rolled silently into the garage, but the two men burst into the house with enough exuberance to wake the town.

"Wee-haw!" Trent shouted, removing his fleece-lined leather jacket and flinging it haphazardly over the back of a kitchen chair. "Was that a kick in the butt or what?"

"That was definitely a kick in the butt," Allen said, swinging his arms wide for emphasis and nearly knocking over the lamp beside the couch. Judy steadied it, then steadied Allen when he lurched backward and nearly fell onto her lap.

"And in the kidneys, and the top of the head, and just about every other part of the anatomy," he added. He turned to Judy. "I tried to explain the purpose of sush . . . pension, but Trent wasn't impressed by the concept."

"Who wants a soft ride in a four-wheeler?" Trent asked.

"Have you been drinking?" Judy asked.

Allen tilted his head sideways. "Yes, I believe what we were doing would qualify for that dish . . . cription."

"Drinking and *driving*?" Donna asked.

"Just a couple o' beers," Trent said. "I was in perfect control the whole time."

Allen laughed. "Control? Half the time we were in the air!"

"Yep," Trent said proudly.

"Sounds like you had fun," Donna said. "Did you find the capsule?"

Their faces lost a little enthusiasm. "We found where it was," Trent said, "but somebody beat us to it."

Allen sat down on the arm of the couch. "We got the

parachute, at least. Whoever took the EDM didn't bother to gather it up. They just cut it loose and left it snagged on the sagebrush."

"Must have been the Feds," Judy said. "Anybody after a ready-made spaceship would have taken the parachute, too."

"Yep. So we, um, came home by a roundabout method, just in case anybody was watching the site." He sounded so proud of himself that Judy couldn't resist smiling.

Neither could Donna, though she rolled her eyes and said, "Men," in a voice that would make a dog hang its head.

Judy told them about the news reports. Donna switched to the channel whose anchor had defied the censors, but the station was back on the air with an old Jackie Chan movie as if nothing had happened.

"Censorship," Allen said. "Who'd have thought they'd stoop to that? All the more reason to get the heck out of Dodge."

"Dodge?" Judy asked.

"Finger of speech. 'Scuse me." Allen staggered off to the bathroom, scattering his coat and hat and gloves along the way.

"So," Trent said, coming into the living room and settling in beside Donna. "Sounds like it's plan B for sure. Allen told me what you're going to use for a spaceship, and I told him he was nuts, but he says the two of you've got it all figured out."

"Pretty much," Judy admitted. "Of course we're open to suggestion if you've got a better idea."

He laughed softly. "I learned a long time ago not to offer advice to a . . . to a person who knows what they're doing."

Donna poked him in the ribs. "Nice recovery, there, Butch."

"Jeez, woman, I said—"

"I heard what you said, and I heard your tone of voice, so don't you 'Jeez woman' me."

If they hadn't been poking at one another and smiling like newlyweds, Judy would have sworn they were about to start throwing crockery, but instead they launched into a ticklefest that had Judy scooting away on the couch to avoid flailing limbs.

"Yow!" Trent shouted. "Hey! Stop that!"

Donna giggled like a teenager and pressed the attack. Trent fought back with a sofa pillow, whacking her on the head and sides with it until she shrieked for mercy. They were still at it when Allen popped open the bathroom door and said, "What's going on out there?" He stood in the hall-way, his hands on his hips.

Judy snatched up another pillow and flung it at him, catching him square in the chest before he could react. His face went through an amazing contortion from surprise to confusion to realization to revelry, then he flung the pillow back at her and followed it with arms outstretched for action.

Judy dodged the pillow, but she couldn't squirm away from his roving hands. "No fair!" she cried when she tried unsuccessfully to tickle him back. "You're still wearing your coat!"

"All's fair in love and war," he replied, pressing the attack.

Trent and Donna were no help. They were engaged in a protracted battle of their own—one which frequently spilled over into Judy and Allen's territory. The house rang with shrieks and giggles, slowly subsiding to hiccups and sniffles as they finally wore out their nervous energy.

Things didn't seem quite so cheery in the morning. Trent and Donna had to go to work again, and so did Allen and Judy. The men had to do it with hangovers, too, which didn't help their dispositions any.

Allen and Judy went over their equipment list again, adding a couple dozen more last-minute items to it. Despite Trent's statement that he didn't offer advice to people who knew what they were doing, he had apparently had some good suggestions on the drive out to the landing site and back, so Allen added those to the list as well, then he stood up from the kitchen table where they were working and took the phone off the wall.

"What do you think?" he asked. "Should we call him?"

Judy grimaced. "I don't like taking bank robbery money, even if we let him charge it to your credit card. But we're in worse trouble than I thought, and the sooner we get back into space, the better I'll like it."

"Was that a 'yes'?"

"I guess so."

Allen dialed the number, blocking the caller ID first.

"Hi, Dale? Allen Meisner. We've got a shopping list. Got a pencil?"

It took nearly five minutes to read everything. When he was done, Allen said, "Yes, I know that's a lot of stuff, and yes, we do need all of it. The cable is to reinforce the tank so it won't balloon out under air pressure, and the foam insulation will provide a cushion so it won't crack when it lands. That's right; we'll be coming down under a parachute. No, we've already got one." He rolled his eyes. "Yes, I know a spare would be nice, but do you know where to *get* one big enough to do the job? A regular sport parachute won't cut it."

He listened for a moment, then said, "Well, I'll be damned. Sure, that ought to do. Get us one. No, wait, get us three. Because we're building a second starship for a friend, that's why."

Allen told him to buy three sets of all the electronic parts in the list he had broadcast, as well. "There *is* a Radio Shack in this town, isn't there? Good. Sure, buy some for yourself, too." He laughed. "Yeah, maybe I'll hold classes."

They discussed logistics, including where to have all the stuff delivered. Trent had suggested the building site where he was working; it wouldn't seem out of the ordinary to have a septic tank delivered there, nor most of the other equipment, for that matter, as long as it was boxed up. Trent could bring it all home in his pickup after dark, and claim it had been stolen if anyone asked where it had gone.

Finally, Allen reeled off a credit card number from memory, and told Dale to charge an extra couple of thousand dollars to it for his trouble. Dale protested, but Allen insisted, and they went back and forth on it until they sounded as if they were about to call off the whole deal and hang up on each other, but Dale eventually gave in and they finished the conversation on a friendly note.

"Why do guys always do that?" Judy asked him.

"Do what?"

"Get all macho about who pays for what."

He grinned sheepishly as he set the phone back in its cradle. "I don't know. I guess it's how we keep score. You don't want to be the one left owing the other guy a favor."

"Why not? It means you're the one who just *got* a favor, doesn't it?"

"Yeah, but . . ." He shrugged. "It's not something I've ever thought out. It's just the way we do things."

She could tell she wasn't going to learn anything more from him about it. "So what was that about parachutes? He's got a source for those, too?"

"Yeah. He's apparently in the National Guard. They've got a whole bunch of 'chutes they use for airlifting supplies into disaster areas. Designed for great big cargo containers."

Judy had seen those before: they were huge. Having one for a backup in case the first one fouled made her feel a great deal better about their impending expedition. The whole setup was such a haphazard affair that she hadn't even been thinking of redundancy, but her astronaut training had made her nervous at the idea of flying without fail-safes. There were still a couple of dozen criticality-one failure modes that they couldn't provide backup for, but at least this one was covered.

"So what do we do until our spaceship is delivered?" she asked.

Allen nodded toward the door into the garage. "I thought I'd go through the hyperdrive and make sure it's okay. Maybe you could do the same for the spacesuits?"

"Sure."

The garage wasn't heated, so they brought their work inside. Allen set the getaway special canister beside the computer desk and opened it up, angling the light into it so he could see the electronics. He didn't have any specialized test equipment, but he did have the computer itself, so he hooked up the serial cable to the hyperdrive's communications port and started querying the status of its various subsystems that way.

The spacesuits were smeared with soot from the EDM and the boots were grimy from their hike, so Judy found a bright blue plastic tarp and unfolded it on the living room floor, then laid the suits on that and set to work cleaning them up and checking them for problems.

It seemed odd to have equipment in someone's living room that was normally allowed only in an environmentally controlled clean room. As Judy sat cross-legged on the tarp and cleaned the spacesuits with a light blue sponge she'd found under the kitchen sink, she imagined herself as a nomadic tribeswoman sitting in her tent and preparing her family's possessions for the summer's travels. When she thought of it in those terms, it didn't seem quite so strange. People had been expanding into new territory for millennia. Going into space had always seemed so daunting that it took an entire nation to do it, but now that Allen had lowered the barrier, things had gone right back to the way they had always been.

It was a lot more comfortable working cross-legged on a padded carpet than in a clean room. Sunlight slanted in through the front window and warmed her as well as cheered her up. She brewed a pot of tea, and she and Allen turned on the TV to keep an eye on the news while they worked.

The news hadn't changed, but the reporting of it had. Commentators were still regurgitating the official story, but they were doing everything in their power to make sure people knew it was a lie. Judy just about laughed up a lung when she heard one anchor say, "This just in from the department of censorship" before reading the teleprompter in a monotone and twitching his head in jerky movements like a robot. Others ended their reports with "Yeah, right," or "Nudge-nudge, wink-wink." One station didn't even report; their cameras merely panned back and forth through the studio, revealing the armed soldiers standing guard in every doorway.

"Jesus," Allen said when he saw it. "How can they get away with that?"

"Who? The army, or the TV station?"

"Both. I mean, don't they have to declare martial law in order to suspend the Constitution? And since they didn't, why are the military guys letting the TV guys film them breaking the law?"

Judy watched the silent exhibition of military presence and media defiance. "I'm guessing Stevenson wants to have his cake and eat it too. He doesn't want the political damage that would come from declaring martial law over something like this, but he can get the same result without it. When this gets hashed out in court in years to come, we'll probably find that all the orders can be traced back to a single fall guy."

Allen nodded. "Ollie North takes the heat, and the President gets off scot-free."

"Right. In the meantime, the individual soldiers are probably just as pissed about their orders as the TV stations are. So until they're ordered to stop this particular kind of broadcast, they're going to let it go."

"This isn't going to work," Allen said, "and Stevenson knows it. The government can't keep a lid on this forever. Hell, they can't even *put* a lid on it. The news is already out there."

That was true enough. This particular genie would never fit back into the bottle, no matter how hard they tried. But someone was certainly going through the motions, and they had to have a reason for it. Was it just a knee-jerk reaction to losing control over the situation, or could they actually be accomplishing something?

She thought about it awhile, then said, "Maybe they're

just trying to scare as many people as possible into staying home and keeping their heads down."

"The ones who would build their own spaceship aren't the kind to scare easily," Allen pointed out.

Judy wondered about that. She was getting plenty scared. But she knew what he meant. "Well, then, maybe they're trying to keep the economic impact to a minimum, or trying to reassure the rest of the world that we're not going nuts over here."

"Or maybe they're trying to keep their tax base from evaporating away." Allen snorted in disgust. "I wouldn't put it past them."

"Whatever their reasoning, you're right: they can't keep the lid on forever." Judy wished she was really as confident as she sounded. She knew intellectually that she was right, but the presence of soldiers in TV studios scared the hell out of her. She'd never seen anything like that before, never even heard of it. Not in America, at least. That, more than anything else that had happened since she'd cast her lot with Allen, made her worry that she had made the wrong decision.

She tried to put it out of her mind and concentrate on what she was doing. Clean off the dirt, check out the air tanks, check the batteries and seals, run the control system diagnostics. . . .

She was still at it when the TV station they had been watching cut to an on-the-scene report of a mysterious explosion in Lancaster, California. There was shaky footage of an old two-story house with piles of junk all around it, but the house didn't seem to be the site of the explosion. There was a crowd of people on the street, all looking toward the back yard, where used cars, bits and pieces of airplanes, various appliances, and tons of scrap metal filled every inch of space—except for a circular gap in the middle of the yard.

A reporter stood in the midst of the crowd and said, "Witnesses at the scene describe a single, loud explosion, like a thunderclap, but there were no clouds in the sky.

There was no smoke, and even more puzzling: no debris. Just this peculiar crater."

It was hard to get a good shot of it through all the junk until the cameraman climbed onto the top of an old refrigerator and focused on the gap, and then its shape became apparent. It was a perfectly hemispherical bowl about fifteen feet across, defined by the sheared-off edges of the junk piled around it. It extended into the ground only four feet or so; the center of the hemisphere was about three or four feet in the air. The exposed dirt had a shiny, glassy look to it, as if it had been fused by tremendous heat, but there was no sign of heat on any of the junk surrounding it. Instead, the edges looked like they had been sliced with the world's sharpest blade. There was half a washing machine sitting there with its tub and electric motor exposed like a cutaway view in a service diagram, sitting on two railroad ties whose ends looked like they'd been carefully polished over days and days of work.

The reporter said, "The owner of the house cannot be located, but neighbors say he is—or was—a noted eccentric who collected anything he could get his hands on at swap meets, and often combined them in unusual ways." The camera panned into the driveway, where an old Ford Pinto had been refitted with a jet fighter canopy instead of its normal windshield and roof.

Judy looked over at Allen. "That explosion. Air filling a vacuum?"

"That's right," he said. He leaned back in his chair and smiled. "The first explorer is away."

18

The news was full of similar reports over the next couple of days, but that was nearly eclipsed by the backlash over the attempt at censorship. As both Judy and Allen had predicted, the news blackout didn't last long, and when it fell, it was like a sand dike under a tidal wave. Every political organization from the American Civil Liberties Union to the Ku Klux Klan filed class-action suits against the government, and since the conspiracy had struck so close to home, TV and radio stations and newspapers across the country gave the lawsuits prime coverage.

Information about the hyperdrive emerged between the lines, and in second-page sidebars. The story was too technical for the front page, but it provided an excellent source for commentary. Economic and sociological analysts argued about what it would do to everything from world trade to population pressure, while technologists discussed the repercussions for the aerospace and defense industries. Nobody agreed, not even on whether there would be repercussions, but everyone had an opinion.

Even Carl Reinhardt had his say. In an interview from the space station, he reiterated his belief that the hyperdrive spelled the end of organized space exploration, but he was practically laughed off the air by Mary Hunter, the station commander. "Are you nuts?" she said. "Launch costs have just dropped from a thousand dollars a pound to something like a penny. Your local high school could put up a space station now! We're going to see more big projects than you can imagine."

Carl begged to differ, but the interviewer went on to ask Mary what sort of projects she envisioned, and her description of classrooms in orbit and geology field trips to Mars trumped his message of gloom and doom.

Gerry Vaughn got his moment in the limelight as well, but he fared even worse than Carl. Nobody loves a traitor, and there was no amount of spin he could put on the situation that made him look like anything else. The idea that Russia still had sleeper agents in America caused an uproar almost as big as the censorship issue, and world tension ratcheted up another notch.

The international picture looked just as fractured as the domestic one. Practically every government had tried to stop the spread of the hyperdrive plans, and some were still struggling to contain them, but it was a lost cause and everyone knew it. The true struggle now seemed to be for control of the high ground. If people were going to go into space, then it would be *their* people who got first pick of the prime real estate, and it would be done in an orderly, government-controlled fashion.

"Yeah, right," Allen said when he heard that. He and Judy were in the garage by then, mounting hardware on their rapidly evolving spaceship and listening to shortwave radio on the multi-band transceiver they had bought for the trip. "Do those idiots have any idea how many planets there are out there? There's something like four hundred billion stars in the Milky Way alone, and the odds are good that most of them have planets. We could have a separate planet for every group who wants one, right down to left-handed theremin players who wear propeller beanies on Tuesdays. Territory is a dead issue."

"What's a theremin?" asked Judy. She was duct-taping a tiny video camera to the end of the plastic tank while Allen fed its data cable through the four-inch-diameter inlet pipe that jutted out of the end. It was part of a home security system: two gimbaled cameras mounted outside where they could swivel around to cover overlapping hemispheres of view, and two monitors inside to display what they saw.

"A theremin is the first electronic musical instrument ever built. It's got an antenna sticking up out of the case, and it generates a tone that rises in pitch the closer your hand gets to the antenna. You wiggle your hand, and it makes a *woo-woo-woo* kind of sound. Sound engineers use them a lot to make spooky noises in horror movies."

"Oh." Judy had never heard of one, but she supposed it would be just the sort of thing for Allen. Maybe there would even be room enough out there for people to play them without annoying their neighbors, too.

But that wasn't a foregone conclusion. "What if those planets are already inhabited?" she asked.

Allen grinned happily. "Then the Universe will be an even more interesting place than we thought."

There were footholds molded into the corrugated side of the tank. He used them to climb up and lean in through one of the two manholes on top. They didn't really need two, but the tank had come with them, and it was easier to use them both as hatches than to seal one up. The lids themselves would need some reinforcement, but the collars were built like regular street manholes; thick enough to drive over. The plastic barely flexed under Allen's weight, but the tank echoed with his voice as he said, "Could you wiggle the wire so I can figure out which one it is?"

Judy obliged, and a moment later the wire slid in until it was snug against the side of the tank. While Allen hooked it to the security system mounted inside, she ran a strip of duct tape along the exposed length to hold it down. They didn't want anything loose to flap around and break during descent. The parachute would keep their airspeed down once they deployed it, but they could pick up a pretty good velocity in the upper atmosphere beforehand. Not enough for thermal effects to melt anything, but certainly enough to tear loose what wasn't held down.

Judy's skepticism about the tank was fading as she helped turn it into an interstellar spacecraft. It had charmed her right from the start with its color and shape: it was like a bright yellow bread loaf with alternating ridges and grooves running up and down its sides every four inches all the way around. It glowed with a cheery warmth from the safelight they had dangled inside, and when she climbed in and sat on the ribbed bottom, there was plenty of head-room. The domed top gave it the feel of a deep-sea submarine, which only added to the aura of scientific authenticity.

There was a sticker on one of the manholes that made her grin every time she read it: "Use only as a septic tank. Any other use will void warranty."

She wondered who would offer the first spaceship actually designed and warranted for the purpose. One of the airplane companies, like Boeing or McDonnell Douglas? Or would it be the auto manufacturers? Modern cars were already sealed and climate controlled; it wouldn't take much to make them airtight and put carbon dioxide scrubbers in the air-conditioning vents. She laughed at the image of American families taking weekend trips into space in their minivans and SUVs, but it might just come to happen.

Or not. A spaceship didn't have to actually fly anywhere, and it certainly didn't need wheels. Plastic tanks were a heck of a lot easier to mass produce than planes or cars, and a lot cheaper, too. The first interstellar spaceships on the open market could easily be built by unskilled labor in an injection-molding plant.

Too bad. Now that she was actually doing it, Judy had discovered that she enjoyed building her own spaceship. It gave her a sense of hands-on involvement that merely climbing aboard a ready-to-fly shuttle had never provided. She had studied every subsystem on board the shuttle until she could diagram the whole orbiter in her sleep, but even so, she didn't know it like this. She knew the tank with her body, felt the orange-peel roughness of the plastic and the sharp edges of its mold lines in her fingertips, heard its hollow echo resonating in her ears, smelled the vinyl and urethane vapors in her sinuses. She had handled every piece of hardware they had bolted, tied, or taped down, and with every component she added she could sense her own excitement building. Hour by hour, piece by piece, she and Allen drew closer to the moment when they would truly break the bonds of Earth and venture out into the cosmos.

Even the most reckless NASA engineer would have gone into shock at the sight of their equipment, but she and Allen had tested every component. It was their lives on the line, after all. They had wrapped the tank itself in quarter-inch steel cable to keep it from expanding and splitting a seam in vacuum, and they had lashed together a separate framework of 4 × 4 posts to help it keep its shape. They had reinforced the thick plastic manhole covers with inch-thick marine plywood and sealed around the edges with heavy silicone rubber. The hatches swung inward rather than outward, so air pressure would hold them closed while in flight. It wouldn't be full atmospheric pressure anyway; they were going to use pure oxygen from a welding bottle and keep it at five pounds per square inch instead of fifteen. They had threaded a pair of simple water faucets into the septic tank's side—with the handles and spouts pointing inward—to serve as pressure relief valves if they had to vent the tank to space or equalize pressure on the ground. They would also be wearing spacesuits in case the tank didn't hold, but after seeing how tough it was, Judy doubted the suits would be necessary.

The biggest danger was going to be on landing. They would be falling straight into the atmosphere from rest, rather than angling into it at just under orbital velocity like the shuttle did, but they were still going to be moving pretty fast when they deployed the parachute. The jerk when it snapped open could rip the mount right off the top, or buckle the floor if they wrapped the shroud lines all the way around. A bungee would solve the impact problem, but too much rebound would throw them right back up into the canopy, where they would tangle with the shroud lines and collapse the 'chute.

Allen had come up with a tie-down system using a web made out of wide nylon cargo straps and twelve inches of foam-core insulation on the bottom of the tank. The straps would provide a little bit of stretch on their own, but the insulation would absorb most of the shock by crushing under the straps' pressure. The deceleration would still be fierce, but it wouldn't be instantaneous, and the foam insulation that hadn't been crushed by the parachute opening would serve as a shock absorber again when they hit the ground.

A week ago Judy would never have believed that she'd be trusting her life to such a contraption, but here she stood in Trent and Donna's garage, happily putting the final touches on it and looking forward to the moment when they could test it out.

That wouldn't be long. Another two days at the outside. They were almost done with the video system; after that they only needed to mount the hyperdrive, load their supplies, and go. They had already installed and charged the batteries, found a used laptop computer to use as a jump controller, and tested the software on it.

Allen was building a spare hyperdrive just in case, and another pair for Trent and Donna. Their hosts were taking notes as the first starship neared completion, asking tons of questions and even offering the occasional suggestion when they figured out something ahead of Allen or Judy. It was Donna who pointed out that seats weren't worth the trouble in such cramped quarters, especially when mounting them could put enough stress on the tank to break it during the impact of landing. She had a much better suggestion: beanbag chairs. They would conform to practically any shape, even a spacesuit with a backpack life-support system attached, and they would provide much a better cushion during landing than a conventional acceleration couch. They could also be used for stuff sacks for anything soft. All a person had to do was remove an equal volume of filler and they had ready-made storage space for sleeping bags, pillows, extra clothing—even toilet paper.

So now the inside of the starship held a bright red beanbag at one end and a bright green one at the other, both duct-taped to the floor and sporting seatbelts made from bungee cords and more duct tape. They weren't elegant, but Judy had to admit that they were far more comfortable than the shuttle seats; especially the little fold-up guys that the payload specialists and the mission specialists had to sit in on launch and landing.

They were going to have to do without ultralight airplanes, at least for their first foray. They had been unable to track down even a single plane that could be folded into a compact enough package to carry along, much less two of them. They could probably have done better if the internet hadn't been so bogged down with the government-introduced "virus-alert" virus, but it was practically impossible to get beyond the local node.

It didn't really matter to Judy. Traveling to a planet circling another star would be accomplishment enough; she didn't really have to fly another dozen miles once she got there just to say she was exploring. They could always pop back into space and drop to the ground again if they wanted to move to another location. Not the most efficient way to travel, perhaps, but it would work. Besides, if they really needed an airplane they could come back in a few weeks, after the chaos had died down, and try it again if they wanted to.

Provided it *did* die down. Judy wasn't convinced it was going to any time soon, especially not for her and Allen. The various governments of the world seemed determined to make the worst of Allen's gift, and they were still looking for him so they could trot him out for people to throw stones at. They hadn't done a house-to-house search of Rock Springs yet, but Judy suspected that was only because most of the people in those houses were armed rednecks who wouldn't take kindly to the invasion of their privacy.

It would be a long time before she and Allen could show their faces in public again. The best thing they could do would be to find a tropical paradise somewhere and hang out for a few months, and that was just what Judy intended to do, just as soon as they finished building their starship.

19

They were only a few hours short of being ready when their luck ran out. It was Saturday afternoon, and Trent was helping them drag their completed starship out into the back yard, where they intended to winch it up off the ground from a thick branch of the Chinese elm tree so they wouldn't take a spaceship-sized divot out of the lawn when they made the big jump. Allen had mounted the hyperdrive engine in the middle of the tank and tightened its jump field to minimize the amount of volume it enclosed, but it was still a spherical field. It would dig a pretty good hole if they didn't raise the tank in the air first.

The sun was shining out of a clear blue sky, and the temperature had risen to nearly fifty degrees. Everyone was laughing and joking as they inched Allen and Judy's ungainly vehicle across the cement driveway, skidding it carefully on waxed 2 × 4s to avoid tearing up the thick pad of foam insulation strapped to the bottom. The yellow plastic shone brightly in the sunlight, and Judy felt lighter than she had in days. The country might be going to hell in a handbasket, but she was going to Alpha Centauri. In a septic tank, to be sure, but still.

They had christened it that morning, and painted its name on the side in big, flowing black letters that followed the four-inch corrugations in and out: *Getaway Special*. Allen had suggested the name, and Judy had laughed at first, but when she realized he was serious she went along with it. Like the ship itself, the name was as functional as it was inelegant.

A small plane flew over at a couple thousand feet. Nobody paid it any attention, not even when it banked around and circled the neighborhood. Judy just figured it was some-body out for a weekend flight, the pilot probably showing his passengers what their house looked like from the air. Not until Donna came out of the house with the cordless phone in her hand and a puzzled frown on her face did she think anything might be wrong.

"Someone named Dale is calling for you," she said to Allen.

Judy stopped pushing against the tank and looked up at him. "Dale? How did he know where to call?"

Allen looked just as puzzled as Donna. "Don't ask me. I didn't give him the number." He took the phone from Donna and said, "Hello, Dale? How did you—what? How? How do you know that? Oh. They got what? But that still shouldn't—Hello? Hello?"

He lowered the phone. "He hung up. But he says the Feds are onto us. They broke through the security on the credit card charge and traced it back to him, and when he went online to get his email just now, they hacked into his com-puter and got the list of supplies he bought for us." He handed the phone back to Donna.

"And here we are pushing a bright yellow septic tank out into the yard," Judy said, looking up at the airplane, which had just banked around for another pass.

Trent followed her gaze. "Time to go," he said.

"We're in the middle of your driveway," she pointed out.

"You're going to be in the middle of a maximum security cell in about ten minutes. Screw the driveway. Just go."

"But we don't have the food loaded! And we need to pre-breathe oxygen for at least an hour before we put on the suits. We can't just—"

Trent turned to Donna. "Get some food. I don't care what; just throw it in there. You two, get in the tank. You pressure-tested it to twenty psi; you'll just have to keep it at full pressure until you can get the nitrogen out of your sys-tems." He moved off toward his pickup, parked at the head of the driveway, then stopped when he realized nobody had moved. "Do it!" he shouted. "There's no other choice!"

There didn't seem to be. Judy slapped Allen on the butt and said, "He's right. Get in."

Allen blinked a few times, looked up at the airplane, then back at Trent. "What about you guys?" he said. "We can't just leave you here to face the cops by yourselves."

"I've faced cops before," Trent said. "They got nothin' on us. Once you're gone, they'll leave us alone, or they'll wish they had. Now go!" He ran off toward his pickup.

Judy climbed up the side of the tank and dropped in through one of the manholes. A moment later, Allen, still protesting, climbed through the other. The hyperdrive in the getaway special canister filled the space between them in the center of the tank, and the spare drive, built into a five-gallon PVC bucket, shared the space below it with their oxygen tank. The video monitors mounted side by side at one end of the hyperdrive took up more space, leaving only a window-sized gap to see each other through, and their spacesuits and beanbag crash couches filled up what little room there was at their feet.

Trent leaned in right after Allen and handed over a short-barreled revolver and a box of ammunition, evidently recovered from the glove box of his truck. "Here," he said. "They'll just take this away from me anyway, and you might need it where you're going."

"A gun?" Judy asked. "We don't need a—"

"You'll think different if the planet you land on's got tigers or something on it. Just take it." He dropped it in Judy's lap, and a moment later he started tossing in food. Boxes of macaroni and cheese, sacks of apples and potatoes, and cans of soup and beans rained down on them, bouncing off the hyperdrive and the monitors and the beanbag chairs and rolling to the sides of the tank. There was no space to put anything; the engines and the spacesuits and the beanbags took up practically all the room.

"Wait!" Judy shouted. "Hold up a sec—ow!"

"Sorry. Watch your head; six-pack of Bud coming through."

"We don't need—"

"Sure you do." He lowered it gently and she set it aside, then reached for the next item, but there wasn't any more. Trent took her hands in his and said, "Good luck. We'll see you in Orion or somewhere."

"Not Orion!" Judy said. "That's all hot new stars, and there won't be any planets. Go for—"

"I know, I know. I've got the list you gave us. And the starmap program for the computer. We'll be fine."

He grasped Allen's hand, then helped Donna up to say goodbye as well. She looked a little shell-shocked, but Judy imagined she looked just as bad. "Thanks for everything," she said. "You're the best people I've ever met."

Donna blushed and said, "Oh, now, we didn't—" but Trent called out, "Cop cars down the street. Seal 'er up and go!"

Donna flew backward with a startled "Oh!" as he lifted her off the side of the tank.

"We're clear!" he hollered. "Go!"

They could hear tires squealing as cars pulled to a stop in the street. Doors slammed, and loud voices shouted, "Get your hands up! Step away from the septic tank."

Judy slammed the hatch above her head and snapped the latch in place. It was a spring-loaded gate latch; it would provide just enough pressure to hold the hatch closed until air pressure took over the job. Allen was already busy powering up the hyperdrive and entering the first set of coordinates, so she closed and dogged his hatch, too. They could still hear voices outside, but they couldn't hear what anyone was saying.

"Diagnostics look good," Allen said. "Ready?"

"I'm not even strapped in! And there's loose stuff scattered all over. We can't launch like this!"

"We're going to have to. Hang on. Jump in five, four, three, two, one." He pushed the "Enter" key.

Weight ceased all at once. The tank creaked ominously, then fell silent. All the food rose up off the floor, along with the spacesuit helmets, the gun and ammunition, and half a dozen other things that they had thought were tied down.

The light grew brighter on Judy's left, but the wall on her right lost its glow. There was no atmosphere outside to scatter sunlight anymore; it was all coming directly from the source.

Judy's heart was pounding worse than it had during her first shuttle launch. "I'm . . . going to lower the pressure to ten psi," she said. They could drop that much without risking the bends, and it would relieve the stress on the tank by a third. She opened the faucet on her end of the tank and listened to the sucking noise as air rushed out, keeping her eye on the altimeter taped to the wall beside it and swallowing to equalize the pressure in her ears all the while. The gauge was just a simple hiker's barometer that Donna had bought for them at the mall, but it read in thousands of feet and inches of mercury. When the needle hit 10,000 feet—20 inches of mercury—she closed the stopcock and said, "Okay, that should be good for now. We'll give it a little time at this altitude before we drop it again. In the meantime, let's get these suits on."

"The walls will hold," Allen said, but Judy pointed to the two security monitors, where the outside cameras showed the hemisphere of ground that they'd brought with them spewing out clods of dirt and rock in a slow motion explosion. The water in the soil was boiling in the vacuum.

"Uh . . . okay," he said. He helped her into her suit, and she did the same for him, as much as they could, anyway, through the tiny opening between the halves of the tank. They kicked floating food every which way, but Allen closed the lid on the computer so they couldn't accidentally trigger another jump and they ignored the drifting debris until they were both suited up. They left their helmets off, and Allen left his gloves off so he could use the computer easier, but they kept them ready to snatch up and put on at a moment's notice. Allen had taped a pencil-style eraser to the side of the index finger on his right glove so he could still press a key at a time, but it was clumsy enough that he didn't want to use it unless he had to.

The pressure relief valves were mounted at opposite

ends of the tank, but not aligned along its axis. They were both aimed out the side, and the same side at that, so escaping air would act like a small rocket and send them into a slow spin. They had planned for that; it would help keep the temperature even on all sides. Judy could hear something bumping into the walls, and she assumed at first that it was the food slowly coming to rest as centrifugal force pushed it outward, but a quick look at the external monitors revealed the true cause: The boiling dirt was pushing rocks away in all directions, and some of them were striking the tank.

She swallowed and forced herself to breathe. It wasn't dangerous. The disk of concrete that they'd cut out of the driveway might have been if it had been moving faster, but it had already bumped into them and was now drifting away into space, its mirror-smooth edges reflecting sunlight as it tumbled. There was a length of pipe that might have caused trouble if it had been aimed at them, but the jet of steam spewing out of both ends had set it spinning away as well.

"I think we cut their water line," Judy said.

Allen peered closely at the screen. "I hope that was just a water line. If it was a gas line, there could be some excitement going on down there."

"I imagine there's some excitement anyway," Judy said. "I hope they don't wind up in too much trouble over this."

"Me too."

She looked at the monitors as they tumbled, hoping for a glimpse of Earth, but if Allen had used their pre-calculated initial jump coordinates then they were two light-minutes away. Earth would be just a bright dot from here. They could find it with the computer's starmap program and the video signal from the outside cameras, running a difference check to find the "stars" that weren't in the database, but there was no point in it. There was nothing they could do to help Trent and Donna now.

The Sun swept through the field of view, and the camera automatically irised down to keep from burning out. It was a far cry from the first TV cameras that had gone to the Moon; those could be permanently damaged by just a second's exposure to direct sunlight. The Apollo 12 astronauts had learned that the hard way. These were designed for automated security systems; they could sweep back and forth across the sun all day and not be damaged.

The food was still drifting everywhere. Judy unzipped her beanbag chair and pulled her sleeping bag out of it, then began sweeping all the loose items into the bag. It made a fairly convincing mummy when she was done. She tied it to the bottom of the tank beside her somewhat-floppier-than-before beanbag, then looked outside again.

Nothing remained of the hemisphere of dirt but a rapidly expanding fog of particles and the flat disk of concrete. The septic tank wouldn't look much different if the walls blew: a little scrap of hard plastic amid a field of debris.

Judy's pulse rate was still bordering on tachycardia, and her breath was coming short. Had she miscalculated with the altimeter? She checked, but the needle was rock steady at 10,000 feet. No leaks, then, either. They couldn't be running out of oxygen yet; they'd only been in space a couple of minutes.

She took a deep breath to calm down. They hadn't blown up yet. They were in a homemade spaceship way the hell and gone out into space, but they were okay.

Allen had opened up the computer again and was letting the sky comparator program collect enough data to calculate their rotation rate. The navigation software would correct for it, but it needed to learn the parameters so it would know when to trigger the jump. Otherwise they could wind up light-years from where they intended to go.

This wasn't quite how Judy had envisioned the beginning of their maiden voyage, but she had to admit that aside from their precipitous departure, things were going pretty much according to plan. A sudden thought made her laugh, and Allen said, "What?"

"I just realized, if we hadn't insisted on paying Dale

back, we would have gotten away without a hitch."

He snorted. "Mom always said my morals would get me in trouble."

The computer beeped. He studied its display for a moment, then said, "We've got a lock. We can make our interstellar jump any time. Shall we try something simple first, like Alpha Centauri?"

20

His words sent a shiver of anticipation down her spine. Alpha Centauri. The closest star to the Sun, and the most similar star within telescope range. The two had almost certainly coalesced from the same gas cloud billions of years ago, and had stayed gravitationally bound ever since. From the time she was old enough to read, Judy had been fascinated by the idea of a companion star, and she had dreamed of someday going there to see if the system held a planet like Earth, too.

There could be more than one. Alpha Centauri was a double star, the Sunlike primary circled by a smaller orange companion in an elliptical orbit that never came closer than Saturn came to the Sun. They were far enough apart for planets to have settled into stable orbits around both stars, though astronomers still debated whether planets could have formed there in the first place.

Judy had always imagined that she would be an old woman before she got the chance to answer that question firsthand, if she ever did, but here she was just minutes away from fulfilling that dream.

Or dying in the attempt. None of the people who had left silvery craters in the ground over the last few days had returned to report on their travels. There could be as many reasons for that as there were explorers, but it could be possible that the hyperdrive was dangerous over long distances. Judy could be closer to answering a religious question than an astronomical one.

She swallowed. Took a deep breath. Nodded. "Nothing ventured, nothing gained."

Allen grinned. "That's right. Here goes."

He pushed the "Enter" key. There was no radio pulse like there'd been on the shuttle. There was no point in it; the signal would take years to catch up to them through normal space. Allen had wired an ammeter in series with the batteries so he could tell how much current the drive was drawing, but Judy kept her eyes on the video monitors. Nothing happened for a few seconds; the computer was waiting for the right moment. Then she felt the by-now-familiar instant of disorientation, no worse than any of the previous jumps, and the light from outside went out like a switch had been thrown.

Allen reached up and switched on the overhead lights: two industrial-strength flashlights shining into frosted plastic bags. "We're there," he said.

The stars hadn't even flickered. "Are you sure?" she asked. "Nothing changed."

"We only jumped four light-years. It'll take a lot more than that to shift the stellar background in any random patch of sky." He called up the comparator program again and let it crunch on the signal from the cameras.

Only four light-years. Merely a hundred million times the distance from Earth to the Moon, nine *billion* times the width of the United States; it was impossible to grasp the magnitude of that distance, yet the stars had hardly changed.

Except the Sun. It was so far away now that Judy couldn't even pick it out among all the others. There was a bright one in Gemini that she didn't remember being there before, but that couldn't be Sol; not if the hyperdrive had taken them the direction they had intended. Sol should be in Cassiopeia from here.

But there was definitely a new star in Gemini, just inside the left knee. "Is that Alpha Centauri?" she asked, pointing.

Allen slid his finger across the touchpad until the arrow pointed at the star, then read the identification at the bottom of the screen. "Nope, that's Procyon. But how about that third head?"

Sure enough, there was another star where there

shouldn't have been one. It was even brighter than Procyon, and just to the left of the two head stars, Castor and Pollux. If it had been visible there from Earth, the constellation would have been called "Trimini."

Allen aimed the pointer at it and waited for the computer to figure out what it was. It took a second, but when the answer flashed on the screen, he said, "Bingo. Alpha Centauri B. The little brother. If we're close enough to see that, we're very close to where we want to be."

A few seconds later the computer confirmed his assessment. It beeped for attention and drew a shimmering circle around another bright star in an otherwise blank patch of sky nearby. "Alpha Centauri A," Allen said. "Just a second while I transfer the data . . . okay, we've got a lock. Triangulating on A, B, and Procyon, gives us . . . ten light-hours. About twice the distance from Pluto to the Sun. Not bad for a first shot, eh?"

"Pretty good," Judy admitted. Her neck muscles loosened up a bit at the realization that they knew where they were.

He tapped at the keyboard for a few seconds. "Okay, I've set it to jump to three AU out. We should be able to spot planets pretty easily from there."

"How was the current drain on that last jump?" she asked. She didn't want to burn out the hyperdrive by jumping too often like they had done on the shuttle.

"Fine. Distance really doesn't seem to matter. And those heat sinks I put on the voltage regulator should let us jump all we want now."

"Okay, then, let's go for it." She gripped the sides of her beanbag chair, even though she knew there wouldn't be any disturbance. She just needed something to hold on to.

Allen hit the "Enter" key, and in the next instant the walls of the tank glowed again with familiar yellow light. Judy looked at the monitor and saw the bright solar disk slide past as the tank's slow rotation swept the camera across the star. They were there.

She bent forward across the getaway special canister

and gave Allen a clumsy kiss. He looked a bit startled at first, then he warmed to the idea.

"Thank you," she said.

He blushed. "I don't think anyone's ever thanked me for kissing them before."

She stuck out her tongue at him. "I'm thanking you for bringing me here. It's one of my biggest dreams come true. But thanks for the kiss, too."

"Any time."

She stretched out for a more serious one, but the motion opened the way for her intestines to vent the gas that had been building up ever since she had lowered the air pressure in the tank. The fart was audible even inside her spacesuit, and the smell that came boiling out of the neck ring killed the mood faster than garlic breath.

"Gack! Sorry." She felt herself overheat with embarrassment.

Allen's response was not what she expected. He sighed in obvious relief and let loose his own back pressure, fanning the air in front of his face with his hands. "Thank god," he said. "I was about to explode."

Judy giggled. "Ah, the romance of space exploration." She looked at her watch. They had been sealed inside the tank for eleven minutes. She wouldn't waste air just to flush out the smell, but it was probably time to refresh the oxygen supply anyway. They didn't have any lithium hydroxide scrubbers to remove the carbon dioxide that built up as they breathed, so they would start hyperventilating from CO_2 poisoning if they let it build up too much. And despite her chagrin at spoiling the mood, she felt so giddy from their accomplishment that she would never know when they ran out of oxygen.

She opened the valve and let the pressure drop to 18,000 feet, then she shut it off and cracked the valve on the oxygen tank. She only pressurized it back to 14,000 feet; that was still enough to prevent the bends, and with the infusion of pure oxygen it was a richer mix than before. It smelled better, too.

The computer beeped again, and she looked over at the screen, where the star comparator program had identified four sources it couldn't account for.

"They almost certainly have to be planets," Allen said. "Let's make a short hop across the system and get some distance figures."

"Okay."

He keyed in the coordinates, hit "Enter," and the angle of the light changed. They waited another minute or so for the computer to find the planets' new locations, then Allen fed the data from the comparator into the navigation program and let it calculate their actual positions in space. Judy pulled herself around so she could see the screen more clearly, but the figures were displayed in table form, and it took her a few seconds to make sense of them.

"You should program that to show us a diagram of the solar system."

Allen pursed his lips and nodded. "That'll be a feature for version 2.0. But it's not too hard to puzzle out. This is the distance from us, and this is the distance from the primary. It's in kilometers, so we want something on the order of a hundred and fifty million."

There was one planet at 70 million, another at 100, and another at 180. Judy's heart fell. The inner two would be too hot, and the next one would be considerably colder than Earth, unless it had a thick enough atmosphere to hold in more heat than Earth did. The outer one was all the way out to 450; the equivalent of Sol's asteroid belt.

She pointed at the third planet. "That's the only candidate, isn't it?"

"Looks like. Shall we take a closer look?"

"Of course we should! I didn't come this far just to turn back because it doesn't look promising."

Allen didn't have to type in the coordinates this time. He cut and pasted them from the navigation program, but then he zeroed out the last two digits of the third coordinate.

"What was that for?" Judy asked.

"I shortened the distance, just in case the software got

a really accurate fix. We don't want to jump into the middle of the planet; we want to be ten or twenty thousand kilometers away."

"Oh. Right." She shivered. Allen had said the hyperdrive wouldn't let them jump into a space that was already occupied, but she didn't want to test it.

He hit the "Enter" key, and the light from outside grew brighter. They watched the monitor as the *Getaway*'s rotation made stars sweep by, waiting for their first glimpse of the planet.

When it came, it nearly took Judy's breath away. She had been afraid they would find another cold, lifeless Mars or a Saturnian giant, but the curved horizon that slid into view held the familiar white swirls of storm systems marching across brown continents and blue ocean.

"It's there!" Judy whispered. "My god, it's real!"

They were only a few thousand kilometers above the surface: close enough to see a chain of mountains along the edge of a major continent directly beneath them. The peaks were covered in snow, but the lower slopes looked lush with greenery.

"There's chlorophyll here," she said. "Plant life!"

The atmosphere looked thicker than Earth's. It might have been just an optical illusion, but the cloud layers looked more complex, and the horizon looked fuzzier than Earth's. And by the looks of the vegetation, something was holding in heat. The planet's extra distance from its sun didn't seem to matter at all.

The camera panned across the entire continent as their spaceship continued its slow rotation. They could see more mountain ranges, river valleys, plains, and even a desert, which only accentuated how alive the rest of the continent was.

Allen switched on the radio. "I wonder if there's anybody home?"

They had brought a shortwave set on the off chance that they might be able to detect alien radio transmissions with it. It had only a fraction of the bandwidth that they needed to search the whole electromagnetic spectrum, but it was the best they could do on short notice, and it would also come in handy if they needed to talk to anyone once they got back to Earth orbit. Allen had used the cable wrapped around the outside of the tank for an antenna, so it was extremely sensitive, but the speaker was quiet as the radio automatically scanned up and down the bands for a signal. There was an occasional crackle, probably from lightning in the clouds below, but that was it.

"Could there be an entire planet just waiting for us?" Judy asked. "That's almost too much to ask."

His eyes twinkled. "Almost?"

"Well, a person can dream, can't they?"

He took the microphone off its clip and spoke into it. "Hello, is there anybody out there? Hello? Testing, testing, testing. This is Allen Meisner and Judy Gallagher broadcasting live from the *Getaway Special*. Is anyone listening?"

He let up the button and listened to the silence for a few seconds, then keyed the microphone again. "Hello! We're your neighbors from next door. We come in peace. Well, actually, we came in a septic tank, but that's another story."

He listened again, but there was still no response. Judy reached for the microphone, and he handed it over to her. "Hello," she said. "This is Judy Gallagher, and I've just got to say one thing to all you people back on Earth who may be listening when this message arrives there in four years: Nya, nya, we got here first!"

She giggled and reached out to hand the microphone back to Allen, but she gasped in shock and let go when the radio crackled to life.

"No you didn't."

21

The microphone sprang back on its coiled cord and clipped the getaway special canister, then bounced off and whacked Allen in the head before he could catch it.

He grabbed the cord before it could do any more damage and reeled it in. "Who's there?" he asked.

The voice was male, and gravelly with time or smoke or garrulousness. "Name's Nicholas Onnescu. I've been here two days already. What kept you?"

Judy heard a ringing in her ears and realized she was clenching her teeth hard enough to hurt. It was a ridiculous reaction, but she couldn't help it. There was somebody else on her planet!

Allen had lost some of his giddiness, too. "We, uh, had a hard time tracking down all the equipment we needed," he said. "Your name sounds familiar. Are you the guy from Lancaster?"

"Yep. 'From' is the operative term. Man, I am so out of there, you can't believe. I may go back for the rest of my stuff, but not anytime soon. I'm too busy fishin' and buildin' a cabin." He laughed. "So my departure made it on the news, eh? I wasn't sure if anybody would report it, considering the lies they were spreadin' around."

Allen waited a second to see if he was done, then said, "They showed the crater you left behind. Boy, you had a lot of junk in that yard!"

"Collectibles," Nicholas said. "Collectibles." Then he laughed again and said, "No, you're right. It was junk. Jeez, that was a lifetime ago. What an artificial bunch of crap we humans drag around with us, eh?"

Allen looked at the interior of the septic tank, festooned

with equipment. His eyes met Judy's, and he gave a little shrug. "You don't know the half of it," he said. "Well, hey, I'm glad you made it here okay. You have any trouble with the hyperdrive?"

"Nope. Worked like a charm. Bit my tongue landing, but that was the worst of it."

"How'd you get here so fast? I mean, what did you do for a spaceship?"

"Hah! I had one already built. I made it a couple of years ago when I found the plans for a Dean drive in an old *Astounding* magazine, but the drive turned out to be a piece of junk. Barely lifted itself, much less a spaceship. Your little gadget, though—that's a honey. Did you come up with that all by yourself?"

Allen grinned with pride. "Well, Einstein and Hawking had a little to do with the research, but the design is all mine, yeah."

"Good for you. And thanks for sharing. A lot of guys would have took out ads in the back of *Popular Science* and sold mimeographed schematics for a hundred bucks a pop."

Judy found her voice. "Ask him how many other people are here."

Allen nodded. "Did you come by yourself?"

"Yep."

"Did anyone else come afterward?"

"Two others that I know of. I may have missed some; this scanner doesn't have the best range in the world. Well, maybe it does, come to think of it, but you know what I mean."

Judy knew all too well. That there were *any* other scanners in the world was almost too much to bear. Who was this Onnescu guy, anyway? And who were the others?

She looked to the monitors. The planet was sweeping past again, a little closer than before. They were falling toward it. Some of that was probably their leftover vector from Earth's orbital motion, but gravity was definitely drawing them down as well.

"Let's go," she said.

"What?" asked Allen.

"Let's go. Everybody and their grandma is going to come to Alpha Centauri first. Inside a week, this place will look like Tokyo."

"Oh, come now. It'll take years before . . . ah, right."

She looked away from the monitor. It was too blurry for her to see much at the moment anyway.

Allen keyed the microphone again. "Uh, well, hey, it's been nice talking to you, but we're going to head on out a few more light-years and see what we can find. Give our regards to whoever else passes through."

Nicholas didn't sound very disappointed to see them go. "Will do. Good hunting."

"Thanks. Um, Allen Meisner, signing off." He stuck the microphone back in its clip. "Well. Where to next?"

"Anywhere but here."

He gave her a look, *the* look, the one she would be seeing off and on for the rest of their lives if they stayed together. The one that asked, "Are you okay?" and answered that question at the same time.

"Well," he said, "there's Tau Ceti not far away, but that's probably going to be overrun with science fiction fans. Same with Sirius and Arcturus and all the other sunlike stars that people have been writing about for years."

"Then let's go farther. You said distance isn't a factor, right? Let's go for the other side of the galaxy and see what's there."

Allen captured a loose screw that was drifting in the air between them and tucked it into a thigh pocket on his spacesuit. "That might be a bit extr—ah, risky. Our star map is just a commercial sky atlas compiled from an astronomical database of nearby stars; it isn't going to be much help beyond a couple hundred light-years. That's a tiny little bubble of space compared to the size of the whole galaxy. If we get lost out there we could have a hell of a time finding our way home again."

He was right, damn him. She took a deep breath and let it out slowly. "Okay, then, how about something still on the map, but a little less likely to have settlers already?"

He bit his lower lip and his eyes got a faraway look. "Well, there's a whole slew of other G-type stars in Cetus. Some of them are pretty close together. There's a cluster of them about fifty light-years out that I've always wondered about."

She tried out *the look* on him. "You've always wondered about it? Like it's kept you awake at nights?"

He shrugged; hard to do in a spacesuit, but at least possible under zero-gee. "Maybe a night," he said. "The point is, they're close enough together to support a nice little interstellar empire even with slower-than-lightspeed travel. If we're looking for something interesting, that's a good prospect, and it's not all that well known."

"Oh." An interstellar empire? Wouldn't the Search for Extraterrestrial Intelligence project have found evidence of it if there was one? Fifty light-years was practically in Earth's back yard from their point of view.

Which meant there probably *wasn't* an empire out there. Or anybody else. At the moment, that was just what Judy wanted.

"Sure," she said. "Let's give it a shot."

They got to the first star on Allen's list in three more jumps: the first to get away from the Alpha Centauran planet's gravity well, the second to cross fifty light-years of space, and the third to close in on their target. They popped into being about five AU out from the star; a little farther than they'd intended, but still close enough to search for planets.

Judy refreshed their air and lowered the pressure a little more while they gave the stellar comparator a chance to assemble a database from that vantage, then they jumped across to the other side of the star and let the program do its work. It took a while, but when it finally made its report, they understood why. It had catalogued 389 planets within ten AU of the primary.

Judy blew a soft whistle. "Holy cow. They must be thick as flies out there." She studied the image in the monitor, but she couldn't tell planets from stars. They were all just bright specks, and this far from the Sun, none of the constellations were familiar. "Can we get a size on any of them?"

Allen looked at the list. "There's a couple that're only half a million kilometers away. Not much farther than the Moon from Earth. We should be able to zoom in on one."

He didn't bother to state the obvious: if either of the nearby planets had been of any size, they would have seen it already as their spaceship rotated and gave them a 360-degree panorama.

He reached out to the camera controls mounted beneath his monitor and upped the magnification, but that merely narrowed his field of view and made the star field slide by faster, so he took the joystick and tried to direct the camera to follow one of the stars. That was tougher than it looked. Judy tried it with her camera, but she had no better luck than he.

"I don't suppose you've got a program that'll do this, do you?" she asked hopefully.

"Nope," he asked. "I could probably cobble something together, but it would be simpler if we just stopped our rotation and let the program we've got point out where we need to look."

"Um, that's going to take a lot of air." Each time Judy had vented air into space, the tank's spin had increased. They weren't rotating all that fast, but there was quite a bit of mass involved, and it would take an equal amount of force applied in the other direction to cancel out all that angular momentum. They could do it with the valve tapped into the opposite side of the tank, but Judy had just refreshed their air; venting more now would be a waste.

On the other hand, waiting for their air to grow stale so they had a good excuse to vent it was kind of dumb, too. "Oh, to hell with it," she said. "We've got six hours' worth; let 'er rip." She got ready on the oxygen tank while Allen opened the faucet next to his elbow, but she didn't crack the valve right away.

"Uh, it's getting a little thin, isn't it?" he asked as the altimeter needle swung past 20,000 feet and began its second lap of the dial. He closed the faucet and swallowed to make his ears pop.

She kept her valve closed. "We can survive for a few seconds at low pressure. Keep going."

"Ooo . . . kay." He let more air out. She let it go up to 24,000, then nodded to him and turned on the oxygen flow while he closed the vent. She stopped at 16,000 this time; they'd been breathing oxygen-enriched air long enough that they were probably safe from the bends at that altitude by now.

Their spin had slowed considerably. Now they could let the program flag the points of light they were interested in and zoom in on them manually. It was still hard to hold the cameras on them at high magnification, but they could do it long enough to learn what they needed to: even at the highest power, they could detect no sign of a disk on either of the two closest planets. Nor did any of the others show as more than bright specks of light.

"Looks like a bunch of asteroids," Judy said.

"It does, doesn't it?" Allen stared at the screen for another thirty seconds or so, then typed in the coordinates for the closest target. "What the heck; we might as well go have a look. I've never seen an asteroid up close."

"Up close" was the operative term. The moment he pushed the "Enter" button, the external monitors filled with a rugged, grayish-green surface that looked like it was only a couple feet away.

"Yeow!" Judy started backward in surprise and banged her head on the side of the septic tank, but she didn't give herself even a moment to register pain; she just immediately pushed herself back down and checked the monitor again to see if they were moving toward it or away. She couldn't tell at first. The image was sliding past too quickly. She grabbed the joystick to try following a landmark for a second, but the moment she moved it and saw how touchy the camera was, she realized she had left the magnification all the way up. When she zoomed out again, the surface didn't look nearly as close.

Nor did it look like an asteroid.

It looked more like a thicket of vines entangling a pile of rocks, boards, and rusty scrap metal. It looked, in fact, like Nicholas Onnescu's back yard. If she hadn't seen the tiny size of the crater in his yard, she would have thought maybe he had come here first on his way to Alpha Centauri, but as her eyes picked out more details she realized that the scale was all wrong. This went on for miles. It wasn't even remotely spherical, either. It was more of an oblong, like a stretched-out football, or maybe a disk seen mostly edge-on. The more Judy looked at it, the more she thought it resembled a cityscape. A cityscape reflected in a lake, with waves distorting the image at all angles, but there was definitely order to it.

Allen was staring at it like a deer staring at a pair of oncoming headlights. "Holy shit," he whispered. "There *is* an interstellar empire."

22

They were moving toward it, but not so fast that they had to dodge immediately. "Try the radio," Judy said.

Allen slowly unclipped the microphone and held it up to his mouth. When he spoke, there was none of the cockiness he'd shown around Alpha Centauri. His voice was a high-pitched squeak as he said, "Hello? This is—" He cleared his throat and tried again. "This is Allen Meisner and Judy Gallagher of Earth. Can you hear us? We, uh, we'd like to come in and say 'Hi.' "

He let off the microphone and said, "Shit, that sounded stupid. They'll think we're morons."

"We got here on our own power," Judy said. "They've got to respect that."

"But look what we got here *in!*"

"Like they're going to know what it's supposed to be used for?" The moment she said *that* she wondered how stupid that was. Anybody who could build structures like this in space—and this many of them at that—could probably figure out in an instant not only what their spaceship was made of, and what the tank's intended purpose was, but where it came from and what it carried as well.

She kept her eyes on the monitors. Hers showed the entire space station, or colony, or whatever it was. Its spiky protrusions cast stark shadows across the irregular core, giving it a sharp-edged, technological look, but Allen's monitor still showed the close-up image, and that displayed a much more organic aspect. The ductwork or transport tubes or whatever they were really did look like vines, complete with a rough green surface that resembled bark much more than it did metal. The lumpy habitat modules they enclosed had a more pebbly coating, like lizard skin.

There was no answer to their radio call. Allen switched the receiver to scan mode and let it cycle through all the frequencies it could pick up, but there were no transmissions on any band.

He picked a frequency at random and tried transmitting again. "Hello, this is the Earth vessel *Getaway Special* calling. Do you copy?"

No response. He tried at least a dozen more times, picking a new frequency for each attempt, but if anyone heard him, they showed no sign.

It looked like they weren't going to hit the station after all. Their motion was going to take them close, but they would pass under it by a few thousand feet. Judy held her breath as they approached, half expecting a missile or a laser beam or some alien death ray to lance out and blow them to smithereens, but the station showed no sign that anyone on board even noticed they were there. She supposed it was possible that she and Allen had slipped in under their radar, so to speak, but that thought only scared her all the more. She knew what humans would do in a similar situation once they *did* detect an intruder; in fact she had experienced it firsthand less than a week ago.

"Get ready to jump," she whispered.

"Where?"

"Anywhere. We don't know they're friendly."

"We don't know they're *they*," Allen pointed out.

"What do you mean by that? This thing's big enough to hold a couple of million people. I don't care how big the guys who built it are; there's more than one of 'em on board."

He clipped the microphone back onto the radio and keyed in a set of jump coordinates. "I don't know. I don't see any evidence of habitation here. No windows, no handholds, no airlocks, no docking ports—nothing like that. If it's a space station, it's not run by beings who think like us. And if they don't think like us, they may not *be* like us, not even on a fundamental level. This could be a big blob of bacteria living off the solar wind for all we know."

Judy had to swivel the camera all the way to its upper limit to keep it aimed at the station as they swept past. It was no blob of bacteria, of that she was certain. But Allen had a point: it didn't look like anything humans would build, either. It was too organic. It had hard edges, but they were the kind of edges you would find on a thorn bush or a seashell.

The camera couldn't zoom out enough to keep the whole thing on the monitor anymore. It was so big, size became an abstract concept. Watching it pass on the screen felt just like scanning a soil sample with an electron microscope. The pipes could be fungal mycelia; the spiky things could be diatoms; the irregular lumps could be cells.

It was growing cold in the tank. They were too far from the star, and radiating too much heat. The plastic walls would grow brittle if they lost much more. Judy's sense of adventure felt like it was already close to cracking. It was fine to imagine meeting aliens when your mental picture of them came from watching *E.T.* as a child, but when she was actually there, floating closer to a city-sized space station— maybe—she didn't feel nearly so enthusiastic about it.

She looked to the lumpy sleeping bag at her feet. Had she put Trent's gun in there? Could she get to it in time to defend herself if she needed it? She was appalled at herself for even thinking that, but it was an involuntary reaction.

A pistol would be useless here anyway. The thing was huge. Their entire spaceship, such as it was, could smack into it at orbital velocity and still not do more than superficial damage.

She and Allen watched it slide past, its irregular surface growing more and more filled with shadow as they moved away from the sunlit side. There could be anything waiting in those pools of darkness. Weapons, predators, antibodies . . .

Or nothing at all. The artifact swept past, then receded into the distance, becoming just a ragged line of backlit extrusions outlining a black oblong that blotted out the sun.

Judy breathed again, but at the same time she felt more disappointed than she had since she'd been the ugly girl at a high school dance. "They . . . 'it' . . . whatever . . . just ignored us."

"Looks like it," Allen said. He consulted the navigation program again and typed in another set of coordinates.

"Where are we going now?"

"I want to have a look at another one. Maybe we'll have better luck there."

Judy looked at the dark mass again. "Yeah, like maybe this one was just asleep or something," she said facetiously, but the moment she said it, she realized she meant it.

The second one looked exactly like the first. They had to make two jumps to get as close to it as they had come by accident before, but it paid them no more attention than its twin. And the more Judy stared at it, the more convinced she became that it wasn't a space station. She wasn't quite ready to believe that it was a living organism, either, but whatever it was, it paid no more attention to them than she would to a dust mite.

They tried a third one with no more success. Judy had relaxed by then, at least as much as possible when she was fifty light-years from home in a spaceship the size of a closet. Her pressure suit was starting to chafe, and her bladder was giving her the one-hour warning. She was normally good for four or five hours, but she hadn't had a chance to pee since she'd gotten up that morning.

And they were already a third of the way through their air supply. That was the critical factor. She could urinate in the suit if she had to, but once she and Allen got down to the end of their air, they would have to go back to Earth and try it again.

As they watched the unresponsive whatever-it-was recede into the distance, she said, "I don't think we're going to learn much more unless we actually match velocities with one and go over for a closer look in our suits. And that would take time we don't have."

Allen reluctantly agreed. "Yeah, matching velocities would be a real trick. We'd have to calculate the vector we need, then go find a planet we could use as a gravity well, then pop back here. We don't have radar, so we'd probably have to fine-tune it with three or four jumps." He looked from the monitor to Judy. "But we can't just leave without figuring out what they are, can we?"

"Do we have a choice?"

He grimaced. "No. Damn it, no, we don't. Shit!" He whacked his hand against the tank. The hollow *bong* sounded like a church bell tolling the death of his dream.

"I'm sorry," Judy said. "We could try again later. Come back with a real spaceship that we can maneuver. But for now, we've either got to find someplace where we can breathe the air, or go back home in about four hours and hope we can avoid the authorities long enough to recharge our oxygen tank."

Allen's angry outburst had propelled him sideways against the hyperdrive. He pushed himself back down onto his beanbag chair and cinched the strap around his waist to hold himself in place. "You're right" he said. "Damn it. This isn't what we came for." He called up the starmap program, got the coordinates for the next star in the cluster of nearby sunlike ones, and keyed them in.

A moment later, they were there. It only took two jumps this time; there had been no need to escape a planet's gravity well.

Judy wished they could escape the aura of gloom that had settled over her, too. She knew she wasn't being logical—she had just come over fifty light-years from home!—but she hadn't bargained on finding incomprehensible artifacts that might or might not have even been artifacts. Their size, rather than filling her with awe, had merely made her feel insignificant. And that on top of finding Alpha Centauri's perfect planet not only discovered already, but in the process of being colonized—it was too much to bear in one day.

But the day wasn't over yet. They went through the same

routine of checking for planets that they had done at both previous stops. Judy braced herself for disappointment, but she allowed herself to hope when the comparator came up with a good prospect about 3 AU out from the star, which was itself almost as good a prospect as Alpha Centauri. It was brighter than the Sun, but it had no close stellar companions to perturb planetary orbits, so the extra brightness just put its habitable zone farther out.

"Third time's a charm," she said when she saw it, then she searched frantically for something made out of wood to knock on before she jinxed it. She rapped the plywood-reinforced hatch overhead, her gloved hands making a soft *thud*.

Allen calculated the jump and took them closer, but the moment she saw the planet, her heart fell again. The atmosphere looked good—swirls of white cloud swept through it just like on Earth—but the surface was all one color: blue. It looked like one huge ocean, even at the poles, which were only evident by the weather patterns.

She zoomed in with as high a magnification as she could get and searched for any sign of land, but if there was any, it was on the night side. This planet could be water all the way to the core for all she knew.

Allen helped search for a few minutes, but then he turned his attention to the comparator reading again. "Hey, there's a moon," he said cheerily.

"So?"

He narrowed his eyes. "So . . . maybe we should go have a look."

"What's the point?"

"To see what it looks like?"

"It's just going to be an airless rock. Or another one of those piles of crap that doesn't give a shit about us one way or the other."

He lowered his voice the way he might speak to a petulant child. "We don't know that. It could be anything. Maybe this is a double planet, and the other one didn't get quite so much water."

"And maybe it's made of green cheese. That would be good."

They stared at one another, Allen obviously unsure what to do with this stranger who had taken over Judy's body, and Judy past caring. She clenched her fists, but the spacesuit gloves resisted even that little bit of comfort.

"Damn it. Damn it all! This isn't the way it's supposed to work. Space is supposed to be full of habitable planets. Enough for everyone, including left-handed theremin players. Where the hell are they?"

"We've only tried three stars," Allen said reasonably. "And we did hit one. It's too small a sample to be statistically significant, but even if it were, that's not such a bad average."

"Yeah, right." Judy took a couple of deep breaths, trying to wash the anger out of her system. When she could trust herself to speak again, she said, "Look, I know it's not your fault, but this isn't working out quite the way I'd hoped. I don't want to spend all our time looking at astronomical curiosities; I want to find another planet we can actually land on."

"Me too." Allen typed in another set of coordinates. "One quick jump to the moon just to see if it's a candidate, and if it's not, on we go."

She took another deep breath. "All right."

The water planet winked out like a burst soap bubble, but nothing else took its place. They weren't rotating nearly as fast as they had been before, so it took a couple of minutes to confirm what Judy already suspected: there was nothing in sight in any direction.

"Where the heck did it go?" Allen asked, but he was already running the comparator program again to find out. It only took a few seconds to come up with the answer: they had overshot, and now it was nearly hidden in the glare of the sun.

"Hmm. Must be smaller than I'd hoped," he said. "Not enough mass to create much of a gravity well. Let me calculate the right correction . . . and here we go."

This time something popped into view when they jumped. It was half in light and half in shadow, giving them a high-contrast view of every bump and groove as they zoomed in on it.

Judy didn't know whether to laugh or cry. It was another artifact, but this one, at least, was recognizable. It was a long cylinder with a rounded nose on one end and four smaller cylinders spaced evenly around the circumference at the other. The nose was peppered with evenly spaced dimples that could only be portholes, and there were more of them along the side. The cylinder grew thicker toward the back, where the four smaller pods were mounted. Those had to be engines, and while it was no design Judy had ever seen, the whole thing had to be a spaceship.

23

"Once more into the breach," she muttered.

They were moving past it at a pretty good clip. At nearest approach they were still a couple of kilometers away, but that was close enough. The thing was huge. It filled the monitors even at the cameras' lowest magnification, and at full zoom they could see the outlines of thousands of airlocks and cargo bay doors and various other less definitive lumps and projections. Everything had a rounded look to it, as if it had partially melted or was made of something soft right from the beginning. There was no writing on it, unless the subtle variations in its brownish color conveyed meaning in some alien script.

It was not human built; that much was obvious. For one thing, the race that was still struggling to keep *Fred* in orbit couldn't build something like that in a decade, much less the week they had had since Allen had dropped the hyperdrive plans in their laps. And the Onnescus of the world notwithstanding, nobody just happened to have one lying around in their back yard, either.

"Try the radio," Judy said, with no trace left of the hesitation she had felt the first time.

"Right." Allen called, listened, called again and listened while the two ships drew apart, but nobody answered. "I'm beginning to think that radio isn't the best way to get someone's attention," he said.

"Have you got a better idea?"

He nodded. "Let's shed some velocity and see if we can actually come up on 'em slowly enough to be seen by naked eye."

Judy didn't really want to waste the time it would take

to do that, but she couldn't see any way around it, short of going back for another pass, depressurizing the tank completely, standing in the open hatch, and simply throwing a can of beans at the ship as they swept past. Considering what even a modestly speeding can of beans could do to a spaceship—even one that size—she didn't suppose that would be a good idea.

"All right, let's see if we can slow down," she said. They needed to see if this "tangential vector translation maneuver" of Allen's would work anyway, preferably before they tried using it to land somewhere. This would be as good a test as any.

He spent a couple minutes at the keyboard, keying in his best estimate of the relative velocity between the two ships and getting an exact distance to the center of the planet, based on triangulation from their current position and the point where they had first showed up next to it. He entered the data into the "TVTM" program, pressed the "Enter" key, and said, "According to this, we've got about twelve minutes to fall, provided I got all the bugs out."

"We can always hope," Judy said as the program shifted them to a point above the planet where its gravity would pull them into just the right vector. She wasn't really that worried about this part; she had great faith in Allen's programming. His planet-finding routine had worked without a hitch, even if the planets themselves had been disappointments.

They fell freely in their new position, examining the planet as they rose away from it, but there was really not much to see. Judy would never have imagined that she could grow bored in so short a time looking at an extra-solar planet, but when all there was to see were storm systems that looked exactly like the ones she'd seen from Earth orbit, there really wasn't much to hold her interest.

She refreshed their air again, lowering the pressure another pound now that they were breathing almost pure oxygen. They used both valves this time, carefully keeping their rotation rate slow enough to allow them to pan the cameras without struggling. When they were done repressurizing, their oxygen supply stood at just over fifty percent.

Her legs were cramping from being bent so long. She wanted desperately to stretch out, but there simply wasn't room with all the stuff wedged in around her. At least she didn't have gravity to contend with; if she were packed this tightly into place on Earth, half her body would be in agony by now.

At last the program beeped to warn them that their velocity change was complete, then it automatically took them back to their starting point. Allen had to find the alien ship again from there, but when the comparator did its thing and he took them close to it, they could hardly detect any relative motion.

Now that they had a chance to examine it at leisure, they could see that the other ship was tumbling end-for-end. The motion was almost too slow to see, about like the minute hand on a watch, but the effect was apparent immediately: the ship's nose had been pointing toward the sun before, but now the tail faced about sixty degrees into the light.

"Jesus, look at those rocket nozzles," Judy said. The entire backside looked like one cavernous exhaust port. The opening looked like it extended inward at least a third of the length of the ship, too. "It's all engine," she said, but the moment she said it she realized that didn't make any sense. A rocket with a nozzle that size would accelerate at dozens of gees if the engine was at all efficient, but even if the passengers could take that kind of punishment, there was no point in it. Rocket engines were most effective when they burned small amounts of fuel over long periods of time, not the other way around, and anybody who could build something like this ship would understand that principle just as well as she did.

And besides, she had seen portholes and airlocks all along the flank during their first pass. The way things looked from here, they would open directly into the nozzle—for about a millisecond until their seals burned through and the exhaust flame ripped the ship apart from the inside out.

But there were the hatches. They were tiny compared to the size of the ship, but she could see them quite clearly down inside. Far more clearly, in fact, than from the outside. They didn't have any of that melted look she had seen before.

"Wait a minute," she said. "This is totally backward."

"It kind of is, isn't it?" Allen zoomed in with his camera until they could count the portholes. They weren't actually holes; from the inside they looked like rubber casts of portholes, and the airlocks looked the same way. He focused the camera on the outside, where the features were less distinct. "It's like the ship has been turned inside out."

Judy focused her own camera on the center of the open end. Sunlight didn't penetrate all the way to the nose, but when she zoomed in until the brightly lit parts of the ship slid off screen, the camera irised open and she could see deeper into the recesses of the ship by reflected light. The interior details went all the way up.

"It's a mold."

Allen narrowed his eyes. "A what?"

"A mold. You spray liquid metal on the inside surface, let it harden, and you've got a ready-made hull. Either that or somebody sprayed this stuff all around an already-built spaceship and then peeled it off."

"Why would they do that?"

"How should I know?"

That had to be it, though. Now that she had the right mental picture, the pods spaced around the tail made more sense. Those *were* engines, and probably fuel tanks as well, or at least that was where they would go. Even then the ship had a hell of a lot of power, but by the size of the body, Judy was willing to bet that it needed it. That thing could hold a couple of thousand people, easy. It was wide enough to spin on its axis for gravity. If the beings who built it were anything like people, the ship that came out of that mold was big enough to live in for months, maybe longer.

"There's got to be a habitable planet somewhere else in this system," she said. "That's a passenger ship."

Allen looked at the comparator screen. "There's five others, but they're not good candidates. One's tucked right up next to the star even closer than Mercury, and the other four are quite a ways out."

"One of them has to be inhabited," Judy insisted. "This thing came from somewhere, and I'll bet money it wasn't here."

He zoomed back out with his camera and swiveled it around until he could see the water world. "I don't know; there could be a whole society of dolphins or something like that down there."

"And how would they build something like this? They couldn't mine anything. And even if they could, they couldn't make a fire to smelt metals. They couldn't build telescopes, so they probably wouldn't even know about planets, or that there was any point in going out to them."

"Fish have eyes," Allen countered. "Clams build shells without fire. It would be harder for *us* to build a spaceship underwater, but who's to say how tough it would be for someone who lived there?"

Judy looked at the cloud-and-ocean-shrouded world. "How many other satellites are there?" she asked.

Allen checked the comparator display again. "Just the one. But we probably wouldn't be able to see communications satellites or smaller spacecraft."

"We'd be able to hear them." She pointed at the radio, still set to receive and still silent.

"Maybe, maybe not. This is a shortwave receiver, not microwave. If they're using high frequencies to pack more information into the signal like we do, we'd never hear them."

This was all just too much. Judy said, "So what do you want to do about it? Parachute down to the water? Then what? How are we going to talk to intelligent dolphins, even if they're down there? What happens if our cameras get wet and short out? We'd have to navigate home by dead reckoning."

He held up his hands, palms out. They looked ridiculously small inside the oversize spacesuit cuffs, like a child's hands stuck on an adult body. "Whoa, slow down there. Nobody's talking about landing in the water. I was just saying maybe we shouldn't write this place off so quickly."

"And I'm saying we've already used up half our air. I'm all for meeting whoever built that spaceship mold, but I'm not willing to hang around searching for flying fish when there are five other prospective homeworlds that we haven't even looked at yet."

"Four," Allen said. "You can't seriously suggest that a planet closer to its star than Mercury could support life. Especially when the star is twice as bright as the Sun."

"All right, then, four. But let's go see."

He thought it over, then nodded. "Okay. No big deal."

No big deal. She nearly threw a can of beans at *him*, but it would have been too much trouble to dig one out of her sleeping bag. She just zoomed her camera back to wide-angle display and waited for him to key in the coordinates.

They hit the planets in order of distance from the primary rather than along the most direct route. "Direct" didn't mean much anymore, Judy supposed. She wondered how long it would be before people stopped thinking in terms of distance altogether. Hopefully longer than it took her and Allen to find something actually worth going to all the trouble of coming out here for.

The first planet was a bust. It was an airless rock with no moons, no satellites, and no evidence that intelligent life had ever visited it. Of course there could have been vast cities underground, or networks of small ones aboveground, and they would never be visible from space, but there was no radio traffic either, and no time to make a more detailed search.

The second planet was a gas giant, nicely ringed and accompanied by several moons of its own, each of which required at least a cursory look. Unfortunately, that was all they required; they were all either rocky or icy or both, and far too inhospitable to human life even if they had sported alien presence, which they didn't.

The third planet was a double gas giant, a Jupiter-sized ball of banded yellow-and-brown clouds and a pale blue one about half its size orbiting one another a couple million kilometers apart. Gravitational perturbations had swept the space between them clean of anything else, so there was no reason to stick around there.

The last planet was another rock, this time with an atmosphere, but at its distance from the sun there was no way that atmosphere could have any oxygen or nitrogen in it except as methane or ammonia. And there were no satellites in orbit around it, either natural or artificial.

That was the last straw. Somebody had to have made the spaceship mold, and a mold implied that there was at least one complete spaceship somewhere in this planetary system, but it seemed to Judy as if they were deliberately hiding from her. They weren't listening to radio and they didn't show any sign of life; what did they expect of her, anyway? To top it off, the farther they got from the star, the colder the *Getaway* became. They could handle it easily enough inside their spacesuits, but Judy didn't like subjecting the tank itself to such extreme temperatures. And besides, cold air made her nose run, and the fluids were already pooling in her upper body from weightlessness.

"I'm fresh out of ideas," she said. "What do you want to do?"

Allen scratched his head. "Well, I hate to leave a solar system that's got such direct evidence of intelligent life, but you're right about one thing: there's no place here for us to land. Even if we could find the ship that came out of that mold, the odds that the crew breathes the same air we do are pretty slim, so unless they can set us up with an environment box, we're going to run out of air and have to go home in a couple more hours anyway."

"I didn't come all this way in this damned tank to spend even more time in a box."

"The thrill is starting to pall a bit for me, too," he admitted.

"So what do we do?" she asked again. "Go back to Alpha

Centauri and stake a claim before it's all snapped up by homesteaders?"

He tapped the fingers of his right hand in a nervous rhythm on the hyperdrive canister. "We could do that. That's actually not a bad idea for a fallback position. But we could be on the ground there in less than an hour from anywhere, so we still have time to explore one or two more stars. We're only halfway through the cluster; why don't we at least give it another shot?"

Judy shrugged, biting back a curse as the spacesuit's neck ring chafed her shoulder blades. "What the hell," she said. "As long as we're here." She rubbed the back of her neck, trying to work the tension out of the muscles. Who would have guessed that interstellar exploration would turn out to be so frustrating?

24

The next star was off to the side rather than farther away from Sol. Its actual position in space didn't really matter to anyone but the computer, but Judy wanted to keep a picture in her mind of where they had been. The stars were just numbers and dots on the map, but it seemed more real to her to imagine a short line from the Sun to Alpha Centauri, then a long line out to the star with the weird pseudo-organic junk in orbit around it, then another line at a bit of an angle to where they were at the moment, and a final jog off to the left to their next attempt.

She tried to work up some enthusiasm for the jump. Captain Gallagher of the Imperial Space Navy explores yet another star! But flying around in a septic tank and finding incomprehensible mysteries was not her idea of a stellar career. She wanted planets she could land on and aliens she could talk to, and she wanted them now. She knew she was being unreasonable. The universe couldn't be expected to answer to her whims, but at the same time she couldn't help wanting it to. One little terrestrial planet, with one little tropical paradise where she could get a tan under an alien sun—was that too much to ask?

Apparently so, at least so far. But they had air enough for one more try, and she wasn't quite ready to give up yet. She took a few deep breaths while Allen prepared the drive, then got ready on the video controls.

Three jumps later, they were at the target star. Another jump after that gave them data for the comparator to crunch. This star was almost a perfect match to the Sun in luminosity and spectral type, and there was a planet dead square in the middle of the habitable zone, but Judy still didn't allow herself to get excited. It could be another airless rock, or a gas giant, or even a passing comet that just happened to be in that spot in its orbit.

Another jump put them within visual distance. Judy panned her camera around in a spiral, waiting for the moment when her hopes would be dashed again, but when she saw the planet, she let out a gasp of surprise.

"Oh! It's . . . it's . . . there it is!"

It was as Earthlike as anyone could ask for, at least at first glance. White sworls of cloud, blue oceans, and this time—this time—there were continents. The distribution of landmasses wasn't the same as on Earth: This planet had a couple dozen continents ranging in size from Australian all the way down to that fuzzy boundary line where they become islands, with narrow seas dotted with smaller islands in between. The poles were covered with ice, and so were the continents down to about 40 or 50 degrees latitude, but where they weren't frozen they were a medley of color.

"I think we want to land fairly close to the equator," Judy said. "It doesn't look as warm here as Earth."

"You're right. How about the one we're coming up on?" Allen pointed at a continent that was just creeping up over the horizon. They watched it approach: an oblong patch of green and brown with a central mountain range running down its spine.

"It looks good to me," Judy admitted.

Their rotation was carrying it toward the middle of her field of view. She zoomed in on it as they swept over it, checking out the coastline, forests, plains—whatever looked interesting. To Judy it all looked interesting; she felt it calling to her like a siren calling ancient mariners to a perilous but irresistible rendezvous. This was her planet. She could feel it.

But it was already slipping away. They were moving across the sunlit face of it maybe two thousand kilometers up, but they were going way too fast to orbit at this distance. They would have to slow down and move closer if they wanted to go into orbit, then slow down some more in order to land. Judy checked their oxygen gauge: under fifty percent now and it was time to refresh the air again. They would have time to adjust their velocity, but that wouldn't leave them much room for error on the way back to Earth. Even if the planet's air was breathable, they had no compressor to refill their tank with.

"Screw orbiting," she said. "Let's just pick a spot and land."

Allen chewed his lower lip. "Mmm, I guess we could do that. The vector translation maneuver assumes we're in orbit over the point we want to land on, but if we can make a good estimate of our vector, we can correct for that."

They didn't have Doppler radar or global positioning satellites to give them accurate numbers, but Judy had been in Earth orbit enough times to know what it looked like to be moving at 27,000 kilometers an hour just outside the atmosphere. It was harder to gauge their speed this far away, but it looked to her like they were crossing the width of the planet at least twice as fast as they should be, and moving away from it as well.

"I'd guess we need to kill about thirty thousand klicks per hour just to put us in orbit," she said. "If we want to come to rest, we probably need to kill fifty or sixty."

"That's going to take a while," Allen said.

"Then we'd better get started."

"Shouldn't we see if there's anybody here first?"

Judy glanced at the radio. It was still on, still in scan mode, patiently sifting through all the channels it could receive in search of a signal, but there had been nothing but crackles. Now that she thought about it, there were more of them here than there had been at the last planet, but that probably meant only that the atmosphere was more active here. There might be a row of thunderstorms on the leading edge of a cold front. She supposed they should call and see if anyone answered, but they would still have to slow down in order to land, and this time Judy was determined to do just that. If there were aliens already living here, so much the better. And if there were humans—well, she was going to set foot on alien soil today even if Nicholas Onnescu and his entire family had already set up a land office.

"We can call while we're slowing down."

"Uh . . . right." Allen set to work at the computer, and a couple of minutes later said, "Okay, this should put us just outside the atmosphere and falling outward, but it's going to be on the night side of the planet, so we won't be able to see for sure. Let me get another set of coordinates ready in case we're headed the wrong way or something. We might need to jump in a hurry."

"We won't be headed the wrong way. We can see our motion."

"Mmm hmm." He copied a set of numbers into the computer's clipboard anyway. "Okay, I guess we're—"

"Do it, already!"

"Here goes."

There was the brief moment of disorientation, and the video image went totally black. No planet, no stars, no anything. Judy tensed up, waiting for them to smack into the atmosphere at thousands of kilometers per hour, but after a few seconds she relaxed. If they were going to hit the planet, they would have done it already.

She swiveled her camera around until she could see the starscape peeking around the curved limb of darkness. New stars kept popping up from behind it as they rose; they were moving at a pretty good clip. It was frustrating not to have an actual velocity figure, though.

"Next time, we bring radar," she said.

"Bingo." Allen stretched, careful to avoid hitting anything vital with his arms. It was hard to do in the close quarters. "Still," he said, "we're doing pretty well, all things considered. I think we've proven pretty definitively that we don't need high-tech gadgets to function in space."

Coming from a guy in a million-dollar spacesuit, that statement seemed laughable on the surface, but when you realized that the only thing the spacesuit had accomplished so far was to get in the way, it didn't seem so outrageous after all. Radar would be nice, and so would a spectrometer to help figure out what the atmosphere down below was made of, but they had a low-tech way to . . . no they didn't.

"Shit!" Judy punched the wall of the tank as hard as she could.

"What?"

"We forgot the fucking mice!"

She watched him realize what that meant. They had intended to bring along half a dozen mice, one of which they would expose to the atmosphere of each planet they landed on. If the test subject lived, they would try the air themselves, but if not, they would go on to the next planet. But of course in their rush to escape the cops, they had left the mice in their cage in the house. They hadn't needed them until now, but they didn't have so much as a housefly to test the air below.

Allen looked as stricken as Judy felt. "What do we do?"

Judy swallowed. "I guess I get to play mouse."

"No way! If anybody should, it's—"

"It's me. You're the pilot. You're also bigger than me. If you keel over, I'd have a hell of a time getting you back inside the tank, and even if I managed it, I'd have to fly us home."

"You could do it. I've shown you how the programs work."

"And I showed you how to land the shuttle, too, but I wouldn't have let you do it unless there was no other choice. No, I'm the one who should test the air."

He didn't like that at all. "We should go home and get some mice," he said.

She shook her head. "I didn't come this far just to turn around and go home. Let's at least give it a try. We can both stay right here inside, and you can put on your suit while I let some air in. I can do it just a little bit at a time, and if I start to get dizzy, I can pop my helmet on and be breathing pure oxygen in a couple of seconds."

"If the atmosphere is cyanide, you won't *get* a couple of seconds."

"It's not cyanide."

"How do you know?"

"Intuition." She stared him down, challenging him to counter that. Forty years of rabid feminism in America had been good for something: like most men, he'd been conditioned not to contest even the most outrageously sexist statement if it came from a woman.

She was starting to feel a little light-headed as it was. She opened the air valve on her side of the tank and bled out a couple of pounds, waited for Allen to do the same with his, then replenished their oxygen from the welding bottle. It didn't help her light-headedness, but she hadn't figured that was from the air anyway. Not directly.

Waiting while gravity slowed them down was the hardest part of the whole trip. They tried calling on the radio for anyone who might be listening, but they got no response. They checked in every nook and cranny for loose food or equipment and made sure everything was tied down, and they pulled themselves down into their beanbag chairs and scooched around to make formfitting cradles to cushion the impact of landing, but when they had done everything they could think of to prepare, they still had twenty minutes to go.

How long had they been in space? It seemed like days, but when Judy checked her watch she saw that it had only been a couple of hours. That was long enough, considering the stress they'd been under. Maybe the light-headedness had a more mundane cause.

"How about some lunch?" she asked.

"I couldn't eat if I had to," Allen said.

Neither could she, but they needed something in their stomachs. She unzipped her sleeping bag and rummaged around through the canned goods until she came up with a sack of red delicious apples, took two of them out of the sack, and handed one to Allen.

He laughed when he took it from her outstretched hand. "Is this fraught with metaphorical significance, or what?"

"What? Oh. Garden of Eden. Well, we can always hope." She took a big bite. It was a fresh, crisp apple, sweet and full of juice. She had to chase a couple of drops with her tongue before they drifted away.

They crunched their way down to the cores, then Judy had to find a bag to hold the remains. The computer beeped for attention while she was doing that, and Allen said, "We're ready. Hang on; I'm going to put us back where we were and see if we need to tweak our vector any more."

Judy stuffed the cores back in the same bag with the whole apples, zipped them into the sleeping bag again, and straightened up to see the sunlit planet on the monitors. It didn't seem to be moving, except through their own rotation, but they were still a couple thousand kilometers away.

"Take us closer," Judy said.

The planet swelled in the monitors, then drifted off to the side, but she couldn't tell if that was rotation or linear velocity. "Let's kill our spin," she said. They were going counterclockwise as seen from above; that meant she needed to blast a few seconds of air from her side. She did that, then a little more when it didn't seem to be enough, and finally the planet stayed put. It was cocked at an angle—or rather they were cocked at an angle relative to it—but that was even easier to fix. Judy made sure she was strapped snugly into her beanbag, then swung her arms around in a circle until the tank slowly tilted into the right orientation. She couldn't make a very wide circle, but it was enough to impart an equal and opposite force to the tank. She stopped swinging when the camera's direction indicator said the planet was straight down, and the tank stopped tilting.

If they were moving tangentially, they were doing it slowly enough that the motion was undetectable. They might have been falling or rising at a few hundred kilometers per second, but that was impossible to see from their altitude, either. Directly beneath them, a multicolored landmass stretched from horizon to horizon.

It was time to land.

25

Judy felt her pulse rate rising again with the significance of what they were about to do. This time, she was pretty sure they were the first. She felt like she should have a recorder going to capture their first words from the surface, but they hadn't brought one and she wouldn't have used it if they had. Recording your own first words was just the sort of pompous behavior she abhorred about some of the glory hounds who had joined NASA for all the wrong reasons. True explorers didn't give a damn what anybody else thought about them; they did it for themselves. If Judy and Allen died in a crash here, no one else would ever hear about it, and even if they made it home safe, nobody would care. Not with all the new planets that people would be reporting in months to come. She and Allen would be like the Vikings who had discovered North America: first, but forgotten in the rush that followed. In a way it was a comforting thought. If they messed up out here, nobody would know.

She cleared her throat. "You ready on the landing sequence?"

"As ready as I'll ever be."

"Then let's do it before we lose our nerve."

"Okay."

She put on her helmet and made sure it was sealed, then helped Allen seal his own. He put on his gloves this time as well, then held his hands over the laptop computer's keyboard and carefully pushed the "Enter" key with the end of the pencil eraser he had taped to the side of his right index finger. He had already loaded the program he had written weeks ago for landing; pressing "Enter" activated it and made the rest of the keyboard control the hyperdrive in preprogrammed steps. Pressing one of the arrow keys would move them horizontally a hundred kilometers in the direction of the arrow, "D" would take them down ten kilometers at a time, "U" would go up, and "Esc" would bail them out 100,000 kilometers at once. He had told Judy that when he was programming it, he had thought about making that only 10,000, but he had thought better of it when he remembered that the hyperdrive didn't necessarily know which way was up, and in an emergency it was highly likely that the pilot wouldn't know, either. With a 100,000-kilometer jump, even if they were upside down when he hit the button, they wouldn't wind up trying to jump inside the planet and falling the rest of the way to the surface with a burned-out hyperdrive.

He tapped the "D" key once. Nothing apparent happened in the monitor, but as he tapped it a few more times the view began to expand.

They were dropping straight down from a standstill, but even so they would pick up too much velocity for a modified septic tank to withstand if they simply fell all the way in. So with each push of the "D" key, the hyperdrive flicked them ten kilometers closer to the surface without the associated gain in velocity. They would descend until the atmosphere became thick enough for a parachute, and then drop normally from there.

"I wish there was a way to adjust kinetic energy in a jump," Allen said as he took them down. His voice sounded thin and reedy through the spacesuit intercom. At least Judy thought it was the intercom's fault. "I tried to figure out how to do it, but kinetic energy just doesn't seem to have any meaning in hyperspace. It's all potential. Which is why we can use it to get from one place to another, so I guess I shouldn't gripe, but—what's funny?"

Judy stifled a giggle. "Nothing."

"Something is. What?"

She hesitated, then said, "The mad scientist discusses his invention. Sorry. I keep forgetting what we're doing here, and then it suddenly hits me."

"Don't apologize. It's too much for me sometimes, too, and I invented it." Allen grinned, an expression that made him look even more the mad scientist, and turned back to the monitor. They were coming in over the mountain range. He pushed the descent key a couple more times, until they were what Judy figured to be about sixty or seventy kilometers up, then he used the cursor keys to move them sideways until the mountains were comfortably off to the side. That put them over the sweeping arc of a storm front, so he moved them perpendicular to its path by one jump. The mountains ran at a diagonal to their path, so that brought them over its foothills again, but the storm was comfortably far away now, and the hills didn't look that rugged.

They fell for a few seconds while they both pondered the view. "What do you think?" he asked.

Rivers made tiny jagged lines leading out into the plains from the mountains. There was snow on the peaks, but the foothills were green. Farther from the mountains the land looked more jagged, like badlands, but the ground directly beneath them was mostly rolling hills.

"Looks like this is about as flat as it gets," she said. "And it's green, but it doesn't look like jungle. And no lakes that I can see. I couldn't ask for much better."

"Me either." Allen pushed the descent key again, keeping his eye on the ammeter connected to the drive as he did. Judy watched over his shoulder. The meter had barely jiggled during their previous jumps, but now it bumped a little bit higher. "We're starting to hit air," Allen said.

According to him, it took extra energy to put one mass inside another. The more mass you were dealing with, the more energy it took, so you could tell how dense your target area was by how much energy it took to put you there. Air at sixty kilometers up was pretty thin, but it was there.

He hit "D" again and the ammeter jumped even more. So did the tank; Judy felt it lurch upward and to the side as the wind hit it. The force was no stronger than the acceleration in an elevator, but after hours of weightlessness, she definitely felt it. She steadied herself against the hyperdrive, and her hand met Allen's as he did the same. "I'm going to try once more," he said, "but then I think it's time for the drogue."

"Sounds good," Judy replied. She reached up between the hatches and grabbed one of the three D-rings that hung there, making sure it was the right one. The green one released a bedsheet on the end of a hundred feet of rope; that would provide just a little bit of drag and ensure that they were oriented properly before they yanked the red or the yellow handles and popped one of the two main 'chutes.

The next jump was obviously the last. Judy could actually hear the engine strain: it buzzed for a second like a bug-zapper with a moth in the grating, and the ammeter bumped halfway across the scale, but the circuitry completed the jump. The tank lurched again, and this time they could hear a high-pitched whistle that immediately changed pitch as they heeled over backward in the wind.

They had put as much of the heavy equipment as they could at the bottom of the tank so the center of gravity would stay low and help keep them upright as they fell. Judy waited for the sideways motion to stop before she popped the drogue; if the tank started tumbling it could wrap the rope around itself and foul the main 'chute before it even opened.

The floor actually felt like a floor for the first time since they had left Earth. They were pulling less than half a gee, which was a good thing, since the entire source of the drag came from friction with the air. After a couple of seconds of stable descent, Judy yanked the handle and felt the knot that held the bedsheet in a tight ball come undone, and a moment later they felt another lurch as the sheet streamed out and caught air.

"Drogue 'chute's away!" Judy said. She had to speak up to be heard over the whistle of the wind. Some of that whistle probably came from the hole in the tank that the ripcord passed through. It was only a quarter-inch hole, and most of that was filled with rope, but Judy let go the D-ring and mashed the lump of modeling clay that had sealed it before back into place.

They began to feel gravity again, growing stronger as they descended deeper into the atmosphere and the bed-sheet streamer caught more air. They came in at quite an angle at first, but their residual orbital velocity slowly gave way to friction, and within a couple of minutes they were headed straight down. "Straight" was an average value; the blunt bottom of the tank wasn't aerodynamic at all, and they rocked back and forth in the turbulence it created as they fell.

They watched the ground draw closer, becoming more and more detailed as it did, until at something like ten kilometers above the surface Judy reached up and yanked the red D-ring that released the main parachute. She felt a moment of panic when nothing happened, then the 'chute hit the end of its shroud lines and filled with a bone-jarring *snap*. Something clanged like a kitchen accident in the space beneath the spare hyperdrive, and Judy sagged into her beanbag chair, but the shock-absorbing web that Allen had designed had done its job. The air pressure remained stable, and now the tank was steady as a rock, descending as majestically as any Apollo capsule under its orange-and-white canopy.

"Thrill a minute, eh?" Allen asked. He kept his finger poised over the escape key on the keyboard. If it looked like they were about to crash, a single keystroke would kick them back into space. They couldn't try another landing because the main parachute would be outside the jump field and would get left behind, but they could at least make it back to Earth orbit and use the reserve 'chute to land there.

The ground took on more and more definition as they approached. Even without zooming in, they could see river valleys and patterns of vegetation on the hillsides. It drew closer, and now they could see individual boulders and trees. The canopies looked like round, green puffballs, but that's what just about any trees looked like from directly overhead. There were a lot of them down there, but there were open spaces between them. With any luck, they would come down in one of the gaps, but Judy didn't know if they could count on luck.

As they fell the last couple hundred feet, she had to bite her lip to keep from saying "Abort!" At the last minute she almost did, but the sight of the ground rushing up to hit them froze her tongue and she was too late. Allen either had more nerve than she did or he was equally paralyzed, because he didn't push the button. The ground swelled until Judy swore she could count the pebbles, then with a thump that jarred them deep into their beanbag crash couches, they landed.

The *Getaway* tilted up on end, spun around, and crashed back down. The image on Judy's monitor gyrated wildly. For a moment she thought they were tumbling, but she didn't feel any more motion, and a second later she laughed with relief when she figured out what had happened.

"The camera pulled loose!" she said.

"I think my *teeth* did, too," Allen replied. "Are you okay?"

"Yeah. How 'bout you?"

"Aside from the heart attack, you mean?" He breathed heavily into his microphone. "Man, it was all I could do to keep from pushing the bail-out button."

Judy reached for her video controls and tried to swivel her camera around so she could see something other than the square foot of ground directly beneath it, but the motor turned the mount, not the camera, and the whole apparatus was hanging by the wires. All they could see in her monitor was dirt and small yellow fern-like plants.

Allen's camera still worked. They both eyed the screen as he panned it horizontally from lock to lock. They had come down on a bit of a slope, but not a steep one. There were trees and bushes and rocks scattered over the hillside, the trees more yellow than green and their branches more fern-like than leafy, but they were trees. The bushes could pass for sagebrush if a person didn't look too closely. The rocks looked like plain old everyday granite. They had a good view of one: they had missed a boulder bigger than their spaceship by about ten feet. The parachute had draped over part of it and spilled into a pile of cloth at its base.

Allen shook his head, and said with a laugh, "Well, that's certainly one giant leap for a septic tank."

26

Both hatches had already popped open against their spring-loaded gate latches. They opened inward; as soon as the air pressure outside exceeded the pressure inside, they had loosened enough to let it equalize.

"I'm going to crack the seal on my helmet," Judy said.

Allen put his hands out to stop her. "Are you sure you want to do that?"

"We've already been through this," she said, pushing his hands gently aside. "It's either this or go home with our tails between our legs." She twisted her helmet sideways and pulled upward on it, but it wouldn't release. "Oh," she said. "Of course. The pressure is higher than inside my suit." Even air halfway up Mount Everest would have more pressure than inside her suit, but she glanced at the altimeter and saw that the needle was reading a couple thousand feet below the zero mark. There was more air here than at sea level on Earth. No wonder she couldn't lift off her helmet; there was at least a hundred pounds of force pushing it closed.

She opened the seal on her right wrist and pried off her glove. That let enough air in to allow her to equalize the pressure, but she left her helmet on and took a couple deep breaths instead. Let the little bit of air she'd already allowed into her suit mix with the rest, and see what a small dose would do to her first.

She had to swallow a couple of times to equalize the pressure in her ears, but she couldn't detect anything wrong with it at all. She took another deep breath and held it in her lungs for a second, waiting for the moment when it would start burning like fire, but it never came.

She lifted her helmet, then set it down again and took another breath. This time she could smell living things, but none of the scents were familiar. Just green.

She felt a sneeze coming on. Was there some kind of allergen that would turn her into a sniffling blob of swelling mucus membranes until her throat closed up and suffocated her? She waited for that to happen, but the urge to sneeze went away.

Allen's voice came through the intercom. "Are you all right?"

"Fine so far."

"No dizziness?"

"Nope." She lifted her helmet and took a breath straight from the tank. Now she could smell something like rosemary, probably from the plants they had crushed. It smelled wonderful, but then rotting garbage would probably have smelled wonderful after all the flatulence they had blown into the air after they had lowered the pressure.

She left the helmet off and took another breath. No allergens, no poisons, no problem at all. The air was fine.

She wished she could say the same for the gravity. Her legs were killing her. Hours of staying bent, and now full gravity—and maybe a little more, by the feel of it—were too much to bear. She couldn't even stand up inside the tank.

"I'm opening the hatch," she said.

Allen waved his hands. "Not yet!"

"Would you lighten up? I'm not even wheezing." She reached overhead and tugged on the hatch, swung it down, and stuck her head outside.

It was surprising how different the reality was from the TV picture inside. The scrubby bushes she had thought looked like sagebrush were actually more like tiny pine trees, and the trees looked like huge ferns that branched into smaller and smaller shoots, like fractal drawings. A breeze rustled some of the fronds and they made a dry rattling sound like gravel skittering down a talus slope. There didn't seem to be any animals around, but that wasn't surprising. She would probably be cowering under a bush herself if a gigantic yellow box dropped out of the sky next to her.

"Hello!" she called out, but the trees and the distance swallowed up her voice without an echo.

The smell of rosemary wafted by on the breeze. It reminded her of her mother's home cooking. She could definitely learn to like this place if the rest of it was as delightful as this. Even the temperature was right: somewhere in the mid to high seventies by the feel of the air on her face.

The hatch next to hers popped open and Allen stuck his head up through the hole. He wasn't wearing his helmet.

"Hey!" she said. "You're supposed to wait until we're sure it's safe."

"I'm not going to let you take all the risk."

"Right, so now if it turns out to be deadly we both croak. That's smart."

He didn't reply. He ducked down again, and she heard him panting and cursing for a few seconds, then he popped back into the hatchway without the upper torso of his suit. He stuck his arms out and pulled himself up to sit on top of the tank, leaving the lower half behind as well.

Judy couldn't really fault him for it. She was so tired of the damned spacesuit she could cut it off with a knife and not feel bad about it. She dropped down onto her beanbag chair again and twisted the waist ring open, struggled out of the top, and kicked off the legs. She felt so free she could probably have floated out of the hatch, but before she stood up again she unzipped her sleeping bag and found the pistol and the bullets that Trent had given her, popped open the cylinder, and slid six of the thumb-sized bullets into the holes. .45 Colt, according to the ammunition box, but it didn't look a bit like the pistol Gerry had been waving around on the shuttle. This one felt more Western, with a fat, stubby barrel and a cylinder that clicked ominously as it rotated and a curved wooden handle that just begged to be twirled around a couple of times before it landed in your hand. Judy didn't really figure she would need it, but Trent would never forgive her if she got eaten on her first foray out of the ship.

"Whoa!" Allen said when she stuck her arms out to pull herself up. "What's that for?"

"Artificial self-confidence."

"Oh. Okay, that makes sense. Cover me." He slid off the side of the tank to land on his feet in the fern-grass.

"I said *self* confidence, not sidekick confidence. You're supposed to be backing *me* up." She climbed out and slid down beside him, but she kept the gun. "Stay here while I go have a look around."

He folded his arms across his chest. "Boy, put a pistol in your hand and suddenly you're Annie Oakley."

She waggled the barrel back and forth, careful not to point it toward him. "Thanks for not saying 'Calamity Jane.' " She had never been a gun enthusiast, but right now the weight of the pistol in her hand was a comfort. It wasn't just the self-defense factor, either. After the last week of hiding out from the government and looking over her shoulder every time she turned around, it felt kind of nice to step out into the unknown with a little bit of a swagger.

She tried not to let it show. She took a couple dozen careful steps, paying attention to the gravelly texture of the ground beneath her suit-liner booties. The fern was too soft to feel through the tough fabric, but she could smell its piquant aroma as she swished through it. She couldn't help but smile. Her planet smelled nice!

She turned around and looked at the *Getaway*. The insulation at its base was crushed, just as they had intended. That had loosened some of the straps holding it on; they would have to tighten those before they jumped again.

The parachute was billowing softly in the breeze, its orange and white nylon fabric whispering softly against itself. That was fine now, but if a gust of wind came up, their spaceship could wind up dragged halfway across the continent. Judy made a quick circuit around it, checking for anything that looked dangerous, but she saw no animal life at all, so she said, "Okay, it looks clear. Come help me fold this up."

Allen took the long way around, checking out the bushes and one of the trees on the way. Judy kept her eye on him while she tugged the end of the parachute out straight. She felt a moment of panic when he turned away and she saw the ventilation tubes on his spacesuit liner; even though she'd seen them a million times before, in this new context they looked for just a second like a five-tentacled alien stuck to his back.

There didn't seem to be any aliens, not even insects. Judy bent down to look between the fronds of the tiny ferns at her feet, but all she saw was brownish black dirt. She grinned at the thought of having the first picnic in human history without ants, but she was still too excited to eat.

A breeze wrapped the end of the 'chute around her legs. "Hey, come on, let's fold this up," she called out, and Allen abandoned his exploration.

"Those bushes have a hell of a thick trunk," he said as he came closer. "They're like barrel cactus with branches and leaves."

"I wonder if they're edible," Judy said.

He held up his hands, palms out. "I don't want you trying it until we know for sure. Breathing the air was bad enough, but I draw the line at that."

"Yes, Mom. Here." She handed him a fistful of parachute.

They had practiced repacking it before, but they'd done it inside Trent and Donna's garage. This was easier in one respect: they had more room to stretch it out, but every time they lifted it off the ground, the breeze would fluff up part of it that they didn't want to move. They had to resort to using rocks to hold it down, but even so it took them fifteen minutes to get it right, and by the time they shoved the last of it inside the stuff sack and re-laced the ripcord, they were sweating like dockhands inside their spacesuit liners.

"Well," Judy said as they leaned against the side of the tank, both of them breathing hard from the exertion, "I think we'd be dead by now if the atmosphere was going to kill us. We might as well get out of these things and into real clothes."

"Amen to that," Allen said. He climbed up onto the tank and dropped inside, and a moment later a pair of jeans and a T-shirt flopped over the edge of the hatch.

Judy set the pistol on the step molded into the side of the tank and peeled out of her suit liner. It felt deliciously dangerous to strip naked on an alien planet, to feel the soft fern tickle her toes and the breeze blow cool and fresh against her skin. She closed her eyes and leaned back against the sunlit warmth of the yellow plastic, savoring the heat and the light and the freedom of this new world.

She heard thumps and curses from inside the tank, then Allen's startled, "Oh! Now that's a sight."

She opened her eyes and tilted her head even farther back to look up at him. His chest was bare, and she was willing to bet the rest of him was, too. She felt her entire body tingle at the sight, and at the thought of what she wanted to do. To hell with a picnic; she had just endured the craziest week of her life, capped by what had to be the craziest day in recorded history, and she'd survived to tell the tale. She'd landed in paradise for her reward, but there was one more thing that would make it perfect, and the risk only added to the allure.

"Hey, sailor," she said in the sultriest voice she could manage. "Want to celebrate our landing?"

27

"Zork," she said, and she giggled as she held the sweating can of Budweiser up to her lips.

Seated cross-legged on the unzipped sleeping bag that they were using for a blanket, still naked as a jaybird, Allen frowned. "Zork? What kind of name is Zork for a planet? It sounds like something out of a nineteen-fifties B-movie."

"Exactly!" Judy said. Her giggles prevented further speech, but a wave at the septic tank, its sides reinforced with steel cable and 4 × 4 posts, illustrated her point.

Allen shrugged. "All right, so it *is* appropriate right now, but millions of people are eventually going to have to put up with the name."

Judy took a long pull at her beer, nearly finishing it. "They'll be millions of people with a sense of humor," she said after she'd swallowed. "My kind of people."

"Not so," he said. "Your kind of people will be out planting bizarre names on every star and planet in the galaxy just as soon as they can get their own tanks sealed up."

"You're probably right," she admitted. "All right, let's not ruin it with a silly name. What do *you* suggest?"

"Hmm. Good question." He cocked his head sideways in thought, then said, "Maybe we're getting ahead of ourselves anyway. There could be natives with their own name for it already."

"I haven't seen any evidence of 'em yet," she said. "But if there are, they're probably ugly little green guys with knobby fingers and antennae. And their name will probably be worse than 'Zork.'"

"Only one way to find out," he said. "What do you say we go for a little walk and see what's out there?"

Judy stretched luxuriously, knowing what the sight was-doing to him. "Oh, I don't know," she said. "I could settle in right here and take a nap just as easily." She drained her beer and threw the can casually over her shoulder, where it hit the big rock behind her with a metallic *donk* and clat-tered to the ground.

His eyes grew even wider. "What are you . . . that's . . . we shouldn't start littering . . ."

She laughed. "Gotcha!"

He closed his mouth and shook his head. "You did."

"Just keeping you on your toes. Sure, let's go for a walk. We're going to get sunburned if we don't put some clothes on anyway."

She retrieved her beer can and shook out the last few drops, then carried it and the remains of their picnic back to the *Getaway*. Allen's clothes were still flopped half out of the hatch; he started putting them on while Judy crawled inside and found some of her own. It was all hand-me-downs from Donna, but she was glad to have something that had a little history. All her history was sixty-some light-years away, and probably confiscated by the Feds by now anyway.

She found a pair of faded blue jeans and a long-sleeve shirt with vertical lilac and green stripes, then dug out un-derwear and socks from another bag and her hiking shoes from where she'd wedged them in next to the spare hyper-drive.

The inside of the septic tank already looked like a teen-ager's bedroom. Judy literally had to dig through layers of stuff to reach her shoes, and she could barely move without banging her elbows or knees into things. If she and Allen had to leave in a hurry again, they would be swimming in junk.

With any luck, that wouldn't be a problem. "Zork" looked like a decent place so far.

She came across the walkie-talkies they had bought when they had still thought they might be able to get ultra-light airplanes, and gathered them up, too. She had no in-tention of splitting up on their first foray, no matter how benign the planet seemed, but radios might come in handy if they got separated by accident.

They didn't have a day pack. She put another couple cans of beer, some apples, and a wedge of cheese in her sleeping bag's stuff sack, then went back outside to get dressed, and in a few minutes they were ready to go. Allen climbed up on the tank and pulled the hatches shut, then dropped back to the ground. "Which way should we go?" he asked.

"How about uphill?" she replied. "Maybe we can find an overlook and see what the landscape's like. And it'll be easier coming back if we go uphill to start."

"That makes sense."

Allen took the sack of food. Judy considered putting the pistol in there, too, but that would make it too hard to reach in an emergency. Trent hadn't given them a holster with it, so she finally just tucked it in her waistband, making sure the cylinder was rotated partway around so the hammer wasn't on a live round. It felt awkward there, but its presence was still a comfort.

They held hands while they walked. Judy hadn't been a big touchy-feely person before, but somehow knowing how far she was from home made her want to remain in contact with the only other human being around. The fact that she was hot for his body probably had something to do with it, too, but whatever the reason, she liked the feeling. He didn't seem to mind, either, though he had to rein in his long natural stride to keep from outpacing her every couple of steps.

They stopped under one of the big trees to check it out. It was maybe thirty feet tall, with a trunk about a foot thick at the base, tapering up for half its height before it split into three branches that split again into three more each, and so on out to the leafy fronds at the ends. The bark was smooth and rubbery, like a gray-green wetsuit, and the branches behaved like soft plastic rather than wood. Judy jumped up and caught one, and it flexed easily when she pulled it down so she could examine the fronds more closely, but when she let go, it didn't spring back into place. Instead it slowly rose up, like a snake out of a basket, until its fronds were next to the others again.

"Hydrostatic pressure?" she asked.

Allen pulled another one down and let go. It, too, rose slowly back into place. "Could be. It would be easy enough to find out." He reached into one of his pants pockets and pulled out a Swiss army knife.

"Wait a minute," Judy said as he unfolded the corkscrew. "Let's not go poking holes in things just yet."

"No?"

"No. Not until we know a little more about the ecology."

"Poking holes in things is one way to *learn* about the ecology," he pointed out.

"And watching it in action is a less invasive way," she said. "There's plenty to see without dissecting the natives."

"It's a tree," Allen said, but he put away his knife.

Judy wondered why she'd been so reluctant to let him do it. It *was* just a tree, after all. By nightfall, if it got cold enough, she might start pulling dry branches off it herself for a fire.

Well, not this particular tree. This one didn't have any dry branches. Nor did any of the others she could see from where she stood. They were all different sizes, but they were equally green from bottom to top. As she and Allen walked uphill through them, she couldn't see a single brown leaf or dead twig.

Maybe that was it. They all looked so perfect, she didn't want to be the person to put the first scar on one.

She wondered if it was spring here. Earth trees always looked perfect in spring, too, before the caterpillars set to work on the leaves. She tried to think how this planet's poles had looked in relation to the sun, but she hadn't spent enough time in orbit to remember.

It didn't look like the explanation was that simple anyway. There were no dead branches on the ground, and no mat of decaying leaves, either. Just the myriad little ferns, none of which showed any more sign of mortality than the trees.

The forest was silent except for the rustle of the fronds in the breeze. Judy and Allen's footfalls hardly even made a noise, but as the ground grew steeper, they began panting enough to make up for it. Gravity was definitely stronger here than on Earth. Not by much, but even a little extra work for every step eventually added up. And the temperature that had seemed ideal when they were picnicking and making love now seemed about ten degrees too hot.

"Gah," Judy said, fluffing her shirt out in front to get some air inside it. "Nobody told me exploring was going to be hard work."

Allen wiped sweat from his forehead with the side of his hand. "I'd kill for a cold mountain stream to stick my feet in about now, but something tells me we're going the wrong direction to find water."

"Maybe we can at least see where there is some when we get to the top." She hoped she was right, but at the same time she wondered how smart it would be to soak their feet in a stream when they didn't know what was living in it. She planned to boil anything they drank, too, but of course they had left the camp stove in the *Getaway* along with the pots and pans. She hadn't expected their first foray to become a major expedition.

They could always go back, she supposed, but she wanted to at least get a look at their new world before they did that. She turned around to check their progress, but they hadn't climbed high enough yet to see much more than what they had already walked through. And the treetops were spaced just wrong to give them a view out to the horizon.

She couldn't see the *Getaway*. They had at least gone far enough for the trees to hide it as well. She felt a little satisfaction at that, but then she felt cold panic slide up her spine when she realized what that meant.

"Allen! We didn't mark our trail."

He turned around, too. "Good point. I'm sure we can find our way from here—it's pretty much straight downhill, after all—but it wouldn't hurt to build cairns from now on."

He nudged a couple of head-sized rocks with his toe until he worked them loose from the ground, then stacked them precariously atop a third rock.

Judy eyed it critically. "That won't stay put very long."

"Long enough. We're not going to be gone all day."

As soon as he said that, she suddenly realized that they didn't even know how long "all day" was here. She looked up at the sun, trying to remember where it had been when they arrived, but she hadn't thought to look then and she didn't know which direction she was facing now anyway.

It was still high in the sky, for what that was worth. They had hours before they had to worry about nightfall.

They continued up the slope, building cairns every few hundred feet as they climbed. The trees were still fairly far apart, so it was easy to spot one pile of rocks from the next, but the farther away from their starship they got, the more nervous Judy became. If they got lost, it was a *long* way back home.

The trees never grew close enough together to become an actual forest. The bushes never joined into thickets, either. Something kept them spaced just about as far apart as they were tall, and after a few minutes of thought, Judy realized they were the perfect distance to keep from shading one another. The bigger trees commanded more space than the smaller ones, and the bushes clustered in the spaces farthest from any of them. It seemed very logical at first, but the more she thought about it, the less sense it made. How did the trees know ahead of time how tall they were going to grow? They were spaced ideally now, but in another ten years they were going to be crowding one another out.

There were still no dead trees, either. She and Allen had walked at least half a mile by now; they should have found at least a couple of fallen logs.

And birds. Shouldn't there have been some sign of them? Nests in the treetops, or a snatch of song off in the distance? So far Judy hadn't heard a sound since they had arrived other than the wind in the trees and the noises she and Allen had made. She hadn't seen a flicker of motion other than the rustling fronds, either. It was like walking through a movie set on an indoor soundstage; it didn't seem real without ambient noise to go with it.

"Could it be possible that there aren't any animals here?" she asked.

Allen shrugged. "Anything's possible, I suppose, but I can't imagine how the ecosystem could work without 'em."

He stopped to build another cairn, and this time when he dug out a half-buried rock, Judy bent down and examined the hole it left behind. No worms. No insects. The dirt didn't even smell of fungus. She didn't expect the same actinomyces that gave Earth dirt its characteristic smell, but there had to be something similar to break down organic matter here, didn't there?

Did there?

"Maybe there isn't an ecosystem," she said. "Maybe the trees get their nutrients straight from the air and the ground, and since there's nothing to eat them, they don't have to grow or reproduce nearly as fast as they do on Earth."

"Looks like they reproduce just fine," Allen said, waving his arms to encompass the couple of dozen trees surrounding them.

"But we don't know how often it happens. These trees could be thousands of years old."

He cocked his head, looking from her to one of the trees and back. "That's a good theory. Appropriately wacky. We need a core drill so we can count rings and see just how wacky."

Judy led off farther up the hill. "If they don't grow much from year to year, the rings would be microscopic, if there are any at all."

"Then that would be pretty good evidence for your theory," he said.

"And if I'm right, proving that theory could mean injuring something older than the dinosaurs."

He laughed softly.

"What's funny about that?"

"I don't think I've ever met a pistol-packin' tree-hugger before."

She looked down at the revolver tucked in her waistband. She had never exactly considered herself a tree-hugger, but there was no denying the pistol-packin' part. It was beginning to look like a useless weight, but she wasn't ready to put it in the stuff sack just yet. There might not be any animals on this planet, or there might be a pack of wolves just over the rise.

Or there might be a cliff. Judy had noticed that the trees seemed to thin out up ahead, but she couldn't see why until she was nearly on top of it. There was an outcrop of rock beyond the last of the trees, then a thousand feet or so of empty space beyond that. It wasn't a sheer drop, but it wasn't a slope she would try descending without a rope, either.

They had climbed the flank of the first mountain in the range. They weren't to the top yet, but they were quite a ways up. There was another mountain directly across the chasm from them, its peak probably no farther away than the valley floor below. A rushing noise came from the valley, almost like the sound of the wind in the trees, but not quite the same. The forest was thicker down there; it took a moment to see anything other than its green canopy, but eventually Judy spotted a few glistening flashes of sliver and white.

"There's your river," she said.

28

"Fat lot of good it does us down there." Allen picked up a rock and overhanded it out into space. It fell far short of the river, but it bounced and rattled its way down the slope, knocking loose more rocks on the way until a couple dozen of them careened through the trees and splashed into the water.

"Maybe we can get to it where it flows out of the canyon." Judy pointed into the foothills, where the river widened and slowed down and the banks were more manageable.

"Not today, we can't," he said. "I've walked just about as far as I want to go in one afternoon."

She sat on one of the flat rock slabs that made up the outcrop. "Me too. But I'm thirsty as a fish, and all we've got to drink is beer."

"Beer'll do fine." He opened the stuff sack and took out a can of Bud, popped the tab, and handed it to her for the first swig.

She wasn't used to having men defer to her, not even after a week in Wyoming. After a lifetime spent competing with men in one of the most macho fields in existence, she didn't really know whether she should let Allen get used to pampering her, but it was easier to just take a sip of beer and hand the can back than to make an issue out of it.

She'd always thought of Bud and all the other light pilsners like it as wimpy beer, but she had to admit it tasted pretty good on a hot day. Trouble was, she might as well have pumped the alcohol directly into her bloodstream, because she could feel it hit almost immediately. The tingly buzz would have been fun in other circumstances, but at the moment she didn't want to mess up her reasoning ability or lower her reaction time. She just wanted to cool off and quench her thirst. Seeing all that water directly beneath her didn't help any, either.

She looked upstream. The canyon wound around behind the next mountain back in the range, but she could see where it led by the placement of the mountains beyond. She and Allen hadn't climbed high enough to see all the major peaks, but there were three or four with snow on top, obviously providing the meltwater that made up the river. It would be cold. Bathing would be a challenge, but Judy felt grubby enough she was willing to try at least a sponge bath.

It would have to wait until morning. They had at least a mile to walk back to the *Getaway*, and by the looks of the river's path once it left the mountains, they had at least another three miles from where they'd landed before they reached water. Judy was no more eager to do that than Allen.

They could always take the *Getaway* back into space and try again, but from the height they would have to jump to, and without a steerable parachute, they would have no guarantee of coming any closer to a stream on a second attempt. They were just as likely to wind up farther away. At least this distance could be walked in a few hours, now that they knew which direction to go.

If she ever needed an object lesson in the limits of technology, this was one to remember. They could cross sixty light-years in an instant, but without ground transport they were still half a day from water.

A cloud slid over the sun; one of the few clouds they had seen in the sky all day. Allen looked up, and after a few seconds he said, "It's so strange not to see contrails."

She followed his gaze. The sky was a lighter shade of blue than on Earth, probably because of the extra thickness of the atmosphere, but the cotton-puff cloud looked exactly the same as a cumulus cloud would back home. Allen was right, though: it was odd to see no sign of air traffic. It was odd to see no sign of civilization on the ground, either, but there were no roads or cities or plowed fields. Not even a cell phone tower. Nothing, all the way out to the horizon.

It suddenly occurred to her that she could actually *see* the horizon. From her height it had to be at least a hundred kilometers away, and it was still distinct as a window frame. When was the last time she'd seen something like that?

"I wanted an untouched planet," she said. "I guess I got what I asked for."

"But?"

She looked over at him, still standing at the edge of the rocks, beer in hand. "But what?"

"I can hear it in your voice. You got what you asked for, but it's not what you wanted, is it?"

She reached for the beer, maybe to give herself time to think as much as to quench her thirst. She savored two good swallows, then handed it back and said, "Exploring on foot is hard, sweaty work, and we're not finding anything particularly exotic. It's nice to take a hike in the woods, but all we've got to go back to tonight is a crowded septic tank. I'd love to sleep out under the stars, but that would be pretty dumb until we learn what kind of night life there is. So . . ." She shrugged.

"So you'd like a hotel room with a nice hot bath and a comfy bed?" The way he said it made the hackles stand up on her neck.

"No. I'd like a bigger spaceship and some ground gear so we can do this right."

He nudged another loose rock off the edge with his toe and watched it bounce down the slope. "Same thing," he said at last. "We've got what we've got. Wishing for more is a waste of time."

"Screwing around with inadequate equipment is the waste of time."

He turned away from the canyon. "Look, I'm sorry I couldn't come up with a motor home and a humvee, okay? I did the best I could. We're here, aren't we? Shouldn't that count for something?"

She had heard that lament from him before. She'd

thought it sounded whiney then, and it didn't sound any better now. "Yes, damn it, that counts for something, but it doesn't count for *everything*. You're a genius, all right? You invented a hyperdrive engine. That's really neat, but now we're three or four miles from water and getting thirstier by the minute. No amount of genius is going to make that okay."

Allen wiggled the beer can. "We've got three more of these, by my count. We'll be all right."

Slowly, as if explaining it to a child, she said, "If we keep drinking beer, mister genius, we're going to get drunk. We haven't exactly been making the best decisions in the world as it is, but at least we've been sober when we made them. I don't want to start trusting my life to our reasoning ability when we're plastered. And tired."

"Lighten up," he said. "It'd take a lot more than a six-pack of beer to get us plastered."

She stood, steadying herself on a rock, then faced him with her hands on her hips. "Lighten up? Lighten *up*? Damn it, Allen, this isn't a camp-out; we're on our own out here! We're light-years from home. Nobody's going to come save our butts if we screw up. Nobody's even going to find our bodies. So I don't want to screw up."

He snorted. "Interesting choice of terms for someone who threw all caution to the winds along with her clothes a couple of hours ago."

"That . . . well, touché, but that's exactly the sort of thing I'm talking about. What the hell were we thinking? We could have been eaten alive."

"I thought that's what—"

"Oh, be quiet." She felt herself blushing now. Losing her self-control was one thing, but talking about it later was even worse. "Come on, let's get back to the *Getaway* before we run out of daylight."

"Now that's a good idea." He held out the beer. "Want to kill it?"

She was still thirsty, but her head had spun when she stood up. Maybe it was fatigue, but maybe it wasn't.

"Go ahead."

He drained it, sucking out the last drops, then held the can out in front of him, his fingers wrapped evenly around it.

"Don't crush—" Judy said, but it was too late. He gave one quick squeeze and the can collapsed with a whoosh. "Damn it, we could have used that to hold water."

"Oh." He looked at the mangled can, all his pride at learning how to crush it one-handed evaporating away. "Sorry. I'll, uh, see if I can knock it back out."

"Don't bother. We've got five more." Without waiting for him to answer, Judy set off downhill, back the way they had come.

It was a much quicker walk back to their landing site. They hardly spoke on the way down; just walked from cairn to cairn until they saw the familiar yellow plastic tank peeking through the trees. Judy didn't know if they were mad at each other or not; they were just quiet.

So was the planet. Judy kept waiting for it to feel like an eerie, just-before-the-monster-pounces kind of silence, but it was just the silence of the wilderness. Except for the shape of the trees and their peculiar spacing, she could be in just about any backcountry nature preserve.

Maybe that was part of the problem. They had seen plenty of bizarre things today, but they hadn't been able to explore any of them, and now that they could explore a little, they had nothing exciting to see.

She knew she was being unfair. They couldn't judge an entire planet by what they found in one spot, and they couldn't even judge that one spot after just a couple of hours. But first impressions were hard to shake.

Maybe tomorrow would bring something a little more otherworldly.

When they reached the *Getaway*, she climbed inside and started packing.

"What are you doing?" Allen asked when he saw her shoving the spacesuits into the corners.

"Making some room for tonight," she answered.

"Oh." He evidently decided that made sense, so he climbed in and helped her stow things. They emptied her sleeping bag and managed to tuck most of the food into nooks and crannies around the edges of the tank, but there was still not room enough to stretch out. The hyperdrive engines filled the center of their space.

"So do we move the engines, or sleep sitting up?" Allen asked.

"Sleep sitting up," Judy answered. "I want a working spaceship in case we have to make a quick getaway."

"So to speak."

She looked up and saw him smiling.

"Right." His expression was contagious, and the bright yellow glow from the evening sunlight hitting the tank was too cheery to let her sustain a bad mood for long anyway. She smiled back at him, then leaned against the side of the tank and said, "This reminds me of the way I used to play spaceship when I was a kid. I'd get a big cardboard box or throw a blanket over a couple of chairs and crawl inside, and I'd pretend I was landing on another planet. Everything was completely familiar inside, but I would convince myself that just beyond the walls were all sorts of alien mysteries waiting to be explored."

She lifted the top of her sleeping bag up to her nose and inhaled the unmistakable smell of nylon and insulation. "This is so close to what it was like, it's hard for me to believe we're really here."

Allen raised up so he could see her over the hyperdrive and said, "It seems kind of surreal to me, too. I never really considered this part; the first night on a new planet, trying to relax enough so I can get to sleep."

"It's going to be tough," she said. "It's been an amazing day." She rolled up onto her knees so she could lean over the hyperdrive and give him a quick kiss. "All the same, the body will do what it has to do. Speaking of which, I'm going to go outside and find a bush."

He frowned. "Huh? We've already found dozens of bushes just outside."

"That was a euphemism, idiot." She picked up the roll of toilet paper from where she'd hung it between the two hatches and held it out for him to see.

"Oh."

"Be right back." She climbed up through the hatch and dropped to the ground. There were plenty of bushes, not that it mattered; with Allen inside, there probably wasn't another pair of eyes to see her on the whole planet. Still, she walked a few dozen paces away before she unzipped her pants and squatted down to pee.

The sun was setting behind the mountain. The clouds overhead were still bright white, but that would probably change within the hour. Judy wondered if the sunset colors would be any different with a thicker atmosphere.

She saw a flicker of motion off to her right, and when she turned her head, she saw a butterfly landing on a branch a few feet away. It was a big one, with bright blue wings maybe three inches across and a fat, yellow body the size of her thumb. It had six or eight legs—Judy couldn't tell for sure—and a single bulbous eye in front. The eye glistened with gold highlights in the evening sun.

Insects! Her planet had animals after all. She wanted to shout to Allen, but she was afraid of scaring it, so she just finished watering the fern at her feet and stayed put.

The butterfly flapped its wings a couple of times, then flew to a closer branch. Judy watched its wings move. They were triangular, and attached point-first to its body. There were three to a side: two in front held one over the other like the wings of a biplane, and a single smaller one in back.

Its eye still glowed, even in the shade of a leaf. Was it actually emitting light, like a firefly?

Then it turned sideways and she saw that the glow came from a little knob at the end of its forelegs, which it was holding up to its eye. Built-in landing lights, she thought, smiling. It was a little early to need them, but maybe the butterfly was practicing for tonight.

The light blinked out, and the butterfly stuck its forelegs into a pouch under its belly. When they emerged again, they were empty. Was the light a separate creature? Maybe the big one carried its young in a pouch, like a kangaroo. And the young glowed so they would be easier to find?

Judy admired the way the pouch was designed: it opened to the front, but it had a flap to make air flow smoothly over it in flight. It even had a little clasp to hold the flap shut. Plus little tendons or cords or something to hold the whole thing snug to the butterfly's body. And . . . buckles on the cords? She leaned in for a closer look.

With a quick, fluid motion, the butterfly reached into a smaller pouch beside the first and withdrew an inch-long needle with a bulb at the base. A detachable stinger, too? Judy suddenly felt the urge to jump back. But the cords— she had to get a better look at those cords.

The butterfly held its ground while she bent forward. She stopped when she was about a foot and a half away, but she could see clearly enough. They were miniature cargo straps, flat webbing with buckles on the end just like the ones she and Allen had used to tie down the foam insulation on the bottom of the *Getaway*. And the bag was covered with even tinier pockets, from which protruded the handles of yet more equipment.

"Take me to your leader," she whispered. Then she remembered to pull up her pants.

29

"It's intelligent," she told Allen. He had come running, pistol held high and cocked, when she called to him. The butterfly had fled at his approach, but it had quickly returned to flutter over their heads, just far enough away that none of its artificial equipment was visible.

"No way," he said. He held the pistol off to the side now, pointed at the ground.

"It's wearing a pack, and it's got some kind of—there!"

The tiny light had come back.

"What's that?" Allen squinted at the butterfly, which hovered surprisingly still while it did whatever it was doing with the light.

"I think it's a video camera," Judy said.

"Oh, come on!"

"Well, what do you think it is?"

He held his free hand upward, palm up. "Come here, little guy. Let me get a good look at you."

It dipped down, but stopped just out of reach. Allen lowered his hand, and it came a little closer.

"See?" Judy said. "It's holding something in front of its face. Something that came out of a little belly pack. It's got a stinger in that long sheath on the side, too."

"Hmm. That's sure what it looks like, all right. But that doesn't mean it's artificial. Something like that could evolve pretty easily."

Then the light blinked once, went out for a second, blinked twice, went out again, blinked three times, another pause, then five.

"It's counting every other number," Judy said.

"Could still just be an instinctive biological thing," Allen replied, but he held his breath as it finished blinking seven, paused for a second, then started blinking again. He began counting with it to keep track. ". . . Eight, nine, ten, eleven. Hah, it missed one."

The light winked out, and the butterfly hovered over their heads, waiting.

"Nine's not prime," Judy said softly.

Allen looked at her, then back at the butterfly. "You're kidding."

"No," Judy said. "I think it's blinking prime numbers at us. Hold up one finger."

"What for?"

"Just do it."

Allen did, and Judy added both of her hands beside his, all ten fingers extended.

"Now hold out three."

He did.

"Now . . . uh . . ."

"Seven," he said, tucking the gun between his knees and holding up two fingers of one hand and all five of the other.

They held that position for a few seconds, then dropped their hands and waited to see what the butterfly would do.

It blinked the light again. Judy counted nineteen, then a pause, then twenty-three.

"I'll be damned," Allen said, carefully lowering the hammer on the gun and tucking it in the waistband of his pants. "It skipped twenty-one. I think you're right. The thing's intelligent."

Judy shivered, thinking, *Be careful what you ask for.* "Now what?" she asked.

"I don't know. How do we communicate with a bug?"

They just had, she supposed, but unless they could teach it Morse code, they were limited to math. Judy thought it over for a few seconds while the butterfly hovered patiently overhead, then she extended her hand out like Allen had done earlier, making a little landing pad. She held her other hand over it and fluttered her fingers like wings, then brought them down into her open palm.

"Let's see if it understands an invitation," she said.

"Even if it understands, it may not be brave enough to—"

Before Allen could finish his sentence, the butterfly swooped down and touched her palm, then backed away. Judy flinched, but she forced herself to keep her fingers extended. The touch had tickled, but if the butterfly saw her clench her fist, it would never trust her.

"It's all right," she said softly. "I'll be careful." She mimed landing again, and this time it followed her fingers down to stand on the muscle at the base of her thumb. It weighed no more than a couple of quarters.

She lowered her hand until her face was just inches from the butterfly. From there she could see its body in detail, but there wasn't a whole lot of detail to see. Its wings were the same color blue from root to outer edge, and its body was shiny yellow, like their septic tank. It had a bulbous yellow head with one big oblong eye that wrapped halfway around, not faceted like an Earth bug's, but smooth all the way across. It had eight legs, two of which were holding the source of the winking light: a metallic silver box with an unmistakable lens in front and an activity indicator above the lens. The butterfly held the box up to its eye again and the light came on.

"It's filming," she whispered. She couldn't have spoken louder if she'd wanted to. She was surprised her voice worked at all. This was an intelligent alien, standing right on the palm of her hand. She swallowed, then said, "H-hello. My name's Judy. What's yours?"

If it replied, its voice was out of the range of her hearing, but it folded all of its wings to point straight up, then lowered them one at a time until all six touched her hand.

"What do you suppose that means?" she asked.

Allen shook his head. "I haven't got a clue."

This was the moment when a properly equipped interstellar explorer would break out the Universal Translator and immediately begin discussing trade relations with the aliens. Or failing that, they would at least start learning each other's language, teaching one another concepts as diverse as love, courage, wonder, and "that's mine" until they could converse like schoolmates. Judy supposed the latter might be possible, given enough time, but it assumed that the aliens at least had a language to learn.

"How about the computer?" she asked. "Can we use it to draw pictures or something?"

"What?"

"We've got to figure out some way to communicate with this guy. It doesn't sound like he uses speech, so I thought maybe we could try pictures."

Allen said, "Good idea, but I don't have a drawing program."

They hadn't brought any paper or pens, either.

The butterfly raised and lowered its wings again; quickly on the upstroke, slowly going down. Judy imagined that was its equivalent of talking loudly for the foreigner, but it didn't help her a bit.

She felt a sudden urge to clench her fist; not out of any desire to harm the butterfly, but merely because this was a fist-clenching moment if ever there was one. Here she was, meeting face-to-face with an intelligent alien, the first one humanity had ever found. This could be the most important discovery in history, even bigger than Allen's, but it could just as easily turn into the most pathetic footnote for lack of a way to communicate.

"We use sound," she said to it. "Words. My name is Judy." She pointed to herself with her free hand, then pointed to Allen. "And that's Allen." For lack of anything better to say, she repeated it a couple of times, pointing back and forth. "Judy, Allen, Judy, Allen."

The butterfly flapped its wings once more.

"How about the radio?" Allen said.

"The radio? But he's right here."

"It's another way to communicate. If this little guy's got a video camera, maybe he's got a radio, too. We did hear a lot of static when we were in orbit; maybe some of that was actual transmissions."

"I suppose it's worth a try," Judy said.

"I'll go fire it up." Allen backed away, then turned and jogged to the *Getaway*. Judy followed him at a slower pace, hoping the butterfly would stay put if she didn't jostle it too much. It grew more and more agitated, flapping its wings and crawling around on her hand, but it didn't fly away.

Nor did it settle down when she stopped beside the yellow plastic tank. Its wings quivered and its feet danced, tickling Judy's skin. She wondered if it was truly excited or if she was reading human emotion into something completely different, but it certainly seemed to be doing a little victory dance on the palm of her hand. After a few seconds it settled down and turned its camera toward the makeshift spaceship, panning from one end to the other, then it did lift off and circumnavigate it once before coming to rest on Judy's hand again.

Allen's voice echoed from inside the tank. "I'm setting the frequency as high as it'll go. That guy doesn't have much room for a long antenna. Hello, this is Allen Meisner. Do you hear me?"

He let up the microphone button, but there was only static.

"Okay, let's try a little lower. Hello, this is Allen Meisner. Do you hear me?"

Still just a little bit of static.

"Lower still. Hello, this is Allen Meisner. Do you hear me?"

The butterfly dropped its camera.

The tiny box bounced off Judy's palm and tumbled over the edge between her thumb and forefinger. She lunged for it with her other hand and caught it just a foot or so down, then tilted her hand until she could grasp it in her fingers and hold it out for the butterfly to take from her, but it wasn't paying any attention. Its wings were quivering again, and all eight legs were moving at once, spinning it slowly around like a radar dish.

"I think he heard that," she said.

"Yeah?"

"Something spooked him."

She took a closer look at the camera. It was no bigger than a watch battery, and a small one at that. The lens was the biggest part of it; an eighth of an inch across and just as long. If the camera were scaled up to human size, that would almost certainly be a zoom lens with macro capability. It connected to a boxy housing with tiny slots in the sides for the ends of the operator's legs to fit into.

The radio crackled with static inside the *Getaway*, then Allen spoke again: "Hello out there. One. Two two. Three three three. Four four four four. Five five five five five."

The static returned, rising and falling in waves, but the waves were the same length, separated by long and short pauses, and they came in sets of six, seven, and eight. Not primes this time, but Allen had simply been counting upward, so the butterfly had apparently decided to continue the same progression.

"Yes!" Allen called out triumphantly. "That's him!"

"Oh, great," Judy muttered. "Now we're doing math over the radio."

Then the receiver crackled again, and a voice like a kids' toy with a string in the back said, "Oh, great. Now we're doing math over the radio."

"Who the hell was that?" Allen yelled.

"That was me. Our friend must have heard me and relayed it back to you."

A second later, the radio echoed that, too.

"All right," Allen said. "Now we're getting somewhere."

Judy didn't see that simple mimicry was all that much better than exchanging numbers, but she supposed it at least proved that the butterfly could hear her and make the same sounds. Over the radio, of course, but it was still sound.

Then the radio crackled again and the pulled-string voice said, "*Skkkkk*, one, two, three, four, five."

"Math again," she muttered, but Allen had already keyed the microphone and said, "Six, seven, eight, nine, ten."

There was a pause, then the voice said, "Three . . . one, one, *skkkkk* three, seven, five, five."

"What the heck is that, a phone number?" Judy asked.

Allen said, "No, it's pi. Provided *skkkkk* is zero."

"Yeah, right. Pi is three point one four one five nine something or other."

"Not in base eight. And base eight is just what you'd expect from somebody who's got eight legs."

Judy stretched up and peered inside the tank at Allen. "You know pi in base eight?"

"No, I calculated it."

"With what?"

"In my head."

The radio crackled, and the scratchy voice said, "Yes! That's him! Three point one four one five nine two six five."

"Hot damn!" Allen said. "He heard you, and he filled it out to ten digits. That means he's already figured out that we use decimal notation. This is going to be a piece of cake."

Maybe for Allen, but Judy hadn't come all this way to trade numbers. What were they going to do, start talking in sines, cosines, and tangents? This could be the trigonometry class from hell if she didn't do something to derail it.

She held the tiny camera in front of the butterfly, and this time it took it from her with its front two legs. "What do you call that?" she asked. "We call it a camera."

"We call it a camera," the voice said over the radio.

She bent down and picked up a rock, then said, "This is a rock. Rock. Rock."

"Rock," said the voice over the radio.

She walked up to the closest tree and rested her hand against its trunk. "Tree."

The radio was hard to hear from this distance, but she could just make out the scratchy reply: "Tree."

"Now we're talking," she said.

30

The sun set way too soon. Judy and Allen and the butterfly had barely gotten into sentences like "I fly to tree" before the clouds over the mountain turned red and the shadows began to deepen. Judy would have gone on with the language lesson all night, but when the light began to fail, the butterfly, whom they'd begun calling "Tippet" as the closest approximation they could manage to its name, lifted into the air and said, "*Tppppt* go *skkkkk* dark."

"You can stay with us," Judy said, but she knew there were too many new concepts even in that short a sentence for Tippet to understand. "Tippet stay here dark," she said, patting the side of the *Getaway*.

The butterfly paused, evidently considering her offer, then said, "No. *Tppppt* go. Come back sun east sky bright."

Judy was getting good at puzzling out the sentences he made with his limited—but fast growing—vocabulary. "Yes," she said. "We'll be here at sunrise. Sun east sky bright is sunrise. Sunrise. Understand?"

"Sunrise. Understand. *Tppppt* come back sunrise." Then the butterfly turned away and flew up over the trees, heading south. That was toward the river. Maybe tomorrow they could kill two birds with one stone: get some water and see where the aliens lived.

Since Tippet had seemed able to hear them just fine without the radio, Allen had left the receiver turned on with the volume cranked up and had climbed out of the *Getaway* to participate in the language lesson. Now he leaned back against the side of the tank and said, "He's obviously not afraid of bats or birds, or he wouldn't be flying up high like that. I wonder if he's at the top of the food chain here."

"Add that to the list of questions," Judy said. She'd been keeping mental note of all the things she wanted to ask when they learned how to communicate well enough. It was a long list. But at the rate they were going, they might start whittling it down pretty soon.

They had given up trying to learn Tippet's language, but that was mostly because he was so much faster at learning English. He only needed to be told the names of things once, and he could pick up simple verbs like "walk" and "run" after only a couple of demonstrations. He didn't have any trouble forming the words, either. His pronunciation was so good, in fact, that Judy suspected he was somehow storing them and playing them back when he needed them, which implied computer technology and digital sampling capability at least as good as humanity's, if not better.

"Intelligent butterflies," she said, shaking her head. "Who'd have guessed?"

Allen crossed his arms over his chest. "Bugs have a pretty well developed social structure, so it's not too surprising that they could develop high-order brains."

"It's the size of the package that amazes me." Judy flexed her hand to get the blood flowing in it again. She'd been holding it out as a landing platform for most of an hour, taking breaks only when Tippet flew over to something to name it. "And all that tiny stuff he was carrying with him. That's some serious miniaturization there."

Allen laughed. "I doubt if Tippet looks at it that way. That's just the size you build things if you're his scale."

"I guess." She looked out into the forest, which was taking on a different character as twilight deepened toward night and the shadows spread beneath the trees. What other sorts of creatures might live here? Tippet was the only animal they'd seen all day, but who knew what might come out at night? Tippet traveled armed, if that little stinger of his was what it looked like. That implied the existence of something at least dangerous to him.

On the other hand, she and Allen had traveled armed

today, too, and that was because they *didn't* know what to expect. But Tippet presumably did.

"Oh," she said out loud.

"What?"

"I just realized something. Tippet must have come looking for us on purpose, after he saw us land. That's why the video camera and the radio and the stinger and stuff. I was wondering why he was so well prepared for a first-contact situation, but it makes sense if he was expecting it."

"Hmm," Allen said. "I never thought about that, but yeah, you could be right. He did seem to be pretty well equipped."

"I wonder if he told any of his friends about us, or if he's keeping the discovery to himself?"

Allen climbed onto the tank and held out a hand to help Judy up. "Well, I don't know about him, but we were broadcasting at a couple of hundred watts. Unless he's the only one with a radio, we could have had an audience for kilometers around."

Judy shivered at the thought of thousands of aliens knowing about them. Even as tiny as Tippet was, if a bunch of his compatriots decided to come after the intruders with pitchforks, things could get ugly. There had been no indication that Tippet thought that way, but humans didn't all think alike; why should butterflies?

"Let's, uh, make sure we're ready to jump at a moment's notice tonight, eh?"

He paused with one foot inside the *Getaway* and one out. "You expecting trouble?"

"No. Just paranoid."

"Ah. Well, there's no harm in being prepared."

They climbed inside and settled in for the night. Judy set the pistol on the five-gallon bucket that housed the auxiliary hyperdrive so either she or Allen could get to it, and he put the computer in landing mode so all he would have to do if they needed to jump was hit the escape button and it would take them 100,000 kilometers into space. They had to switch on the flashlights so they could see what they were doing, but as soon as they had zipped themselves into their sleeping bags and snuggled into place, Judy switched the lights off. Their plasma batteries would last for months, but she didn't want the tank glowing like a beacon in the night. They were high-intensity halogen lights; even shining into the milky-white bags to diffuse their beams, they were bright enough to light up the inside of the tank like day.

She wished they could close the hatches, but then they would have to use their internal oxygen supply to keep the air from growing stale. They couldn't afford to do that; they needed the rest of their oxygen for the trip home. Closing the hatches wouldn't offer much protection anyway, since they opened inward. She and Allen would just have to stay alert.

"I'll keep first watch," she offered. Her voice echoed in the enclosed space. It might have been the only sound on the whole planet as far as she could tell.

"Oh, sure," Allen said. "Very generous of you, considering we're both too wired to sleep."

"All right, then, let's draw straws."

"Why don't we just see who drops off first, and the other guy can stay awake for a while longer."

She snorted. "That's the stupidest idea I've ever heard. What if we both fall asleep?"

"Then we both get some sleep. Nothing's going to happen."

"Famous last words."

Allen didn't reply right away, and when he did it was to say, "This is when my mother is supposed to stick her head in the room and say, 'You kids knock it off and go to bed.' "

Judy giggled. "It is kind of like a slumber party, isn't it?"

"It is. I definitely feel like a little kid again, that's for sure."

"Me too." Judy felt a lump under her butt, and twisted around so she wasn't sitting on it anymore. She pulled the sleeping bag up to her neck and inhaled its familiar aroma. It took her right back to childhood, back to the times when she would go car-camping with her dad. They always pitched a tent, and she always intended to spend the night in it, but rain or wind or night noises would keep her awake until she crawled into the back seat of the car.

"You know," she said, "I haven't felt this good since . . . heck, I don't know if I've ever felt this good. We've discovered aliens!"

Allen let out a long breath. "It's been a busy day, that's for sure. Running from the cops this morning, and talking to alien butterflies by nightfall."

Judy could still hear the squeal of tires as the cars pulled up in front of the house. "I wonder how Trent and Donna are doing?" she asked.

"I'll bet they're okay. In a town that size, they probably went to school with half the cops. They're probably having more trouble with the pipe we cut than anything else."

"I hope it wasn't a gas line." Judy imagined the fireball that could have engulfed the house, and suddenly her euphoria fell away into guilt. What if they'd been hurt? She'd been so caught up in her own problems and her own adventures that she hadn't really considered the mess they'd left behind, but now that she had time to think about it, she realized she and Allen had been agents of chaos on a personal level as well as a global level. Somehow, thinking that they might have hurt Trent and Donna seemed the worse of the two.

And Dale. If the Feds had hacked through his security, he could be behind bars by now. They might not link him to the bank robberies, but they would know he was laundering money, and they would probably accuse him of drug running if they couldn't pin anything else on him.

Shit. Why did things always have to work out like that? Trent and Donna hadn't done anything wrong, and neither had Dale, at least not to Judy or Allen. But because of their generosity, now they were all in trouble.

She wondered what was going on elsewhere. Was the government messing with her family, or Allen's? She hadn't even called her dad the whole time she'd been in Wyoming, for fear the call would be traced. She'd meant to call him before they left, but there'd been no time.

Damn the government and their paranoia anyway. Things could have gone so smoothly if they hadn't over-reacted. But no, they had to panic, and now everyone was running around in circles. She imagined the various other governments of the world were doing the same. Instead of building spaceships, they were probably all frantically building hyperdrive bombers. What if someone actually nuked New York, or London, or Paris? That would be bad enough, but she could just imagine the flurry of retaliation from it.

"You still awake?" Allen asked softly.

"Yeah." Judy sighed. "I'm sitting here beating myself up over all the trouble we've caused."

"Hmm?" He cleared his throat. "Weren't you feeling good just a minute ago?"

"I was, but then it hit me how much confusion we left behind."

"Oh. Every silver lining has its black cloud, eh?" He said it in a joking tone of voice, but it still stung.

"I'm just thinking about things, that's all."

"Okay." She didn't need light to see the gesture that went with that one word: hands held out in front of him, palms toward her.

She hated it when people did that, but she didn't want to get into it with Allen. Not now. She just settled back against the wall of the tank and rested her head in the groove between two of the wide corrugations.

She might have fallen asleep, or she might have just been drifting, but a noise from outside brought her upright in an instant. It was a sucking sound, like someone pulling their foot out of the mud, and it sounded so real and so close that she half expected to hear whoever was out there say "Damn it!" as they lost their shoe.

It happened again.

"Did you hear that?" she whispered.

From Allen's side of the tank came only soft breathing.

She stuck her feet under the auxiliary hyperdrive and jostled his beanbag. "Allen! Wake up!"

"Mmm?"

The sucking noise came closer.

"Something's out there! Something big."

"What? Where?"

"Outside!" She felt for the gun, but couldn't find it on the top of the bucket where she had left it. She patted around among the food and spacesuits at the base of it, but she couldn't find it there, either.

"Where's the gun? Have you got it?"

"No, I—"

Something scraped against the side of the tank, and they both yelped in terror. "Yaah!"

Allen banged against something. "Ow! Should we jump? Should we jump?"

"Not yet." If they did that with both hatches open, they would lose all their air in one big whoosh. Judy reached up and felt for Allen's hatch and slammed it closed, but instead of closing her own, she snatched one of the flashlights mounted between them, ripped it loose from its duct-tape loop, and stood up, flipping on the light and aiming it out into the night.

It still had the plastic bag on the end. The sudden glare was like a strobe going off right in front of her face; she yanked it free and shined the light outward again, hoping whatever was out there had been blinded just as badly.

When her eyes recovered, there was nothing to see. She swept the beam around in a full circle, but all she saw were trees and bushes. No eyes glowing in the light, no shadowy figures slipping furtively into cover; just the same fernlike trees they had seen during the day. One of the rubbery branches on the closest tree had drooped down toward the tank, and that was apparently what had scraped against it. She couldn't see what might have made the sucking sound, but nothing was moving now. She couldn't hear anything, either, but the pounding of her heart could have masked a jet engine.

"What's out there?" Allen asked. "Do you see anything?"

"No. Just the forest." She waved the light around, trying to spot anything that might be trying to sneak up on them, but the only motion she saw was the shadows she created.

Her sleeping bag had slid down around her ankles. She kicked it off, instinctively freeing her feet in case she had to run, even though she knew that flight in this case meant a completely different thing.

The light was bright enough to make her squint, even after her eyes had adapted. She waved it overhead and it cast a widening searchlight cone into the sky, but there was nothing up there, either, so she shined it back on the tree.

"It's gone."

"You sure?"

"No." Whatever had made that noise hadn't made a peep since. If it could move away silently, it would have approached silently.

She shined her light at the branch that had brushed the tank, a rubbery, maybe-hydraulic branch like the one that stayed put for a few seconds after she had flexed it. This one angled down from the trunk toward her, the tuft of greenery at its tip just a foot or so from the plastic.

She didn't remember any trees being that close before. In fact, she was nearly certain the closest one had been twenty or thirty feet away.

How had Sherlock Holmes put it? "When you've eliminated the impossible, whatever remains, however improbable, must be the truth." Something like that.

If that was the case, then the trees were sneaking up on them.

31

"I think it's the trees," Judy said.

"The trees?"

She risked a glance down into the tank. There was enough light reflecting off the fronds overhead to illuminate Allen's face in pale green. He was half out of his sleeping bag, hands hovering over the computer, its screen providing a bluish counterpoint to the green light from above.

"There's nothing else out here. And I'd swear one of 'em's closer than it was before." She looked back out, but nothing had moved since she'd switched on the light. At least she didn't think so. It was hard to wrap her mind around the concept that something like a tree *could* move. Millennia of evolution had hard-wired her brain to accept plants as part of the landscape, not as something that could walk around.

But that sucking sound . . . She shined the light down at the roots, and sure enough, she could see where they had pulled free of the ground. They lay on top of the soil now, but they were slowly working their way back into it, like earthworms in a freshly spaded garden. And behind the tree, thirty or forty feet back where Judy remembered one standing before, was an open spot with gouges in the mat of tiny fern where the roots had ripped free.

"Jesus," she said. "Have a look at this."

Allen popped open his hatch and pulled the second flashlight from its tape, then stood up and shined it out into the night.

"There," Judy said, aiming her beam at the roots and the torn-up ground behind them.

They watched the tree nestle into place. Judy kept an

eye on the branches, ready to duck if one of them took a swipe at her, but they stayed put.

Allen swept his light around in a circle. "Is it just that one?"

"I don't know. It's the only one I actually saw moving, but they all look closer to me."

"That could just be the light."

She supposed it could. All those shadows behind them made them look like they were leaning forward. And she didn't remember exactly where they were to begin with. It was like when she rearranged the furniture in her apartment; it was hard to remember how it looked before.

But the tree standing next to the *Getaway* was unmistakable. If it had been there when they landed, their parachute would have snagged in its branches. And they had seen its roots in motion.

It wasn't doing anything now. The branch that had brushed the side of the tank was still there, still stretched out toward them like the arm of a kid poking at an anthill with a stick. The tiny fronds at the end of it fluttered softly in the breeze—except the air was dead still.

"Hello?" Judy said. Her voice sounded small and flat.

She reached out to the end of the branch and gingerly touched a frond. It was soft, velvety, like a moth's wings. A little shudder passed through the entire tree, and the branch slowly rose back into the air to join the others.

This was totally outside Judy's realm of experience. "What now?" she asked.

"I don't know." Allen shined his light to either side, then turned and swept it behind him again, but none of the other trees had budged since he and Judy had switched on their lights.

The tree's roots had stopped moving. They weren't buried all the way in the ground, but it didn't look like it was going anyplace soon. Of course until a few minutes ago, Judy would have sworn it never *had* moved.

"I don't think we're being attacked," Allen said. "Do you?"

"No. It looks more like . . ."

"What?"

She had to struggle to say the words. This was a tree they were talking about! But she had heard it move, and had seen it anchor itself down again. And that outstretched branch. "I . . . I think it's just curious."

Allen took a deep breath, then nodded slowly. "I would be, if something dropped out of the sky right at my feet. But it's had all afternoon to check us out. How come it didn't do anything until now?"

"I have no idea."

They watched the tree for more signs of animation, but nothing moved. After maybe five minutes of standing there in the hatch holding a flashlight, her shoulders growing cold in the night air, Judy said, "I don't think it's going to do anything more."

"You want to go back to sleep?" Allen asked incredulously.

"No, but I don't want to stand here all night waiting for a tree to move, either. Let's try something else."

"Like what?"

"Well, it waited until we'd gone to bed before it moved before; let's try switching out the lights and hunkering down again. Maybe it'll think we've gone to sleep again and come a little closer."

Allen thought that over for a few seconds. "Do we want it to come closer?"

"I want it to do *something*."

He looked at the tree, then back at her again. "This is nuts, you know that?"

"You got a better idea?"

In lieu of an answer, he simply switched off his flashlight and ducked down so his head was even with the rim of the hatch. Judy did the same, dropping all the way down and hunting around in the dark until she found the pistol. It had fallen off the auxiliary hyperdrive into her spacesuit helmet. She pulled her sleeping bag up over her shoulders, leaving her feet free to move, and stood back up.

They waited. Five minutes seemed like forever. Ten became an eternity. She was just about convinced that they might as well settle back in to sleep when the tree made a soft creak like the noise of a door swinging open. Judy rose up just enough to look over the edge, but even with her eyes adapted to the dark again, there wasn't enough light to see more than faint shadows in the deeper darkness.

The creak sounded again, and this time she could tell it was coming from the ground. It grew louder until it became a rumble that could be felt as well as heard, then there was a slurp and a pop. A moment later the whole sequence repeated, then a third time, and a fourth.

Judy rested her thumb on the hammer of the pistol, ready to cock it and fire if the tree reached in through the hatch. She had no idea what part of its anatomy to shoot for, but from inside the tank she didn't exactly have a wide field of view to choose from. Fortunately she didn't have to try; the squelching noises picked up their pace and a dark shadow moved away overhead, leaving stars in its wake. The ground shook with heavy thumps, like the footsteps of a giant. Judy stood up a little higher, and as long as she didn't look straight at it, she could see motion in the darkness. Receding. The tree was running away.

There was a loud crash and a splintering of branches. Judy flipped on her flashlight just in time to see the tree smash headlong into one of the others that hadn't moved. It teetered, nearly falling over, then stretched out a root and caught itself. It lurched to the side, roots rippling like snakes and branches waving wildly for balance, and it staggered another couple of steps before coming to a stop.

"Turn that off!" Allen hissed.

"Why?" Judy asked, but she killed the light.

"Because I don't want it to come back and trample us, that's why."

"I don't think there's much chance of that," Judy said. "It's terrified of us."

"Yeah, right. That's why it stops every time we turn a light on it."

He had a point, but it wasn't necessarily the right one. "Maybe the light blinds it, and it doesn't want to move if it can't see."

"And maybe the light attracts it. Plants are phototropic, after all."

"Earth plants are." But she left her light off, straining to see by starlight alone.

The tree remained motionless for another minute or two, then, just as Judy thought to turn on the video cameras and see if they could pick up an image in this dim a light, it creaked to life again. She held her breath, gripping the pistol tight in her hand, but she relaxed when the tree thumped off deeper into the forest.

To heck with the video cameras. When they could no longer hear or feel the vibration from the tree's headlong flight, Judy flipped on her light again and shined it at the ground around the tank. The fern carpet was ripped up like a bus seat after a street gang had tagged it. She checked the base of the other trees, but they hadn't moved an inch.

"Well, that's a relief," she said softly. "At least all of 'em aren't mobile."

Allen sat back down inside the tank. "One is crazy enough. You happy now?"

"What's that supposed to mean?"

"You wanted strangeness. I'd say you got it."

She knelt down and put the gun on the bucket again, then tucked her feet into her sleeping bag and settled back against the wall. "I certainly can't complain."

There was a tiny flash of blue-green light from Allen's half of the tank: his wristwatch's backlight.

"What time is it?" she asked. She had taken her watch off when she'd settled in to sleep, and didn't want to hunt for it in the dark.

"About three."

"A.M.?"

"Yep."

It wasn't nearly that late local time, but it had already been afternoon when they'd left Rock Springs. They should have picked a landing spot closer to the night half of the planet if they'd wanted to keep their biorhythms in synch with the day/night cycle. Of course they had no idea how long this place's days were, so that might not have lasted through the night anyway.

It didn't matter. In her years as an astronaut, Judy had learned how to adjust to practically any schedule. As long as she got a couple hours of sleep for every ten or so she spent awake, she could function indefinitely.

She was falling behind tonight, but there were still hours of darkness to go. Provided no more inquisitive trees came to see who had landed in their midst, she should be okay.

Just as soon as her heart rate came down again.

32

The sun had just cleared the horizon when Judy woke. She stretched lazily as the first rays lit up the *Getaway*, then found her watch in the corner where she'd put it last night and checked the time. 10:38 A.M. Here was another dream come true: she'd found a planet where there were more than twenty-four hours in the day.

Allen was already awake and bustling around outside. Judy heard him muttering to himself, or so she thought at first, but then she heard the squawk of a radio and another voice answering him.

Tippet! He'd come back already!

She had never undressed last night; now she slid her sleeping bag down over her feet, put on her boots, and climbed out of the tank.

The air was chilly, but not so bad that she needed a coat. She looked at the trees, half expecting to see them all gathered in a circle around the *Getaway*, but they weren't. They were spaced evenly, their canopies giving each other plenty of room to collect sunlight, just like they had been yesterday. Judy couldn't find the one that the curious one had smashed into last night. None of them had broken branches or gaps in their foliage.

The ground cover had repaired itself, too. A couple of tons of tree running amok had ripped up the fern and left big gouges everywhere, but that was all smoothed over now and covered with fresh greenery. That stuff would be worth its weight in gold for no-maintenance lawns if it could be imported safely, but Judy doubted it could. Non-native plants that spread by seed or vine were bad enough; plants that actually picked up and walked from place to place would be an ecologist's nightmare.

Allen was sitting on the ground with his back against the big rock, holding the computer in his lap, and Tippet was standing on his right hand, riding the top knuckle of his index finger while he typed and manipulated the mouse pointer with his thumb on the glide pad.

"Good morning," Judy said, walking toward them.

Allen looked up at her with a big grin. She had seen that look on his face before, and she was just about to ask him what new kind of mischief he'd dreamed up when the radio—a walkie-talkie that he'd propped up on the rock beside him—crackled with momentary static, then a clear voice said, "Good morning, Judy. Allen and I have been discussing the Copenhagen interpretation of quantum mechanics and the ramifications of Bell's inequality. Would you care to join us?"

She stopped with one foot still upraised to take a step, then slowly lowered it to the fern. "You what?"

"Allen and I have been discussing the Copenhagen interpretation of quantum mechanics and the ramifications of Bell's inequality. Would you care to join us?"

There was a moment of silence while she tried to bring her brain up to speed, but Allen burst into laughter before she could think of a response that wouldn't make her sound like an idiot.

"Gotcha!" he said.

"What?"

"I just taught him to say that. He doesn't understand a word of it."

She resisted the urge to hit him. Tippet might think she was going for *him*. So she just stuck out her tongue at them both and sat down beside Allen. The fern was cool and damp underneath her butt, and the rock was cold against her back; she immediately wished she had brought her sleeping bag to sit on, but she ignored her discomfort and said, "So what else have you taught him?"

"Quite a bit, actually."

Allen pointed at the walkie-talkie, and Tippet said, "Radio." He pointed at his right foot, and Tippet said, "Boot."

"Right or left?" Allen asked.

"Right."

Then he pointed at the computer screen, and Tippet said, "Wheel."

Judy leaned over to see what was on the screen, and sure enough, it was a picture of a bicycle. Allen's finger rested on the front wheel.

"Where'd you get that?"

"The screen saver. It's got a ton of image files." Allen clicked the mouse pointer on the "Demo" button and the bicycle started pedaling itself around the screen.

"Roll," Tippet said.

"Yes, that's right. He's got nouns down cold," Allen said. "He picks 'em up as quick as I can display 'em. And he gets verbs almost as fast, once he realizes I'm interested in the action. I'm thinking of trying him on the alphabet and turning him loose with a dictionary."

He didn't sound like he was kidding. "You're serious?"

"Hey, it's worth a shot." Allen opened a text document and typed the word "Tree," then said it out loud: "Tree." He pointed at one for good measure.

Tippet did his little victory dance on the back of Allen's hand. "Yes," he said. "Understand."

Allen typed half a dozen other words, naming them as he did, then he pointed out the similar letters, sounding them out within the words. Tippet echoed the sounds, stumbling a little over long and short vowels, but it was clear that he was already familiar with the concept of writing.

Judy left them at it and went off to pee and freshen up as best she could without water. She stopped beside one of the trees and reached out cautiously to touch it, half expecting it to shy away like a nervous horse, but it stood there like any other tree. She laid her palm against its bark and felt for a pulse. None. The branches bent when she pulled on them, and lifted back into place slowly rather than springing up like an Earthly tree branch, but that was the only major difference she could see between it and any other bushy-looking palm.

She whacked the trunk with her hand, ready to leap away if that got a response, but it absorbed her blow with hardly a sound. A knife might get its attention, but she wasn't ready to try that yet. So she just hunkered down out of sight of Allen and Tippet and did her business, then went back to the *Getaway* and dug around in the grocery bag until she found a couple of apples and a can of beans. It was the most breakfast-like food they had brought with them unless she wanted to cook potatoes, which she didn't. Not without some water to clean up with afterward. She looked at the three remaining cans of beer, but left them where they were. The apples would have to be enough liquid for now.

She took the food back outside and gave one of the apples to Allen, then opened the can with her Swiss army knife and stuck a spoon in the beans. Tippet learned the names for everything while they ate, and Allen spelled out the words for him.

"We've got to go get some water today," Judy said.

Allen nodded. "Yeah. Maybe we can carry the computer with us and keep up the language lesson while we do it."

"Have you asked him about the trees?" she asked. "Is it safe to walk around in the forest?"

"I tried, but we got hung up in the vocabulary. He doesn't seem to get it when I talk about them moving around."

"Hmm. That's kind of strange. Maybe it's not all that common."

"Or it's so common he doesn't get what I'm asking about. When I told him one of the trees was checking us out last night, maybe he was like, 'So?'"

"Maybe. Well, we didn't get eaten yesterday, and we've got to get some water if we want to stick around, so I think we're going to have to risk it."

"Yeah. Let's see if we can get that idea across to him." Allen switched the computer display to the screen saver again and searched through the image files until he found a picture of a stream. "Water," he said.

"Water," Tippet echoed through the walkie-talkie.

"Judy and Allen go water," Allen said.

Tippet thought about that for a moment, then said, "Judy go water before dark."

She blushed. He'd recorded it, too. "Not that kind of water," she said. "We need fresh water. To drink." She mimed scooping some up in the empty bean can and drinking from it. "New water."

"What is new?"

Oh boy. How could she get that across to him? She fished in her pocket for some coins, thinking she might have a shiny one and a worn one that she could use for comparison, but she didn't have a cent on her. She looked around her, thought about using rocks, but there were too many other interpretations. Apples? Sure! Allen hadn't eaten his yet—he was too busy playing with the computer—but she'd wolfed hers down in about six bites. She picked up the gnawed core that she'd set on ground beside her and said, "Old apple," then she picked up Allen's whole one and said, "New apple."

Tippet said, "Maybe understand. Before dark is old day; this light is new day?" His voice over the radio even got the inflection right to make it a question.

"Got it!" she said. "We go get new water."

"Got it," Tippet echoed.

They didn't have canteens or bottles or even Ziploc bags to carry it in. Judy climbed back inside the *Getaway* and dug through their equipment for anything that would work, but the best things she could come up with were the empty beer and bean cans. She and Allen would drink that much just walking back from the river.

She eyed the white plastic bucket that housed the auxiliary hyperdrive engine. They had drilled holes in the lid for wires to pass through, but they had intentionally left the bucket intact just in case they needed it. And five gallons would be enough water for a couple of days, if they could just carry it back without killing themselves. That would be the trick.

Unless . . . "Hey." She stood up and stuck her head out through the hatch. "Allen, ask him if there's any water closer than the river."

He looked up from the computer. "Oh. Sure. Good idea. Tippet, where is the closest water?"

"Closest?" Tippet asked.

Allen answered by pointing at trees. "Far. Closer. Closest." He repeated it with pebbles to make sure it was clear he was talking about the concept of distance, and not something to do with trees.

"Closest water?" Tippet asked. "Not understand."

"We want to know where it is. Where closest water?" Allen pointed around in a wide arc. "Where closest water?"

"*Tppppt* understand question. Not understand where closest water. You tell *Tppppt*."

Judy frowned. "He lives here and he doesn't know where the creeks are? That seems odd."

Allen said, "Maybe he doesn't drink water. Or maybe he doesn't live nearby. He could be from way out in the plains for all we know." He turned back to the butterfly. "Where do you live?"

"Live?"

"Where you go when the sun sets?"

"You go water when sun set?"

"Oh, bugger. Too many concepts at once. No, no. We go water now, but we don't know where water is."

Tippet flexed his wings. "Don't is not? You not know?"

"Got it. We're new here."

"You . . . new?"

"That's right. We just got here yesterday. We live on a planet that goes around another star."

That was too much all at once. "Stop," said Tippet. "Slower. What is planet? What is star?"

Judy laughed. "You got yourself into it that time."

But Allen did an amazing job of explaining elementary

astronomy in just a few words. He waved his hands all around, touched the ground, then pointed at the sky, saying, "This, this, this, far, near, everything; this big, big, big rock is a planet. Understand? Trees, rocks, air, everything together is the planet."

Tippet caught on fast. "Planet is *skkkkp*. Big rock, fly around sun."

"Right! And the lights in the sky at night; those are stars."

"Stars are suns far away."

"That's right. Good, you know that already. We live on a planet that flies around another star."

Tippet tilted all his wings toward the *Getaway Special*, its wooden framework and reinforcing cables giving it more the appearance of an outhouse on its side than an interstellar spacecraft. "I not understand as much as I think I do. You live there, yes?"

"No, no. That's what brought us here. That's our spaceship. We climb inside, go from star to star very fast."

Tippet mulled that over for a few seconds, then said, "No. Big far lot many no."

The look on Allen's face was priceless. He'd invented hyperdrive, built a spaceship, and flown it to another star, but even the aliens weren't impressed. He stammered, "It's—it's true! We did!" but Tippet wasn't having any of it.

"No go from star to star," the butterfly said. "Not in that."

Judy laughed. She knew just how he felt. But there was an easy way to prove it, and it didn't even involve a demonstration. Not of the hyperdrive anyway. She merely reached down to her feet and extricated her helmet from the pile of stuff there, set it on the top of the tank between her hatch and Allen's, then tugged the rest of her spacesuit out as well. She had to climb out first and drag it through the hatch behind her, then lower it to the ground.

Tippet was totally silent while she split open the waist ring, stepped into the legs, wriggled into the top, and rejoined the two pieces. She put the helmet over her head and locked it down as well, then stepped away from the *Getaway* and did a slow pirouette.

She pulled off the helmet again. No sense in wasting oxygen. "This is my spacesuit," she said.

Tippet had taken out his camera. He flew up and filmed her from all angles, then landed on her right shoulder and focused on the inside of her helmet as well. His walkie-talkie voice said simply, "Spacesuit."

"Right. It holds air when I'm in space. Way up high above the sky, there's no air. We call that space. You understand space?"

Tippet did a little dance. "Understand space? Understand space? *Skkkkt*."

He flew back to the computer on Allen's lap, set his camera down on the "H" key, and said, "Watch."

Judy knelt down until her face was only a couple feet away. Allen was already that close. Tippet stood there on the keyboard for a few seconds, not moving a muscle, then just as Judy was about to say, "Well, what are we supposed to see?" he reached up with his forelegs and pulled off his head.

Except he still had a head. It was a smaller one, wrinkled and dark like a raisin, and for a horrible moment Judy wondered if that was his brain, but then Tippet popped the smooth yellow bulb back over it and gave it a twist and the picture came clear.

"He's wearing a spacesuit too," she whispered.

"Son of a bitch," said Allen.

Tippet's radio voice squawked and honked for a few seconds while his suit refilled with his own air, then he gave a very human-sounding snuffle and said, "*Tppppt* understand space. *Tppppt* live in space! Whole life in space, move slow from star to star."

Judy looked at the tiny butterfly standing there all aquiver on the laptop computer keyboard. His whole body barely covered four keys. How could something that small be an interstellar astronaut, especially on a ship that actually traversed every kilometer between stars? The energy required to accelerate to a useful velocity and to decelerate when he reached his destination would be enormous.

Of course the smaller the payload, the less energy it would take, but still. It would require controlled nuclear fusion at the very least, and probably total conversion of matter to energy to make it practical. The image of butterflies fooling around with those kind of elemental forces seemed ludicrous.

But he was wearing a pressure suit, or at least an environment suit, and there would be no reason for that if he'd evolved here.

"Well, that explains why he doesn't know where the watering holes are," Judy said. She was trying to decide whether this was good news or bad news. Finding intelligent aliens was one thing, but finding another spacefaring race opened up a whole different can of worms. For instance, if Tippet had come here slower than light, that implied a higher level of technology than humanity's. Earth had been at least a century away from being able to field a sublight interstellar vessel before Allen changed the rules. There was no need for that particular kind of ship now, but the technology behind it was still well beyond what humanity had. Maybe beyond what they would ever have, if Carl Reinhardt was right. But Tippet and his people had already done it.

Suddenly he didn't seem so small and cute as he had before.

"Where's your spaceship?" she asked.

He was still recovering from his dose of air. "What is . . ." *sniff* ". . . spaceship?"

Judy pointed at the corrugated yellow *Getaway*. "That. Spaceship is where you live while you move from star to star."

Tippet took a few seconds to reply. Maybe he was parsing out what she'd said, or maybe he was just trying to convince himself that a yellow plastic tank could be a spaceship. At last he said, "*Tppppt* spaceship above sky. Go around planet in space. Understand?"

"It's in orbit," Allen said. "Sure. Go around planet in space is orbit. How many more of you are up there? How many Tippets on spaceship?"

Tippet said, "Lot many, but number not matter. Same *Tppppt* there. All one *Tppppt*."

"Oh."

Oh, indeed. Judy hadn't considered that possibility. She wondered how that worked, if it was some kind of clone-style gestalt where all the separate little Tippets added together to make one big organism, or if there was a queen who controlled all the little worker Tippets. She wanted to ask, but she didn't have the vocabulary for it.

"We've got to learn how to communicate better," she said. "And unfortunately, we've got to go get water today, too."

"Maybe not," Allen said. "How about your landing craft?" He held out his hand and made rocket noises while he brought it to the ground. "Landing craft. Comes down from spaceship. Where is your landing craft?"

Tippet tilted all his wings to the left. "There. South. Lot fly south."

"That's the same direction the river's in. Can you bring water here in your landing craft?"

Again it took him a few seconds to answer. Judy had assumed he was just thinking when that happened, but now she wondered if he was receiving a translation from some supercomputer in orbit. Or instructions from the queen. "No," he said. "Landing craft only come down. Not fly again."

Allen said, "Oh. Then how do you get back up to your ship?"

"Not go back. *Tppppt* stay."

"You're setting up a colony here?"

"Not understand."

"A colony. That's when you live here, build houses, have children, and . . . never mind. We'll talk about that later."

"Not understand," Tippet said again. There was no change in his tone of voice, but something felt different than it had a minute ago. Maybe it was just the longer pause between responses, or maybe the change was in Judy's reaction to what he said. Learning just how technologically advanced he was had changed the picture for her considerably.

"Learn more words," Tippet said. "Show me new words."

"Right." The computer's screen had timed out and gone blank; Allen reached around Tippet and tapped it on again. "Let's see if this thing's got a dictionary."

•   •   •

Judy removed the spare hyperdrive from the five-gallon bucket, nestling its unprotected wad of circuitry into a hollow in her beanbag chair. She put a couple more apples and the cheese they hadn't eaten yesterday and a can of chicken noodle soup into her stuff sack, plus the spare walkie-talkie in case something happened to the first one. She stuck the portable camp stove and a cook pot in the sack, too, so they could boil the soup and any water they drank on the way home, and she put in all three remaining cans of beer in case they didn't make it to water. She was getting tired of carrying the pistol everywhere she went—it had to weigh a couple of pounds—but she remembered the tree running amok last night, so she tucked it in her waistband. Who knew what they might find today?

She put the stuff sack in the bucket, climbed out of the *Getaway* and pulled the hatches closed behind her, then the three interstellar explorers set off for the river.

The forest was just as they had seen it yesterday: frond-topped trees standing well apart, with the occasional bush interspersed among them and fern-grass blanketing the ground. There was no motion while they walked through, no sense that anything was even aware of their presence. If she hadn't seen a tree in motion last night, Judy would have sworn nothing had moved here for years. The place had a timeless, static feel to it, like a movie set on a soundstage. Even the sky seemed painted on, with only a couple of tiny clouds drifting over the mountains to the west.

Judy navigated while Allen held the computer and scrolled the dictionary up the screen one definition at a time for Tippet, who stood on the spacebar and filmed it with his video camera, presumably relaying the image directly to the mothership overhead. Judy wondered if that was such a good idea—after all, words like "war" and "genocide" were in there along with all the others—but there didn't seem to be much choice. It was either turn him loose to learn at his own rate, or teach him a word at a time the way they'd been doing and watch their tongues around him forever after.

She'd had enough experience trying to hide stuff from her parents to know how well that worked.

At least Tippet wasn't reading an encyclopedia. Not yet. But at the rate he was plowing through the dictionary, he might very well graduate to an encyclopedia within the hour. Of course there was a difference between uploading the language and learning how to speak it, but in Tippet's case that wasn't as big a gulf as it would have been for Judy or Allen. He seemed to have a natural aptitude for language, or a translation program on line that could assemble the pieces of an alien tongue in seconds. He would pause in his filming every now and then and the walkie-talkie at Allen's waist would crackle to life with a question about verb tenses or parts of speech or grammar, and the questions grew more complex each time.

The defining moment, as it was, came when he reached "Zymurgy," stared at the blank screen below it for a moment, then said, "That was very illuminating. But it leaves several questions unanswered. Specifically, what is Copenhagen? And what is the significance of unequal bells?"

"What?" asked Allen, nearly dropping the computer in surprise.

Tippet leaped into the air until he got it under control, then landed again and said, "Do we not use the words correctly? We have inferred the rules of grammar from usage examples within the dictionary and from the recordings I have taken of your speech. We believe our comprehension to be extensive, if not exhaustive, but perhaps we are mistaken."

"No, you've . . . you've got it right. But I don't—"

" 'Good morning, Judy. Allen and I have been discussing the Copenhagen interpretation of quantum mechanics and the ramifications of Bell's inequality. Would you care to join us?' This is what you taught me to say this morning, is it not? We understand quantum physics, but this dictionary does not list 'Copenhagen,' nor any definition of 'bell' that would elucidate the greeting."

Allen blushed. "I . . . that was a joke. I just had you say it to surprise Judy."

"Ah. Humor. Specifically the prank, or perhaps the practical joke. We understand. We see. We comprehend, follow, get, make out, take in, catch, conceive, grasp, fathom, compass, and grok. Ha, ha, ha."

34

It was an easy walk to the river. For one thing, they were crossing the foothills to the mouth of the canyon this time rather than climbing up into the mountains, but they could have been scaling a cliff and Judy would hardly have noticed the effort. Now that they could actually talk with Tippet, the floodgates burst open on both sides, and they peppered each other with questions.

This was the fourth port of call for Tippet's ship, but the first habitable planet. He had been growing discouraged as star after star proved barren of life, but when he had arrived here, he had been ecstatic, even when he discovered that the atmosphere held too much oxygen for him to breathe safely.

Judy had been thinking of Tippet as "him" since their first meeting—either out of habit or because her subconscious mind thought only a male would take pictures of a woman urinating—but the concept of "him" versus "them" proved even more slippery than gender. There were thousands of individual Tippets on board the ship, and hundreds of them on the planet's surface, but they weren't all autonomous. They could be for short periods of time when abstract thought wasn't required, but even then they would link with the others every few hours to share their experiences. And when they needed to solve a problem, they could all join into a single intelligence far greater than the sum of its individual parts.

"That's how you learned English so fast," Allen said when he heard that.

"Partially," Tippet replied. "Even our combined intellect would have taken days to assimilate all the concepts, so we enhanced it artificially. Our mind is less than half biological at the moment."

"Jesus," Judy said softly. "Committees that are actually smarter than their individual members. And plug-in intelligence to boost it even further. If you could teach humanity that trick, you could name your price."

"I suspect you would have to evolve the brain structures for linking first, but we can investigate the possibility."

That led to a discussion of trade, and what each had to offer the other. Judy suggested music, then had to sing a song to demonstrate what she meant. She felt totally self-conscious, especially knowing that this would be the first exposure to Earth music for an entire race, but she took a deep breath and sang the Beatles' "With a Little Help From My Friends." She picked it for the opening line about singing out of tune, but the deeper she got into it, the more appropriate it seemed for the whole situation. Themes of loneliness, friendship, and love wove all through the song. After the first verse, Allen joined in and sang harmony, and she lost her embarrassment and gave it a lilting, happy tone that carried them all the way through to the end, which they stretched out until they burst into giggles and gasped for air.

"Wonderful!" Tippet said, and he clapped his wings together in silent applause. "We have music, but ours is very different. We use a sixteen-tone scale, and since our language is not verbal, all of our compositions are instrumental."

"Not verbal?" Allen asked. "How do you communicate?"

"Directly through our neural link when we are in physical contact; otherwise by radio, but even then we send and receive the same nerve impulses that we would use directly."

"You mean you learned a totally alien *concept* of language as well as the vocabulary when you learned English?"

"Not entirely. We have audiolingual species on our world as well."

"Hey," Judy said. "Before we get sidetracked into that, I want to hear one of your songs."

Tippet hesitated a moment, then said, "We will have to lower it in frequency for you to hear it. Some of the nuances will be lost. But here is one that might interest you."

The walkie-talkie had the acoustic fidelity of a rotting stump, but the foreignness of the music came through even so. It sounded all electronic, like experimental synthesizer music full of buzzes and beeps and warbling sine waves, and the notes were too close together. Judy kept waiting for a satisfying resolution, but measure after measure left her hanging, almost but not quite reaching the note that would have concluded the phrase. When the song ended, maybe ten minutes after it began, she had to hum the final note to keep from going nuts with frustrated expectation.

"Yes!" Tippet said. "You understand!"

"It's supposed to end like that?"

"Yes. That was called 'The Solitary Scout.' An isolated explorer searches, and occasionally finds novelties, but without a hive to share them with, cannot find resolution."

"That sounds like your own experience. Did you make it up just now?"

"No. We composed it on board the ship on the way here from the last star we visited."

We composed it. Judy wondered how many Tippets he was talking about. Did something like that take the entire hive mind, or was it the work of a few individuals? Just how smart were these guys on their own? She supposed it didn't really matter if they could link up when they needed to boost their brainpower. God, what an advantage that would give them!

She wondered if there was an upper limit. The fact that they hadn't discovered hyperdrive implied that there was, but even so, Tippet's upgradable intellect scared the hell out of her. What if his race weren't the easygoing xenophiles they seemed to be? If they came into conflict with Earth, would humanity even have a chance?

The back of her neck prickled. She tried to tell herself she was being silly, but she couldn't calm down, and the farther they got from the *Getaway Special*, the worse the feeling became. She told herself it was just fear of being stranded on an alien planet, but she knew that wasn't it. She hadn't felt this way yesterday when she and Allen had hiked up the ridge. This was a much more focused anxiety, centered directly on Tippet and his hive-mates overhead.

They were almost to the river before she realized why: Tippet hadn't asked about the hyperdrive.

Allen was busy talking with him about the natural harmonic overtones of a vibrating string, but he must have seen her stiffen in shock, because he suddenly turned to her and said, "What's wrong?"

"Nothing," she lied. "I, um, I just understood something for the first time, that's all."

"Oh." He ducked his head in a little shrug of pleased acknowledgment. "Glad to have been of service." He turned back to Tippet. "So the second overtone gives us what we call the dominant note in the musical scale, and the fourth gives us the mediant, which I'll bet are the very same notes you use for your sixth and tenth in your sixteen-note scale . . ."

Judy glanced over her shoulder while he babbled happily on. She didn't see anything but forest and blue sky, and she hadn't heard any rocket engines or sonic booms from decelerating spacecraft, but how big would a landing craft full of Tippets need to be? It could decelerate way the hell up in the upper atmosphere and glide down the rest of the way and she would never notice.

Maybe she was just being paranoid, but she and Allen had left the *Getaway* unattended, with the hyperdrive not just there for the nosy but spread out on her beanbag chair like an exhibit in a museum. She could imagine a whole army of butterflies busily studying it while she and Allen were away. Hell, last night's curious *tree* could have come back and learned the secret by now.

The pistol in her waistband mocked her with its useless weight. Humanity's most valuable discovery since the wheel lay open for grabs a couple miles away, and there was nothing she could do about it.

She would have turned around and gone back, but if Tippet hadn't thought of stealing it, she didn't want to give him the idea. Besides, she could hear running water up ahead. They had nearly reached the river; they might as well get what they came for and head back with a full bucket.

The forest grew denser the closer they drew to the river. The competition for water apparently overrode whatever evolutionary signals kept the trees spaced so generously up in the hills. There were a lot more low bushes to contend with, too, sometimes blocking their path in long, heavily entwined rows, but Tippet took to the air and directed Judy and Allen through the maze until they were able to scramble down the last few dozen feet of bank to the streambed.

It was heavily shaded down there. Big, stately trees hugged the bank, stretching their branches out over the river, which looked to be about thirty feet across and two or three feet deep. It was still moving fast on its way out of the mountains; the roar of water cascading over boulders made it hard to hear Tippet's voice on the walkie-talkie, and Judy and Allen had to shout to make themselves heard even a few feet away from one another.

Judy didn't bother trying. She just pried the lid off the bucket, took her stuff sack out, dipped the bucket in the stream—

—and the next thing she knew she was in the water. She screamed in surprise, got a mouthful of ice cold snowmelt that she swallowed before she could stop herself, then smacked her shoulder into a rock.

She didn't let go of the bucket. The water was freezing and the same shoulder clipped another rock as she thrashed around trying to get her feet under her, but she kept a death-grip on the handle. She wasn't about to lose it now. She had walked all morning to fill that bucket, and in the process left the hyperdrive unguarded for anyone who came along to steal it; she wasn't going to compound her ineptitude by going back empty-handed.

The rocks were at least rounded from erosion. Judy caromed off one after another, bouncing along like a boulder herself while the bucket dragged her downstream like a parachute in the wind. She pulled it up against her stomach and rolled over it, bringing her head out of the water for a second before she tumbled on around.

"Judy!"

She gasped a quick breath and saw Allen reaching for her, but when she stretched out an arm for him to grab, there was still a foot of space between their fingers.

She went under again, rolled sideways, and managed to get her feet beneath her. Momentum carried her upright, and even though she knew the reaction would push her even farther into the stream, she flung the bucket toward the bank.

Water sprayed out in a wide fan as it flew through the air. Judy had just enough time to think *Good, it will hit the ground empty* before she lost her footing and splashed into the stream again.

The current carried her around a boulder the size of the *Getaway*, then dropped her into the pool in the lee of it. She swirled around a time or two before she found her footing again, then braced herself with her legs wide apart and stood up.

"Yeeeow!" she screamed, flinging her head backward to throw her wet hair out of her face. "God, this is cold!"

Allen was scrambling over tree roots to reach the point on the bank opposite her. "Are you all right?" he shouted.

"I think so." She looked at the torrent that rushed past between them. The swath of white water was at least eight feet across: too far to jump even if she wasn't thigh-deep in a pool. If she tried to swim it, she would just get swept even farther downstream, and there were a couple more boulders down there she would just as soon not hit.

But she had to do something before she froze to death. She was already growing numb; it wouldn't take long before she lost control of her legs and went under again. And besides, who knew what lived in the water?

She looked up at the canopy of branches overhead, but they were way too high for her to reach. No vines, either.

And of course there were no dead sticks on the bank for Allen to pull her to shore with. The forest was as clean here as everywhere else.

Tippet fluttered up to one of the branches overhead. Allen followed Judy's gaze, then suddenly crouched down and leaped. For an instant she thought he was going for Tippet, but he grabbed the branch a foot past where the butterfly stood. Tippet sprang into the air, and the branch flexed under Allen's weight, but he did a quick hand-over-hand until he hung out over the water.

"Be careful!" Judy shouted.

He didn't reply, just kept coming one grip at a time, the branch swaying up and down with the motion until his feet bobbed up and down in front of her.

"Grab on!"

"I'll pull you in!"

"No you won't. Grab on! Hurry!"

There wasn't much choice. The branch was slowly drooping under his weight; if she didn't do something, he would wind up in the drink with her. She reached up and took hold of his ankles, but instead of adding her weight to his, she pushed upward instead, using his weight to push her feet firmly against the streambed while she walked across to the bank.

He kept pace with her, pulling himself along hand-over-hand above her and helping her steady herself when her feet slipped on the smooth rocks. When he made it to the trunk he let her drag herself onto dry ground before he let go and collapsed beside her, panting heavily.

"Are you okay?" he asked.

Judy felt her shoulder where it had hit the rocks. There would be a hell of a bruise there, but it didn't feel broken.

"Other than feeling like a total idiot, I think I'm fine. What a dumb shit! I might as well have pitched an anchor in instead of that bucket. Hell, I'd have been better off with an anchor; it wouldn't have carried me so far downstream."

Tippet flew down to land on a rock beside her. The walkie-talkie at Allen's waist crackled with his voice, but

Judy couldn't hear the words. At the moment she didn't care. She just stood up, gave Allen a hand up as well, then squelched over the tree roots to the bucket. It lay on its side in the crevice between a root and a rock, undamaged. She picked it up and braced herself against the root, then dipped it cautiously into the water and lifted it out full, straining against its weight.

Allen helped her stand up with it, then he retrieved the computer and her stuff sack while she snapped the lid on tight.

"Let me carry that," he said, holding out the lighter equipment for her.

"No," she said. "I can get it. Let's just go. I need to get back in the sunlight before I freeze."

"What?" He bent closer.

"I've got it! Let's go!"

"Okay." He started up the bank, and as soon as Tippet realized what they were doing, he flew up ahead of them to lead the way.

When they could hear one another again, Tippet said, "Are you sure you are unharmed? You received several blows that would have killed a being of your size from my planet."

"I'm fine," Judy replied. "I'm more worried about the water I swallowed when I went under." She set the bucket down on the ground at the top of the steep incline, then took a couple of steps away and shook like a dog. Allen's eyes nearly bugged out of his head when she did that, and she realized that her shirt was clinging to her body. She shook again just to taunt him, but she certainly didn't feel sexy at the moment. In fact, the thought of alien microorganisms swimming around in her stomach made her feel like throwing up, but years of astronaut training had given her a steady stomach. She could probably make herself do it if she had to, but she already felt miserable enough as it was, and she didn't imagine it would do much good anyway. Liquids didn't stay in the stomach long; if she'd swallowed anything dangerous, it was already spreading through her intestines.

"Do you know anything about what lives in the water?" she asked Tippet.

"I have tested samples of it for lifeforms," he said. "There are several different types of single- and multi-celled organisms, none of which are inimical to my health, but I don't know what their effect will be on you."

"Inimical? Is that a word?"

"I believe so. Did I not use it correctly?"

"I don't know. I've never heard it before."

"The dictionary defines it as 'injurious or harmful in effect.' It seemed the most appropriate word for the situation."

"It probably is," Judy said. "I just never learned that one." She felt a little embarrassed to admit it. An alien who'd only learned the language an hour ago had a better vocabulary than a native speaker. He had no idea which words were common and which were obscure, but he knew every shade of meaning available. And what more did he know from reading between the lines?

She couldn't shake her unease at his mental capacity, especially now that she stood before him dripping wet after a stupid mistake that could have gotten her killed. A mistake that could kill her yet if the alien bacteria proved deadly. His impression of the human race couldn't be good, and she wasn't doing anything to help it out.

She checked the pistol, still tucked in her waistband. It was as wet as everything else, but she bet it would still fire if she needed it. It had the look of something that could take a lot of abuse and still work.

Hah. Their weapons technology was probably the one thing humanity possessed that would impress Tippet's people, and that was exactly the wrong kind of impression to give them.

She lifted the bucket again. Gah. Forty pounds. Maybe a little less here, but in a mile it would feel like eighty. If they had a pole to run through the handle, she and Allen could carry it on their shoulders, but she had seen no dead branches in the entire forest, and the live ones acted more like rubber hoses than branches. Besides which, she didn't know how to tell a mobile tree from a regular one—assuming *any* of them were normal trees. Cutting off a branch could be like amputating an arm.

Neither she nor Allen could carry the bucket far alone, though. She set it down again and said, "Let's try both grabbing the handle. Maybe we can carry it between us." She took the stuff sack from him, leaving him with the computer in his left hand and his right hand free to help carry the water.

It was awkward at first, but they soon discovered that it worked better if they leaned outward and walked in step on alternate feet. When they did that, they fell into a smooth gait that let the bucket glide along between them without jostling or even swinging much.

They had to sidle around clumps of bushes at first, but within a few minutes they had cleared the thicket around the river and had smooth sailing back home. Tippet called out directions, not even flying up above the trees to get his bearings as Judy would have expected, but doing it either by dead reckoning or by using some internal navigation equipment.

She felt her stomach rumble within the first quarter mile, but she didn't suggest stopping to fix lunch. If that rumble wasn't just hunger, she wanted to be as close to the *Getaway* as possible before she got sick. And the less time they left the hyperdrive unattended, the better she would feel.

For the first time since this whole business had started, she understood why the governments of every nation on Earth had reacted the way they did. They might be glad to have the secret for themselves, but they were afraid, just as she was, that others couldn't be trusted with it. Her definition of "other" was a little more broad than theirs, but it all came down to the same thing: fear. She didn't like what it said about her, or about humanity in general.

She wondered if Allen was having the same doubts. He had wanted to give his discovery to everyone on Earth, but did that generosity and trust extend to aliens, too? *Should* it? Judy could argue both sides of that question, but she knew the safe answer.

Tippet undoubtedly did, too, but he was either too polite or too circumspect to mention it. He chattered on like a child about his explorations since he had arrived here—only a few days before Judy and Allen, it turned out—and he asked endless questions about human society and life on Earth, but he steered clear of the hyperdrive.

They made it a mile or so back the way they had come

before Allen called a halt, saying, "I've got to drink something or I'm going to fall over."

He hadn't had the inadvertent mouthful of water Judy had gotten in the river. That and her anxiety over leaving the *Getaway* unguarded had kept her going, but he was operating on a single apple for breakfast.

"Time for a break," she admitted.

They set the bucket down and got a beer out of the stuff sack. Allen popped the top and drank half of it in one go, then handed it to Judy, who took a more cautious sip and handed it back. She dug out the cheese and tore off a hunk for each of them, then said to Tippet, "What about you? Can you eat or drink any of this?"

He had been riding on Allen's right shoulder while they walked. For a moment Allen thought she was talking to him, and he said, "Of course I—oh," just as Tippet said, "I have my own food supply, but thank you for the offer."

"How long can you go in that environment suit before you have to resupply?"

"That depends on my exertion level. With you carrying me, I can last two days before dipping into emergency reserves. Otherwise I must return to my lander every night."

"Oh. You, uh, want to spend the night with us, then?"

"If you are amenable to that, yes. It would allow us more time to get to know one another. And perhaps I will see the mobile tree you discovered last night."

Judy laughed. "It discovered *us*, and I'm not sure if I want it to come back, but you're welcome to hang out with us and see if it does."

"You haven't seen any of them move before?" Allen asked.

"No," Tippet replied. "I have not seen any ambulatory lifeforms since I got here, other than you."

They must not be all that common, then, Judy thought. She wasn't sure whether to be relieved or disappointed. Mobile plants were definitely the sort of exotic life she'd wanted to find, but a full-sized tree could be dangerous to someone her size even if it wasn't hostile.

She glanced over at Tippet, still riding on Allen's shoulder. Was that how he felt about her? Or did the existence of the hive mind reduce his individual fear of mortality? She couldn't think of a delicate way to ask him. *Are you afraid of me?* Not good. The only thing worse would be to ask, *So, what's it like to be so small?*

She and Allen finished their beer and cheese and picked up the water bucket again. It seemed to have doubled in weight just sitting there, but after a few hundred steps it was no worse than before. If nothing else, exploring was going to keep her and Allen in good shape.

They were puffing too hard to talk much, but Tippet regaled them with more stories of his exploits, describing the land to the south of the river and the vegetation he had found near his landing site there. He was telling them about the different kinds of bushes he had found in the drier badlands to the east when he suddenly stopped speaking.

"Tippet?" Allen asked. Judy looked down at the walkie-talkie on his hip, thinking maybe the battery had suddenly died, but the power light was still glowing red.

"Wait," Tippet said. "Something . . . happen . . . in space."

Allen stopped walking. Judy took another step before she realized he wasn't keeping up with her, and nearly wrenched her arm before she could let go of the bucket. It hit the ground with a thump and tipped sideways, but the lid held. A handful of water glugged out of the holes in the lid, but Allen righted it and turned his attention to Tippet, "What's the matter?"

"Wait. Not sure. Mind . . . busy now."

Judy immediately imagined some kind of onboard disaster going on overhead. A fire, or a blowout, or a leaking fuel tank; in space, there were a million dangers just waiting to happen at any moment. Whatever it was, it was apparently demanding enough of the hive mind's attention that there wasn't any to spare for its members on the ground.

Tippet's wings quivered, and Judy realized she was shivering as well. Some of that was from her clothing, which was still damp even now, but not all of it.

"Can we do anything?" she asked, but she already knew the answer. They were still at least a mile from the *Getaway*. By the time they could get there and get into orbit, whatever was happening on board Tippet's ship would be over.

"Wait," Tippet said again. "Wait. Linking . . . again. Oh."

"What? What's happening?"

"Another spaceship has suddenly appeared in orbit."

36

"What kind of ship?" Judy asked. "What does it look like?"

"Not like yours," Tippet said. "This is much larger and more streamlined. It's cylindrical, with one rounded end and one tapered end. It has a single large fin about a third of the way from the blunt end, and four smaller fins spaced equally around its circumference near the narrow end."

She tried to visualize it, and came up with a ballistic missile. Had someone converted a Titan or a Minuteman into an interstellar spaceship? But the guidance fins were on the wrong end for that, and what was the extra fin on the side?

Allen laughed. "Does it have a propeller on the narrow end?"

"A propeller?" replied Tippet. "In space?"

"If it's what it sounds like, then it wasn't built for space. I think it's a submarine."

Judy flashed on the image of a sub suddenly jumping from the ocean into vacuum, carrying a sphere of water a couple hundred feet in diameter along with it. That must have been a sight. The water would instantly start to boil, throwing off a cloud of vapor kilometers across, but the loss of heat would freeze the middle of the sphere solid long before it all boiled away. The sub would be encased in ice until the sun melted it off, which would probably create a comet bright enough to be seen by day. That must have turned some heads back home.

Tippet considered Allen's guess for a few seconds, then said, "It does seem well adapted to maneuvering in water.

But why would a submarine be used in space? How *could* it be used in space?"

Judy picked up the bucket and started walking again. Allen quickly joined her, saying, "It actually makes a lot of sense when you think about it. It's already airtight. And it's designed to hold up against enormous pressure from outside, so the hull is more than strong enough to withstand one atmosphere pushing outward from inside."

"Yes, but how did it get into space? How did it get *here*?"

"Hyperdrive," Allen said.

"That word isn't in the dictionary."

"It means faster-than-light travel."

Tippet made a hissing sound; part of his link with the hive mind leaking onto the audio channel? Or maybe it was deliberate commentary, because his next words were: "That's impossible."

"That's what I thought, too," said Allen, "until I figured out how to do it."

"You? Individually?"

Allen beamed. "That's right."

"I have a hard enough time believing that your '*Getaway Special*' is actually a spaceship," Tippet said. "Believing that it travels faster than light is . . . considerably more difficult."

So he hadn't accepted their story when they'd told him they had traveled from another star in it. Judy wondered if that meant his companions had left it alone these last few hours. If they hadn't thought there was anything valuable there, maybe so.

But he was hot on the topic now. "How does it work?" he asked.

Judy cleared her throat in as theatrical a manner as she could. Allen looked over at her, and she shook her head slightly, but he just frowned at her and said to Tippet, "Do you understand quantum tunneling?"

There was a long pause, then Tippet said, "Yes. Enough to know that the effect cannot be applied to large objects."

Allen nodded vigorously. "That's true. But it can be applied to a lot of small ones at once. That's how I made the electron plasma battery, and then I got to thinking about what would happen if I tried tunneling everything, not just electrons, and giving them a little kick on their way from point A to point B. When I tried it, I discovered that you can make the barrier arbitrarily large. Light-years across, if you want."

Tippet didn't reply. Maybe Allen's explanation was too full of unfamiliar technical terms.

He apparently thought the same thing. Before Judy could think of something to say that would steer the conversation in another direction, he said, "Did you follow that?"

"Theoretically. As I said, believing it is difficult, even when faced with physical evidence of its veracity."

Judy said, "Have you tried talking to the sub yet?"

Tippet took another few seconds to answer. Judy wondered if these pauses were simply because the hive mind was busy on other fronts, or if it was mulling over its answers before it gave them its reply. Had it quit trusting them? Had it ever trusted them?

At last Tippet said, "We haven't. They have broadcast a greeting, but the language is neither ours nor yours."

"Oh?" Judy wondered if it was completely alien, or just not English. "Can you replay it for us?"

"We can do that. Wait." Another pause, then a deeper, more resonant voice said, "Bonjour. Est-ce qu'il y a quelqu'un ici?"

An icy shiver ran up her spine. "Well," she said. "There's a classic case of good-news/bad-news. They're not the government coming after us, but they're not exactly friendly with Americans these days, either."

"Who are they?" Tippet asked.

"They're French." Then she realized that probably wasn't enough of an answer. "They're people from Earth, just like us. But they're from another nation that's hostile to ours. They won't be happy to find us here."

"What about us?"

She considered her own response to Tippet: excited at

first, then more wary when it became clear that he wasn't just a cute little butterfly who could speak.

"I don't know," she said. "It depends on what they're here for."

"Should we answer them and try to find out?"

"Not yet," she said, just as Allen said, "Sure."

He looked over at her. "Why not?"

"Because we're still half an hour from the *Getaway*, for one thing," she said. "I'd like to be able to make a run for it if they're not friendly. And because they probably won't tell us the truth even if we ask. We'd be better off watching them in action." She asked Tippet, "How big is your starship? Have they spotted it yet?"

"It is much larger than yours," Tippet said. "Or theirs. But they show no sign that they have discovered it. And if they continue to use radar as a location method, they are unlikely to. It is much farther away from the planet than they are, and it is mostly organic in composition."

"Oh?" She would love to know more about that, but not at the moment. But if it was big . . . "Turn it end-on to them so it presents the smallest cross-section," she said. "That way they won't be able to spot it optically. And how about your radio transmissions? Are they directional, or—"

"This is silly," Allen said. "We gave the hyperdrive to everyone, including the French. Hiding from them now is hypocrisy."

"It's prudence," Judy replied, "which is something we haven't been exercising enough of lately."

Tippet didn't reply, except to say, "Our transmissions from the ship to the ground are directional. My relay to your radio is not, but the power level is far too low to be detected from space. And speaking of direction, we are drifting a bit to the left of a direct path back to your . . . spaceship."

"Thanks." Judy and Allen adjusted their course by a few degrees.

Allen said to Judy, "I thought you agreed that giving the hyperdrive away was the best thing we could do."

"It seemed like a good idea at the time. Now I'm not so sure."

"You gave it away?" Tippet asked. "I don't understand. How did you get here if—"

"Just the plans. We told everyone on Earth how to build their own engine. I didn't want soldiers to be the only people in space."

"Soldiers," Tippet said. "Professional fighters. Is that who has joined us?"

Allen sighed. "Probably. Unless the Cousteau Society decided to retrofit a sub."

Judy adjusted her grip on the bucket. All this work for five gallons of water, and someone out there had brought a submarine! "I wonder if they're going to try landing it in the ocean," she said.

Allen shook his head. "I can't imagine how you could lower anything that heavy by parachute."

"Parachute?" Tippet asked. "Why would they need that?"

"The hyperdrive won't put something into a space that's already occupied," Allen explained. "We had to pop in as close to the top of the atmosphere as we could and drop from there under a parachute. Unless these guys have figured out a better way, that's what they'll have to do, too, but a sub is too big for that."

"Ah." Tippet made another hissing sound, then said, "This hyperdrive . . . it is still experimental?"

"No," Allen said. "We tested it a couple of weeks ago."

"Weeks? Your race has only had this technology for two weeks?"

Allen shrugged. "I've known about it for over a year, but it took me that long to get a ride on the space shuttle to test it."

"Yet here you are already. In force. And how many other stars did you visit before you came here?"

Allen squinted and wrinkled his nose in concentration. "Uh, let's see, there was Alpha Centauri, then the place with the weird organic-looking asteroids, then the—"

"Three," Judy said. "But we were starting to run out of air by time we got here. If this hadn't worked out, we would have had to go home."

She had meant to downplay the significance of it, but Tippet wasn't fooled. He made a sound like a bicycle wheel with a playing card flapping on the spokes, then finally stopped and said, "You would have gone home. You could do so right now, couldn't you?"

"Well, not *right* now, but yeah. As soon as we get back to the *Getaway*. That's what we call our ship."

"Of course you do."

Judy looked over at him: a fat-bodied butterfly in a yellow pressure suit clinging to Allen's shoulder and flapping his wings as if he was trying to lift him into the air by sheer force of will. At last he slowed down and said, "After we decided to attempt an interstellar flight, we spent nearly a century developing our starship. It took decades to cross the immense distance to our closest neighboring star, and years more exploring each of its planets in turn, but none of them were habitable. We went on to another star, and another. This was our fourth try as well. We have been away from our homeworld for over thirty generations; we remember it only through the collective mind. And you were on yours when?"

Allen looked at Judy, then at Tippet. "Uh . . . yesterday."

"*Tptkpk.*"

Judy could imagine well enough with that meant. If the trip from there to here had eaten her entire life, only to find someone else who had done it in an afternoon, she'd have said more than just "tptkpk."

But these guys had built a starship the hard way. And they could augment their own intelligence at will. They had learned English in less than a day; she had no doubt that they could build their own hyperdrive in little more just from the clues Allen had already given them. And what else could they do that she didn't know about?

They walked for a while in silence, each of them no

doubt contemplating the things to learn—and to fear—from the other.

And now there was another factor in the equation. Another human one, but Judy had hoped to leave all that behind, at least for a while. She should have known she couldn't do that. She had learned at an early age that she couldn't run away from her problems; why should she have expected it to work now?

37

The *Getaway* looked just the same as they had left it. If Tippet's alter-egos had studied it while they were gone, they had cleaned up after themselves, but Judy doubted they had ever been there. The hatches were still shut tight, and the air smelled stale and plasticky from being closed up all morning.

While Allen hooked up the computer to the hyperdrive again and made sure it would be ready to go when they needed it, Judy set up the stove and heated up a can of beef stew, with a canful of their hard-earned water and a couple of sliced-up potatoes thrown in to bulk it out into a meal for two. The stove had a tiny butane tank that seemed too small to hold enough fuel to boil even a cup of water, but when she opened the valve and gave the flint lighter a spin, it flared to life with a *whoosh* that singed her knuckles and wrapped flames all the way around the pot. She had to turn it down to practically nothing to keep the burner from overdoing it; at that rate she could probably boil the entire five gallons of water and have plenty of fuel left over. She'd had no idea camp stoves were that efficient.

A breeze rustled the fronds of the trees all around her. Judy couldn't feel it on the ground, but that was fine with her. She was just now warming up again after her dip in the river.

She had intended to change her clothing once she got back to the *Getaway*, but her pants and shirt had dried out during the walk back, and the sun had warmed the ground and the rock beside the tank enough that she felt comfortable enough as she was. She took off her shoes and set them on the rock to air out, then spread out her sleeping bag for a picnic blanket and started taking apart the pistol while the stew cooked.

Every inner surface had been coated with oil. She didn't have any to replace it with, so she was careful not to wipe the water off. She just blew it dry as best she could and let the rest of the moisture evaporate.

Tippet sat on her knee and watched her work. "Pretty primitive, eh?" she asked him as she removed the bullets from the cylinder and dried them with her shirttail.

Allen still carried one of the walkie-talkies on his hip, but Judy had set up the other one beside her. Tippet's voice came to her in stereo; faintly from inside the *Getaway*, and more directly from near her feet.

"Perhaps," he said, "but nonetheless it looks effective. The projectile alone masses more than I do."

"It wouldn't do you any good, that's for sure." She blew through the cylinders one at a time, then said, "When we first met, you had a little pointy stinger in one hand. Is that a weapon?"

"Yes," he replied. He pulled it out of its holster and held it up for her to examine. She had to squint to see it.

"How does it work? You don't actually have to stab your target with it, do you?"

"No, it can be fired from a distance. It creates an electrical discharge that interferes with neural impulses. It does so with lifeforms from my world, at least. Whether it would do the same to you remains to be seen."

"I'm not volunteering to be zapped."

"I wouldn't suggest it." Tippet put the stinger away.

Judy finished drying the pistol and put it away as well. With any luck, they would never find out how effective their weapons were on one another.

The stew was bubbling softly. She gave it a stir, then tasted one of the hunks of potato. It was soft all the way through, and on an empty stomach it tasted wonderful.

"Soup's on!" she hollered to Allen.

He didn't need to be called twice. He hopped out of the tank and sat down next to her on the sleeping bag, and the two of them dug in. After their six-mile walk, they slurped it down with ravenous delight, eating directly from the cook pot and fighting over the bits of beef, which they as often as not fed to each other once they'd won. Even Tippet tried a bite, after analyzing it chemically and deciding it wouldn't poison him, but the taste set him to gagging for a full minute. If his reaction was typical, then food was one aspect of their cultures they wouldn't be sharing.

"Unless it's just my cooking," Judy said when he had recovered.

"I doubt—*skkllk*—if that's the problem," Tippet said graciously.

"Well, thanks for saying so." She rinsed out the pot with a quarter cup or so of water, then dried it by holding it in the camp stove's open flame until the last of the water drops sizzled into steam. It was easier than using a towel, and probably safer: the heat would sterilize it for the next time.

A breeze rustled the treetops again. She was glad for the sound; it was one of the few noises she'd heard since she and Allen had landed here. It reminded her of lazy afternoons when she was an undergraduate in college, when she would sit out in the grass on the quad and let the world go by.

She hadn't done that in way too long. When she was done drying the pot, she shut off the stove, leaned back on the sleeping bag, crossed her arms behind her head, and settled in for a long bout of cloud-watching. Allen lay crosswise with his head in her lap, and Tippet landed on her knee.

"So what are the French doing?" Allen asked.

"The submarine is still in space," Tippet replied. "They have refined their orbit into a stable circle just outside the atmosphere, and now, from the radar pulses reflecting off the ground, it seems clear that they are mapping the surface."

Why here? Judy wondered. There were hundreds of stars closer to home with planets they could explore, starting with Alpha Centauri. She and Allen had come this far to get away from people, but the French Navy wouldn't need to do that. Hell, given their belligerence of late, she would have expected them to kick Onnescu and the other early arrivals off Centauri's planet and claim it for themselves.

Apparently they wanted one they could claim without a fight. Maybe she and Allen should have told them to go away when they first showed up, but she didn't really want to claim the planet for herself. She just wanted to explore one that didn't already have people on it, but after meeting Tippet, even that didn't seem so important anymore. Let the French land. If their intentions were benign, she and Allen could contact them any time. And if they were setting up a secret military base or something, well, the U.S. had two pairs of eyes on site that the French didn't know about. Or several thousand, if you counted Tippet and his brethren.

They spent the afternoon talking about Earth's sudden exodus into space. Tippet wanted to know the political situation that had led to Judy's decision not to greet her own people sixty light-years from home, and how it had come to be that way. Judy was reluctant to talk about it, mostly because she was so embarrassed for humanity, but Allen answered the alien's questions and asked dozens of his own. How did Tippet's people handle disagreements among nations? Did they even *have* nations, or was their whole planet covered by one huge networked mind?

"Neither," Tippet replied. "There's a practical limit to the number of nodes in a link. Beyond a few thousand, the coordination effort overwhelms any further gain in intelligence. But any of us can link with any others, so the composition of a mind will shift over time, and disagreements between minds are usually settled by exchanging members until they reach consensus."

"Usually?" Allen asked.

Tippet said, "Some overminds become protective of their identity. It's probably a throwback to our evolutionary roots, when hives were discrete entities that competed for resources. It's uncommon now, but it happens."

"So how do those minds settle differences?"

"They seldom do."

That didn't sound encouraging. "What do you do with them, then?" Judy asked.

"It depends on how disruptive they are to the rest of us. If they become dangerous, we swarm and disband them, but if they're merely eccentric, we allow them to pursue their own destiny. They occasionally prove useful."

"How?"

"They sometimes provide new insight that the rest of us miss. And . . ." He paused. "And they make good starship crews."

"Aha!" Judy laughed. "You're a mad scientist too!" Then she had to explain about INSANE. She made Allen show Tippet his membership card to prove she wasn't kidding.

Tippet didn't find it amusing. "You actually worry that your race will exterminate itself?"

"Not anymore," Allen said. "But yeah, before I gave away the plans for the hyperdrive, it was looking pretty inevitable."

Tippet said, "Apparently singleton societies react differently to outside stimulus. On our world, such a revelation would increase the tension between hives, rather than ease it."

"It did on ours, too," Judy said.

"That's just a short-term reaction," said Allen. "Once people have a chance to think it through and realize we're not all stuck on the same planet anymore, things will settle down."

"I am not convinced," Tippet said. "The economic repercussions alone will destabilize your nations' governments for years to come. If things are truly as volatile as you say, your 'gift' could provide the final push into chaos."

"You sound like Carl."

"Who is Carl?"

Somewhat reluctantly, Allen described the mission specialist on their shuttle flight, and his objection not only to the way Allen had distributed the plans for the hyperdrive, but to the hyperdrive itself. He made it sound like Carl was a classic head-in-the-sand Luddite, but even so, Tippet said, "His fears are well grounded. Even if your nations avoid war, the loss of population could lead to an industrial decline that may never recover."

"So what if it does?" Allen said. "We've been spoiling the planet with industry as it is. Maybe slowing down a little would be a good thing."

"Maybe," said Tippet. "I would not wish to experiment on my own homeworld in such a way."

"You don't want the hyperdrive?" Allen asked.

"I have not been offered the hyperdrive," Tippet replied. "And no, that is not a veiled request for it. But even if you were to offer it, and I were to accept, I would not take it back to my homeworld without preparing them for it in advance."

Allen sighed. "I honestly don't get it. I thought people would be excited by the prospect of getting around the light-speed limit, but the only things they can think about are the economic and political consequences."

"Those are significant concerns." Tippet paused a moment, then said, "There is also the quarantine issue to consider. The immense distance between stars has until now served to keep the galaxy's intelligent races from interacting. What will happen now that the barrier is gone? You and I have become friends, but will our entire societies react the same way to one another? That remains to be seen. And . . . wait. Something just happened."

Judy had actually been relaxing, despite the topic of discussion, but now she felt her pulse rate climb. "What? Not *another* ship?" She raised up on her elbows so she could look at Tippet.

"No, but the French submarine has expelled several landing vehicles. They are firing rockets to reduce their orbital velocity."

"What?" Allen asked. "Retro-rockets? That's stupid. They've got to have hyperdrive engines on board if they want to get back to the submarine. They could do a tangential vector translation and they wouldn't have to waste the energy."

Judy laughed. "It's the military, Allen. They don't care about efficiency."

"But—"

"They've probably got the emergency descent modules from *Mir*. They have a standard procedure for using them, so that's what they're going to do, even if they launch them out of torpedo tubes." She imagined what that must be like: roaring out of the sides of the sub one after the other, lining up in formation, and lighting the engines. It would be a kick and a half! Maybe that's why they were doing it that way: for the sheer fun of it.

Allen sat up and turned around to face her and Tippet. "How many of them are there?" he asked.

"Ten," Tippet replied. "They seem to be aiming for a continent about a third of the way around the planet to the west of us."

"That's smart, at least," Judy said. "That'll give them most of a day to explore before dark. What's surprising is that they're launching so many at once. They're all going to wind up coming down in the same place."

"That's how the military does things," Allen said.

Judy couldn't decide if he was mocking her or not, but either way, he was right. They might send a single scout if the situation demanded it, but if not, they would send a squad.

She looked over at the bright yellow *Getaway Special* resting on its pad of crushed foam insulation, its 4×4 framework and steel reinforcement cables clinging to its sides like bargain-basement scaffolding. That was about as far from the military way of doing things as a person could get.

The thought of a military invasion force landing on her planet—even if it was a continent away—raised the hair on the back of her neck. She had never taken the French very seriously, even when they had broken off diplomatic relations and closed their borders to Americans, but now that they had mounted a military expedition all the way out here, they didn't seem quite so insignificant.

"How are they doing?" she asked Tippet.

"They're just entering the atmosphere now. We can see plasma trails forming behind them as their passage heats the air. Their radio signals are beginning to deteriorate, but we're following them down telescopically." He continued to report on their progress as they slowed down through the upper atmosphere, then regrouped using their attitude jets and free-fell to within a kilometer of the ground before opening their parachutes. They were clearly trying to land as close together as possible.

"They've got guts, I'll give them that," Judy said.

"Perhaps, but their targeting skills could be improved," Tippet replied. "Their formation flying is impressive, but the whole fleet is going down in a forest, one much more densely overgrown than this. The first of them is approaching the top of a large tree now . . . and has crashed through it. The parachute has been drawn tight over the tree's canopy, which would indicate that the vehicle has fallen through and is hanging by the shroud lines above the ground. The others are going in as well, some punching through and some getting hung up in the branches. One has vanished, leaving a spherical hole in the treetop it landed in. The tree . . . *skkkkt* . . . the tree is thrashing its remaining branches back and forth. Amazing."

"They bugged out with the hyperdrive," Allen said. "And they took the top of the tree with them. I wouldn't be happy about that, either."

"You are speaking of the tree," Tippet said.

"Right."

"I remain skeptical that a tree can feel anything, but the evidence does seem to support your claim. It is now bending over . . . no, it is falling. It has ripped two of the landing vehicles from neighboring trees on its way down. Now it is on the ground and . . . 'twitching' is the only word to describe it."

Judy looked up at the trees around them. If she hadn't seen one moving last night, she would never have believed what Tippet was describing now. But this was an alien planet, and the rules apparently weren't the same here as they were back home.

"How about the astronauts?" she said softly. "Can you see if they're okay?"

"None have emerged from their vessels yet. There are several simultaneous radio transmissions, but they all seem to contain only one word. It is not in the dictionary."

"What is it?" Judy asked.

"It sounds like 'Merde,'" Tippet replied. "Just 'merde, merde, merde,' over and over again."

Judy's first impulse was to go help them. They were fellow astronauts in a bind, after all, no matter what their nationality. But they were also a third of the way around the planet, and even if she and Allen could locate them precisely enough to land anywhere nearby, they would only wind up dangling from the treetops with them.

She sat cross-legged on her sleeping bag while Tippet described the unfolding situation as the French astronauts on the ground emerged from their capsules, cut down the ones caught in the trees, and helped their companions out. There were two per capsule, which made eighteen in the landing party. The tree that had been topped by the hyperdrive had quit twitching, but the humans milled around on the ground next to it for a while, the other treetops obscuring all but the most general impression of their motion that could be detected through infrared sensors.

After fifteen minutes or so, during which Judy supposed they were testing the air and cleaning out their spacesuits, they began dragging their landing vehicles together. That must have been a huge job, but they managed it one capsule at a time, six of the landing party going out for a lander and hauling it into the clearing made by the dead tree, then another six going for the next one, then the last six, and so on until they had retrieved them all.

Then they started cutting down more trees.

"What the hell do they think they're doing?" Judy demanded when Tippet reported another tree flailing its limbs, then falling over. "Didn't they see what happened the first time?"

"They apparently don't care," Allen said.

"I believe they have orders to create a secure perimeter that they can defend," Tippet said. "We are making a little progress deciphering some of their language, based on English cognates, and that seems to be the gist of the transmissions from orbit."

"Military thinking again," Judy said. "Never mind if the trees are sentient beings; if they're in the way, cut 'em down."

"Calling them 'sentient' might be overstating their abilities," Tippet said. "They react to injury, but they don't seem to be able to defend themselves, or even to notice that their neighbors have been killed."

"The one we saw last night was curious, and when we shined our flashlights at it, it took off like a scared rabbit. That's sentient behavior as far as I'm concerned."

"Perhaps so," Tippet said, but he didn't sound convinced.

Judy grew more agitated as he continued to relay the French soldiers' actions. They felled a dozen more trees, then cut them into sections and dragged the trunks into a circle around their landing vehicles. By that point, the butterflies on Tippet's starship could see directly into the camp through the gap in the forest, and they could see in detail as the soldiers also cut the limbs into lengths, which they attempted to use for tent poles. The rubbery branches proved too flexible for that, so they tried setting one on fire, and when that worked satisfactorily, they cut the rest into smaller lengths and stacked them in the middle of the camp.

"Holy shit," Judy said. "The trees burn when they're green. How can that be?"

"There must be a lot more oxygen in the atmosphere than we thought," Allen asked.

"It is nearly one part in three," said Tippet.

"That would explain it. We're used to twenty-one percent."

Judy wondered if that was why the stove had burned so hot. She would have thought the fuel would be the limiting factor, but maybe the burner design wasn't totally efficient and the extra oxygen had reacted with the unburned excess.

That still didn't answer her first question. "If green wood burns here, how could the forests keep from burning down? There'd be nothing to stop a fire. The first lightning strike would set off the entire thing, wouldn't it?"

"Maybe the trees run away," Allen said.

Maybe they did. But if that was the case, then why didn't they run away from people with axes? And why had the one last night run away from them when they simply shined a light at it?

They might get the chance to answer that question soon, or at least gather some more data. The sun was setting behind the mountains; in another hour or two, it would be dark.

Not a moment too soon, either. The hike to the river and back had evidently taken more out of Judy than she had thought; she was definitely ready to call it a day.

While it was still light enough to see, she set to work boiling water, then pouring it into the three empty beer cans where it could cool off and remain sterile. That way they would have water ready to drink in the morning, and they wouldn't have to carry the stove with them if they decided to explore some more. The wind in the treetops picked up while she was doing that, and she made sure the stove was stable. She didn't want it tipping over and catching the ground cover on fire, especially not with the air thirty percent oxygen—and at higher air pressure than on Earth at that.

Allen puttered around the *Getaway Special*, tightening straps and checking the parachutes to make sure everything was ready to go, then as the sky darkened and the shadows deepened beneath the trees, they climbed inside the tank and settled in for the night. Judy put the water bucket back where it had been before, and carefully nested the open circuitry beside it. The open beer cans fit tightly into the corrugations in the side of the tank, where they wouldn't get knocked over in the night.

Judy's watch said 3:42. That seemed awfully early for sunset, but then she realized it was 3:42 A.M. The longer day here had lulled her into forgetting the time. And she had only eaten one real meal today. No wonder she was so tired.

She wondered how Tippet was holding up. "How long is the day on your home planet?" she asked him. For all their talk today, there were still a million things they didn't know about each other.

He had settled in on top of the main hyperdrive engine, where he would be safe from human clumsiness in the dark. Allen had set his walkie-talkie on the water bucket so its speaker wouldn't blast Tippet's ears every time he spoke. "Our day is nearly twice as long as here," Tippet said. "What about yours?"

"Shorter," Judy said. "It's already early morning by our clocks."

"Does that cause difficulties for you?" he asked.

"A little. We'll be okay after a little sleep."

Allen had already crawled into his sleeping bag. "That's exactly what I intend do if you two will quit yakking," he said. "Wake me up if anything interesting happens."

Tippet waited a few seconds, then said, "Allen! A member of my overmind has just confirmed the reliability a new method to differentiate between *skkttp* and *sttkkp* during power-up."

"What?"

"You said to wake you if—"

"Interesting to *me*," Allen said.

"You didn't specify that. Ha, ha, ha."

"Very funny."

Judy giggled, only partially at Tippet's joke. There was an alien staying the night in her spaceship! And they were lying low to see if an ambulatory tree would come for a visit again tonight. When she stopped to think about it, she either had to laugh or scream.

She switched out the light and settled into her own sleeping bag, leaving it unzipped so she could get out of it in a hurry if she had to. She listened for sounds from outside, but the forest was silent save for the soft whisper of air moving through the tops of the trees. She focused on it, letting it soothe her jangled nerves, until she drifted off to sleep.

The smoke was thick enough to mask the neon *Open* sign in the window, and the jukebox was blasting out a rap rampage at top volume, but Judy didn't care. She was just diving into her second helping of batter-fried butterfly with hearts of palm on the side when Tippet's voice cut through the dream.

"Wake up! Wake up! It's coming!"

She sat up, instantly awake, her heart already hammering. There was a deep bass rumble that came through the ground more than the air, accompanied by the same creaking noise and wet slurping sound that she had heard last night. It seemed much louder than before, as if the entire forest were on the move this time.

She yanked her flashlight free from its duct-tape loop and made sure the plastic bag wasn't in the way of the beam this time, but she didn't turn it on yet.

She couldn't see a thing in the dark. She couldn't hear Allen moving, either. "Allen?" she whispered. "Allen, wake up."

"I'm up," he said. Soft blue light blossomed from his side of the tank: the computer waking up from "suspend" mode.

Tippet was on the rim of Judy's hatch.

"What do you see?" she asked.

"Three trees are approaching us from uphill. The others are moving out of their way."

Judy felt for the pistol with her left hand, got her finger on the trigger and her thumb on the hammer, then stuck her head up through the hatch. There was just enough starlight to see the forest opening up like a crowd of peasants when the king passes through, leaving a wide avenue for the dark silhouettes of three short but bulky-looking trees that shook the ground as they stomped down the slope toward the *Getaway Special*.

"I don't like the looks of this," she said. "Get ready on that hyperdrive."

Allen snorted. "If we jump now, you'll get blown out into space in your pajamas."

"I didn't say 'jump'; I just said get ready. I'll close the hatches if we have to bail out."

"You'd better." Allen turned on his video monitor and swiveled his camera to face the oncoming trees. Judy looked down at it once and saw three ghostly images on the screen, then she looked back out into the night again. The surveillance cameras gave a clearer image, but if she had to shoot, she needed to keep her eyes dark-adapted.

Tippet was filming, too. The trees slowed down when they came within fifty feet or so, but they kept advancing one cautious step at a time.

"What do you think?" Judy asked him. "Are they just curious, or are they going to try to trample us? Or both?"

"I don't know," he replied. "I hear a great deal of high-frequency vocal communication between them, and in the surrounding forest. Hold up a walkie-talkie and let's see what they do if I echo some of it back to them."

"They're *talking*?" After seeing the trees' reaction—or lack of it—to the French landing party, Judy had figured them for the vegetable equivalent of cows, but cows didn't talk.

Tippet said, "It has the give and take of speech, but that's not necessarily what it is. It could also be mating calls, or territorial warnings, or simple echolocation."

Judy couldn't hear anything but their footsteps—or was that "rootsteps"? But Tippet evidently had a wider hearing range than she did. Whether the walkie-talkies had the fidelity to handle it was anybody's guess, but she tucked the pistol in her waistband long enough to grab the one on the water bucket and set it up on the flat spot between her hatch and Allen's, thumbing the volume all the way up as she did. Then she transferred her flashlight into her left hand and took the pistol in her right. That felt a little less awkward, but she couldn't say it was comfortable either way.

The walkie-talkie screeched like a public address system going into feedback. She plugged her ears with the ends of her thumbs and waited to see what would happen, but she didn't have long to wait. The three trees hooted like monkeys, their branches waving like semaphores, then they leaned forward and rushed the tank.

"What did you say to them?" she asked.

"I have no idea," Tippet replied, "but it apparently wasn't good."

The ground shook and squelched beneath the trees' weight. Judy imagined the sound the *Getaway Special* would make if they stepped on it, but she didn't intend to let them get that close. When they were still thirty feet or so away, she aimed her flashlight at them and flicked it on.

They definitely didn't like that, but unlike the tree she had pinned down with it last night, these didn't stop. All three of them whipped their branches backward, as if they were leaning into a hurricane, and kept coming.

"All right, then," she muttered. "Let's try plan B." She cocked the pistol with her thumb, aimed it high in the air, and pulled the trigger.

A tongue of flame shot about six feet out of the barrel, and the report echoed off the surrounding forest like a clap of thunder. That did what the flashlight hadn't: the three charging trees split apart like magnets with their same poles shoved together, and with a roar like a mile-wide strip of Velcro tearing loose, the rest of the woods yanked up their roots and leaped a few steps backward as well.

Judy's hand tingled from the recoil. What a rush! For just an instant, while the gates of Hell had opened up at her command, she had felt like a god. An omnipotent and impatient god at that. No wonder some people liked guns so much; it gave them at least a fleeting sensation of mastery over an otherwise indifferent universe.

But "fleeting" was the word. Two of the three trees had fled, but the one in the middle kept coming straight for the *Getaway Special*.

39

Judy fired again, aiming toward the tree this time, but it didn't even hesitate. She couldn't tell if she'd hit it or not, but even if she miraculously struck a vital organ with a third shot, momentum would carry it as far as it needed to go now.

She didn't waste time trying. "Jump!" she shouted. She dropped the pistol and lunged for Tippet, sweeping him inside as gently as she could, then she slammed the hatches closed and shouted again: "Jump!"

"We're not—" Allen began, but the tank lurched violently to the side. Judy whacked her head against the hyperdrive, lost her balance, and fell toward the beanbag chair, but she never connected. The tank lurched again, and they were in free fall.

The sudden flash of sunlight on the side of the tank nearly blinded her, but when she squinted she could see pitch-black shadows crisscrossing the yellow wall in every direction. The creak of plastic stretching to its limit made her think at first that they were stress lines about to give way, but then she realized what it was: the shadows of tree branches.

"Tippet?" she called softly. "Tippet, are you all right?"

There was no answer. Debris was rising into the air all through the tank, but none of it looked like a butterfly in a spacesuit. She raised both feet and looked at the soles of her shoes, but she hadn't stepped on him. Where had he gone?

There was a scrabbling sound, then a heavy thump. The shadows moved across the plastic, their thick ends going for the dark side of the tank.

"Holy shit," Judy said. "It's still alive." Either she hadn't hit it, or a bullet in the trunk didn't matter. And apparently neither did vacuum.

"It can't be," Allen said. "The jump field wasn't set nearly wide enough. We must have cut it in half."

"Then what's that outside?"

"Just—I don't know. Muscle contractions." He looked at his video monitor, and Judy followed his glance, but the image was spinning wildly. The tree must have knocked the camera loose.

Something soft smacked her in the face. She reached up to brush it away, stopping just in time when she realized it was Tippet. "There you are! Are you okay?"

He flapped his wings a couple of times to keep himself in place, but still said nothing. Then Judy realized why: his walkie-talkie was on the other side of the hatch, no doubt tumbling away into space.

"Just a sec," she said, digging among her things for the other unit. She found it still beside the water bucket and flipped it on.

Tippet's voice immediately filled the tank. "Let's not do that again."

"What's the matter? Are you hurt?"

"I . . . don't believe so. Not now. But the jump cut me off from the overmind, and I was terrified until they located my signal again."

"Oh." She had no idea how that would feel, but it didn't sound fun.

The tank screeched again as tree branches slid across its rough exterior, then something started banging rhythmically on the side right next to Judy's head. More muscle contractions? She looked at her video monitor, then at her spacesuit, still crumpled up on what had a minute ago been the floor. "First things first," she said. "Suit up."

"Uh . . . right," said Allen.

"Tippet, can that suit of yours stand up to vacuum?"

"In an emergency," he said.

"If whatever it's banging on the outside of this thing

manages to punch through, I guarantee you it'll be an emergency."

Judy wasn't wearing her suit liner, but she didn't want to take the time to put it on, either. She just pulled on the bottom half of her outersuit, wriggled into the top, locked the waist ring, then put on the communications carrier and the helmet and gloves. She sealed it up tight this time, and made Allen do the same.

"Testing, testing. Allen? Tippet, can you hear me?" she asked.

"Loud and clear," Allen replied.

"Tippet?"

Nothing.

"Tippet?" She looked around for him, saw him gently flapping his wings to keep himself from drifting into the way of their flailing arms and legs.

"Tippet, can you hear me?"

"There you are," he said. "I had to find your intercom frequency."

"Oh. Sorry. I should have thought of that."

She turned on her monitor. Her camera was still taped down; she zoomed out to extreme wide angle and swiveled it around until she could see what they'd dragged into space with them.

It was the whole tree. Either the jump field was wider than Allen had thought, or the tree had been reaching down to grab them when he hit the escape button, but Judy couldn't see any missing limbs. It clung to the *Getaway* with its gnarly, tubular roots, and its trunk was bent nearly double, shoving the green fronds at the end of its branches down into the tank's shadow. The whole works was rotating slowly, about twice the speed of a second hand on a clock, and the tree kept shifting around to keep its fronds in darkness. It kept one root free to whack against the side of the tank.

"Jesus," Judy whispered. "It's definitely alive. And it doesn't like direct sunlight."

Allen slapped his gloved hand against the side of the tank.

"What are you doing?" Judy asked him.

"Answering." He whacked the tank twice more, then paused, then three times.

She laughed, more from nerves than anything. "Oh, come on. You can't honestly expect a *tree* to do fill-in-the-blank math problems. Especially while it's hanging on for dear life in interplanetary space."

Then the tank rang with four distinct blows. They were muffled inside the sealed spacesuits, but still clearly audible.

Allen whacked the wall five times.

Judy counted the response: one, two, three, four, five . . .

If there was a sixth, they never heard it. Above-normal atmospheric pressure from inside and the stress of a tree gripping it from outside was too much for even a lifetime-guaranteed septic tank to withstand. The end seam right next to Judy peeled open like a zipper, and in a single *whoosh* like a fighter jet passing low overhead, all their air rushed out into space.

Everything that wasn't tied down also raced toward the crack. Judy watched her sleeping bag slither out like an oil slick down a drain, followed by her spacesuit liner, the pistol, and half a dozen smaller items. The stuff sack full of food wedged itself up against it, but wouldn't fit through.

Tippet, on the other hand, sailed out with room to spare.

"Tippet!" Judy yelled.

"Tptkpk!" The radio hissed and popped with words in his his native tongue, then he said, "I—I'm all right. I caught a branch."

"Thank God," she said.

Tippet said, "Ha. I had thought the notion of a deity rather quaint when I found it among the words in your language, but in this instance I will thank anyone I can."

"Can you make it back in?"

"I believe so. Just don't do anything to alarm the tree."

Judy couldn't imagine anything alarming it more than it already was, but she said, "We won't."

With no air to carry sound, the tank was totally silent now. Judy's spacesuit hissed softly as it bled off air to put its internal pressure within its design limits, but that soon stopped. She put her hand against the wall, but she couldn't feel any vibration from the tree, either. The outrushing air had acted like a rocket, setting tank, tree, and all spinning a full revolution every five or six seconds; centrifugal force had probably stretched the tree out to full height again, and it didn't want to risk slipping just to whack on the tank with a root.

The tree was heavier than the *Getaway*; the center of gravity was somewhere outside, partway up its trunk. Judy and Allen and all their loose gear had drifted up against one wall, and the short radius of their spin kept threatening to give her vertigo when she turned her head too quickly. Steam boiled out of the water bucket and the open beer cans. Water in vacuum would boil until it froze. And the nitrogen in Judy's and Allen's blood would boil, too, under the reduced pressure in their suits.

"We're going to get the bends," she said. "We've got to land."

Allen shook his head. "We can't do that with a tree hanging on to us. It's got to weigh at least a ton. Even if we deployed both 'chutes, we'd still hit like a bomb."

She looked at the monitor. Sure enough, the tree was standing out to its full height. It wasn't moving anymore, either. She could see Tippet out near the end of one of the branches, slowly working his way back. However inadvertently, the tree had saved his life. But it could still cost her and Allen theirs. "Then we'll have to cut it loose," she said.

"No," Tippet said.

"I know it sounds cruel, but the tree's going to die anyway," she said. "It's probably as good as dead already, and even if it's not, we can't put it back. And we can't keep full atmospheric pressure in these suits, which means we've got maybe half an hour at best before we start getting embolisms in our blood. When one of them plugs an artery in our hearts or our brains, we're dead."

"There is another option."

"What?"

"Go for my starship instead."

Neither Judy nor Allen said anything for a second, then they both spoke at once. "Can we breathe your air?" Judy asked, while Allen said, "It would take too long to match velocities."

Tippet actually laughed; not the "Ha, ha, ha" he'd used before, but the real thing. It was an obvious mixture of Allen's and Judy's laughter, but it sounded genuine. "Yes, you can breathe our air. From what you've told me of Earth's atmosphere, ours is closer to normal for you than what you've been breathing here. And Allen, you forget what you are dealing with. Our starship has engines enough to boost us to a third of lightspeed. We can accelerate to match your vector, while you use the planet's gravity to bring yours closer to ours. Within a few minutes at most, we will be able to dock and bring you on board."

"But do you have any space that's big enough for us to stay?" Judy asked.

Tippet laughed again. "We are aerial creatures. Of course we do."

40

That was an understatement. When they matched course with Tippet's ship, it was hard to imagine how there could be anything *but* open space. The thing was over a mile long, and at least a third that wide. If it had the density of a wiffle ball, it would still mass millions of tons. Even with the four oversized engines sticking out the back, it would take forever to accelerate to any fraction of lightspeed unless it was mostly air.

Judy's blood felt like it was mostly air, too. Her legs ached, and her right hip felt like somebody was twisting a knife blade in the joint. It had taken only twelve minutes to rendezvous with the starship, but that was about five minutes too long for comfort.

They were almost there now. She watched the video feed from the one good security camera as it approached, the immense vessel doing all the maneuvering just to match velocity with their tiny tank. The situation seemed odd enough, but as the starship drew alongside them she kept feeling little hits of déjà vu. The *Getaway*'s rotation gave her only a momentary glimpse every few seconds, which only heightened the effect. Tippet's ship looked a little like a blimp, with its blunt nose and long cylindrical body, but that wasn't what felt familiar. Its four engines mounted evenly around the circumference looked a little like a Russian rocket with all its strap-on boosters, but that wasn't it, either. She had seen something like it before, though.

Then its shape registered, and she gasped in surprise.

"Judy?" Allen sounded worried. "Are you all right?"

"Yeah. I just . . . Tippet, did you guys find a planet that was all water at one of the other stars you visited?"

He had crawled back into the tank through the same seam that he'd been blown out of. Now he clung to the wires leading from the hyperdrive engine to the laptop computer, a vantage that let him see what was going on and also afforded a good grip now that his wings were useless. "We did," he said. "Why?"

"Was it about fifteen light-years from here?"

It took him a second to make the conversion from his own units. "Yes. Why?" he asked again.

"The last star we visited had a water planet. We found this thing that looked like a spaceship in orbit around it, but the ship was hollow, like a mold. We couldn't figure out where it came from, because there wasn't any evidence of life anywhere else in the system, but it looked an awful lot like this."

Tippet said, "Hmm. Interesting. Describe the rest of the planetary system."

She tried to remember. It was only yesterday, but it seemed like a lifetime ago. "Let's see, there were four other planets, weren't there Allen?"

"Yeah. One was an airless rock close to the star, then there was the water world, then farther out there was a gas giant with rings and moons, a double gas giant, and a ball of ice with an atmosphere that was probably methane or ammonia. Does that sound like the place you guys were at?"

"Yes," said Tippet. "It was methane, by the way. We spent several years in that system, exploring each of the planets in turn, but none of them were habitable. Eventually we gave up and came here. But our starship was old and battered from collisions with interstellar dust and gas from the previous voyage, so before we took it back into deep space we let it metamorphose a new body. What you found was its cocoon."

Judy looked back out at the ship, now just a flat wall dimpled with portholes and hatches. "Your starship is alive?"

"Of course. How else could beings of my stature create

something large enough and powerful enough to carry us between stars?"

"Wait, wait, wait. You genetically *engineered* it?"

"We did. From spaceborne lifeforms that already exist in our home solar system, but yes, we modified them to suit our purpose."

"Ho-ly shit." She'd already been daunted by their level of technology; now she felt the last vestige of anthropocentric pride vanish under the sheer magnitude of their accomplishments.

When she'd seen the shell around the water world, she'd assumed the rows of round circles along its flanks were portholes. She'd been partly right; they were windows for looking out of, but they were not butterfly-scale windows, nor even human-scale. These were dozens of feet across, revealing huge sunlit parks and grottos filled with vegetation. Judy wouldn't have been surprised to see dinosaurs casually peering out without bothering to stoop down. She did see smaller animals, brightly colored and curious, with their faces to the windows as the *Getaway* drifted in toward a cavernous docking bay.

Allen was looking over the hyperdrive engine at her monitor, his face stretched wide in a big, goofy grin. "Where's a camera when you need one, eh?" he said.

"In Trent and Donna's living room." They had planned to bring a couple disposable Digimatics with them, but those had still been in the house with the rest of their last-minute gear when they'd made their hurried escape from the law.

It didn't matter. Even with photographic evidence, nobody would believe this.

The whirling septic tank with its arboreal passenger cleared the landing bay door without scraping a twig. The door irised closed behind them, and a moment later air rushed in through the crack in the tank. Moments after that, their rotation began to slow until the image in the monitor was steady.

All the loose junk that had been tossed up against the walls drifted free again. Judy's spacesuit deflated as the outside pressure matched the inner, then it began to wrinkle and press against her. She could have left it on and let it squeeze her body without risking contact with another alien atmosphere, but she would run out of oxygen in a couple of hours anyway. If the air was going to kill her, she might as well get it over with. And if it didn't, well, then she should save what was left in her suit for the next emergency.

She popped off her helmet before the inrushing air made it too difficult to lift, then took a cautious sniff.

Green. It smelled of living things, both vegetable and animal. It was chilly, but that might have been just a consequence of expanding out of storage tanks to fill the landing bay.

Tippet pulled off his helmet, too, then tossed it into the rising cloud of debris. "*Sppzzz!*" he said, his voice still coming through the communications carrier on her head. "Real air! I was certain I would never breathe it again." He scrabbled at something on his chest, then peeled off the rest of his suit, the motion so resembling an Earthly butterfly emerging from its cocoon that Judy watched in delight, momentarily transported back to her childhood. His wings came off with the suit, and she suddenly realized they were mechanical, but he had his own beneath, which he unfurled as soon as he pulled himself free.

They were gorgeous: iridescent blue with swirls of green and red and gold all through them. His body was equally colorful, not at all like the monotonous yellow of his suit.

"You're—you're beautiful!" she whispered.

"I feel like I've been coughed up by a *plkktt*." He used all eight legs to comb his wings and scratch his body simultaneously. "Ahh, that feels better." He flapped his wings a couple of times, then did a figure-eight loop around Judy's helmet and the hyperdrive.

Air continued to rush into the tank. "We're over-pressurizing the atmosphere to match what we just left,"

Tippet said, settling down to hover between the hatches. "Will that stop the progress of your bends?"

"Yeah," Judy said, swallowing to help her ears pop. "We should be all right if nothing in the air kills us. How about the tree?" She could hear plastic protesting and see shadows moving as its roots shifted their grip on the tank.

At least they were still in free fall. If Tippet's ship had had artificial gravity, that would have been one surprise too many, both for her and the septic tank. And probably for the tree as well.

"It seems to be trying to find the ground. Do you object if we move your spaceship into one of our gardens, where our passenger might feel more at home?"

"Go for it," Judy said. What did it matter? They weren't taking the *Getaway* anywhere else anytime soon, not with a blown seam.

Allen had removed his helmet as well. Now he pulled open his hatch and pushed his head out. Judy did the same on her side, ready to duck back if a root or a branch came too close, but the tree was only moving the ends of its limbs. Its trunk stood straight out from the tank at a sixty-degree angle or so from the hatches, and its somewhat bedraggled-looking fronds waved slowly from side to side like seaweed in a tide pool. A dirt-covered root the size of Judy's leg had wrapped itself across the top of the tank between the two hatches, and it was squeezing so hard it was making a dent in the plastic.

She couldn't see any bullet holes in its trunk. That was no surprise; given her lack of experience with guns and her agitation at the moment, she would have been surprised if she'd hit anything. At the time she'd been trying to kill it, but now, even after all the damage it had done, she was glad she hadn't.

A couple of dozen butterflies riding in the middle of basketball-sized metal frameworks moved in on tiny puffs of compressed air, bumped up against the sides of the tank and the tree, and pushed them toward a slowly widening circular doorway into one of the green oases they had seen from outside. The chamber was irregularly shaped, like a natural cavern. The sides were concave in places, and convex elsewhere, as if other rooms were pushing inward from beyond, and the end opposite where they had come in angled upward for maybe fifty feet in a cascade of ragged terraces like a tumbled-down cliff face. Everything was covered in plants, their leaves glistening with dew, and raindrops floated lazily through the air, softening the edges of the distant corners and glowing like tiny diamonds in the sunlight that flooded in through the huge window off to the left. There weren't any animals in evidence; either there weren't any in this "garden" or they were hiding under the bushes.

Judy was glad for the sunlight. The air didn't feel that much warmer in here, and the humidity felt like it was at least ninety percent. She thought about all the trouble she had gone to on the ground to boil water to kill any microbes that were living in it, but that would be pointless here. Here she would be inhaling the water with every breath.

The thought didn't scare her as much as it might have. Even if she got sick, she imagined Tippet and his cronies could just send some bio-engineered bug into her bloodstream to root out the problem.

The cargo handlers zipped around to the other side of the *Getaway* and brought it and its passengers to a gentle halt against the wall opposite the window. They even oriented it bottom-first. Judy's worldview did a somersault when they bumped the ground; they were still in free fall, but suddenly the window felt like a skylight, with the sun shining down from overhead.

The end of one of the tree's roots found the dirt. A little shudder ran all the way up the trunk, then the roots slowly slid away from the tank and burrowed into the ground, pulling the whole tree down until it was anchored in the soil as if it had been there for years.

The butterflies fired their air jets and pushed the *Get-*

away across the garden to put some space between it and the tree.

"Thanks," Judy said.

"You're welcome," Tippet said. She wondered if it was actually Tippet who had spoken, or one of the others.

They swirled around, swooping playfully in their framework cargo pods, then flew back into the landing bay, closing the door behind them and leaving Tippet, Judy, and Allen alone with the tree. Didn't they have any curiosity? But then she realized that they were getting everything Tippet saw and heard, without the danger. They *were* Tippet, almost as much so as he was. They could go on about their business and remain here at the same time.

Tippet fluttered out into the air above Judy's head. "The tree seems to have survived its experience," he said.

"It'll have a hell of a story to tell its grandchildren," Allen replied.

Judy snorted at the image that conjured up: a circle of trees standing around a campfire while they told spooky stories to one another.

Tippet said, "Let's see if it's more amenable to conversation now. Do we still have the walkie-talkie?"

41

Despite his multiple components, sometimes Tippet had a real one-track mind. But Judy supposed he had good reason at the moment: he and his hive-mates had no idea how the tree would behave on board their ship, and the sooner they could learn to communicate with it, the sooner they could relax. Or toss it out the airlock.

She looked up/out at the porthole. It wasn't exactly an airlock, but she bet it could be opened if necessary. Maybe she would keep her spacesuit on a while longer. . . .

She said, "Transmit on the walkie-talkie's frequency," and pushed herself back inside among the debris.

"What do you want me to say?" The voice came from somewhere low in the tank.

"Anything. Recite the Gettysburg address."

"I don't know what that is."

"Then sing me a—never mind." The walkie-talkie was slowly tumbling past Allen's legs. She snagged it in her left hand and pulled herself partway through the hatch again, holding it out toward the tree.

Tippet said, "Should I echo some of the speech I recorded on the ground?"

Allen shook his head. "Given how it reacted last time you did that, maybe you should say something else."

"That would be difficult," Tippet replied. "I don't even know the structure of its language yet, much less any of its individual words. But you have a good point. You were getting a response with cardinal numbers; perhaps I should try prime numbers and see what happens."

Oh, great, Judy thought. Math again. Why did it always come down to math? She wondered if Columbus had tried prime numbers on the natives when he landed in the Carib-bean.

"It's worth a shot," Allen said.

The walkie-talkie peeped like a sparrow going for the record on ascending trills. Judy heard no response, and evidently neither did Tippet.

"Nothing at all," he reported. "Let me try something simpler."

The beeps and twitters didn't sound any different to Judy, and apparently the tree wasn't any more excited by these than the earlier ones.

"Trying simpler yet," Tippet said. This time Judy heard the ascending pattern of beeps, but after a few seconds Tippet said, "Still nothing. This is odd."

"It's probably going catatonic with shock," Judy said. "After what it's just been through, I wouldn't blame it a bit."

"Yet Allen got results by banging on the wall while we were still in space."

He had, hadn't he? And the tree had been active the whole time, trying to hide its head—well, its leaves—from the sun while the *Getaway* rotated beneath it. Judy looked at the window, then back to the tree, remembering the way the tree last night had frozen under her flashlight beam, and the way this one and its companions had held their fronds behind them, out of the light, while they charged.

Now it held them up to the light, leaves spread wide to gather the sun like any tree.

"Wait a minute," she said. "Does that window have a shade?"

"Yes," Tippet answered. "Is the light too bright for you?"

"Not for me, but I think maybe it is for the tree. We've never seen them move except at night. During the day, they just stand there, even if you cut one down right next to them. I think maybe they only wake up at night."

Tippet pondered that for a few seconds, then said, "I would have thought of that eventually."

The window's inner frame bulged inward, then slowly constricted, covering the clear lens like the iris of an eye.

Judy wondered if the space they were in had started out as an eye before Tippet's ancestors had genetically engineered the ship for their own needs. She shuddered at the thought, but she supposed it was better than some of the alternatives. The iris wasn't the only contractile muscle in a living body, after all.

It grew darker in the garden. The iris stopped just short of closed, then a translucent membrane slid across the rest of the gap, leaving a pale white glow about as bright as a crescent Moon.

They waited for the tree to react, but after five minutes with no change, Judy found herself growing impatient. And thirsty. She tucked the walkie-talkie under one of the straps holding the parachute to the tank, then ducked back inside and found one of the cans she had filled with water, still wedged into its crevice in the wall. It hadn't boiled dry, but what was left was a lump of ice. She supposed she could melt it with her hands, but she was already too cold. It didn't seem worth it just for a drink of ice water.

On the other hand, the camp stove could solve both problems at once. Normally she wouldn't even think of lighting an open flame on board a spaceship, but Tippet's ship had air to burn. Literally. She patted around with her hands until she found the stove, then stuck her head and arms outside again and set the stove on the flat space between her hatch and Allen's. Heating things could be tricky in zero-gee, but at least the can was mostly enclosed. If she set it spinning above the flame, the heat would be fairly evenly distributed, and the meltwater would flow out to the side of the can. There was enough of a lip that it wouldn't pour out the mouth-hole immediately, and when it did start to escape, she could drink what had liquified and set the can back in the flame.

"Here," she said to Allen. "Help me hold this down."

He obligingly took the butane canister in his hands and pushed it down so the bottom of it was flat against the top of the *Getaway*. The reaction tried to push him outward, but his spacesuit's backpack wedged against the underside of his hatch and held him in place. Judy braced her feet against the sides of the tank and pushed herself upward until she felt her suit hold fast as well. She made sure Tippet was out of range—he was drifting eight or ten feet above her head and still trying to talk to the tree—then she opened the gas valve and flicked the flint wheel.

The stove lit with a loud *whoosh*, and a cone of bright yellow flame roared out six or eight feet from the burner.

"Yow!" Judy yelled.

Allen jerked his hands back with a startled "Whoa!"

Tippet frantically flapped away from the flame, his walkie-talkie voice repeating *"tpt-tpt-tpt-tpt-tpt-tpt!"*

And across the garden, the tree thrashed its branches and yanked its roots out of the ground with a wet *slurp*.

Judy twisted the gas valve off again. "Sorry. That was stupid. I should have realized it would spray liquid butane out the burner."

"You sure got the tree's attention," Allen said.

Judy fielded the tumbling can of ice, then looked over at the tree. The silvery light from overhead seemed even dimmer after the bright flash of flame, and its afterimage left a bright blue triangle in her field of vision when she blinked, but she could see well enough when she held her eyes open for a second. The tree's flinch had pulled it completely free of the ground; now it was drifting into the air and tipping slowly backward as it did. Fortunately, it was close enough to the irregular wall that its branches brushed the native bushes growing there, and the moment they made contact, the tree wrapped the tips of its branches around the bushes and pulled itself back. It did a complete somersault, then its roots hit the wall and they dug in. The tree held fast for a moment, and Judy thought maybe it had gone catatonic again, but then it let go with its branches and slowly stood away from the wall.

Now its trunk was sticking straight out at them. There was still at least thirty feet of space between it and them, but Judy got ready to duck if it tried to jump.

"I'm going to try another series of prime numbers," Tippet said. The walkie-talkie beeped its ascending trill again, and this time the tree rustled its leaves and tilted them flat toward the source of the noise.

"Very good!" he said. "It's echoing my numbers back to me."

Judy hadn't heard its response. The walkie-talkie squeaked again, then they waited a few seconds, then it squeaked some more, but she couldn't hear a thing coming from the tree.

"Are you sure it's saying anything?" she asked.

"Yes, I hear it quite clearly. And now it's responding with the next prime numbers in the sequence."

"Oh." And it wasn't attacking. That was good. Yet . . .

She stood in the hatchway, the cold air chilling her face and hands while the screeching radio sent chills of an entirely different nature down her spine. The trees were intelligent. She'd met two new alien species in two days. She was all for expanding her horizons, but things were moving a bit too fast for her at the moment.

Actually, at the moment they seemed to be moving right past her. Tippet was the one learning to talk with the tree. How could she talk to something she couldn't even hear?

Her thoughts must have shown even in the dim light. Allen reached out with his free hand to touch the side of her face. "Are you okay?" he asked.

"Yeah," she said automatically, then she said, "No, that's not true. I think I'm about to collapse into a gibbering ball of goo."

"Good."

"What?" She hadn't expected that.

"I thought maybe it was just me."

"Oh. No, I think anybody would, after what we've been through." She shoved the stove and the can of ice back inside the tank, then took his hands in hers and squeezed.

"If you would like to rest," Tippet said, "that would be fine. I suspect it will be some time before we can communicate with any useful degree of facility."

Any useful degree of facility. Right. And he'd learned English how long ago?

The foot or so of space between Judy's and Allen's hatches prevented them from getting any closer. That was intolerable.

Judy looked out at the tree, over at Tippet, then back to Allen. "Tippet's right. At the moment, we're as useless as propellers on a rocket. Let's get some rest while we can, 'cause there's no telling when we'll have the chance again."

He didn't argue. He just let go her hands and pushed himself inside. She did the same, moving by feel after her head cleared the hatch. The dim light from the shuttered window didn't even provide a hint of illumination inside.

"We've only got one sleeping bag left," he said.

"That's fine with me." She started stripping off her spacesuit. "It's warmer with two people in one bag anyway."

"It's going to be pretty cramped, too." She could hear him fumbling with his own spacesuit as he spoke.

She banged her elbow on the hyperdrive, and the reaction sent her spinning until her head and shoulder met the beanbag chair, still strapped to the bottom of the tank. "At least we don't have gravity pulling us down to the floor," she said. "We can shove the water bucket aside and stick our feet through the gap. That ought to let us stretch out."

"Yeah." She heard more thumping and bumping, and a helmet clonked her gently in the back. She couldn't tell if it was his or hers, and at the moment she didn't care.

It was cold without her suit, but she stripped on down to bare skin. The best way for two people to get warm in one sleeping bag was to get naked, and besides, she wanted the human contact. At the moment she wasn't sure she would ever let go.

"Foot of the sleeping bag coming through," Allen said.

He must have already moved the bucket aside. Judy reached into the opening where it had been and pulled the bottom of the sleeping bag through into her half of the tank, then stuck her head and shoulders through into his side. There was a pleasant few minutes of fumbling in the dark while they climbed into the bag, then they zipped it up and wrapped their arms and legs around one another to hold themselves together. She could feel his arousal as he pressed up against her, and she thought briefly about losing herself in a few minutes of pure animal joy, but she wasn't sure if she could handle the extra emotion at the moment. She pressed her face into the hollow where his neck met his shoulders and tried to relax instead.

Neither of them had bathed in days, unless you counted her unplanned dip in the river, but they were both too cold to give off much aroma. What scent she did get off Allen was actually kind of comforting. It was a human smell: honest sweat, a faint hint of shampoo in his hair, the indescribable *maleness* of his skin.

Outside, the walkie-talkie piped more of Tippet's shrill math lesson at the tree.

"Sounds like a modem trying to connect out there," Allen said softly.

"Mmm." It did. Not surprising, she supposed: a modem was basically a device for encoding numerical data into sound waves, and that's exactly what Tippet was doing. She wondered if the sound would change when he started learning the tree's language. She couldn't believe she was falling asleep with that going on just outside—after all, Tippet was talking to a tree!—but her capacity for wonder was just about maxed out, along with her ability to keep her eyes open any longer. Even her ears seemed to blank out for long seconds at a time; a sure sign that her brain was about to shut down whether she wanted it to or not.

She kissed Allen softly on the side of his neck. "Wake me up if anything interesting happens," she said.

He snickered.

"To *me*," she added, but if he said anything, she was already asleep.

42

If there were dreams, she didn't remember them. The next thing she knew, Allen was rubbing her back and whispering her name.

"What?" she asked. It was way too soon to get up. For one thing, it was still dark out. Then she remembered what had been going on when she went to sleep.

"Has Tippet figured out—"

"Something's going on in the French camp," Allen said.

She tried to sit up, but the sleeping bag only let her lean away from him a little bit, sucking cold air into the space between them. She pulled herself close again. "What kind of something?"

Tippet's voice came from outside, where the walkie-talkie was still wedged in under the parachute strap. "The forest has closed back over their encampment," he said. "We can hear frantic calls over the radio. They're speaking French, so we can't decipher much of what's going on, but it doesn't sound good."

She shook her head, trying to wake up. She couldn't see whether Tippet was in the tank with her and Allen or if he was still outside, but it sounded like the modem was still trying to connect even while he spoke to her.

"Is someone else talking to the tree now?" she asked.

Without a pause in the bleeps and twitters, Tippet said, "No. The radio's speaker can duplicate a complex waveform with adequate fidelity to talk to it and to you at the same time."

"Oh." She shouldn't have been surprised. While he was linked with the hive mind, Tippet could probably handle dozens of conversations at once, in a dozen different languages. "Are you . . . actually speaking with it?" she asked.

"My vocabulary is still limited, and my understanding of the parts of speech is full of conjecture, but yes, I'm making progress in learning its language."

Allen cleared his throat. "Does it, uh, does it know anything about what's happening to the French?"

Tippet said, "No. It seems to have little concept of distance, and no way to communicate that far even if it did. But I have learned enough to make an educated guess."

"Oh?"

"The trees who approached us seem to be leaders, or perhaps 'herders' is a more accurate term. They maintain the forest. I haven't yet determined if it's a farm that they grow for a specific purpose, or if their function is a natural ecological niche that they have evolved into, but whatever the reason, they were afraid that we would harm the trees under their care."

So the big trees were shepherds, eh? Or maybe alpha males. Judy wondered if they kept all the female trees to themselves, and for a moment she had the ludicrous image of two trees locked in a coital embrace. Then she remembered what she and Allen had done beneath one of them right after they had arrived, and she felt her body temperature skyrocket. They didn't need to imagine anything about human sexuality.

Nor, unfortunately, about the danger humanity posed for them.

She said, "So if the forest that the French landed in is protected by guardians . . ."

"Just so. I believe they are defending their herd."

Her mouth tasted awful. She unzipped the sleeping bag and felt along the edge of the tank until she found one of the beer cans full of water that she had wedged into a corrugation. The ice had melted, but it was still cold enough to make her teeth ache. That and its crisp, fresh flavor helped her wake up.

She thought about retrieving the walkie-talkie and bringing it inside, but she could hear it well enough where it was, and Tippet was still using it to talk with the tree.

She cleared her throat. "Why did they wait until now to go after the French camp?"

Tippet said, "As you guessed, the trees are nocturnal. When they wake and when they sleep is not a choice, as with our animals, and presumably with yours. From what I understand, they can't even remain sentient in daylight."

"So they woke up at dusk and found a couple dozen of their friends murdered."

"Worse," said Tippet. "Some of them were on fire. Nothing seems to scare the trees worse than fire."

"Yeah, we saw that." And no wonder, if even green branches would burn.

"There's no animals," Allen said.

"What?"

His voice was distant, distracted, the way he got when he was thinking just a few words ahead of his mouth. "Without animals, there's no balance. Atmospheric oxygen builds up until something catches fire. The only renewable carbon source is the same vegetation that produces the oxygen, so it's always living right on the edge of burning up." He whistled softly. "I'll bet their ability to move around evolved as a way to turn oxygen back into carbon dioxide at least as much as a way to run from fires."

Tippet said, "Perhaps. There could be other explanations."

"What about the French landing party?" Judy asked. If she let these two start speculating on the evolution of the local flora, it could be hours before they remembered that someone else was in deep trouble.

One nice thing about Allen: he could switch gears in a heartbeat. He pushed himself up beside Judy, pulling the sleeping bag up around both of them again, and said, "Tippet, can you speak enough of the tree language to talk to the ones that're attacking the camp?"

"No," Tippet replied. "And even if I could, it's not likely that they speak the same language on a separate continent."

"Good point. Well, we should at least radio the submarine and tell them what we've learned. You could bust in on the same frequency they're using to communicate with the ground, right?"

"That much would be easy," said Tippet.

"Judy? What do you think?"

She thought it over for a few seconds. They probably should have done that as soon as they saw the French cutting down trees in the first place, but the landing party had seen for themselves that the trees could move, which was about all she and Allen could have told them at the time. She hadn't thought the trees could fight back. It certainly hadn't looked like it then. Besides, the French were supposed to be America's enemies. Neither side had actually declared war, but even talking to them felt like fraternizing with the enemy. And this particular batch of them had brought their troubles on themselves. On the other hand, she and Allen had managed to get in trouble with the forest, too; and Allen, at least, had been trying to reduce international tension with his hyperdrive. Maybe it was time to consider anyone who made it beyond the Solar System simply "human" and leave nationality out of it.

"Yeah, what the hell, go for it," she said.

"Okay," Allen said. "Tippet, how do we go about this?"

"Simply speak," said Tippet. "I will relay your words to the submarine." All the while, his conversation with the tree had never wavered.

Allen said, "Okay, here goes. Hello, this is Allen Meisner calling French submarine. Allen Meisner calling French submarine. Do you read, over?"

There was a pause, then an astonished voice came over the walkie-talkie. "Allo? Allen Meisner? Vraiment?"

He gave Judy a quick squeeze. She knew just what he was thinking: International celebrity! "Yes, it's me," he said. "Does anybody there speak English?"

She imagined the tangled web of communications that were flying back and forth: from Allen to Tippet to the hive mind to the sub, and who knew what further relays on board before the final link in the chain up there replied down the same pathway.

"Yes," a different voice replied. "I speak English, but you must wait. We have an . . . urgent situation to attend to." The man's accent was as clichéd as Inspector Clouseau's.

"We know," said Allen. "And we've got some information you need. The trees are intelligent, and you've pissed them off by cutting down their buddies. They're not going to back off."

"The trees? Intelligent? You joke."

"They're running roughshod all over your base camp, aren't they?"

"How do you know this?"

"We've got friends in high places. Look, the shepherd trees aren't going to stop until your people are out of there. They've got to jump back into orbit."

"They try. Not everyone can make it to the capsules." There was a moment of dead air, then, "We must leave this frequency open for the rescue effort. Go up ten kilocycles and we will talk more, yes?"

"Tippet, can we do that?" Allen asked.

"Yes," Tippet replied. "No problem."

"Okay, moving up."

Tippet had only been giving them the signal from the submarine, but Judy could imagine what it must be like on the ground, with trees stomping around all over the place and people running for cover. The human instinct would be to run *toward* the trees, but that would be the exact wrong thing to do now.

She felt a moment of disorientation, as if she were there herself, her head spinning with confusion. She fought it down, but the sensation wouldn't go away completely. Apparently the sight of moving trees had affected her more than she thought.

"Are you there?" the Frenchman asked.

"Yes," Allen replied. "Tell your ground crew to try spotlights. The trees don't seem to like bright light."

"No!" Tippet said. "That terrifies them. It puts them to sleep against their will."

"Isn't that a good thing?" Allen asked.

At the same time, the Frenchman asked, "Who is that?"

"His name's Tippet," Allen said. "He's, uh, been studying the trees."

Tippet said, "A spotlight isn't bright enough to put a tree to sleep unless you surprise it. The tree can fold its leaves back in order to stay awake. In the meantime, it becomes desperate to stop the threat."

More dead air, then, "Oui, that fits what we have seen. But what can we do?"

The guy probably had no idea he was talking to an alien. Judy wasn't ready to give away that much information, either. But Tippet apparently didn't care. "Use a bigger spotlight," he said. "Tell your people to shield their eyes."

"What do you mean? What are you going to do?"

"You will see. Allen, Judy, prepare for thrust."

"What?" Judy said. "Wait a—"

The disorientation she'd been feeling for the last few seconds stopped, then there was a deep rumble that she felt more than heard, followed by thumps and rattles as all the floating debris inside the *Getaway* drifted toward Judy's feet. She reached out to grab the walls to keep herself from sliding under the hyperdrive to the other side of the tank. Fortunately the thrust was only a tenth of a gee or so; she and Allen were in way too awkward a position to hold themselves up in full gravity.

"Mon Dieu!" the Frenchman said. A babble of voices rose up in the background, then cut off.

She would have killed for an outside view, but she could see it clearly enough in her mind's eye: The butterflies had turned their ship, then lit the drive. The huge engines at the back were no doubt aimed at the planet, spraying their exhaust directly at the French encampment. Not that they'd have to be that accurate. With the kind of power those engines could unleash, the whole night side of the planet was probably lit up like day, and auroras would be flashing like neon lights from pole to pole even so. And the trees would be freezing in place like bugs caught in amber.

"Move quickly," Tippet said. "We can't keep this up for long."

The Frenchman they'd been speaking to didn't reply for a moment, and when he did it was only to say, "Just a few more seconds."

Something thumped hard against the *Getaway*, or perhaps that was the *Getaway* smacking up against the aft wall. "Down" was along the axis of the ship, and they had been resting against a wall when the drive had come on line. They were lucky they hadn't tumbled.

"How's the tree?" Judy asked. "Is it hanging on?"

"They have stopped moving," the Frenchman said, then Tippet said, "Oh. I relayed that before I realized you were asking me. It is hanging on. But we must cut our thrust soon. We had no time to prepare the ship for it; we will cause damage if we persist."

"Just a few more seconds," the French radio operator said. "They are loading the wounded."

"Ten," Tippet said. "Nine. Eight." He counted on down to zero, then the thrust let off.

"Are your people away?" he asked.

"Oui! Yes. Merci, merci! You have—how did you do that?"

Before Tippet could reply, Judy said, "Answer me a question first. What were you guys trying to do down there?"

"Who is this?"

"Judy Gallagher." She felt a small shot of smug satisfaction at the knowledge that they would know who she was, too. "That didn't look like any exploration party. What were you trying to do, set up a military base?"

"No! We—" The radio went silent, save for Tippet's continuing conversation with the tree, then a few seconds later the Frenchman said, "We attempt to start the colony."

Had he been checking the official story, or just checking to see how much of the truth he could tell? She would probably never know. She said, "That's a damned strange way to set up a colony. And you're a long ways from home, too. Alpha Centauri's a hell of a lot closer."

"We did not want to be close. We wanted someplace our enemies would not find until well after the holocaust."

A shiver ran up Judy's spine, and it had nothing to do with the air temperature. "Holocaust?" she asked. "What holocaust?"

"The one that will surely engulf the Earth before the week is finished," the Frenchman replied.

43

"Wait a minute," Judy said. "We've only been gone for two days, and it wasn't looking that bad when we left. What the hell have you people been doing?"

"Fleeing for our lives," the Frenchman replied. "Since Monsieur Meisner gave everyone the hyperdrive, we have all been waiting for bombs to appear over our cities. Until now, the threat of—how do you say—of mutual assured destruction has prevented war, but once our enemies build colonies elsewhere, mutual destruction is assured no more."

"So you're rushing to build a colony of your own," Judy said.

"Yes."

"Thereby triggering the very war you're trying to avoid."

"It doesn't work that way," Allen said, his voice filled with the same disdain he'd shown Carl Reinhardt back on board the shuttle. "As soon as people see that there's room enough for everybody—"

"They will strike first to prevent their enemies from establishing a presence outside their control." That was Tippet.

"They—the United States wouldn't," Allen said.

"Of course they would," the Frenchman replied.

"It is the logical thing to do," Tippet said. "Once your enemies escape your grasp, you have no more influence over their actions. Their beliefs and their way of life will spread unchecked. If you truly consider them enemies, then the most logical course of action would be to eradicate them before they can escape."

"But . . . but . . ." Judy felt him quiver beside her in the sleeping bag. "That's insane!"

"Perhaps," Tippet said. "But it is the most logical course of action for beings who cannot subvert their enemies as we do."

"Jesus H. Christ!" Allen shouted. "What the *fuck* is wrong with everyone? Nobody has to fight anybody ever again! That was the whole *point* of this whole goddamned *thing*." He pounded the side of the tank with his fist. "The *logical* thing to do is to spread out until we're not in each other's faces anymore. There's more than enough room! People should be dancing in the streets, but everyone who even hears about the hyperdrive seems hell-bent on making the absolute worst of it at every turn."

Judy put her arms around him, as much for her own protection as to comfort him. In the dark, he couldn't see where he was swinging his fists.

The Frenchman said, "We understand reality. The frottement—the friction—between nations is not always about land. It is often the idea. How do you say—the culture."

Judy muttered, "Yeah, right. We're going to snuff ourselves because I say tomato and you say what? Pommes frites?"

The Frenchman laughed softly. "Pommes frites are what you call French fries," he said. "And you serve them in your despicable fast-food restaurants as an insult to our national cuisine. To a chef, that is cause enough to go to war."

"All right, bad example," she admitted, "but still. We're not going to wipe out the planet to keep food snobs from getting a toehold somewhere else, and you're not going to bomb us because we eat fried potatoes, are you?" She slid out of the sleeping bag and began feeling around for her clothes. It didn't look like she would be sleeping again for a while.

The accented radio voice said, "Perhaps not. Who knows what madness lies at the root of our own government, much less someone else's? But we have been ordered to carry at least one egg out of the nest just in case. We were supposed to establish our colony far enough away that we would not be found, but we obviously didn't go far enough. We will not be so conservative on our next attempt."

"You're not going to try it again, are you?" Judy asked.

"We are. And this time we will go across the galaxy. Let you American spies try to find us then!"

"We're not spies, and we don't give a flying f—"

"Thank you for your assistance," he said. "We must now recover our landing party, and then we will go. Adieu."

"Wait a minute!" Allen said. "You can't just run away. If you're right about what's going to happen back home, then we've got to do something to stop it."

The Frenchman laughed again. "So humorous that you would say this, no? Is not running away just what you had hoped everyone would do? Eh bien, you have opened the gates of hell; now there is nothing else to be done."

"We've got to try," Allen said. "Damn it, we can't let the whole planet go up in flames!"

Tippet said, "He has stopped transmitting. The submarine has shifted position to recover one of its landing craft."

"Hail them again," Allen said.

A few seconds passed. "They do not respond," Tippet said. "Not even on the original frequency."

The warbling background had never wavered, though. While Judy pulled on her pants, she asked, "What are you telling the tree, anyway?"

"I'm trying to explain what's happening in terms it can understand, but that is proving difficult. It uses echolocation rather than optical vision, so it has no concept of space other than as a place that can't be seen. It knows nothing of stars, or of vacuum—other than the few minutes of exposure it got. It knows that we're inside an enclosed space now, but it doesn't understand why it has no weight. And so on."

"Did you tell it about the French landing party?"

"I tried. It's having a difficult time comprehending why a tree would deliberately kill another, and why it would set the dead one on fire."

"It thinks the French are trees?"

"It thinks anything that moves is either a tree, a bush, or ground cover."

Not exactly a cosmopolitan worldview, but then Judy had met plenty of people who weren't much better. Including the ones back on Earth who were itching to blow away everyone who didn't think the way they did.

"So, Allen, what are we going to do now?" she asked.

He let out a long sigh, "I don't know. Go back home and try to talk some sense into people, I guess."

She fished around in her beanbag until she found a sweater and pulled it on over her shirt. "I don't think talking to them is going to do any good. I think Tippet's right; we're dealing with the devil's logic here. The only way we can stop them from blowing everything up is to change the equation."

"How can we do that?"

She tried to think of a way, but no bright ideas lit up the darkness. "You don't have any more surprise inventions up your sleeve, do you?"

"Nothing that would help here."

"Tippet? How about you?"

"We have many inventions that may come as a surprise to you, but none of them seem likely to divert your entire species from their chosen course." He paused, then added, "The tree says, 'Sometimes it's better to leap into the fire.'"

"*What?*"

"They seem to think of everything in terms of fire. It's their biggest enemy. If I understand correctly, a tree's usual instinct is to run from fire, but if the flames are too close to escape, a brave tree will run *toward* them instead, leaving a gap that might save the others."

"Huh," Judy said. Altruism as a way of life. That sounded admirable, but how could it apply to the situation on Earth? Should she and Allen go home so they could go up in smoke along with everyone else? That didn't make any sense. The tree obviously didn't understand the circumstances.

Neither did Judy. She didn't have Allen's blind faith that hyperdrive would solve all the world's problems, but neither had she expected this reaction to it. Tippet's endorsement of the logic notwithstanding, it didn't seem logical to her.

She tried to imagine anyone she would want to kill rather than allow them to spread out into the galaxy. People who talked on cell phones in movies? Racists? How about religious fundamentalists? If ever there was a plague on humanity that shouldn't be allowed to continue, they were it. But Judy couldn't imagine nuking even the militant Islamic nations just to prevent them from spreading their beliefs to the stars. For one thing, they wouldn't last a generation if their populations could escape their oppressive rulers, but even if they did manage to persist, that was their business.

Allen had been dressing in the dark as well. She heard him clonk into the hyperdrive and stifle a curse; then he said, "How about we give everybody something else to worry about?"

It took her a moment to shift gears. "Like what?" she asked.

"Like a big honking asteroid aimed right at the middle of the Pacific Ocean. Make every nation on Earth use up all their bombs busting it apart."

"Wouldn't they just hyperdrive it away?"

"Oh." He sighed. "Yeah, they would. Duh."

"Good thought, though. Give them a bigger threat than each other."

She listened to Tippet still communicating with the tree, and felt a shiver of paranoia. What if they were plotting to wipe out these upstart humans while they had the chance?

What if they were?

Her heart started to pound. What if they were? Would Earth be any worse off than it already was?

It might be. It wasn't absolutely certain that humanity would do itself in. But for the French to retrofit a submarine for space and send it out to start a colony on such short notice, they had to believe there wasn't much time left.

Time was all people needed. Once enough of them got

away, what did it matter who blew up the Earth? Judy cringed at the thought, but she was trying to look at it logically. Humanity as a whole only needed Earth for another week or so; after that, they wouldn't have all their eggs in one basket anymore. And paradoxically enough, a war with Tippet's people would probably give humanity the week it needed.

Tippet had to know that. All he and the rest of the hive mind needed to do was sit tight, and the human problem would take care of itself. Since they didn't have the hyperdrive technology to mount an invasion, and probably couldn't build it soon enough to matter, it was a moot point, except for one detail: the French were poised to make their escape right *now*. One submarine full of colonists was probably too small a group to make a successful go of it on their own, but they might manage it. If Tippet really wanted to wipe out humanity, he wouldn't let the French leave here alive.

She took a deep breath. "How, um, how are the French doing?"

"They're recovering the last of their landing craft," Tippet replied. "I'm still trying to get them to respond, but they continue to ignore my broadcasts."

"Keep trying," she said. "Tell them it's an emergency."

Allen said, "What emergency? Other than the obvious one, I mean."

"I think maybe I know a way to stop it, but . . ."

"But what?"

"I need to know something only the French could know."

"What?"

Anything, Judy thought. She just needed to know that they were still alive. Tippet could have already blown their submarine to smithereens as soon as he realized it would be to his advantage. She didn't think he'd done that, but she had to be *sure*.

"I'll know it when I hear it."

Allen snorted. "Quit with the theatrics and tell us already."

Judy hesitated. What could she tell him that wouldn't give away her questions about Tippet?

The French radio operator saved her the trouble. "What do you want now?" he asked. At least it was someone with a French accent. Could Tippet fake that? Easily.

"Are you ready to make your hyperspace jump?" Judy asked.

There was a moment's pause. "Why do you ask?"

"Before you go, I have one last question for you."

Again the pause. "What question?"

"I can't tell you until you're ready to go."

Pause, then: "What silliness is this? You waste our time." Was he checking with his superiors on everything? Or—no. It was speed-of-light lag. The submarine was a light-second or two distant. That was reassuring. But not reassuring enough. Tippet could fake that, too.

"No, it's important. Believe me. Tell me when you're ready to jump, and then I'll ask my question."

Tippet said, "You do not trust us."

She was sweating despite the cold. Zero-gee had never bothered her before, but now she felt as if she were falling headfirst into oblivion. "I trust you," she said. "But the fate of my whole planet is at stake here. I have to know for *sure*."

"Know what?" Allen asked. She could practically hear his frown.

Tippet answered for her. "That the French will be allowed to leave unharmed."

"The what? Who's worried about—"

The accented voice said, "Very well, we are ready to leave, but we will not tell you where we are going."

"I don't want to know that," Judy said.

"Then what do you want to know?"

"I want you to answer me just before you push the button. Within the second, okay?"

"Oui, oui, d'accord. What is this burning question?"

"Are you ready?"

"Yes! Ask it and we go!"

She swallowed. The fate of the world hinged on the stupidest things. But it was the best question she could think of. She took a breath, then said, "What—what's the airspeed velocity of an unladen swallow?"

The Frenchman was silent for a moment, then he laughed. "African, or European?"

The radio hissed with static for a second, then went quiet. Judy sighed in relief.

"What the hell was that?" Allen asked. " 'Airspeed velocity' is redundant. And what did he mean, 'African or European'? It didn't make any sense."

"You haven't seen *Monty Python and the Holy Grail?*" she asked incredulously.

"No."

"Nor have I," Tippet said. "But that was what you were counting on, wasn't it?"

"That's right," she admitted. "And now I know that the French actually got away alive. So now I know we can trust you at least that much."

"Ah," Tippet said. "Now I understand. Your spaceship is damaged, so you need a ride home, but you wanted to know if we could be trusted with both the secret of hyperdrive and the location of your home planet."

"Almost right," Judy said. "I needed to know if I could ask an even bigger favor once we get there."

"What favor?" She could definitely hear the frown in Tippet's voice.

No help for it. In for a penny, in for a pound. "Oh, nothing much," she said. "Just declare war on humanity."

44

The silence stretched out for long seconds. Even the twitter of communication with the tree had stopped. Then Tippet said, "That is a very big favor."

"It's the only thing that'll keep them from killing one another."

"No."

"No, it won't work, or no, you won't do it?"

"Just . . . no. No. We left our homeworld to explore. We don't have the authority to make war. We don't have the desire to. We don't have the capability, either, so the question is academic. Think of something else."

Allen said, "Wait a minute. It could work."

"I just said 'No,'" Tippet reminded him. "I decline, dismiss, deny, refuse, reject, spurn, and veto Judy's request."

"But—"

"No."

"Just listen a—"

"No."

"—minute. You don't have to actually *fight* a war. Just declare one. Rattle your saber until the U.N. pisses their pants. Once they band together to—"

"No! Your fake war could easily become real. What if one of your people finds our homeworld?"

"Oh."

Oh indeed. Judy hadn't thought of that angle. It was one thing to ask a single starship crew to risk themselves to save a planet, but it was another thing entirely to ask them to risk their whole race.

"So fake it," Allen said. "You can send a video signal just as easily as audio, can't you? Make up some slime-dripping, tentacled monster and let *him* send an ultimatum to Earth. Do it from out past Mars, so by the time the signal gets there, we can be hiding in the asteroid belt."

Tippet didn't say "No" again. He didn't say anything at all for a few seconds, then he finally asked, "Nobody would take such a threat seriously, would they?"

Allen laughed. "They would if we dropped a couple of boulders into the Great Lakes and the Mediterranean and the Australian outback. Wouldn't kill anybody, but it'd sure get their attention."

"And the purpose of all this would be to allow more of your people to escape your homeworld before their governments go to war with each other. Would these governments not see through the deception?"

Judy said, "Not if we threaten to hunt down and eliminate all the colonies, too. Of course that would just strengthen people's resolve to get away, but that's exactly what we want."

Tippet didn't speak for nearly a minute. Not to Judy and Allen, anyway. The walkie-talkie began twittering to the tree again, and the hive mind was no doubt busy arguing the question as well. Finally he said, "The tree says 'Herd them apart before the flames engulf them all.'"

Judy wondered how much of the situation it understood. Enough to give the right answer, at least. "What do you say?" she asked Tippet.

"We say maybe. We will take you home—provided we can even move our ship at all with your hyperdrive engine— and when we get there, we will decide whether or not to participate in this scheme of yours. Beyond that, we promise nothing."

"Fair enough," Judy said. "That's as much as we could ask."

"No," Tippet replied. "You asked for more. But that is what we will do."

"All right then," Allen said. He fumbled around in the dark on his side of the tank, then cursed and reached for the flashlight. "Watch your eyes," he warned.

"Don't shine it outside!" Tippet warned.

"I won't." He held his hand over the lens while he flipped it on, then moved a single finger aside to cast a thin beam of light onto the wall beside him. After the total darkness, the bright yellow glow lit up the tank like day. He pushed aside floating debris until he found what he was looking for: the spare hyperdrive. He picked up the bundle of wires and batteries, switched out the light, and pushed himself out through the hatch.

"Okay," he said. "Let's see how quickly we can beef up the circuitry to handle the extra field size."

The butterflies' engineering shop was a mad scientist's dream. When Tippet led them inside, Allen's eyes glittered in delight, and even Judy had to admit it was pretty cool. It was the size of a warehouse store, and packed with gadgetry of every description. Judy recognized metalworking lathes, electronic test equipment, power generators—everything a spaceship would need to keep itself in good repair during an interstellar flight. Most of the stuff was tiny, to match the butterflies' own proportions, but some of it was on a more human scale, and some of the industrial tools dwarfed even that. Robotic arms provided control for anything too large for the butterflies to manipulate on their own.

Tippet led the way into the middle of it. They had brought the walkie-talkie with them so he could talk with them, but he hadn't abandoned the tree; another butterfly had come into the garden to continue the conversation with a speakerphone that could produce the same frequency of sound that the tree did. Tippet was just as much a part of that conversation as the one he carried on with his human guests, but Judy was glad he had come along with them anyway. She knew it was silly, but no matter how inter-changeable the individual butterflies were, she felt more comfortable with the same one she had come to know.

They quickly met more members of the hive as curious engineers came to see Allen's invention. There were easily a dozen of them crawling around on the circuitry while he explained what each part did, and what they needed to do to make it move a ship the size of theirs.

It took them less than an hour to grasp the concepts and make the modifications. Their circuitry looked like fungus spreading tendrils through a barrel full of bread loaves, but it accepted the output from Allen's patchwork construction and amplified the size of the jump field a thousandfold. Allen and the engineers spent another hour testing it with an automated maintenance pod—automated because none of the butterflies wanted to be cut off from the group mind—but when they were satisfied that it actually worked and that the field was large enough to take the whole starship with it, they all trooped inward to the center of the ship and mounted it on a wall there.

If there had been any doubt that the ship was alive, the deep interior removed it. The corridors were tubular and meandering, and they pulsed with constant motion. They glowed with a greenish bioluminescence that gave them a ghastly, spoiled-ham sheen, and fluids moved sluggishly through parallel tubes that pressed against the walls. Gurgling noises came from all sides, growing louder the deeper they went into the ship's belly.

"You, uh, genetically modified all of this?" Judy asked at one point.

"That's right," said Tippet proudly.

"Starting with what?"

"A *swssht*. An eater of comets. They already use rocket propulsion, so it wasn't that radical a change. We added extra stomachs and vessels for our own use and modified its nervous system to take our commands, but that was relatively easy."

"For you, maybe." She wondered if there were *swsshts* around the Sun. There could be all sorts of things out in the comet belt beyond Pluto that people knew nothing about. Not that it mattered now, except for curiosity. People wouldn't need huge spaceships, even if they could be grown like fish in a hatchery. Neither would the butterflies, any-more.

Just as well, she thought as they negotiated a tight passage that reminded her just a little too much of a gullet.

At least it was warm in the heart of the ship. They finally reached the very center of it: a wet, smelly oblong chamber with three-foot-long protrusions sticking out at all angles like thin stalactites from the ceiling of a cave. A host of electronic gadgetry was already mounted to the spines; evidently more than just the hyperdrive needed to be located in the middle of things.

They found an unused stalactite and tied the modified hyperdrive engine to it, tested the remote control circuitry, then backed away a few feet. "No sense in waiting," Allen said. "Go ahead and give it a try."

He had already shown them where Earth was. Tippet said, "We are measuring the field axis. Correcting our aim. Translation in three . . . two . . . one . . . now."

Judy felt an instant of disorientation, gone as soon as she became aware of it.

Tippet made a hissing sound, then said, "This is not going to be a popular method of travel among my kind."

"You *still* got cut off from the hive mind?" Allen asked.

"Not cut off this time," Tippet replied, "but our thoughts were . . . scrambled . . . for a moment. Perhaps it was from the sudden loss of our members on the planet."

Judy had completely forgotten about them. They had just been doomed to die as dumb animals.

"I'm sorry," she said. "I—I hadn't even thought about them. We should have picked them up first."

"That would have taken more time than we have. Don't worry; they knew they would end up alone when they left the ship. Their thoughts are still part of us. The mind goes on."

"Did, uh, did the modifications work?" Allen asked.

"We have gone somewhere," Tippet said. "It will take a moment to determine if we went where we intended to."

They waited. There was no sense leaving until they were sure the drive didn't need adjustment. But within a few seconds, Tippet said, "We are on target. Twenty-six billion of your kilometers to galactic north of your sun."

One light-day. That was over four times Pluto's distance and they were out of the plane of the ecliptic to boot; there was no way anybody could spot them there.

They worked their way back out to the periphery of the ship. That's where most of the living space was, either because it was the easiest part of the organism to modify or because it let more rooms have windows; Judy didn't know which. Whatever the reason, by the time they got there, she was glad to get back into a chamber that was cold and damp.

Tippet led them toward the communications center, which was near the nose of the ship. Judy expected a dizzying array of equipment, something like a cross between a television studio and mission control, but when they got there, it was surprisingly small and austere. It was a spherical chamber maybe twenty feet across, with a couple of dozen butterfly-sized workstations scattered around it seemingly at random. One whole side was given over to green space, and there was even a two-foot pond in the middle of it. That would be the floor during thrust, then, but for now it would make a good background for their computer-generated alien.

"Here's what we have come up with," Tippet said, fluttering up to the biggest of the workstations, at which another butterfly stood, his eight legs gripping the controls. There was a flat monitor about the size of her hand mounted on the wall, from which a triangular head with a face like a bat stared out at them. Judy and Allen nearly clonked their heads together getting close enough to see it, and Tippet had to cling to Judy's collar to stay out of their way, but she supposed this was a theater-sized screen for a butterfly.

The galactic overlord had six eyes on stalks and nostrils where a bat's eyes would be, and the mouth was a round hole with teeth all around, but it was closer to a bat than anything else Judy had seen. The hive mind had created it from her and Allen's descriptions of their nightmare images, and embellished it from there.

"Pretty good," Allen said, "but make it hairier."

The technician tweaked a couple of controls, and the creature's forehead and cheeks sprouted thick, spiky hair.

"No," Judy said. "Now it looks like a teenager. Besides, hair is too mammalian. We need alien. How about tentacles?"

The hair morphed into thicker tendrils about half the length of the eyestalks. "Good. Now put some drool on those teeth. Make it slobber when it speaks."

That was the work of another few seconds. Now the thing looked like it wanted to bite someone's head off just sitting there. "What does it look like in motion?" she asked.

"If you will provide the template, we will show you," Tippet said.

"Template?" Judy asked.

"Yes. In order to give it truly lifelike behavior, we will overlay it on a real-time image of you."

"Oh," she said, startled at the sudden realization that they expected *her* to play the actual overlord. "I . . . well, okay. Where do you want me?"

"Over by the pond." Tippet took a camera from the workstation and flew out to the middle of the room.

Judy pushed herself into position, then said, "What do you want me to do?"

"Whatever you want our simulation to do."

"Right." She felt even more self-conscious than she had the first time Tippet got her on camera, but she took a deep breath and said, "Okay, this is just for practice, right?"

"Of course," Tippet said.

"Okay, here goes." She threw her head back in what she hoped was a haughty attitude and said, "People of Earth! You have intruded upon the domain of the Federation of Galactic Societies. Normally you would be welcomed with knotted tentacles—" she held up her arms and wiggled them back and forth "—but you are in violation of section forty-two, paragraph twelve, subparagraph three of the charter of member races, which strictly prohibits the construction, transport, or use of weapons of mass destruction, or the export of hostile attitudes into Federation territory. You must immediately dismantle these weapons and cease your hostilities toward one another, or we will be forced to subdue you before you disturb the galactic peace with your uncivilized behavior. This is your only warning!"

She tried to hold a stern expression on her face, but it only lasted for a second before a giggle slipped past and she burst into laughter.

"God, that was terrible!" she said.

Allen shook his head. "No, no, it was wonderful! Look!" He reached out for her and helped pull her over to float in front of the tiny screen. "Play it again," he said.

The technician backed it up to the beginning and let the clip run. Judy shuddered when the face took on life; it suddenly looked like a real creature, mad as hell and eager to kick ass. Its lips moved in perfect synch with her speech, which had been lowered in pitch and altered with echoes and harmonics until it sounded like it came from the bottom of a mile-deep pit and out of a throat that was used to howling at the moon. "People of Ya-arth!" it bellowed.

The plants in the background had all been altered, too. Perhaps taking a cue from the intelligent tree they had discovered, the technician had made them all quiver when the overlord spoke. The pond had been morphed into a nimbus of light in their midst, and it rippled with multicolored waves that varied with the intensity of the voice.

When it came to the line about "knotted tentacles," the creature raised four sinuous arms entwined in a ball, but they slid apart as he spoke, scraping a layer of slime off one another until it dripped off their ends and out of the frame.

"Eewww! Disgusting," Judy said.

"Did we overdo it?" Tippet asked.

"No, that's perfect. It'll scare the bejeezus out of practically everybody, and gross out the rest."

They watched it through to the end, then Allen said, "That was perfect. I thought the 'subparagraph three' bit was particularly inspired. I don't see any reason to do another take."

Judy had to agree. She would never be able to match the spontaneity of that one.

"Okay," she said. "Let's go see how it plays in Peoria."

45

They jumped to within two light-minutes of Earth. Their message was only forty-three seconds long; that left them plenty of time to send it and be gone before anyone even knew they were there. And it was far enough away that the ship would only be a speck in the best of telescopes, even if anyone managed to get one pointed in the right direction in such a short time. Plus the closer they were to Earth, the more signal strength they had. They were broadcasting on every commercial television and radio frequency at once, plus the microwave downlink frequencies the satellites in geosynchronous orbit used. Those signals would probably be fuzzy and distorted from coming in at the wrong angle, but what they lacked in direction they made up for in power. The starship's communication equipment had been designed to punch a signal across a dozen light-years or more in order to make regular reports to the homeworld.

Judy waited by the window when they jumped. The stars didn't shift, but a new one popped into view directly in front of her: a double star, both members showing tiny half-moon crescents. The smaller one was indeed the Moon. The other one was Earth.

She wasn't prepared for the pang of homesickness that shot through her when she saw it. Her breath caught in her throat, and her eyes misted up so badly she had to squeeze them shut and shake the tears away. She was home.

Well, actually she was still farther away than any astronaut had ever gone until the last couple of weeks, but after where she had just been, what was a few light-minutes?

"Deploying relays," Tippet said. The ship's engineers had built a fleet of baseball-sized satellites that would stay behind and listen for any response to Judy's message that people might send from Earth. They were small enough to be virtually undetectable, but they could record incoming transmissions and then jump to within useful radio distance of the starship and deliver their recordings in a compressed burst, and they would relay back and forth so there wouldn't be any gaps in coverage. Even if nobody replied, they would listen in on radio and television signals so Judy and Allen and Tippet could learn what was going on.

They had decided to hide the ship in the asteroid belt beyond Mars. There were thousands of free-flying rocks out there, ranging in size from grains of sand all the way up to spherical bodies hundreds of kilometers across; nobody would notice if one of the medium-sized ones suddenly acquired a companion.

"Broadcasting message," Tippet said.

From the workstation behind her, the voice of the Galactic Overlord growled, "People of Ya-arth!" Judy grinned as she listened to it. She could see her own image reflected in the window, a ghost-Judy superimposed over Earth and Moon like a protective angel while her evil twin's ultimatum raced outward at the speed of light to stir up trouble.

The message finished, and Allen, still hovering near the control board, let out a whoop. "Hah! Take that, foul minions of chaos!"

They didn't replay it. A true Galactic Overlord would never repeat himself. Of course a true Galactic Overlord wouldn't say what Tippet said next, either: "Heading for cover."

Earth and Moon blinked out like headlights dropping behind a distant hill. Judy turned away from the window. Now they waited to see what people would do.

"How's the tree holding up?" she asked Tippet.

"Very well," he replied. "Our vocabulary improves by the minute. It finds our subterfuge amusing, and the reason for it horrifying. It wants to know, if your people treat each other so poorly, how do they treat the other trees on your planet?"

She and Allen exchanged a worried glance. By "other trees" it probably meant "all the other lifeforms," but the answer was the same in either case. Judy said, "Um, it probably doesn't want to know."

Tippet said, "I told it as much. I find many alarming terms among the words I learned from your dictionary. 'Clearcut.' 'Genocide.' 'Desertification.' It's a wonder your species has survived as long as it has."

Judy nodded, feeling the crush of world pressure squeeze the joy out of her life again. "Well, it's anybody's guess whether we'll make it through the next few days."

The first burst of news from the relay drones wasn't encouraging. The message had interrupted programming even better than they had hoped, but the United States had quickly branded it a hoax, and the rest of the world had accused the U.S. of doing it on purpose to confuse their enemies.

Allen snorted when he heard that. "Hoax, eh? That's what they said about the hyperdrive plans, too. They apparently got a quantity discount on stupid excuses when they decided to start lying to the public."

"So what are we going to do about it?" Judy asked.

"Just what we planned to do," Allen said. "Throw rocks."

"I'm not enthusiastic about this part," Tippet said.

Allen shrugged. "Me either, but we've got to convince 'em we mean business. Have you mapped the orbits of the asteroids we need?"

The butterflies' stellar comparator equipment was designed to detect debris in the ship's path while traveling in the darkness of interstellar space; they could spot a lump of coal a million kilometers away. Tippet said, "We have determined the orbit of every asteroid larger than . . . well, larger than your head, roughly. There are thousands of candidates with the required mass and vector to use as projectiles."

"Good. Call up an image of Earth and let me show you what we want to hit."

That proved to be more difficult than it sounded. Allen didn't have the experience in space that Judy did, and didn't realize how difficult it was to recognize familiar landmarks when they were partially obscured by cloud or stretched out at odd angles across the curving surface.

She edged closer to help him, squinting to see the tiny screen without bumping her nose on it or on the butterfly operating the controls. It reminded her of her first computer, an Osborne 1, one of the first portable computers ever built. In its day, "portable" meant it was the size and weight of a suitcase full of rocks, but it was a complete, functional computer—provided you had a magnifying glass to see the five-inch diagonal monitor.

"That's the Atlantic Ocean," she said, pointing at the blue-and-white swirls of cloud and water in the middle of the screen. She pointed to the right, at a hint of green and brown amid the blue. "There's the U.S. coast. Lake Michigan. Gulf of Mexico." On the left, she pointed out the Mediterranean.

"Oh," Allen said. "It's upside down."

Judy rolled her eyes, then braced her feet against the wall, took him by the shoulders, and rolled him 180 degrees. "There. Now it's right side up." She pointed at the Earth again. "Asia and Australia are on the night side. We'll have to wait for them to swing around into daylight before we can pick targets for them, unless you want to use your engines to light up the night side of the planet the way you did back at Zork."

"Zork?" Tippet asked.

"My name for the trees' planet."

"Oh," Tippet said. He fluttered his wings a time or two. "We could do that. If we only stayed for a few seconds, it should be safe enough. Perhaps that would be a better course of action than throwing rocks anyway. It would prove we were real without causing damage."

"Never underestimate the human capacity for denial," Judy said. "But yeah, it's worth a try."

This time they prepared the drive for use before they

fired it up. It only took fifteen minutes or so, during which time Judy recorded another message. When everything was ready, Tippet had her and Allen move to the aft end of the communications room, then said, "Here we go."

There was the moment of disorientation, followed within a couple of seconds by thrust. It was only a tenth of a gee or so, just enough to push them gently to the floor, but when Judy looked up at the monitor she saw the Earth suddenly blaze with light. She whistled softly. It was brighter than sunlight.

The Overlord growled, "Hoax, are we? Perhaps we should roast you slowly and see how long it takes you to decide we are real. But we feel magnanimous today; we will will give you one more chance. Disarm yourselves, and you will be allowed to join the rest of the galactic federation. Continue to bicker among yourselves, and you will die!" That much was true enough, anyway.

The drive went out with her last word, and a moment later they were back in the asteroid belt. Judy pushed herself up to the command center and pointed out the Persian Gulf, the Bay of Bengal, and the Australian outback in the image they had recorded during their demonstration.

A flash photograph of a planet, she thought. That was a cool trick.

The next relay satellite brought them the result: Television and radio reports from all over the world showed the bright new sun in the sky and the hysteria it had caused on the ground. Nobody called *that* a hoax, but the Arab nations still accused the U.S. of masterminding the whole situation, and a panel of scientists from the European Coalition agreed that it might have been nothing more than a thermonuclear explosion in space. It had only lasted for a few seconds, after all, and the Galactic Overlord had spoken English.

The U.S. denied everything, accusing first Russia and then France of using the confusion over the hyperdrive to maneuver for global control, and vowing to keep their military on red alert.

Japan broadcast a reply to the Federation: "Hey, don't look at us; we've got no military."

In the middle of it all, one tiny voice suggested banding together to fight the invaders. Judy nearly swallowed her tongue when she heard the report from the United Nations: Cuba, of all places, had taken the bait.

As usual, they were ignored. As the hours passed and world tension continued to escalate, Judy and Allen reluctantly agreed: it was time to knock some sense into people.

The butterflies had already picked their weapons and their targets. The chosen asteroids were only fifty meters across—big enough to make a big bang when they hit the atmosphere, but small enough to vaporize before they hit the ground—and they were in the right position in their orbits that they could be shifted into a collision path with Earth with a minimum of maneuvering. It took a couple of hours to pick them up and set them into the right trajectory, timing them so they would all arrive at the same time. While that was being done, Judy recorded one more message.

"What part of 'disarm' don't you understand?" she demanded, crossing her arms in front of her chest. The Overlord would be writhing his tentacles at that point. "You try our patience. We hear your petty squabbling, and we see your weapons aimed at one another. Very well, then; fire them! We will help you along. Here, let this be the first shot in your demise!"

When Tippet lowered the camera, she burst into a fit of laughter. Allen, hovering near one of the workstations and helping calculate the asteroid vectors, looked over at her and said, "What's so funny?"

"It just hit me. Dumb dreams do come true; just not the way you expect them to. I actually *am* Captain Gallagher of the Imperial Space Navy, but I'm fighting for the wrong empire. If anybody ever finds out what we're doing, we'll both be executed for treason."

"So you're laughing. Ooo-kay." He turned back to his work, and she pushed off to watch the video tech graft the overlay to her performance. Maybe it wasn't funny after all.

When the asteroids were all in position, they jumped to another spot only a few light-minutes out to broadcast the challenge, timing its arrival so people would have about five minutes to wonder what the Overlord was talking about before the rocks hit. Allen wanted to cut the time down to just a few seconds, but Judy argued against it. "We need to give them time to stand down from launch-on-warning status. Otherwise it really *will* trigger the war."

Earth and Moon appeared in the window again when they jumped. Three times in a row wasn't coincidence. At first she thought the butterflies must be orienting the ship that way just for her, but then she realized they probably liked to see who they were talking to as much as she did.

The message started playing. That meant the rocks were only a few thousand kilometers from the atmosphere. They were probably showing up on radar now, but it would be way too late to do anything about them. Laser satellites might melt the top few meters as they flashed past, but that wouldn't make a bit of difference. A nuclear bomb might fragment one, but it would take a direct hit, and their high relative velocity—the rocks were coming from all directions at about 70,000 kilometers per hour—made that practically impossible.

Judy imagined the scramble that must be going on in war rooms all over the globe. Presidents and generals would be arguing whether it was a trick or a real threat from an authentic extraterrestrial government. They would be making frantic phone calls to observatories and science advisors, and probably a few priests and imams as well. Nobody would know what to do; all they would know for sure was that they couldn't afford to be wrong.

There was only one logical choice. To shoot at each other meant certain death, and nobody had had enough time to set up a viable off-planet colony yet. There were probably dozens of attempts being made, but nobody could know for *sure* that their people would survive, not this early in the game. Not even a tin-pot dictator could be insane enough to start a war now, but Judy found herself holding her breath as her latest ultimatum played out. Counting on politicians and military leaders to make a logical decision was a dangerous gamble. She half expected to see mushroom clouds sprout from the planet like roll-up party whistles.

But the Earth floated on, a serene lapis sphere against the star-spangled velvet of space. The flash came from much closer, and off to the left, toward the aft of the ship. The ship lurched, and Judy had just enough time to wonder why the butterflies had lit the engines again before the entire outer wall, window and all, flexed inward and slapped her across the room.

46

She awoke in another spherical garden, this one mercifully warmer than the others. Her head hurt, and her tongue felt like a dry sponge wedged in her mouth. She raised her right hand to rub her temples, but her arm wouldn't bend at the elbow, and when she tried to turn her head to see why, sharp pain shot through her neck and shoulders.

This was when the doctor was supposed to say, "Don't move," and then proceed to tell her that she was all right, but it would take a few days for the superficial wounds to heal. Judy waited, but nobody seemed to have noticed that she was awake. She turned her head to the side, wincing at the pain, but she didn't see anyone there. Just green and violet bushes, turquoise grass or moss or some such, and a cat-sized creature that looked like a Frankenstein surgical project involving spoiled potatoes and a turkey's head. It shied away from her when she moved, and blinked its single eye.

"I hope you're not their equivalent of a buzzard," she said, her voice barely a whisper.

She turned her head the other way, slowly, so it wouldn't fall off, but there was nobody on that side of her, either. Just more greenery, a small pond, and a window with black space beyond. The cratered curve of the Moon took a nip out of the lower edge of the window's view. No, not the Moon. The curve was too tight, and the surface way too dark and rough. This was an asteroid.

She breathed in as deeply as she could before her chest began to protest, then said loudly, "Hey! Is there anybody here?"

The maybe-buzzard squeaked and leaped across the room, doing a mid-air somersault, and disappeared from sight. She reached back with her left arm and pushed herself forward just enough to see that there was a doorway down past her feet a ways, then a few seconds later a butterfly flew through it and hovered a few feet over her face.

"Tippet?" she asked.

He didn't reply. Then she heard Allen's voice from outside, coming from quite a distance. "Tell her I'm on my way! I don't care how you—oh. Never mind." A few seconds later there was a thump and a curse, then Allen stuck his head up through the doorway.

"You're awake!" he said.

"Yeah," she croaked. She might as well have been gagged with a dirty sock, the way her tongue felt. She tried again: "Got any . . . water?"

"Yeah. Here." He reached to his belt, where a softball-sized yellow gourd—or something very much like one—was clipped next to the walkie-talkie. He pulled it free and held the stem to her lips, then squeezed a glob of water into her mouth. She swallowed greedily.

"More."

She still felt like she was talking around a wad of cotton, but it was loosening up. She drank the whole gourdful, feeling the cool water slide all the way down her throat. She hadn't been aware how much her stomach had been hurting, either, until the knot started to loosen.

"That's better," she said at last. "Thanks. How long was I out?"

"Almost two days," Allen said.

"Two days! Holy shit, what happened?" She reached out with her left hand and took his hand, pulling herself around until they were both oriented the same way. It was easier to talk when their heads were on the same level, and she didn't feel quite like such an invalid as she did when he was looking down at her.

"They nuked us," he said. "Tippet figures they must have salted the entire volume of space around the planet with relays a couple of light-minutes apart, just waiting for us to jump in to broadcast another message. As soon as one picked up our signal, it popped home with our location, and they spit a bomb back at us."

"Who's 'they'?"

"Who knows? Every nation on Earth is claiming credit for it, even the ones who didn't have the bomb." He reached up to scratch his head, and she realized he had a big gash between his right eye and ear.

"You're hurt!"

"Tell me about it. So are you. You've got a broken arm, two broken ribs, and a concussion, but Tippet swears you'll live. I damned near pulled his wings off for not letting me take you home to a real hospital, but he's right; there's no way we could get you to the ground without killing you even if we didn't get shot down trying."

That would explain why her elbow wouldn't bend. She raised it and saw a brownish cast from wrist to shoulder, then suddenly what he'd told her soaked in. "We actually survived a nuclear strike?" she whispered.

"Yeah. The only reason we're alive is because they didn't account for the ship's mass. The bomb went off about a quarter kilometer behind us. The aft section took most of the blast, and the rest of the ship actually flexed with the impact, so that helped, too, but the main engines are toast and the ship is metamorphosing to rebuild what it can with what's left. It's a real mess."

"And Earth?"

Allen laughed softly. "Well, we managed to divert their attention. They're strutting around like a bunch of sailors after they've busted up a bar, slapping each other on the back and bragging about how tough they are. Tippet and the rest of the hive are starting to have second thoughts about letting us loose on the rest of the galaxy."

"I don't blame them."

The radio at Allen's hip hissed softly, then Tippet said, "Are you serious, or was that sarcasm?"

"I—I don't know. Are *you* serious?"

"We don't know either. We're not happy with the situation. Your species seems congenitally insane. Allen didn't tell you that they bombed themselves as well as us."

A little shiver ran up her spine. "They did? Who?"

Allen said, "Just who you'd suspect. India and Pakistan. Israel and Palestine. And of course somebody tried to drop a bomb on New York City, but they didn't correct for the rotation of the Earth, so New York moved out from under it before it hit. It wound up in western New Jersey instead."

"That's still not good," Judy said.

"No, it's not, but it could have been a lot worse."

Tippet said, "Not to the inhabitants of western New Jersey."

There was no denying that. "Do they know who did it?" Judy asked.

Allen shook his head. "No. From the trajectory, we know it came from about a hundred degrees around the globe to the east of where it hit, give or take about twenty degrees."

Judy had orbited the planet enough times to know where that was, and how big the margin of error was. "That means it could have come from anywhere in the mid-East or Europe. That's helpful."

Allen snorted. "Well, in a way it is, because the U.S. doesn't know who to shoot back at."

She closed her eyes. Jesus, it had been close. And they weren't out of the woods yet. Now that people on Earth thought they'd killed the Galactic Overlord, the situation was right back where it had started.

"What did our rocks do?" she asked.

"Nothing," Allen said. "Which was just what we planned, of course. They made nice big flashes and loud bangs when they vaporized in the atmosphere, and the concussion rattled a lot of windows, but that was it. They didn't scare anybody for more than a few minutes, because the news after that was all about the bomb that killed the alien ship."

Judy could feel her injuries starting to catch up with her. She hurt everywhere, and she felt as tired as if she'd been working out all day. Her body probably had been, just not the usual way. It took energy to heal.

Zero-gee was a rotten place to feel sick. Fluids accumulated in the upper body, and your stomach always felt close to heaving. She wanted to sleep again, but she forced herself to concentrate. "You should have thrown more rocks afterward," she said. "Shown them we're not dead yet."

Tippet said, "We would rather they weren't looking for us."

"Oh. Yeah, I guess that makes sense. But what are we going to do, then?"

Neither Allen nor Tippet answered right away. Finally Allen said, "Well, that's kind of up to Tippet. I've suggested—"

Tippet said, "Another 'demonstration' from our fictitious overlord would be counterproductive unless we caused actual damage this time. Believe me, we are contemplating just that, but if we do, we won't stop the bombardment until your species is truly extinct. We have our own survival to consider."

Judy felt her skin prickle at his words. That was the trouble with enlisting aliens for allies. Hell, that was the trouble with *any* allies: they always had their own agenda.

She closed her eyes again. The ship had been nuked, she was busted up bad enough to hurt two days later, Earth was still on the brink of war, and now Tippet—and by extension his entire hive mind—was pissed as well. "Is there any *good* news?" she asked.

Allen grinned. "People are slipping through the cracks like sand out of a fist. In another couple of days, it'll be too late to stop us."

Another couple of days, Judy thought. In post-hyperdrive time, that was practically an eternity.

Or it could pass in the blink of an eye. She suddenly realized part of why she felt so awful; she probably hadn't eaten in two days, nor bathed. Nor peed, by the pain in her abdomen.

"Is there anything remotely like a bathroom on this ship?" she asked.

"I'm sorry," Tippet said. "We haven't had time to create one for you."

"They did give us some jugs to put . . . ah . . . stuff in," Allen said. "And we can give you a sponge bath right here."

"Oh, joy," Judy said. "How about food?"

"There's still plenty left in the *Getaway*," he said. "That's right next door. Want me to get you something?"

"Yeah," she said. Then she remembered something else. "Hey, how's the tree?"

Tippet said, "Asleep. We turned the lights on. It was injured, too, and it heals best while it's photosynthesizing."

"Oh. I guess I don't have to ask what it thinks about humanity breaking out of the cradle, do I?"

"Actually, it's ambivalent. It likes the idea of sharing its world with other trees that consume oxygen and excrete fertilizer, but at the same time, it very much dislikes the idea of chainsaws."

She didn't blame it. Nor could she blame Tippet for his attitude, either. She wished she could think of some way for humanity to redeem itself in the aliens' eyes, but at the moment she wasn't feeling all that charitable herself.

Of course, she would probably bite the head off a nun right now, the way she felt. "I need something to eat," she said.

"I'll get it." Allen was gone before she could even ask him what was left. While he was away she used the empty water gourd for a chamber pot and splashed cold water on her face from the aft-wall pond, and by the time he returned she felt almost human again.

He brought a can of chicken soup and a butterfly-built gadget that looked like a thermos bottle. He opened the can and held it next to the thermos, then spun around a couple of times to centrifuge it across from one container to the other. He added water from another gourd, shook the thermos to mix it up, and held down a button on the side with his thumb, holding the thermos at arm's length and spinning around slowly to provide artificial gravity to hold everything inside. A minute or so later, steam wafted out of the top, and he handed it to her.

Her mouth watered at the aroma. Food!

"Careful, it's hot."

She shook a shimmering glob of it out into the air and blew on it softly, guiding it back toward her face with the fingers of her left hand until it was cool enough to swallow. For the moment, at least, all her problems faded into the background.

47

Allen was washing her back when the radio at his hip crackled to life and Tippet said, "Listen to this." The speaker hissed with static, then a different voice, much fainter, said, "Mayday, Mayday, Mayday. Is anybody listening? Mayday, Mayday, Mayday."

"Sounds like somebody's in trouble," Allen said.

"Yes, we gathered that much," said Tippet. " 'Mayday' was the same word that the French used. Could this be the same submarine needing rescue again?"

"Not likely," Allen said. "They're speaking English between the Maydays, for one thing. Where's it coming from?"

"Near your home planet. About one hundred thousand kilometers from the surface, above the center of the North American continent. One of our relay satellites picked it up."

"Sounds like somebody hit the escape button on landing," Judy said. She was floating in front of Allen, wearing no clothing except her panties and the cast on her arm while he gave her a bath.

"Mayday, Mayday, Mayday," the voice said again. "This is Trent Stinson, calling Mayday, Mayday, Mayday. Can anybody hear me?"

Judy flinched so hard when she heard the name that she nearly doubled over with the pain in her ribs. "Wait a minute!" she said when she could breathe again. "We know him!"

"Impossible," Allen said. "I mean, what are the odds?"

"Pretty good, actually," she replied. "You built him a hyperdrive engine before we left." She turned around and listened through another set of "Mayday"s to be sure, but the voice was unmistakable. "It's him. We've got to go help him."

"Someone from your own planet will rescue him, won't they?" Tippet said.

"With what? It would take a hyperdrive ship to reach him, but they'd need regular docking equipment to bring him back. NASA's the only outfit with the gear for it, but if I know them they're a mile deep in paperwork without a ship to show for it yet. Besides, he's out there because of *us*. We've got to go get him."

"No," Tippet said. "Not in this ship. It could be a trap. Even if it's not, the moment we appear that close to Earth, we'll be attacked."

Allen shook his head. "We only need to be there for a couple of seconds. Jump in, move close enough to make sure he's inside our jump field, and jump out again. Then we can take him on board just like you did us."

Tippet thought about that for a moment, then said, "This ship doesn't need to go anywhere."

"You can't leave him out there to—"

"Of course not. But you can bring him here with your own spaceship, can't you?"

Allen narrowed his brows. "It's got a blown seam. And I can't maneuver it in regular space."

"Your pressure suit still contains enough air for the short time you would be away," Tippet said. "And if you put yourself in the right spot, your relative velocity will bring you together. You could then bring him back here with your hyperdrive and let us dock with both of you."

"Do we know his position that closely?"

"In another three minutes we will. When the next relay satellite reports in, we can triangulate on his broadcast."

Allen rubbed his chin. "Hmm. I'd have to expand the jump field so I was sure to pick him up on the way past, but that's easy enough." He reached out absently and handed Judy the sponge he'd been using to bathe her. "All right. I'll be right back."

"Wait a minute," she said. "You've got to breathe oxygen for at least an hour first."

"Trent may not have an hour. I'll be fine. It'll only take a few minutes."

"Famous last words," she said, but she couldn't think what else to do. If Trent was in serious trouble, they needed to get him to safety *now*.

She wished she could go with Allen, but she couldn't fit inside a spacesuit with her arm in a cast, and with two broken ribs she would be useless anyway, even in zero-gee.

"Be careful," she said, leaning forward cautiously to give him a kiss.

"Always."

She went with him at least as far as the *Getaway* and watched him push it from the garden back into the cargo hold. He positioned it right up against the airlock so the escaping air would blow him away from the ship, then climbed inside and donned his spacesuit, handing her the walkie-talkie at the last minute before he sealed it inside with him. Judy made sure he got all his joints sealed correctly, then Tippet gave him the coordinates for Trent's location and helped him calculate an intercept jump and figure out when to trigger their return. Allen spent a few minutes adjusting the jump field, then gave the thumbs-up.

She saw his lips move, and Tippet relayed his words through the walkie-talkie: "Back in a flash."

"Good luck," she replied. She was still holding the wet sponge in one hand and the radio in the other, naked except for her cast. It was less than ten minutes since they'd heard the distress call.

She and Tippet went back into the garden they'd just been in, and the door sealed behind them. They heard a hollow thump that had to be the airlock opening up and the *Getaway* blowing out into space. Judy went to the window and watched the yellow tank dwindle into the distance. It was tumbling slightly, and she wondered how Allen would stop the rotation without the air release valves, but then she saw him stick his arms out through the hatch and throw something into space. A can of beans, maybe? Whatever it was, the reaction from tossing it slowed the tank's rotation, and he did it again until it stopped.

"That was smart," she said.

"Of course it was smart," Allen's voice said through the walkie-talkie. Tippet had relayed her comment.

"Are you okay out there?" she asked.

"Fine. Let me get a little farther away from—holy cow. The whole back half of the ship is covered in a gooey-looking layer of gunk." He must have realized how that sounded, because a moment later he added. "It's actually kind of pretty, in the right light."

Tippet said, "That's the cocoon. The metamorphosis is nearly done; if you think this is pretty, wait until you see the finished spaceship underneath."

"Neat. Okay, I'm definitely far enough away now. Here goes."

"Good luck!" Judy called out. If he heard her, he didn't reply. The yellow speck winked out, and space was empty again, save for the dark, cratered surface of the asteroid they were using for cover.

She finished her bath one-handed, then dressed in her old clothes, since her fresh ones were in the *Getaway* with Allen. While she was doing that, she asked Tippet, "Are you seriously considering . . . what you said about Earth?"

"Yes," he replied. He was hovering near the door. "I'm sorry, but it doesn't seem safe to let your species loose in the galaxy."

"We're already loose," she said.

He was staying well out of her reach, she noticed. Was he afraid of her, now, too? Personally?

He said, "The total number of emigrés is not yet large enough for your race to survive without continued support from Earth. We could still stop you if we choose to do so."

"Using the hyperdrive we gave you."

"There is that irony."

She looked out the window to see if she could spot the *Getaway Special* when Allen returned. He should have had time to get there and back by now, shouldn't he? But there was only black space outside. Even the asteroid looked dark and cold.

"You know," she said, "there are times when I think humanity's too stupid to live, too. Whenever I have to deal with politicians, for instance. Governments seem to bring out the worst in people. So do fifty-percent-off sales in department stores. But for every jerk, there's a hundred decent people who will help you out in a pinch. And even the people you think are hopeless can surprise you. Did Allen tell you about Dale Larkin, the guy who bankrolled us?"

"No," Tippet said.

"He's a thief. Makes his living stealing money from banks. That's not a good thing," she added, just in case finance was different on Tippet's world. "But when he heard we needed money to build our starship, he offered to just give it to us. No strings attached. We had to talk him into letting us pay him back."

Tippet apparently understood the concept well enough. He said, "I'm not impressed by his generosity with what was never his in the first place."

"It was his by the time he gave it to us," Judy pointed out. "He didn't have to part with it."

"It wasn't a hardship for him. Generosity when it's easy isn't as significant as generosity that costs the giver."

"No, it's not," she agreed. "But isn't that the same question you're up against? Letting us out of the cradle is going to cost you some security. So are you going to—"

"It's not the same."

"Sure it is. The stakes are bigger, but it's the same argument."

It seemed strange to discuss the fate of humanity so calmly with an alien who could snuff it out if he decided that was in the best interest of his own race, but Judy didn't think hysterics would help her case any. Besides, she'd never been much good at hysterics anyway.

When Tippet didn't answer, she said, "I'm sure there will be problems if you let us loose. That's practically guaranteed. But it won't be all of humanity causing trouble. The vast majority of us are going to want to be good neighbors, and we're going to help stop the ones who don't. We don't want con men and carpetbaggers out there any more than you do."

"*You* don't," Tippet said. "You individually. But you don't speak for your species. You can't! You're physically unable to. We're having a very hard time puzzling out how this will affect negotiations with you as a group."

"That's why we have governments."

"Which you have just admitted are composed of the worst specimens humanity has to offer. And from what's happening on Earth right now, it's also obvious that governments don't heed the wishes of the people they ostensibly serve. Therefore, negotiating with a government would be an immoral act, by our standards."

"But blowing us all up wouldn't be?"

"It would be the worst thing we have ever done in the entire history of our race. But it may also be necessary. We still don't know."

And the longer they took to decide, the harder it would be to accomplish. Judy didn't need to remind him of that; she was sure he knew it all too well. The fact that he and the rest of his hive had refrained so far was good news, but she suspected they had set a deadline: if they didn't come up with a decision soon, they would err on the side of caution. Unfortunately for humanity, that meant they would start bombing before it was too late.

A flicker of motion out in space caught her attention. Two tiny specks of light had popped into being. They were too far away to see any detail, but it had to be Allen and Trent.

"Allen?" she asked.

"Here," he said. "Keep an eye on Trent. He's moving fast."

It didn't look like it. The two dots weren't separating very quickly. Allen's vector wouldn't have changed much since he left, so he shouldn't be moving more than a few meters per second away from the ship, but if Trent was moving relative to him, there should have been some proper motion. Unless . . .

"Holy shit, he's coming straight for us!"

She barely had time to get the words out before the speck of light loomed into the distinct image of a four-wheel-drive pickup tumbling end-over-end as it swept toward them.

48

"Brace yourself!" Tippet said.

Judy grabbed on to the window frame, which yielded under her fingers like high-density foam rubber, but she kept her eyes glued to the pickup outside. It was obviously Trent's: deep red with every chrome accessory he could bolt on to it. There was a new addition this time: a big metal box in back, faceted like the top half of a Lunar Module and polished to as bright a shine as everything else. He'd welded together an interstellar camper shell.

They had maybe five seconds until impact. There was no way the starship could get out of the way in time, not even with the hyperdrive. The truck was already inside the jump field. There was a little sideways drift, enough to see that it would hit somewhere toward the back of the ship. That might save the ship, but the pickup was moving fast enough to smash itself flat.

Four seconds. Three. Judy could see two faces through the windshield, Trent in the driver's seat, and Donna sitting right next to him. Their mouths were gaping wide as airlocks.

Then they vanished, pickup and all winking out like they had never been.

Judy let out her breath. A second later, Trent's voice came over the radio. "Whoo-ee! That was close enough to leave skid marks. Sorry 'bout that. Couldn't hit the button quick enough."

"Trent!" Judy yelled. "Trent! Are you and Donna all right?"

"Judy?"

"Yes!"

"Well I'll be a son of a . . . Yeah! We're fine. How'd we get . . . hell, I don't even know where we are. And how did you get that big-ass spaceship?"

"Allen brought you here," she said. "Allen, can you hear us?"

"I can hear *you*," he said, "but not Trent. And I'm sure he can't hear me, either. That was one little detail we forgot in the rush to go after him. The shortwave radio's useless in vacuum."

"Oh." He was right. Without air, the microphone couldn't pick up any sound and the speaker couldn't make any. There was probably a way to patch it into a spacesuit's intercom, but it would take cables Allen didn't have.

"We hear him just fine now," Trent said.

"Hey, I hear you now, too!" Allen said.

"Tippet must be relaying your signals."

"Who's Tippet?" Trent asked.

"It's a long story. Hang on a second. Tippet, how are we going to pick them up?"

Tippet said, "Our relative velocity is not that great. We can use Jupiter's gravity well to change our own vector and dock with them within half an hour. Trent, do you have enough air to last that long?"

"Yeah, easy," he said. "We've got a tank and a half of that left. It's parachutes we're short of. The fuckin' laser satellites nailed both of 'em when we tried to land. Pardon my French."

"They shot at you?" Judy said. "I'd swear too. Well, hang tight, then, and we'll be right there."

"Uh, guys?" Allen said. "Maybe you could swing by and pick me up first? As long as you're in the neighborhood, and have the right relative velocity and all. Just a thought."

Judy grinned. "I don't know," she said. "How about it, Tippet?"

He was flying in tight little circles near the door. "Are you insane? Of course we'll pick him up first. He would die of the bends if we—oh. That was humor."

"Pretty lame," she admitted, "but yeah."

A moment later the *Getaway* blinked into existence a kilometer or so away—or rather Tippet's ship moved that close to it—and then there was a minute or two of light thrust while the pilots matched velocity and brought the plastic tank in through the airlock.

As soon as the docking bay filled with air again, Judy and Tippet went to greet Allen. He was cursing at his spacesuit as he tried to take the helmet off against air pressure.

"Wrist seals first," Judy reminded him.

"Oh. Yeah." He pried off a glove, and after that the rest was easy.

They barely had time for Allen to push the *Getaway* back into its garden before Tippet announced that they were ready to pick up Trent and Donna. They watched out the window while the huge starship maneuvered to meet the tumbling pickup. The airlock was only thirty or forty feet from their window, so they got a good look as it approached. The truck looked incongruous as hell out there, even with a pressurized camper shell. Its four fat tires had looked silly enough on the ground; here they were a caricature of themselves. The passengers looked a bit out of place as well: Trent still wore his black Stetson, and Donna still sat right next to him on the bench seat and chewed gum like her life depended on it. The only thing that looked different was her hair, which had puffed out all around her face like a yellow halo.

They drifted closer to the airlock, their tumbling motion reminding Judy of the thighbone-to-spaceship transition scene in *2001: A Space Odyssey*. Then they disappeared from view, and a few seconds later there was a loud *thud* and a deep vibration ran through the ship.

"That was them hitting the back wall," Tippet said.

They waited until the docking bay was filled with air, then opened the connecting door and swooped in. The pickup was slowly drifting back toward the closed airlock, and Trent and Donna were struggling to open the doors.

"Open a window first!" Judy called out to them.

Trent slapped himself on the forehead, then cracked

open his window. Air whooshed in, ruffling his beard and nearly blowing off his hat, then he popped open the door. Judy could see crisscrossed reinforcing bars welded on its inner surface and an extra layer of rubber molding around the edges to seal it tight against vacuum.

Allen caught Trent as he stepped out and helped steady him, but then the two tried to shake hands and they both wound up wobbling around and laughing. Donna pushed herself out of the truck and floated more gracefully toward Judy, her arms outstretched for a hug. Judy held up her arms and said quickly, "Careful! Broken ribs."

"Oh!" Donna tried to stop her forward motion, but there was nothing to grab except for Judy herself. The two women held one another's hands and did a slow pirouette, Judy's chest and right arm aching under the stress, but they managed to come to a stop without breaking anything more.

"Man, you two are a sight for sore eyes," Trent said. "We was startin' to get worried. Nothin' like comin' home from a thirty-light-year road trip and gettin' shot at on your own doorstep."

"Everybody's gone to red alert with their missile defenses," Allen explained. "They're shooting first and asking questions later."

Donna snapped a little bubble of gum. "That definitely sucks."

"Yeah," Allen agreed.

Trent looked around appreciatively. "This is one hell of a ride you've got here. How'd you score it?"

"It's Tippet's," Judy said. She held her good arm out toward the butterfly, who fluttered up to land on her palm. "Tippet, this is Trent and Donna. They're the ones who helped us build the *Getaway*." To them, she said, "We met Tippet on a planet way out in Cetus."

Trent nodded toward the butterfly. "Pleased to meet'cha."

"Likewise," Tippet said through the walkie-talkie.

Trent looked at Judy's waist, where the radio was clipped, then back up at her face. "We were in Cetus, too.

We met some guys who looked like strings of beach balls on sticks."

"You did?" Judy tried to imagine Trent and Donna making first contact with an alien race. "How, uh, how did it go?"

He grinned. "They picked up a little English, and Donna picked up enough of their language to get along. We mostly went fishin' during the day, and you don't want to talk much while you're doin' that anyway."

"Fishing?" Allen asked.

"Yeah. They've got trout the size of your leg just *dying* to take a fly." He shrugged. "Well, they're not really trout, but close enough."

Tippet said, "These aliens—the beach balls on sticks—did you form a political alliance with them?"

Judy felt the back of her neck tingle. She knew what Tippet was getting at. If humanity already had allies, killing them off could be even messier than he thought.

Trent didn't realize what was at stake. Before Judy could say anything, he shook his head and said, "No, we just made friends and had a good time."

Tippet didn't reply, but Judy could imagine the conversation going on in the hive mind.

While they had been talking, the pickup had continued its drift toward the airlock door and bounced off. Now it was coming back toward them, cab first. Trent nodded toward it and said, "Hey, we ought to tie that down before it hurts somebody. Where can I park it?"

"Let's put it next to the *Getaway Special*," Tippet said.

Allen and Trent grabbed the truck and brought it to a stop, bracing themselves on the walls, then pushed it toward the door into the garden.

"Careful!" Judy said as they both gave it a hearty shove. "It's going to be just as hard to stop as it was to get it moving."

It turned out to be harder, since there wasn't a convenient wall to push against. The truck came in at an angle, digging a trench in the ground with its right front bumper and flipping end-for-end before they brought it under control, but they finally—with much whooping and laughter amid the curses and grunts—managed to orient it with its tires against the ground. Trent went inside the camper and got some rope, which he threw over the top and tied to the bushes on either side. Then he leaned back against the driver's door, tucking one foot under the step to hold himself in place, and crossed his arms over his chest. "I gotta say thanks for coming along when you did. When those military bastards zapped our parachutes, I thought we were genuinely screwed."

"Thank Tippet," Allen said. "He's the one who heard your 'Mayday.' He's been monitoring transmissions from Earth for the last few days, trying to figure out what's going on down there."

Donna had been about to go into the camper, but she stopped herself against the door frame. "What *is* going on down there?"

"Long story," Allen said. "I don't know how long you've been away, but things have apparently been getting crazier and crazier since we left."

Trent laughed. "They were crazy enough *when* you left. You nicked our water line on your way out, so we had us a fountain right in the middle of the driveway. All the cops got soaked, and then a bunch of news guys showed up and started taking pictures, so all our neighbors came over to see what all the ruckus was about, and somebody called the fire department so *they* showed up with a truck, and by the time we got everything sorted out it seemed like half the town was millin' around in our yard."

"Did the cops arrest you for harboring fugitives?" Judy asked.

Trent shook his head. "Are you kiddin'? They weren't after us. Once they realized you were gone for good, they took one look at the crowd and lit out for greener pastures."

"And so did you, apparently."

Trent nodded. "It looked like a good time to be makin' tracks. But hey, if we're going to swap stories, I'm gettin' a beer."

49

Trent unhooked his foot and pulled himself toward the camper door, but Donna said, "We gave the last of it to the roly-polys, remember?"

He slapped himself on the forehead. "Oh, dang, that's right." To Allen and Judy and Tippet, he said, "They loved the stuff. Didn't get 'em drunk, near as we could tell anyway, but they took to it like cats to milk. I figure the first guy who sets up a brewery there will probably wind up runnin' the place."

"Is that your intention, then?" Tippet asked.

"Huh? Oh, hell no." He looked at the radio on Judy's waist, then at Tippet, no doubt trying to figure out which to address. He settled on Tippet himself. "Beer's for drinking, as far as I'm concerned, and brewin' the stuff is too much like work."

"Even if you would wind up 'runnin' the place,' as you put it?"

Trent shook his head. "That sounds like an even bigger headache to me. No sir, I'll leave the runnin' to people who like that sort of thing. Me, I just want to see what's out there."

Tippet made a low whistling sound over the radio, but didn't offer any translation.

Judy was only a few feet from the *Getaway*; she reached out and pulled herself inside headfirst. The place was a disaster area—literally, she supposed, given that it had suffered explosive decompression—but she sorted one-handed through the debris until she found the stuff sack she and Allen had carried food in on their walk to the creek. There were still two cans of Budweiser there, still intact and even relatively cold. She took one in either hand and wriggled outside with them.

"Here," she said, reaching out toward Trent.

"Whoa!" Trent said when he saw what it was. "You still got some of that?"

"That's the last of it, but yeah." She handed one to Trent, and held out the other one for Donna.

Donna put her hands up, palms-out. "No, I'll share Trent's. You guys have the other."

Judy didn't argue. A beer would taste great, and she had no idea when she'd get the chance again. "Careful when you open it," she said to Trent. "In zero-gee, it comes boiling out like nobody's business." She showed him what she meant, popping the tab and immediately slurping up the jet of foam that sprayed out. When she couldn't hold any more in her mouth, she handed the can to Allen and let him take the rest.

Trent tried the same trick, but he got beer all over his beard, and when he handed the can to Donna, she let go of the camper shell and wound up doing a slow spiral into the air, amber droplets of beer making a miniature galaxy around her. Everyone burst into laughter, especially when Donna started going after the loose beer drops and slurping them down one at a time.

"I've got to get a picture of this," Trent said, opening the driver's door of the truck and retrieving a disposable Digimatic from inside. Donna hammed it up for the shot, sticking her tongue out and stretching her neck forward.

Trent took the shot, then rubbed his nose-print off the screen in back and showed the image to Judy and Allen. "This is your camera, by the way," he said. "It was still in the house when you left."

Allen shrugged. "That's all right. We wound up bringing souvenirs home with us." He took the camera and flipped through the images while Judy and Tippet watched over his shoulder. There were shots of an Earthlike planet from space, more shots from the ground of trees and rocks and flowers, shots of Trent standing next to the pickup with the parachute dangling from a tree branch overhead, shots of Donna with the beach-ball-on-stick aliens (who apparently came in varying shades of yellow, green, and red), and one group shot of Trent, Donna, and a bunch of aliens together, standing on a dock in front of a sleek metal boat, all of them holding stringers of fish and grinning like fools. At least Judy assumed that's what the aliens were doing with their mouths open in wide ovals.

When Tippet saw that one, he said, "Were you certain these fish weren't intelligent creatures as well?"

"Yeah," Trent said, "we thought about that, but the roly-polys were catchin' 'em and eatin' 'em, so we figured it was okay."

"And you weren't worried about allergic responses, or poisoning?"

He shrugged. "We were careful, but nothing ventured, nothing gained, you know?"

"Yes," Tippet said. "Yes, I do know that."

There was an embarrassing moment of silence, then from overhead Donna said, "Hey, nice tree. Every spaceship should have a tree in it."

Judy looked over at the tree they had brought with them, now dormant in the light. "Actually, we picked it up on the same planet we found Tippet," she said. "It's intelligent, too. It only wakes up at night, but when it does, it can walk around."

"Yeah? That must have been spooky."

Judy laughed. "It was."

Donna reached out for a hand back to the ground, and Trent stretched out toward her, but it took him and Allen together to bridge the gap.

When she was on the ground again, Trent took a sip of beer and said, "So, bring us up to speed. What's happening on Earth?"

They weren't happy to hear about the escalating tension between nations, or about the almost-war after the attack on the "overlord's" ship. "The dumb shits," Trent muttered when he heard about that, but when Judy described how Tippet felt about letting humanity loose in the galaxy, his eyes narrowed to little slits. With his dark beard and black hat, he looked like he might avenge his race's death ahead of time. "You do that, buddy, you better get us *all*," he said, staring straight at the little butterfly, who once again hovered well out of reach.

They were still in the garden with the *Getaway* and the pickup and the tree. Donna had brought out cookies and corn chips from the camper, and everyone was floating at odd angles around the open door like football fans at a zero-gee tailgate party, but the conversation was anything but festive.

"We could track you down if necessary," Tippet said. "But we would rather not."

"Then don't," said Trent.

"It's not that simple."

He shook his head. "It's exactly that simple. If you don't want to get into a fight, then don't start one."

"We have already started one," Tippet pointed out. "At Judy and Allen's urging, and reluctantly even then, but our masquerade has become real."

"Only to you. The people on Earth think they blasted you out of the sky. They won't come lookin' for you unless you cause more trouble. But if you do, I guarantee you they will."

Tippet bobbed up and down over the chrome camper, his wings quivering. "This is only slightly less terrifying than the thought of what humanity could do to us if we don't strike first. We don't like either option."

Allen, anchored to the side of the pickup by one hand, said, "You have a possibility on one hand and a certainty on the other. It seems like the choice is pretty clear to me."

"It isn't," Tippet said. "Ours aren't the only races involved."

Judy looked over the top of the *Getaway* at the tree, wondering what it would say if it were in on the conversation.

Wounded by a human nuclear attack, other members of its species cut down by would-be colonists; if it had spaceships and the hyperdrive, she didn't think it would be as generous as Tippet.

The beach balls that Trent and Donna had discovered might be a little more sympathetic, but once people started dropping out of their sky by the thousands, building houses in their parks and catching all their fish, they would probably wish Tippet had prevented it while he could.

There were undoubtedly more species out there who would feel the same way. Even if Tippet did let humanity out of the cradle, they might still band together to stop the plague from spreading throughout the galaxy.

Judy nearly laughed at the irony of it. They had threatened the Earth with a fictitious galactic federation, but it wouldn't be fictitious much longer. The only question was whether Earth was going to be around to join it once the dust settled.

Not that it would matter to anyone but humanity in the long run. The hyperdrive was out there. Even Tippet's people couldn't keep the secret from spreading like wildfire throughout the universe. Any contact with a spacefaring race was likely to make an intelligent but not-quite-there-yet race develop the capability, especially now that the hyperdrive had lowered the bar so drastically. And with every new race who learned how to use it, the same situation would arise.

"Holy shit," she said. This was a much bigger problem than she had thought. Far from preventing war, Allen's discovery could ignite it on a galactic scale. *Would* ignite it, over and over again, unless the cure could somehow be spread faster than the disease.

That was impossible. But what if the cure were at least spread *with* the disease? Would that be fast enough?

Everyone looked at her. Allen said, "What?"

"Give me a second." She hadn't thought it through, but there seemed only one logical thing to do. Humanity had started the problem; it was only fitting that they help stop it. And maybe save their own skins in the process. "It might work," she whispered.

Tippet said, "You see a solution to our dilemma?"

"Maybe."

"Yeah? What is it?" Allen asked.

She had to swallow before she could speak. This wasn't the sort of thing she could back away from once she set it into motion. If she opened her mouth, she would just dig herself deeper into the very political mess she had been trying to leave behind. Her life, personally, would probably be much simpler if she just shut up now and let Tippet make up his own mind. But she had brought this on herself. She had brought it on all of humanity, back when she had decided to let Allen spread his secret. And if she had learned anything from the last couple of weeks, it was that running from her problems only made them worse.

So maybe it was time to run headlong into them instead. She took a big breath, then said, "Somebody's going to start a real galactic federation; why shouldn't that somebody be us?"

50

Her companions merely stared at her. "It's going to happen anyway," she said. "We know of four intelligent races so far, and there's undoubtedly more out there. All of them are going to have the same worry that Tippet does, even if we've been bombed back to the stone age. Hell, Tippet, if you do that to us, everybody else will be afraid of *you*—at least until somebody succeeds in wiping you out. And then somebody will wipe *them* out, and it'll escalate until there's only one race left. The only way to prevent that is to band together so the federation is stronger than any one race. They can keep the peace."

Trent snorted. "Just like the U.N. does on Earth?"

"They're not perfect," Judy admitted, "but they've kept us from getting into another world war."

Tippet flew up to hover near her right shoulder. "Humanity has already shown what it thinks of the Galactic Federation."

"That's because we were trying to provoke a war. If we give them a chance to work together instead of fight, they'll do it."

"Would they not think we were bluffing again?"

She shook her head. "They don't know it was us the last time. If we just show up and ask to talk, they'll listen." Assuming they didn't shoot first, but she didn't mention that possibility. Tippet no doubt understood that danger.

That didn't seem to be his major concern anyway. "You would voluntarily give up your autonomy to join a group mind?" He sounded incredulous, almost offended by the idea. Then she remembered that he was from a hive that wouldn't link with the others on its homeworld for fear of losing its identity.

"It wouldn't be a group mind," she said. "Just an alliance of partners."

"An alliance whose purpose is to threaten its members with retaliation if any of them causes trouble. Would humans join such a thing?"

"We already have," she pointed out. "The United Nations isn't the strongest political force in the world, but it's strong enough to make even the United States think twice about getting too far out of hand. The U.N. will join the Galactic Federation in a heartbeat if they can get in at the outset, because they'll figure they can wind up running it."

"What if they do?" Tippet asked.

"So what if they do? It'll still work. Once there are enough members to keep the others in line, it won't matter who plays host."

"Perhaps not. I'm not convinced." Tippet whistled for a moment, and the garden window began to constrict.

"Hey, what's going on?" Trent asked.

"I need to confer with another potential member of the Federation." As the garden darkened, Tippet said, "In the meantime, while we wait for it to wake up, I have a question for you."

"Shoot," said Trent.

"What?"

"Ask your question."

"Oh. I see. Very well; you said 'I'll leave the runnin' to people who like that sort of thing.' What about this? Would you help run the Federation if we decide to implement it?"

Trent ran his fingers through his beard, then took off his hat and scratched his head under his matted-down hair. He looked over at Donna, then back at Tippet, now just a shadowy night moth in the twilight. Judy knew just how he felt. No pressure.

But he finally shook his head and said, "Nope."

"You wouldn't do it."

"That's right. Sorry, but I'm not the type."

"And how many of your fellow humans do you think would feel the same way?"

"Hell, I don't know," he replied. "Probably a lot of 'em. Most of us just want to live our lives in peace, you know?"

"No," Tippet said. "We did not know. But it's encouraging to hear that."

Whether he was being sarcastic or not was anyone's guess, but he didn't provide any more clues. The high-frequency speaker near the tree squealed to life with sound too high-pitched to register as more than a twitter of distant birds, and a moment later the tree's leaves rustled in response.

Judy wished she could give the same answer to Tippet's question as Trent had. She hadn't gone into space to spread politics to the stars; she wanted to explore. But if Tippet went for her proposal, then she would bet money that she would have to have to play diplomat for years to come.

Better than playing Overlord, she supposed, though probably not as satisfying.

Tippet talked with the tree for nearly ten minutes, during which time he ignored the humans completely. While he was absorbed in conversation, Trent leaned forward in the dark and whispered, "Should we make a break for it?"

They could bug out in the pickup. It would leave a hole in the starship, and they couldn't land when they got to Earth, but they might at least be able to warn people that their fate was being deliberated by aliens out in the asteroid belt. On the other hand, what could Earth do about it even if they knew? Come out here and bomb the ship again? Hell, if they just wanted to do that, she or Allen could simply leave in the *Getaway*. With its jump field set wide enough to collect the pickup in passing, it would probably yank the guts right out of the starship and kill everyone on board.

Even so, she couldn't believe that would be enough to stop the threat. Tippet hadn't said anything about sending a hyperdrive-equipped scout back to his home planet, but he would be a fool not to. He and the other hive minds were probably in constant communication with relay satellites by now. And if they were still trying to decide what to do, the loss of the ship would probably sway them toward war.

She shook her head. "We've got to see what he decides first."

Trent obviously didn't like it, but he stayed put. She didn't like it either. Now she knew how Tippet felt: Waiting to see what happened might doom her whole race, but acting too soon could be even worse. She would never have believed how frustrating it could be to sit tight and wait while the clock ran out, but that was the best option. She could only hope that Tippet would think so, too.

And if he didn't? She steeled herself to leap for the *Getaway*. If it was going to be war, she could at least take out the flagship. She wouldn't be able to get into a spacesuit, but Trent and Donna and Allen could at least get to safety in the pickup before she jumped, and they could warn Earth what was coming.

She slipped her good arm around Allen and gave him a squeeze. He squeezed back, and she nearly cried out from the pain of her broken ribs, but she wanted to feel his embrace no matter what the cost. It might be the last time.

At last Tippet spoke over the walkie-talkie again. "The tree says, 'The larger the forest, the bigger the fire.' "

That didn't sound good. Judy glanced toward the shadowy bulk of the *Getaway*, gauging the distance and flexing her legs, getting ready to make her move.

"It also says, 'A healthy forest is more than just trees.' " Tippet added.

"So which is it?" she asked nervously. It was hard to force the air out through the tight muscles in her throat. "Do . . . do we have a galactic federation, or not?"

Tippet flew up to hover between her and the *Getaway*. "Considering that the critical moment in the human exodus from Earth has passed," he said, "we have no choice but to try it."

"What critical moment?" Trent asked.

"We estimate that enough members of your species have left your planet that your race will survive no matter what happens to Earth. At this point we would have to forge a galactic alliance to bring you back under our control anyway; therefore the most expedient measure would be to allow you to join the Federation to begin with."

Judy slowly relaxed the tension in her legs. It seemed she might live to see another day.

51

She floated before the window, looking out at Earth less than two hundred miles below while the camera crew packed up their things. It was hard to tell for sure through the clouds, but she thought that was Florida sliding up into view over the horizon. Or maybe it was Italy. It didn't matter; she was home again.

A roly-poly named Bzzweet floated to her right, admiring the view through the compound eyes in each of his four bulbous yellow-and-green body sections. In the week he'd been on board, he had spent nearly every moment staring out the windows, even while cramming his English lessons so he could participate in the summit meeting.

He seemed almost as shell-shocked as Judy over the speed of events. A week ago he had been an itinerant musician, the closest thing his society had to a global ambassador; now he was their representative as a charter member of the Federation.

Allen floated at an angle to Judy's left, and Trent and Donna drifted behind her, gripping the branches of the tree, which had shuffled forward to be in the camera's field of view during the negotiations. Nobody had bothered to tell the Secretary-General that the tree couldn't see a thing during the video conference; Tippet had kept a running translation going and had described anything nonverbal it needed to know about. That was still better than the situation might have been. One-third of the alien delegation would have been asleep if the butterflies hadn't made dark sheaths for its leaves so it could stay alert during the daytime.

Judy suspected that would be a minor adjustment compared to some of the things they would have to do to accommodate the alien races who would soon join their emerging union. People were finding new species everywhere. Dozens of reports had come in already, and the pace was accelerating as more and more people finished their homemade spaceships and headed out into the unknown. Televised news reports were full of video clips from alien planets, and whole programs were dedicated to showing the myriad different vessels that people had devised to hold air long enough to get from planet to planet.

Judy imagined them dropping down through foreign skies like a rain of frogs and snakes. Heck, in a week it probably *would* be raining frogs and snakes, or something like them. Plenty of the newly discovered aliens were ready to take the plunge on their own; all they needed was the hyperdrive and they could join in the fun.

She shivered a little, and slipped her arm around Allen. "So how does it feel to know you've started the first interstellar civilization?" she asked him.

He looked over at Tippet, then at Bzzweet, then at the tree. "Not bad," he said. "Considering that wasn't even what I was trying for when I invented the hyperdrive. I was just trying to bust humanity out of the cradle."

"Well, you managed that." She snuggled into him and watched the Earth roll by. It was a familiar view, made exotic by the company, but to most people it had only been a dream until now. How long before it became commonplace to everyone?

She couldn't imagine anyone ever taking this sight for granted, but then her grandparents probably had never imagined anyone closing the window on an airplane, either. One generation's wonder was the next generation's yawn.

"You know," she said, "it never occurred to me until just now, but when you fulfill a dream, that's one less thing to strive for."

Allen pulled away from her. "What, you're saying around every silver lining, there's a dark cloud?"

"No, no, I don't mean it like that. It's just . . . I don't

know. I've always thought of space as the final frontier, but now it's within reach for practically anybody. What's left to strive for?"

He chuckled. "Oh, ye of little imagination. There's alternate dimensions, different timelines; heck, there's probably whole different universes just waiting for us to discover 'em."

"Yeah, but that's all theoretical. Not like the stars. We can *see* the stars."

"Who says we can't see alternate dimensions? I've been working on a gadget that can do just—hey!"

Quick as a whip, the tree had bent a branch down and wrapped it around his chest, just as the roly-poly leaped on him and stuffed one of its pillowy body sections into his face.

"Mmmph!" he yelled, struggling to pull them off.

Judy laughed, then winced when her ribs twinged. They had started to heal, but they still had a long way to go.

Allen managed to get his mouth free long enough to gasp for breath and shout, "Call 'em off!"

Tippet said, "Not until you promise you'll submit the plans for your interdimensional device to the Federation."

"No!" He struggled some more, and Judy could see Trent thinking about coming to his aid, but she shook her head and poked Allen in the ribs herself. "Promise," she said.

"What, you too?" he demanded when Bzzweet gave him room to speak.

"Damn right, me too," she said. "I learn from experience."

"And I don't?"

"Not if you want to drop another magic gadget on everybody."

"It's not magic; it's science. And it's a logical extension of the hyper—mmmph!"

Judy watched him turn red, then purple, as the roly-poly cut off his air. She was just starting to get worried when it pulled away and Tippet said, "Promise."

"All right, all right, I promise! Jeez, you don't have to strangle me."

"That would no doubt be the safest course of action," Tippet said. "But we'll settle for your word of honor."

Bzzweet backed off. The tree withdrew its rubbery branch, and Judy reached out to smooth Allen's wrinkled shirt. He was breathing hard and frowning, but she couldn't keep from grinning. The Galactic Federation had just averted its first crisis.